Captain Future and the

President Carthew was in his office when t
hunched creature, bizarrely hideous ... The President gaped as a guard appeared in the doorway and pointed his weapon at the fanged being.

'Don't shoot!' Carthew cried, but too late. The beast lay dead on the floor.

Carthew signed deeply as he confirmed his fears. The corpse on the floor was Sperling, his best secret agent, transformed into this hairy brute by the dread peril that threatened to destroy them all.

Only one man left alive might be able to ward off total doom. The President flashed an emergency call for Captain Future ...

The Star Kings

Flung across space and time by the sorcery of super-science, John Gordon exchanges bodies with Zarth Arn, Prince of the Mid-Galactic Empire 2000 centuries in the future!

Suddenly John is trust into a last-ditch battle between the democratic Empire World and the tyranny of the Black Cloud regime. Only one weapon – the terrifying Disruptor – can win the struggle for the Empire Forces. But it is so powerful that unless John uses it correctly it could destroy not only the enemy but the cosmos.

Could his 20th Century mind cope with the technology of 200,000 years from now?

The Weapon from Beyond

Morgan Chane was an Earthman by parentage, but he had been born on the pirate-world Varna, whose heavy gravity had developed strength and incredibly quick reflexes in him. When he was old enough, he joined the raider-ships that looted the starworlds, and fought side by side with the dreaded Starwolves of Varna. But then there was a fight among them. Chane killed their leader, and the other Starwolves turned on him. He barely got away alive – wounded near death, his Starwolf pursuers following him across the galaxy. And there was nowhere he could seek refuge, for no world would lift a hand to save one of the hated Starwolves.

Also by Edmond Hamilton

Captain Future

1. Captain Future and the Space Emperor (1969)
2. Calling Captain Future (1967)
3. Galaxy Mission (1967)
4. Danger Planet (1968) (aka Red Sun of Danger)
5. The Magician of Mars (1968)
6. Quest Beyond the Stars (1968)
7. Outlaws of the Moon (1969)
8. The Comet Kings (1968)
9. Planets in Peril (1968)
10. The Tenth Planet (1969)
11. Outlaw World (1968)
12. Captain Future's Challenge (1969)

Starwolf

1. The Weapon from Beyond (1967)
2. The Closed Worlds (1968)
3. World of the Starwolves (1968)

Interstellar Patrol

1. Outside the Universe (1964)
2. Crashing Suns (1965)

John Gordon

1. The Star Kings (1949) (aka Beyond the Moon)
2. Return to the Stars (1970)

Other Novels

Tharkol, Lord of the Unknown (1950)
The Monsters of Juntonheim (1950) (aka A Yank At Valhalla)
The City at World's End (1951)
The Star of Life (1959)
The Sun Smasher (1959)
The Haunted Stars (1960)
Battle for the Stars (1961)
The Valley of Creation (1964)
Fugitive of the Stars (1965)
Doom Star (1966)

Edmond Hamilton
SF GATEWAY OMNIBUS

CAPTAIN FUTURE AND
THE SPACE EMPEROR
THE STAR KINGS
THE WEAPON FROM BEYOND

GOLLANCZ
LONDON

First published in Great Britain in 2014 by
Gollancz
An imprint of the Orion Publishing Group
Orion House, 5 Upper St Martin's Lane,
London WC2H 9EA

An Hachette UK Company

A CIP catalogue record for this book
is available from the British Library

ISBN 978 0 575 09281 5

1 3 5 7 9 10 8 6 4 2

Typeset by Jouve (UK), Milton Keynes

Printed and bound by CPI Group (UK) Ltd, Croydon CR0 4YY

The Orion Publishing Group's policy is to use papers
that are natural, renewable and recyclable products and
made from wood grown in sustainable forests. The logging
and manufacturing processes are expected to conform to
the environmental regulations of the country of origin.

www.orionbooks.co.uk
www.gollancz.co.uk

CONTENTS

ENTER THE SF GATEWAY . . .

Towards the end of 2011, in conjunction with the celebration of fifty years of coherent, continuous science fiction and fantasy publishing, Gollancz launched the SF Gateway.

Over a decade after launching the landmark SF Masterworks series, we realised that the realities of commercial publishing are such that even the Masterworks could only ever scratch the surface of an author's career. Vast troves of classic SF and fantasy were almost certainly destined never again to see print. Until very recently, this meant that anyone interested in reading any of those books would have been confined to scouring second-hand bookshops. The advent of digital publishing changed that paradigm for ever.

Embracing the future even as we honour the past, Gollancz launched the SF Gateway with a view to utilising the technology that now exists to make available, for the first time, the entire backlists of an incredibly wide range of classic and modern SF and fantasy authors. Our plan, at its simplest, was – and still is! – to use this technology to build on the success of the SF and Fantasy Masterworks series and to go even further.

The SF Gateway was designed to be the new home of classic science fiction and fantasy – the most comprehensive electronic library of classic SFF titles ever assembled. The programme has been extremely well received and we've been very happy with the results. So happy, in fact, that we've decided to complete the circle and return a selection of our titles to print, in these omnibus editions.

We hope you enjoy this selection. And we hope that you'll want to explore more of the classic SF and fantasy we have available. These are wonderful books you're holding in your hand, but you'll find much, much more … through the SF Gateway.

www.sfgateway.com

INTRODUCTION

from The Encyclopedia of Science Fiction

Edmond Moore Hamilton (1904–1977) was a US author, married to fellow author Leigh Brackett from 1946 until his death, thirty mutually productive years later. With E. E.'Doc' Smith and Jack Williamson, he was one of the prime movers in the development of American SF before World War Two, sharing with those writers in the creation and popularization of classic Space Opera as it first appeared in Pulp magazines from the mid-1920s. His first story, 'The Monster-God of Mamurth' for *Weird Tales* in August 1926, which vulgarized the florid weird-science world of Abraham Merritt, only hinted at the exploits to come, even though Hamilton found Science Fantasy a fertile vein, collecting this story and others in his first book, *The Horror on the Asteroid & Other Tales of Planetary Horror* (1936). His early work is also assembled, more comprehensively, in *The Collected Edmond Hamilton, Volume One: The Metal Giants and Others* (2009).

Hamilton's importance to SF was only properly signalled two years later, with the publication of 'Crashing Suns' (1928), one of the founding texts of the kind of Space Opera with which he soon became identified: a Universe-spanning tale, often featuring in early years an Earthman and his comrades (not necessarily human) who discover a cosmic threat to the home Galaxy and successfully – either alone, or with the aid of a space armada, or both – combat the Aliens responsible for the threat; it would be left to E. E. Smith a few years later to transform adventures of this sort into larger-scale narratives involving Galactic Empires and their seemingly inevitable concomitant: structures based on (and presuming to comment upon) human history. Though he never created a full-blown sequence of this sort, 'Crashing Suns' is closely linked to the six Tales of the Interstellar Patrol stories, which followed over the next two years, and which are comfortably set *within* a vast inhabited universe. The 1960s partial book publication of the sequence – comprising *Outside the Universe* (1964) and *Crashing Suns* (1965), was useful; these two volumes have recently been superseded by *The Collected Edmond Hamilton, Volume Two: The Star-Stealers: The Complete Tales of the Interstellar Patrol* (2009), which also includes two similar but unrelated book-length tales, 'The Hidden World' (1929) and 'The Other Side of the Moon' (1929). In Hamilton's early work, science or pseudoscience served as a magically enabling doubletalk for the easier presentation of interstellar action, and the scope, colour and dynamic clarity of this liberated action did much to define the Sense of Wonder for a generation of readers, who rewarded Hamilton with several nicknames in recognition of his gift: 'World-Destroyer', 'The World Wrecker', 'World-Saver Hamilton'.

Much of this material remained in magazines, or was erratically put into book form; but from the 1990s a revival of interest in Hamilton has inspired more sustained efforts to make this early era available to a larger audience. An ongoing project, *The Collected Edmond Hamilton*, the first two volumes of which are cited variously above, is projected to contain all his short work. Earlier volumes designed to recapture his early career – including *Kaldar: World of Antares* (1998), which assembles the three Kaldar tales from 1933–5; *Invisible Master* (2000), which assembles two 1930 stories; and *The Vampire Master and Other Stories* (2000), which mostly includes 1930s SF with a Horror cast – have already assembled sizeable samples from these prolific years, when his exuberance was untrammelled but occasionally lacking argument.

Riskily for his career, Hamilton also occupied much of his time in the early 1940s with the smoother but significantly less over-the-top Captain Future series, published 1940–50 by Standard Magazines in *Captain Future* (1940–4) and afterwards in *Startling Stories* (1945–1946 and 1950–1). Each tale was written to a rigorous formula in which the super-Scientist protagonist, backed by three aides (one Robot, one Android and one brain in a box), brings an interstellar villain to justice; it is worth noting that Captain Future himself is not a Superhero in the Pulp tradition, though he is a man with abnormal powers of cognition. Hamilton eventually wrote twenty-seven Captain Future titles released in book form; with copious introductions and notes, the publication has begun of the entire series in collected form, beginning with *The Collected Captain Future Wizard of Science: Volume One* (2009) and *The Collected Captain Future Man of Tomorrow: Volume Two* (2011). The first tale of all, *Captain Future and the Space Emperor* (1969), which first published in *Captain Future* in January 1940, is typical of the series as a whole (see below).

The original idea for *Captain Future* had come from Mort Weisinger, a senior editor with the Standard Magazines group. Later, in 1941, Weisinger shifted over to DC Comics, and took many of his top writers with him, including Hamilton, who worked for some time in the mid-1940s as a staff writer on Superman, along with Henry Kuttner and others; a job role he could have embraced permanently. But Hamilton seems to have been acutely aware that his early 1940s absence from the mainstream of SF, through his work in comics and his involvement with *Captain Future*, might make it initially somewhat difficult for him to be accepted after World War Two as the competent and versatile professional he had in fact been for years, for he was a writer with a much wider range than was generally realized, one who had already produced several stories whose comparatively sober verisimilitude prefigured post-World War Two requirements.

After his marriage to Brackett in 1946, it may be no coincidence that his very sizeable output began to diminish, and its quality increased, a fact obscured by the publication in book form over the next years of material from his pre-War career – like *Tharkol, Lord of the Unknown* (1950), in which Martians invade Earth for its water – and by his habitual rehashing of older space-opera conventions in archaic epics like *The Sun Smasher* (1959), *Battle for the Stars* (1961) and *Fugitive of the Stars* (1965). At the same time, though, he was writing novels which, though in the space-opera tradition, were more carefully composed and darker in texture. It is for these novels that he is now mainly remembered. They include *The Monsters of Juntonheim: A Complete Book-Length Novel of Amazing Adventure* (1950); *City at World's End* (1951), in which a super-Weapon temporally dislocates a contemporary small city à la Clifford D. Simak into a far future Dying Earth (the term is specifically used) where the survivors must cope with Alien Invasions and a demanding Galactic Empire; *The Star of Life* (1959); and *The Valley of Creation* (1964), a strongly written Sword-and-Sorcery tale with an SF denouement.

The best of them are probably *The Haunted Stars* (1960), in which well-characterized humans face a shattering mystery on the Moon, the secret of star travel left by long-dead Aliens, along with dark warnings; and *The Star Kings* (1949) (see below), which forms the beginning of the Star Kings sequence. Along with its sequel, *Return to the Stars* (1970), it was assembled as *Chronicles of the Star Kings* (1986); both novels were also included in *Stark and the Star Kings* (2005) with Leigh Brackett, along with unrelated material by Brackett, plus the only known collaboration between the two, the previously unpublished 'Stark and the Star Kings', which attempts to conflate Hamilton's Space Opera with his wife's Planetary Romance tales featuring Eric John Stark. *The Star Kings* (1949) stands best alone.

Hamilton wrote one final Space Opera series, the Starwolf tales about tough interstellar adventurer Morgan Chane, which may be antiquated in premise, and told in a clean-cut trimmed-down language which has won supporters for its returning to old ways without succumbing to them. The sequence comprises *The Weapon from Beyond* (1967), *The Closed Worlds* (1968) and *World of the Starwolves* (1968), all three being assembled as *Starwolf* (1982). Hamilton shared with his long-time colleague Jack Williamson a capable and flexible attitude towards the post-World War Two genre and its markets, in contrast to the third great originator of US space opera, E. E. Smith (see comments above), who was a generation older, and who never adjusted. Through his ability to evolve a cleaner and more literate style to meet these new demands, and to apply this style to his old generic loves, Hamilton published novels at the end of his long career that read perfectly idiomatically as tales of the 1960s, and also wrote his best stories during these years, as demonstrated in two compendiums of his shorter work: *What's It Like Out There? and Other Stories* (1974) and the posthumous *The Best of Edmond Hamilton* (1977), the latter edited by his wife just before her own death. In the end, it can be said of Hamilton that he took Space Opera seriously enough to make it good. He was a writer of honour.

Captain Future and the Space Emperor (1969), the first of the Hamilton Space Operas to be presented here, may be the only work of science fiction to have received a review by the great American humourist S. J. Perelman, whose 'Captain Future, Block that Kick!'(15 January 1940 *The New Yorker*) made fun, but not mercilessly, of the kind of story Hamilton had begun to master. Nowadays, we can laugh with Perelman, and thrill with Hamilton. The tale of young Curtis Newton, whose brilliant parents have been murdered on the Moon, pulls all the stops: fast sentiments, high purpose (under the assumed name Captain Future he defends the solar system from various enemies), and propaganda: at a time of war, Americans (and the rest of us) were happy to be assured that the future would be grander than seems likely in 1940. We remain happy to share that dream.

The Star Kings (1949) is the second novel selected here, and shows Hamilton's increasing range. The plot of the tale reflects that of *The Prisoner of Zenda* (1894) by Anthony Hope: the protagonist (in Hamilton's case via a combination of mind transfer and time travel) must take the place of a missing or dead ruler of a Ruritanian kingdom (in Hamilton's case a galactic empire) and defend it against merciless foes. It is, perhaps, a day dream, but a potent one; and it ends in an awakening back on Earth. But there is hope of a sequel.

The Weapon from Beyond (1967) closes this volume with neatness and panache. All of Hamilton's old skills, here honed and tightened, are on display. The young protagonist is brought up orphaned on a heavy-gravity planet, is exiled, hunted through the galaxy, finds companions, becomes a mercenary in the star wars. Not a word is wasted. Once again, in Hamilton's trained and honest hands, Space Opera is given its due, and honoured.

For a more detailed version of the above, see Edmond Hamilton's author entry in *The Encyclopedia of Science Fiction*: http://sf-encyclopedia.com/entry/hamilton_edmond

Some terms above are capitalised when they would not normally be so rendered; this indicates that the terms represent discrete entries in *The Encyclopedia of Science Fiction*.

CAPTAIN FUTURE AND THE SPACE EMPEROR

CHAPTER I

Doom on Jupiter

The chill, uncanny breath of a dark menace millions of miles away pervaded the spacious, softly-lit office high in the greatest of New York's mighty towers.

The man who sat there at an ebonite desk was worried. Facing a broad window which framed the stupendous pinnacles of the moonlit city, he could feel that cold, malign aura. He shuddered at the thought of what he knew was happening even at this moment.

'It can't go on,' he muttered sickly to himself. 'That horror must be stopped, somehow. Or else—'

James Carthew, President of the Earth Government which had ruled all humanity since the last World War, was not an old man. Fifty was considered the prime of life, in these days. But the appalling responsibilities of guiding the destinies of all mankind had aged this man before his time.

His gray-shot hair was thinning around his high forehead. There were deep lines of strain in his keen, powerful face, and his dark eyes were haunted by haggard weariness and lurking fear.

As the door of his office opened his thin hands gripped the edges of his desk convulsively.

North Bonnel, his slender, dark young secretary, entered.

'The liner from Jupiter just landed, sir,' he reported. 'I had a flash from the spaceport.'

'Thank heavens!' Carthew muttered. 'Sperling should be here in five minutes. He knows I'm waiting for his report.'

Bonnel hesitated.

'I hope he's reached the bottom of that mystery out there. The special committee of Jupiter citizens called by televisor again this evening.'

'I know – calling to protest again about conditions on Jupiter,' Carthew said bitterly. 'Each one of them trying to voice a louder complaint than the others.'

'You can hardly blame them, sir,' the young secretary ventured to say. 'Things must be pretty horrible out there on Jupiter, with that hideous thing spreading as it is.'

'Sperling will have found out what's causing it,' the President asserted confidently. He looked at the perpetual uranium clock on his desk. 'He ought to be arriving any second—'

A scream from somewhere in the lower levels of the great Government Tower cut him off. It was a woman's scream.

There were many girl clerks employed here in the huge Government Headquarters for Earth and its planet colonies. Even at night, some of them were always in the building. But what had frightened one of them into uttering that agonized scream?

James Carthew had risen to his feet behind his desk, his aging face paling with sudden apprehension. The secretary started violently.

'Something wrong, sir! I'd better see—'

He started toward the door. It was suddenly flung open from outside.

Young Bonnel recoiled wildly.

'My God!' he cried.

In the open door stood a hideous and incredible figure, a monstrosity out of nightmare.

It was a giant, hunched ape, hairy and abhorrent. Its squat figure wore a man's zipper-suit of white synthesilk. In the too-tight garment, the creature looked like a gruesome travesty on humanity, its brutish, hairy face a bestial mask, jaws parted to reveal great fangs. Its eyes blazed with a cold glitter as it started into the room. 'Look out!' Bonnel yelled frantically.

A white-faced guard in the dark uniform of the Planet Police appeared in the door. He leveled his flare-gun swiftly at the monstrous ape.

'Wait – don't shoot!' James Carthew cried suddenly, as he looked into the monster's hairy face.

His warning was too late. The guard had seen nothing but an incredible, menacing creature advancing toward the President. He had squeezed the trigger.

The little flare from the pistol struck the ape's broad back. The creature's bestial face contorted in sudden agony. With a deep, almost human groan, it collapsed.

James Carthew, with a cry of horror, jumped forward. His face was paper-white as he bent over the creature.

The ape's eyes, strange *blue* eyes, had a dying light in them as they looked up at the President. The creature strove to speak.

From the hairy throat came a hoarse, gurgling rattle – dying words, thickened to a brutish growl, but dimly recognizable.

'Jupiter – the Space Emperor – causing atavism –' the thing gasped hoarsely in dying accents.

It sought to raise its head, its fading blue eyes weirdly human in agonized apprehension and appeal as they looked up at the President.

'Danger from—'

And then, as it sought to form another word, life ebbed swiftly, and the creature sank back, its eyes glazing.

'Dead!' Carthew exclaimed, trembling violently.

'My God, it talked!' cried the white-faced guard. 'That ape – talked!'

'It's not an ape. It's a man!' said James Carthew hoarsely.

He got to his feet. Guards and officials were running alarmedly into the office.

'Get out – all of you,' Carthew whispered, making a gesture with his trembling hand.

Horrified, still staring at the monstrous, hairy corpse on the floor, they withdrew and left the President and his secretary alone with the macabre corpse.

'Good God – those blue eyes – it couldn't be Sperling!' cried the shuddering young secretary.

'Yes, it's Sperling all right,' James Carthew said softly. 'I recognized him, by his eyes, a moment too late. John Sperling, our best secret agent – transformed into that dead brute on the floor!'

'You sent him to investigate the horror on Jupiter, and he fell prey to it!' Bonnel exclaimed hoarsely. 'He changed, like those others out there, from man to brute. Yet he was still man enough to try to get here and make his report!'

The pale young secretary looked beseechingly at his chief.

'What *is* it that's causing that horrible wave of monstrosities out on Jupiter? Hundreds of cases in the last month – hundreds of men changing into apish brutes!'

'Whatever it is, it's something bigger than just Jupiter,' Carthew whispered haggardly. 'Suppose this strange plague spreads to the other planets – to Earth?'

Bonnel blanched at the hideousness of the suggestion.

'Good God, that must not happen!'

The President looked down at the hairy body that a few weeks before had been the keenest, most stalwart man in the whole force of the Planet Police secret agents.

'Sperling may have written out a report,' Carthew muttered. 'Secret agents are not supposed to do so, but—'

Hastily, the young secretary searched the clothing of the hairy creature. He uttered a little exclamation as he drew forth a paper.

It was covered with crude, almost illegible writing, like the scrawl of a child. It was headed, 'To the President.' Carthew read it aloud:

Ship only one day from Earth, but feel myself changing so fast, I fear I won't be able to talk or think clearly by then. Was stricken by the atavism on Jupiter, days ago. Tried to get back to Earth to report what I learned, before I became completely unhuman.

I've learned that the blight on Jupiter is being caused by a mysterious being called the Space Emperor. Don't know whether he's Earthman or a Jovian.

How he causes this doom, I don't know, but it is some power he uses secretly on Earthmen there. I felt nothing of it, until I noticed myself changing, becoming foggy-minded, brutish.

Can't write much more now – getting hard to hold pen – haven't dared to leave my cabin on this ship, I've changed so badly – mind getting foggier – wish I could have learned more—

The young secretary's eyes had horror and pity in them as James Carthew read the last words.

'So Sperling failed to learn anything except that this horrible flight was being deliberately caused by some human agency!' he exclaimed. 'Think of him huddling in his cabin all the way back to Earth, becoming more brutish each day, hoping to reach Earth while he was still human—'

'We've no time to think of Sperling now!' Carthew explained, his voice high and raw. 'It's the people out there on Jupiter, and on the other planets, we must think of now – the arresting of this terror!'

James Carthew was feeling the awful weight of his responsibility, in this moment. The nine planets from Mercury to Pluto had entrusted their welfare to his care. And now he felt the approach of a mysterious, dreadful peril, a dark and unguessable horror spreading like subtle poison.

The first reports of the blight had come from Jupiter, weeks before. Out on that mightiest of planets, whose vast jungles and great oceans were still largely unexplored, there flourished a sizeable Earth colony. Centering around the capital of Jovopolis were dozens of smaller towns of Earthmen, engaged in working mines, and timbering, and in great grain-growing projects.

From one of those colonial towns near Jovopolis had come the first incredible reports. Earthmen – changing into beasts! Earthmen inexplicably being transformed into ape-like animals, their bodies and minds becoming more brutish each day. A horrible retracing of the road of human evolution! The victims had become atavisms – biological throwbacks hurled down the ladder of evolution.

Carthew had hardly believed those first reports. But soon had come ample corroboration. Already hundreds of Earthmen had been stricken by the dreadful change. The colonists out there were becoming panicky.

Carthew had sent scientists, men skilled in planetary medicine, to fight the horrid plague. But they had been unable to stop the cases of atavism, or even learn their cause. And neither had the secret agents of the Planet Police been able to learn much. Sperling, ace agent of them all, had learned but little, despite his sacrifice.

'We've got to do something at once, to check this blight,' Carthew declared shakenly. 'We know now, at least, that these atavism cases are being caused deliberately, by this being Sperling called the Space Emperor.'

'But if Sperling, our best agent, couldn't succeed, who in the world can?' Bonnel cried.

James Carthew went to the window and stepped out onto the little balcony. He looked up at the full moon that sailed in queenly splendor high above the soaring towers of nighted New York.

There was a look of desperation in the President's aging, haunted face as he gazed up at the shining white face of the lonely satellite.

'There's only one thing left to do,' he said purposefully. 'I'm going to call Captain Future.'

The secretary stiffened.

'Captain Future? But the whole world will know this is a perilous emergency, if you call *him!*'

'This *is* a perilous emergency!' exclaimed his superior. 'We've got to call him. Televise the meteorological rocket-patrol base at Spitzbergen. Order them to flash the magnesium flare signal from the North Pole.'

'Very well, sir,' acceded the secretary, and went to the televisor.

He came back a little later to the balcony, where James Carthew was gazing in anxiety toward the moon.

'The flare is being set off at the North Pole,' he reported.

They waited, then, in tense silence. An hour passed – and another. The uranium clock showed it was past midnight.

Far out beyond New York's towers, the moon was declining from the zenith. They could see the distant rocket-flash of liners taking off from the spaceport for far Venus or Saturn or Pluto.

'Why doesn't Captain Future come?' North Bonnel burst out, unable to keep silent longer. 'That ship of his can get from the moon to Earth in a few hours – he should be here by now.'

James Carthew's gray head lifted.

'He will be here. He's never yet failed to answer our call.'

'As a matter of fact, I'm here now, sir,' said a deep, laughing voice.

It came from the balcony outside the window. A big, red-headed young man had miraculously appeared there, as though by magic.

'Curt Newton – Captain Future!' cried the President eagerly.

Curt Newton was a tall, well-built young man. His unruly shock of red hair towered six feet four above the floor, and his wide lithe shoulders threatened to burst the jacket of his gray synthesilk zipper-suit. He wore a flat tungstite belt in which was holstered a queer-looking pistol, and on his left hand was a large, odd ring.

This big young man's tanned, handsome face had lines of humor around the mouth, crinkles of laughter around the eyes. Yet behind the bantering humor in those gray eyes there lurked something deep and purposeful, some hidden, overpowering determination.

'Captain Future!' repeated James Carthew to this big young man. 'But where's your ship, the *Comet*?'

'Hanging onto the wall outside by its magnetic anchor,' answered Curt Newton cheerfully. 'Here come my comrades now.'

A weird shape had just leaped onto the balcony. It was a manlike figure, but one whose body was rubbery, boneless-looking, blank-white in color. He wore a metal harness, and his long, slitted green unhuman eyes peered brightly out of an alien white face.

Following this rubbery android, or synthetic man, came another figure, equally as strange – a great metal robot who strode across the balcony on padded feet. He towered seven feet high. In his bulbous metal head gleamed a pair of photoelectric eyes.

The robot's left hand carried the handle of a square transparent box. Inside it a living brain was housed. In the front of the case were the Brain's two glittering glass lens-eyes. Even now they were moving on their flexible metal stalks to look at the President.

'You know my assistants,' Curt Newton said shortly. 'Grag the robot, Otho the android, and Simon Wright, the living Brain. We came from the moon full speed when I saw your signal. What's wrong?'

'We've need of you, Captain Future – dire need.' James Carthew said haggardly. 'You'll have to leave for Jupiter, at once.'

'Jupiter?' The handsome young man's brows drew together. 'Has something popped out there?'

'A terror is growing out there!' the President cried. 'A black horror that you must stop, immediately. Listen—'

CHAPTER II

Out of the Past

The name of Captain Future, the supreme foe of all evil and evildoers, was known to every inhabitant of the Solar System.

That tall, cheerful, red-haired young adventurer of the ready laugh and flying fists was the implacable Nemesis of all oppressors and exploiters of the System's human and planetary races. Combining a gay audacity with an unswervable purposefulness and an unparalleled mastery of science, he had blazed a brilliant trail across the nine worlds in defense of the right.

He and his three unhuman comrades, the living Brain, the metal robot and the synthetic man, were the talk of the System. Everyone knew that the scientific wizards' home was in some obscure crater on the desolate moon. People looked up at the lunar orb at night and felt safer because they knew that Captain Future was there, watching and ready. They knew that should any sinister catastrophe threaten the System, he would come forth to combat it.

But who *was* Captain Future? What had been the origin of his trio of unhuman comrades? And how had he come to achieve his super-scientific powers?

That was a story that only the President knew. And it was perhaps the strangest story in the history of the Solar System.

Twenty-five years before, a young Earth biologist named Roger Newton had dreamed a great dream. His dream was to create life – artificial, intelligent living creatures who would be able to think and work to serve humanity. He had already made great strides toward that goal, and felt on the verge of success.

But a certain unscrupulous politician with sinister ambitions had heard of Roger Newton's potent discoveries. He had made several daring attempts to steal them. There was danger to humanity if those discoveries passed into such hands. So Newton decided to seek a safe refuge in which he could work secretly.

On a night in that June of 1990, the young biologist communicated his decision to his only intimates, his young wife Elaine, and his loyal co-worker, Simon Wright.

Restlessly pacing the big, crowded laboratory of their secluded Adirondack farm, his red hair disordered and his lean, sensitive young face and blue eyes worried, Roger Newton addressed them.

'Victor Corvo's agents will find us here sooner or later,' he asserted. 'Think of my discoveries in Corvo's hands! We must leave Earth – go to a place where he'll never find us.'

'But where can we go, Roger?' appealed Elaine Newton anxiously, her soft gray eyes fretful, her small hand grasping his sleeve.

'Yes, where can we go?' echoed Simon Wright in his metallic, unhuman voice. 'To one of the colonized planets?'

'No, Corvo's agents would be sure to find us in any of the planetary colonies, sooner or later,' Newton replied.

'Then where is this refuge you speak of, if it's not on Earth or any of the planets?' demanded Simon Wright, his lenslike artificial eyes boring questionably into Newton's face.

Simon Wright was not a man. He had once been a man. He had once been a famous, aging scientist whose body was racked by an incurable disease. To save his brilliant brain from death, Newton had acceded to the old man's plea and had removed Wright's living brain from his body and had encased it in a serum-case in which it could live indefinitely.

The case stood now on a table beside Newton and his wife. It was a transparent metal box a foot square. Made of a secret alloy, it was insulated against shock, heat and cold, and contained a tiny battery that could operate its compact perfusion pump and serum purifier for a year.

Set in its sides were the microphones that were Simon Wright's ears. In front was the resonator by which he spoke, and his artificial lens-eyes, mounted on little flexible metal stalks he could turn at will. In that box lived the greatest brain in scientific history.

'Where can we find refuge, if not on Earth or any of the planets?' Wright repeated in his rasping, metallic voice.

Newton went to a window and drew aside the curtain. Outside lay the peaceful, nighted hills, washed with silver by the effulgent rays of the full moon that was rising in glorious majesty.

The white disc of the great satellite, mottled by its dark mountain ranges and plains, shone starkly clear in the heavens. Newton pointed up to it, as girl and brain watched wondering.

'There is our refuge,' Roger Newton said. 'Up there, on the moon.'

'On the moon?' cried Elaine Newton, her hand going to her throat. 'Oh, no, Roger – it's impossible!'

'Why impossible?' he countered. 'A good interplanetary rocket can make the trip easily. We have enough money from my father's estate to buy such a rocket.'

'But the moon!' Elaine exclaimed, deep repulsion shadowing her eyes. 'That barren, airless globe that no one ever visits! How could anyone live there?'

'We can live there quite easily, dear,' her young husband replied earnestly.

'We shall take with us tools and equipment capable of excavating an underground home, with a glassite ceiling open to the sun and stars. Atomic energy will enable us to heat or cool it as we need, and to transmute rock into hydrogen and oxygen and nitrogen for air and water. We can take sufficient concentrated food with us to last us for a lifetime.'

'I believe your plan is good, Roger,' said Simon Wright's metallic voice slowly. 'Corvo is not likely to think of looking for us on the moon. We will be able to work in peace, and I feel sure we'll succeed there in creating a living being. Then we can return and give humanity a new race of artificial servants.'

Elaine smiled bravely.

'Very well, Roger,' she told her husband. 'We'll go there, and maybe we'll be as happy on the moon as we have been here on Earth.'

'*We?*' echoed the young biologist astoundedly. 'But you can't go, Elaine. When I said "we" I meant Simon and myself. You could not possibly live on that wild, lonely world.'

'Do you think I would let you go there without me?' she cried. 'No, if you go, I'm going with you.'

'But our child—' he objected, a frown on his face.

'Our child can be born on the moon as well as on the Earth,' she declared. And as he hesitated, she added, 'If you left me here, Victor Corvo would find me and force me to tell where you had gone.'

'That is true, Roger,' interjected the Brain's cold, incisive voice. 'We must take Elaine with us.'

'If we must, we must,' Newton said resignedly, his face deeply troubled. 'But it's a terrible place to take anyone you love – a terrible place for our baby to be born—'

Ten weeks later, Newton, Elaine and Simon Wright – man, woman and Brain – sailed secretly for the moon in a big rocket crammed with scientific equipment and supplies.

Upon the moon, beneath the surface of Tycho crater, they built their underground home. There a son was soon born to the man and woman – a red-haired baby boy they named Curtis.

And there in the laboratory of the lonely moon home, a little later, Newton and Simon Wright created their first artificial living creature – a great metal robot.

Grag, as they named the robot, stood seven feet high, a massive, man-shaped metal figure with limbs of incredible strength. He had supersensitive photoelectric eyes and hearing, and a brain of metal neurones which gave him sufficient intelligence to speak and work, to think and to feel primitive emotions.

But though Grag the robot proved an utterly loyal, faithful servant, he was not of high enough mentality to satisfy Newton. The biologist saw that to create more manlike life he must create it of flesh, not of metal. After more weeks of work, they produced a second artificial creature, an android of synthetic flesh.

This synthetic man they named Otho. He was a rubbery, manlike creature whose dead-white synthetic flesh had been molded into human resemblance, but whose hairless white head and face, long, slitted green eyes, and wonderful quickness of physical and mental reactions, were quite unhuman. They soon found that Otho, the synthetic man, learned more quickly than had Grag, the robot.

'Otho's training is complete,' Newton declared finally. His eyes shone with triumph as he continued, 'Now we'll go back to Earth and show what we've done. Otho will be the first of a whole race of androids that soon will be serving mankind.'

Elaine's face lit with pure happiness.

'Back to Earth! But dare we go back, when Victor Corvo is there?'

'Corvo won't dare bother us, when we return as supreme benefactors of humanity,' her husband said confidently.

He turned to the two unhuman beings.

'Grag,' he ordered, 'you and Otho go out and remove the rock camouflage from the rocket, so that we can begin to make it ready for the return trip.'

When the huge metal robot and the rubbery android had gone out through the airlock chamber to the lunar surface, Elaine Newton brought her infant son into the big laboratory.

She pointed up through the glassite ceiling which framed a great circle of starry space. There amid the stars bulked the huge, cloudy blue sphere of Earth, half in shadow.

'See, Curtis,' she told the baby happily. 'That is where we're going – back to the Earth you've never seen.'

Little Curtis Newton looked up with wise gray baby eyes at the great sphere and stretched his chubby arms.

Newton heard the airlock door slam. He turned surprisedly. 'Grag and Otho – are you back so soon?'

The voice of Simon Wright rasped with sudden alarm.

'That's not Grag and Otho – I know their steps,' the living Brain cried. 'It's men!'

Elaine uttered a cry, and Newton paled. Four men in space suits, carrying long flare-pistols, stood in the doorway.

The face of their leader was revealed as they took off their helmets. It was a hawklike face, darkly handsome.

'Victor Corvo!' Newton cried appalledly, recognizing the ruthless man who had coveted his scientific discoveries.

'Yes, Newton, we meet again,' said Corvo exultantly. 'You thought I'd never find you here, but I finally tracked you down!'

Newton read death in the man's triumphant black eyes. And the sight of his wife's bloodless face and horrified eyes galvanized the young biologist into desperate action.

He sprang toward a locker in the corner in which his own flare-guns were stored. But he never reached it. Jets of fire from the pistols of Corvo's men hit him in mid-air and tumbled him into a scorched, lifeless heap.

Elaine Newton screamed, and thrust her baby onto a table, out of range of the guns. Then she leaped to the side of her husband.

'Elaine, look out!' cried the Brain.

She did not turn. The flare from Corvo's pistol struck her side, and she toppled to the floor beside her husband.

Little Curtis Newton, upon the table, began to whimper. Corvo ignored him and strode past the two still forms toward the square metal serum-case that held Simon Wright's living brain. He looked triumphantly into the glittering lens-eyes.

'Now to finish you, Wright,' he laughed, 'and then all the powers gathered in this laboratory belong to me.'

'Corvo, you are a dead man now,' answered the Brain in cold, metallic accents. 'Vengeance is coming – I hear it entering now – terrible vengeance—'

'Don't try to threaten me, you miserable bodiless brain!' Corvo jeered. 'I'll soon silence you—'

Two figures burst into the laboratory at that moment. Corvo and his men spun, appalled, unable to believe their eyes as they stared at the two incredible shapes who had entered.

The huge metal robot and the rubbery android! They stood, their unhuman eyes surveying the scene of death.

'Grag! Otho! Kill!' screamed the Brain's metallic voice. 'They have slain your master. Kill them! Kill them!'

With a booming roar of rage from the robot, a fierce, hissing cry from the synthetic man, the two leaped forward.

In less than a minute, Corvo and his three men lay horribly dead, their skulls smashed to pulp by the robot's metal fists, their necks broken by the android's rubbery arms. Then Grag and Otho stood still, gazing around with blazing eyes.

'Set me down by your master and mistress!' ordered Simon Wright urgently. 'They may still live!'

The robot put the Brain down by the two scorched forms. Wright's lens-eyes rapidly surveyed the bodies.

'Newton is dead, but Elaine is not dead yet,' the Brain declared. 'Lift her, Grag!'

With ponderous metal arms, the huge robot raised the dying girl to a sitting position. In a moment she opened her eyes. Wide, dark and filled with shadows, they looked at the Brain and robot and android.

'My – baby,' she whispered. 'Bring me Curtis.'

It was Otho who sprang to obey. The android gently set the whimpering infant down beside her. The dying girl looked down at it tenderly, heart-breaking emotion in her fading eyes.

'I leave him to the care of you three, Simon,' she choked. 'You are the only ones I can trust to rear him safely.'

'We'll watch over little Curtis and protect him!' cried the Brain.

'Do not take him to Earth,' she whispered. 'People there would take him away from you. They would say it is wrong to let a human child be reared by a brain and robot and android. Keep him here upon the moon, until he grows to manhood.'

'We will,' promised the Brain. 'Grag and Otho and I will rear him here safely.'

'And when he is a man,' whispered Elaine, 'tell him of his father and mother and how they died – how his parents were killed by those who wished to use the gifts of science for evil ends. Tell him to war always against those who would pervert science to sinister ambition.'

'I will tell him,' promised the Brain, and in its toneless metallic voice was a queer catch.

The girl's hand moved feebly and touched the whimpering infant's cheek. Into her dying eyes came a strange, far-seeing expression.

'I seem to see little Curtis a man,' she whispered, her eyes raptly brilliant. 'A man such as the System has never known before – fighting against all enemies of humanity—'

So Elaine Newton died. And so her infant son was left in the lonely laboratory on the moon, with the Brain and the robot and the synthetic man.

Simon Wright and Grag and Otho kept their promise, in the years that followed. They reared little Curtis Newton to manhood, and the three unhuman tutors and guardians gave the growing boy such an education as no human had ever received before.

The Brain, with its unparalleled store of scientific knowledge, supervised the boy's education. It was the Brain who instructed Curtis Newton in every branch of science, making him in a short period of years into a complete master of all technical knowledge. And together the bodiless Brain and the brilliant, growing youth delved far beyond the known limits of science and devised instruments of unprecedented nature.

The robot instilled some of his own incredible strength and stamina into the boy, by a system of super exercises rigidly maintained. In mock struggle, the red-haired youth would pit himself against the great metal creature who could have crushed him in a second had he wished. Gradually, thus, Curt's strength became immense.

The android endowed the growing lad with his own unbelievable swiftness of physical and mental reactions. The two spent many hours on the barren lunar surface, engaged in strange games in which the lad would try to match the android's wonderful agility.

And as he grew older, Curt Newton started secret voyages through the Solar System, in the little super-ship Simon Wright and he had devised and built. The four secretly visited every world from scorched Mercury to Arctic Pluto, and so he came to know not only the Earthman colonies of each world, but much of the unexplored planetary wildernesses also. And he visited moons and asteroids that no other man had ever landed upon.

Finally, when Curtis Newton had grown to full manhood, Simon Wright told him how his father and mother had died, and of his mother's dying wish that he war always against those who would use the powers of science for evil ends.

'You must choose now, Curtis,' the Brain concluded solemnly. 'You must decide whether you will make your purpose in life the championing of mankind against its exploiters and oppressors, or whether you will seek happiness for yourself in normal, comfortable life.

'We three have given you the education and training you would need for such a life-long crusade. And we three will stand by you and fight at your side, if you take up that cause. But we cannot decide for you. You must do that for yourself.'

Curt Newton looked up through the glassite ceiling at the starry vault of space in which bulked Earth's cloudy sphere. And the big, red-haired young man's cheerful face grew sober.

'I believe it's my duty to take up the cause you speak of, Simon,' he said slowly. 'Men such as killed my parents must be crushed, or they'll destroy the nine worlds' civilization.'

Curtis Newton drew a long breath.

'It's a mighty big job, and I may go down to defeat. But while I live, I'll stick to it.'

'I knew you'd decide so, lad!' exclaimed the Brain. 'You will be fighting for the future of the whole Solar System!'

'For the future?' repeated Curt. The humor came back into his gray eyes. 'Then I'll call myself – Captain Future!'

That very night, Curt had flown from the moon to Earth and had secretly visited the President, offering the service of his abilities in the war against interplanetary crime.

'I know you've no faith in me now,' he had told the President, 'but a time may come when you'll need me. When that time comes, flash a signal flare from the North Pole. I'll see it, and come.'

Months later, when a mysterious criminal was terrorizing the inner planets and the Planet Police were helpless, the President had remembered the red-haired young man who had called himself Captain Future, and as a desperate last hope had summoned him.

Captain Future and his three unhuman comrades had smashed the menace in a few weeks. And since then, time after time the signal flare had blazed from the North Pole – and each time Curt Newton and his comrades had answered. Each time, the fame of the mysterious foe of evil had become greater throughout the Solar System, as he destroyed one supercriminal after another.

But now, Captain Future had been called to face the greatest and deadliest antagonist he had ever confronted. The mysterious being who was striking down the Earthmen of Jupiter with a fearful horror that changed men into primeval beasts!

CHAPTER III

Ambush in Space

Out beyond the orbit of Mars, out past the whirling wilderness of the asteroidal belt, flew a queer little ship. Shaped oddly like an elongated teardrop, and driven by muffled rocket-tubes whose secret design gave it a power and speed far beyond those of any other craft, it was traveling now at a velocity that lived up to its name of *Comet*.

Inside the *Comet*, in the transparent-walled room at the nose where its controls were centered, Grag the robot sat on watch. The great robot sat utterly rigid and unmoving, his metal fingers resting upon the throttles that controlled the flow of atomic energy to the rocket-tubes, his gleaming photoelectric eyes staring unswervingly ahead.

Curt Newton stood beside the robot, his hand resting familiarly on Grag's metal shoulder as he too peered ahead, toward the largening white sphere of Jupiter.

'Twenty more hours at this speed will bring us there, Grag,' the big young man said thoughtfully.

'Yes, master,' answered the robot simply in his booming mechanical voice. 'And then what?'

Curt's eyes twinkled.

'Why, then we'll find this Space Emperor who's behind the terror out here, and take him back to Earth. That's all.'

'Do you think it will be so easy, master?' asked the robot naively.

Captain Future laughed aloud.

'Grag, irony is wasted on you. The truth is that it's going to be a pretty tough job – the toughest we ever faced, maybe. But we'll win out. We've got to.'

His face sobered a little. 'This thing is big – big enough to wreck the Solar System if it isn't stopped at once.'

He was remembering James Carthew's haggard face, the desperate appeal in his trembling voice.

'You'll do your best out there on Jupiter, Captain Future?' the President had pleaded. 'That horror – men retracking the path of evolution to brutehood – it mustn't go on!'

'It won't go on if I can stop it,' Curt had promised, his voice like level steel. 'Whoever or whatever this Space Emperor is, we'll track him down or we won't come back.'

Curt was thinking of that promise now. He knew well how difficult it was going to be to fulfill it. Yet the prospect of the perilous struggle ahead exhilarated him strangely.

Peril was like a heady wine to Curt's adventure-loving soul. He had met it in the poisonous swamps of Venus, in the black and sunless caverns of Uranus, in the icy snow-hell of Pluto. And always, when the danger was greatest, he had felt that he was living the most.

Grag broke the silence, the robot still looking ahead with his strange photoelectric eyes toward Jupiter.

'Jupiter is a big world, master,' he boomed thoughtfully. 'It took us long to catch the Lords of Power when they fled there.'

Curt nodded, remembering that relentless hunt for the outer-planet criminals who had sought to hide on the giant planet. That had been the end of a blazing battle and chase that he and his three comrades had taken part in and that had reached from far Pluto to this mighty world ahead.

'It may take us even longer to find this Space Emperor, but we'll do it,' he said resolutely.

There was silence, except for the droning of the cyclotrons in the *Comet*'s stern, and the muffled purring of the atomic energy they produced, as it was released by the rocket-tubes. Then into the control-room came the synthetic man.

'You are late, Otho,' boomed the robot, turning severely toward the android. 'It was your turn to take over a half hour ago.'

Otho's lipless mouth opened to give vent to a hissing chuckle. His green eyes gleamed mockingly.

'What difference can it make to you, Grag?' he inquired mockingly. 'You are not a man, and so you do not need rest as we men do.'

Grag's voice boomed angrily. 'I am as much like a man as you are!' he declared.

'You, a metal machine?' taunted Otho. 'Why, men are not of metal. They are of flesh, like myself.'

The gibing, hissing voice of the android awakened all Grag's rudimentary capacity for indignation. He turned his unhuman metal face appealingly toward Captain Future.

'Am I not as near human as Otho, master?' he appealed.

'Otho, quit teasing Grag and take over,' Curt Newton ordered sternly.

Yet there was a merry spark in Captain Future's gray eyes as the android hastily obeyed.

Curt loved these three unhuman companions of his, the great, simple robot, the fierce, eager android and the dour, austere Brain. He knew they were more loyal and single-hearted than any human comrades could have been.

Yet he derived a secret amusement from these ceaseless quarrels between

Otho and Grag. Both the robot and the android liked to be thought of as human or nearly human. And the fact that Otho was more manlike was a continual irritation to big Grag.

'I can do almost everything that Otho can do,' Grag was saying to him anxiously. 'And I am far stronger than he is.'

'A machine is strong,' sneered Otho, 'but it is still only a machine.'

'Come along with me, Grag,' Curt told the robot hastily as he saw that the big metal creature was really angry.

The robot followed him back into the main-cabin that occupied the middle section of the *Comet.*

Simon Wright's lens-eyes looked up inquiringly at them. The Brain's transparent square case rested on a special stand, which embodied an ingenious spoolholder that automatically unreeled the long micro-film scientific work the Brain was consulting.

'What is wrong?' rasped Wright.

'Otho was just deviling Grag again,' Curt told him. 'Nothing serious.'

'He is not *really* more human than I am, is he, master?' appealed the big robot anxiously.

'Of course not, Grag,' answered Captain Future, his eyes twinkling as he laid his hand affectionately on the metal shoulder. 'You should know enough by now to ignore Otho's taunts.'

'Aye,' rasped Simon Wright to the robot. 'It is nothing to be proud of to be human, Grag. I was human, once, and I was not as happy as I am now.'

'Go back and check the cyclotrons, Grag,' Curt told the robot, and the great metal creature stalked obediently through the cabin into the power-room at the stern.

Captain Future's gray eyes looked inquiringly into the glittering glass ones of the Brain.

'Have you found any clue yet, Simon?'

'No,' the Brain answered somberly. 'Not in all the records of human science can I find any hint of how that ghastly method of causing this strange doom – this atavism – could be achieved.'

'Yet it has been done – it is being done now,' Curt muttered. 'And that means that this time we are up against an antagonist who somehow has gone far beyond known science – further than we ourselves have gone!'

With brooding, unseeing eyes, the red-haired adventurer stared around the cabin, his mind far away.

The cabin was a marvel of compactness, with facilities for research in all fields of science. There was a chemistry alcove, with containers of every element known to science; an astronomical outfit, including an electro-telescope, electro-spectroscope, and a file of spectra of all planets, satellites, and stars above the fifth magnitude.

There were samples of the atmosphere of every planet, satellite and asteroid. And a botanical division contained specimen plants and vegetable drugs from various worlds.

Besides this equipment, there were many instruments which Captain Future and Simon Wright had devised, unknown to conventional science. A small locker contained every valuable scientific book or monograph ever published, reduced to micro-film. It was one of these micro-film spools the Brain had been consulting.

'I know of every biologist of note in the System today,' the Brain was saying. 'Not one of them could have discovered the secret of reversing evolution.'

'Could such an epochal discovery have been made by a wholly unknown scientist?' Curt demanded.

'That seems unlikely,' the Brain replied slowly. 'There is some great mystery about this which I cannot understand, lad.'

Curt's tanned face hardened.

'We're going to understand soon,' he affirmed. 'We've got to, to stop this thing.'

Thoughtfully, he reached into a locker for a little hemispherical musical instrument. Absently, he touched its strings, bringing forth queer, shivering, haunting tones.

The instrument was a twenty-string Venusian guitar, two sets of ten strings each strung across each other on a metal hemisphere. Few Earthmen could play the complicated thing, but Captain Future had a habit of plucking haunting tones from it when he was lost in thought.

Wright's eye-stalks twitched annoyedly.

'I wish you'd never picked up that thing,' the Brain complained. 'How can I concentrate on reading when you're making that dismal whining?'

Curt grinned at the Brain.

'I'll take it into the control-room, since you don't appreciate good music,' he said jestingly.

Twenty hours later saw the little teardrop ship decelerating in velocity as it hurtled toward the world now close ahead.

Jupiter now loomed gigantic before them. It was a huge, spinning white sphere, attended by its eleven circling moons, belted with the clouds of its deep atmosphere, and wearing like an ominous badge the glowing crimson patch of the Fire Sea which men had once called the Great Red Spot. A world that was hundreds of times larger than Earth, a world whose fifty great jungle-clad continents and thirty vast oceans were still almost wholly unexplored.

Only on the continent of South Equatoria, Curt knew, had Earthmen settled. There they had cleared the steaming, unearthly jungles enough to build towns and operate plantations and mines, using the Jovian inhabitants for labor. But only a small part of even South Equatoria was known to them. The rest was unexplored, brooding jungle, stretching northward to the Fire Sea.

Curt Newton held the controls, and his three unhuman comrades were in the control-room with him as he expertly fingered the throttles. They flashed close past the gray sphere of Callisto, outermost of Jupiter's four biggest moons, and plunged on toward the giant planet.

'You're going to land at Jovopolis?' rasped Simon Wright inquiringly.

Captain Future nodded.

'That's the capital of the Earth colony, and there, I think, must be the heart of this menace.'

Suddenly a bell rang sharply from the panel of complicated gauges and scientific tell-tales.

'The ship-alarm!' Curt exclaimed. 'There's some other craft near us in space!'

'There it is behind us!' Otho cried out. 'It's an ambush!'

Curt glanced back through the rear curve of the control-room's transparent wall. A dark little space-cruiser had just darted out from behind Callisto, and from its bows a big flare-gun was loosing a flare of atomic energy that sped toward the *Comet*.

No other space-pilot in the System could have moved quickly enough to escape that leaping flare. But Captain Future had reflexes trained since boyhood to superhuman speed.

The *Comet* lurched sideward from a blast of its starboard tubes, just enough to let the flare shoot past it. Before the attacker on their tail could fire again, Curt Newton had acted.

His tanned hand slammed down a burnished red lever beside the throttles. Instantly an astounding thing happened.

From the *Comet*'s tubes shot a tremendous discharge of tiny, glowing particles. Almost instantly they formed a huge, glowing cloud around the little teardrop ship, hiding it from view and streaming back in a vast, shining tail.

The *Comet* had become, to all appearances, what it was named after – a comet! This was Curt Newton's method of camouflaging his ship when he wished to avoid discovery in space, or when he wished to confuse an enemy craft. It was operated by a powerful discharge of electrified atoms, or ions, produced in a special generator and released through the regular rocket-tubes.

'I'm banking around on them!' Curt called to the android. 'Stand by to use our proton beams on them, Otho!'

'I'll blast them out of space!' exclaimed the android fiercely as he leaped to the breech of the proton guns.

'No, I want those men alive if we can get them!' Captain Future snapped. 'Try to cripple them by blasting their tail – that will force them down on Callisto.'

As Curt swung the *Comet* sharply around, the black attacking ship rose viciously to meet it, letting go another burst of atomic energy from its flare-guns.

'So you still want to play, do you?' grinned Curt. 'That's fine!'

Captain Future had avoided the leaping flares by a lightning roll of the *Comet* that did not change its direction of flight for more than a moment.

Now he sent the little ship, still wrapped in its glowing cloud, swooping down upon the enemy, before it could turn.

'Now – let go our beams, Otho!' Captain Future cried.

The android obeyed. The pale proton beams lanced from the *Comet*, grazed past the tail of the black enemy.

'Missed them!' hissed Otho in bitter disappointment.

'They're trying to escape, master!' boomed Grag, pointing a metal arm.

The black enemy craft, its occupants apparently unnerved by the closeness of the proton beams, was diving sharply to flee away through space.

'It's easier to start a fight than to quit it, my friends,' muttered Curt, jerking open two of his throttles. 'Here's where you find that out.'

Like a streak of glowing light, the *Comet* dived after the fleeing enemy. Pursued and pursuer rushed down through the dizzy depths of space at nightmare velocity.

Curt felt his pulse pounding with excitement as he guided his craft in that terrific swoop. To Captain Future, this was living – this wild whirl and flash of battle out here in the awesome solar spaces where he felt most at home.

'Try again now, Otho!' he cried a moment later.

The *Comet* had pulled almost abreast of the other swooping ship. The android now loosed their proton beams again.

The beams sliced away a third of the black ship's tail. Crippled, its rocket-tubes blasted and useless, it slowed in its wild rush until it was merely floating. Then it began to drift with ever increasing speed toward nearby Callisto.

'That got them!' Captain Future exclaimed, his gray eyes snapping with excitement. 'They'll drift in to Callisto and we'll land there with them, and capture whoever's in that ship.'

'You think they were sent by the Space Emperor – the mysterious figure behind the Jupiter horror – to ambush us?' rasped Simon Wright inquiringly.

'They must have been!' Otho declared. 'The Space Emperor, whoever he is, didn't want Captain Future coming to Jupiter to investigate him.'

Curt Newton interrupted, his gray eyes lit.

'But this may give us a lead right to the Space Emperor! If we can capture the men in that ship and make them talk—'

The black enemy craft was now drifting in a spiral around Callisto, ever approaching nearer to that barren-looking gray moon. Curt kept the *Comet* trailing the other ship, but far enough away to be out of range of its flare-guns, and with the ion-discharge apparatus now cut off.

'But lad,' said Simon Wright's harsh voice, 'how could the Space Emperor know that Captain Future was coming to Jupiter? The only person there whom the President would notify of our coming would be the Planetary Governor.'

'Yes,' said Curt meaningly, 'and that may give us another lead to him. But right now our best chance is to wring information out of the men in that ship.'

Curt's mind was vibrant with eager hope. His mysterious foe had struck at him already, even before he reached Juipiter. But it might be that the attack of the unknown plotter was going to recoil on his own head.

'We near Callisto's surface, master!' came the booming voice of Grag.

Captain Future's gray eyes lit with a reckless gleam. 'Get ready for a scrap then, Grag!'

Down through the thin atmosphere of Callisto the black ship was sinking, falling faster and faster. Still the *Comet* clung to its trail, grimly following it down toward the barren surface of the big moon …

CHAPTER IV

World of Creeping Crystals

At ever increasing speed the small black space-cruiser and its grim pursuer sped down toward the surface of Callisto. This was the sunward side of the big moon, and in the pale sunlight it presented a drear and desolate landscape.

A forbidding desert of drab gray rock, rising into low stony hills, it was infinitely repellent. The air here was barely breathable, as on all the larger moons, but because of its barrenness and also because of the grotesque, dangerous forms of life known to exist on its surface, few Earthmen had ever visited this world.

Now the black ship was only a mile from the glaring gray rock surface. It hurtled downward at slowly increasing speed.

'They won't crash with much force,' Curt observed. 'Callisto's gravitation is not strong. It'll be enough to shake them up and stun them for a moment, though, and we'll jump them before they make trouble.'

'I'd enjoy seeing their ship hit hard enough to splash them all over Callisto,' hissed the emotional android.

Captain Future grinned.

'You're too bloodthirsty, Otho.'

Otho stared at him puzzledly. 'I can't understand you humans some times,' he complained.

Curt chuckled. Then he turned his attention below, ready for action.

The black ship was falling toward the rocky plain. A moment later it struck the stony desert, bounced violently, then hit the ground again with a sharp impact and lay still.

Instantly Captain Future sent the *Comet* speeding downward in a gliding swoop that brought it to a jarring landing close to the other ship. He jumped up from the controls.

'Come on, Grag!' he shouted. 'Otho, you stay here at our proton beams, just in case.'

'Be careful, lad,' cautioned the Brain.

Curt paused to adjust the gravity equalizer he wore on his belt. Every interplanetary traveler owned one of these clever devices. Its 'gravity charge' of magnetic force of selected polarity and strength made its wearer feel exactly as light or heavy as he was on Earth.

Then Captain Future and the big metal robot emerged from the *Comet* into pale sunlight and a thin, pungent atmosphere that rasped the lungs. Curt led the way toward the black craft on a run, the barren desert's sterile surface reminding him strongly of the drab lifelessness of Mercury's Hot Side.

The black, torpedo-shaped space-cruiser lay a little on its side on the gray rock. There was no sound from inside it, indicating that the men within had been temporarily stunned by the crash. Curt and the robot reached the circular door.

'You'll have to open this door, Grag,' Captain Future said rapidly. 'Use your drills.'

'Yes, master,' boomed the big robot.

Grag's big metal fingers were removable. The robot rapidly unscrewed two of them and replaced them with small drills which he took from a kit of scalpels, chisels and similar tools carried in a little locker in his metal side.

Then Grag touched a switch on his wrist. The two drills which had replaced two of his fingers whirled hummingly. He quickly used them to drill six holes in the edge of the ship's door.

Then he replaced the drills with his fingers, hooked six fingers inside the holes he had made. He braced his great metal body, then pulled with all his strength at the door.

They could hear the men inside stirring as they recovered from the shock of crashing. But the colossal strength of the huge robot now ripped the door bodily off its heavy hinges. Instantly Captain Future leaped inside, the robot following.

Two men sprang fiercely to meet them. They were hardbitten, brutal-faced Earthmen, one with a bald head and pale eyes, the other a shock-haired giant. The bald one held a flare-pistol and fired swiftly at Captain Future.

Curt swerved, with a fierce, low laugh, as the man pulled trigger. Before the bald one could fire again, Captain Future had leaped in and seized his gun-hand. They struggled tensely.

In this moment of conflict, Curt's mind reverted to his super-fast games with Otho on the moon, as a boy. How slow seemed this swearing man beside the blurring speed of the android!

And how puny seemed the man's strength compared to the giant power of the mighty robot against whom he had pitted himself in boyhood!

The bald man suddenly went limp. Curt Newton, with his unerring knowledge of anatomy, had pressed and paralyzed a vital nerve center at the base of his skull.

'That will hold *you*, my friend,' Captain Future exclaimed. He turned quickly. 'You have the other one, Grag?'

'Yes, master,' boomed the big robot calmly.

Grag had grabbed the other Earthman in his huge metal arms before he could use his gun, and was holding him as helpless as a baby. Captain Future touched the same vital nerve-center of this man, and he too went limp and helpless.

'Now,' Curt said grimly to the two, 'you will tell me just who you are and why the Space Emperor sent you out here to ambush me.'

'The Space Emperor? I never heard of him,' answered the bald-headed Earthman loudly. 'I'm Jon Orris and this is my partner, Martin Skeel. We're honest traders, going to Saturn.'

'Traders, in a ship that looks to me like a stolen police-cruiser!' Curt Newton commented contemptuously. His gray eyes snapped. 'Silence is better than such a clumsy lie.'

'Try to make us talk then, Captain Future!' snarled Orris, defiant.

'Shall I make them, master?' asked Grag eagerly, clenching his great metal fist ominously.

'Not that way, Grag,' Curt said quickly. He stiffened. 'Listen! I hear Otho coming.'

He sprang to the open door of the ship. Out in the pale sunlight, Otho was running toward him. The rubbery android carried the handle of Simon Wright's brain-case.

'What's wrong?' Curt demanded, sensing trouble.

The Brain answered.

'Crystals coming, lad. Look yonder.'

Curt spun and peered westward, where the Brain's eyes had turned. His lips tightened at what he saw.

Over the brink of low rock hills there, a slender, shining mass was slowly flowing. It was like a brilliant cataract of diamonds, dazzling in the sun as it flowed slowly down the rock hill toward the two parked ships.

Curt recognized that slowly approaching mass as one of the grotesque, dangerous life-forms that existed on Callisto. This strange, bizarre variety of life had developed in inorganic crystalline forms, as semi-intelligent, mutualistic crystal colonies. These crystal colonies had limited powers of movement, which enveloped and killed any luckless living thing unable to evade their slow approach.

'The things can always sense any living creature who lands on their world,' Simon Wright was rasping. 'They'll reach us in a quarter hour.'

Curt Newton's gray eyes lit.

'That gives me an idea! Grag, drag out our two prisoners.'

The big robot obeyed. He emerged from the black ship in a moment, half-carrying the two paralyzed, helpless men.

Curt pointed out the distant, approaching crystalline cataract to Orris and Skeel.

'I guess you two know what those Callistan crystals do to anything they catch,' he said grimly. 'If we take off and leave you here paralyzed as you are now, they'll reach you in about fifteen minutes.'

The two men paled with horror.

'You wouldn't do that, Captain Future!' gasped the bald-headed Orris wildly.

'I would, unless you tell what you know of this horror that's going on at Jupiter!' Curt snapped.

His bluff worked. Sight of the crystals approaching had broken the nerve of the two as nothing else could.

'I'll tell you – but I don't really know much!' Orris stammered. 'The Space Emperor told us to steal a Planet Police cruiser. We were to wait here in ambush for you and blast you out of space. We had to do what he said.'

'Why did you? Who is the Space Emperor?' Curt demanded, feeling a harp-string suspense as he awaited the answer.

Orris shook his bald head shakily.

'I don't know who he is. Nobody knows who the Space Emperor is. I don't even know if he's *human*,' he added fearfully. 'He's always concealed in a big, queer black suit, and he speaks out of it in a voice that don't sound human to me. He does things no human *could* do!

'Skeel and I have criminal records,' he continued hastily. 'We fled out here to Jupiter after we got into a murder scrape on Mars. Somehow the Space Emperor found out we were wanted by the Planet Police. He threatened to expose us to them unless we obeyed his orders. We had to do it! He's forced other fugitive criminals like ourselves to do his bidding, by the same threat.'

'How does he cause that reverse evolution in Earthmen?' Curt demanded.

'I don't know that. I've never seen him do it, if it's he who does it,' Orris answered, dread in his pale eyes. 'I do know that the Jovians worship the Space Emperor, and obey his every order. He's stirred them up to wild unrest to do his bidding.'

'The Jovians worship the Space Emperor?' echoed Simon Wright's metallic voice. 'That is strange—'

'There's the devil of a lot about this story that's strange!' Captain Future declared crisply. 'If you're lying—'

'I'm not!' Orris declared fearfully, glancing nervously toward the approaching cataract of crystals.

'Where were you to report to the Space Emperor when you'd succeeded in destroying me?' Captain Future demanded.

'He was to meet us tonight in our cabin in Jovopolis,' Orris replied. 'It's beyond the Street of Space Sailors, at the edge of the city.'

Skeel, the other man, interrupted.

'Aren't you going to let us go now?' he pleaded hoarsely. 'Those crystals will be here in a few minutes!'

Curt paid no attention to the approaching stream of dazzling crystals which had awakened panic in the two would-be murderers. A quick plan had been born in the red-haired adventurer's mind.

'Otho, I want you to make yourself up as a double of this man Orris,' he told the synthetic man.

'What is your plan, lad?' rasped Simon Wright keenly.

Newton's gray eyes snapped.

'The Space Emperor will come to that cabin on the edge of Jovopolis tonight, to receive the report of these two men. Well, one of them is going to report with Captain Future as his prisoner – only it won't be really Orris who reports, but Otho!'

'I see!' muttered the Brain. 'The Space Emperor will be thrown off guard by Otho's disguise, and we may be able to capture him.'

'Hurry, Otho!' Curt exclaimed. 'Those crystals are getting close!'

'I am hurrying, Chief,' the synthetic man replied.

Otho was clawing in the square make-up pouch that hung at his belt beside his proton pistol. He brought out a small lead flask with a sprayer attachment.

From the flask, the android sprayed a colorless chemical oil onto his own face and head. Then he waited.

In a moment a strange change came over Otho's face. His rubbery, white synthetic flesh seemed to lose its elastic firmness and to soften like melting wax.

Otho's synthetic flesh was so constituted that an application of the chemical oil would soften it and make it as plastic as putty. It would harden again in a few minutes, but before it hardened it could be molded into any desired features.

Now that his flesh was softened to plasticity, Otho himself began molding it. With firm, deft fingers the android pressed and touched the softened white flesh of his face. Modeling his features into different ones, as a sculptor might model a new clay mask from an old one!

As he worked, Otho's green eyes steadily watched the panicky, brutal face of the man Orris. And swiftly, Otho's face *became* the face of Orris, in every line and feature. The android, through long practice, could remake his face into an exact replica of any other face in a few minutes.

A minute after he had finished, the flesh of his face began hardening again into elastic firmness.

'Now for the make-up,' Otho muttered, clawing in his square pouch again.

'Hurry!' urged Captain Future.

With a tiny hypodermic, Otho injected a drop of fluid into each eye which changed their color from green to a pale hue. Thin stain from a tube changed his new face from dead-white to a space-tanned color. A little fringe of artificial brown hair around his new tanned, bald head completed the amazing disguise.

Otho darted into the ship of Orris and Skeel. He returned in a moment clad in a zipper-suit of drab synthesilk like that worn by Orris. Then the android turned to Curt Newton.

'Is it good enough?' he asked in a voice that was an uncanny replica of the voice of Orris.

'It's perfect!' Curt declared. Before him were *two* Orrises – indistinguishable from each other.

'Good God, that creature's made himself into *me!*' gasped Orris horrifiedly.

'Lad, it's time we left,' rasped Simon Wright's warning. 'The crystals are coming too near.'

Curt whirled. The cataract of brilliant crystals was now pouring steadily across the rocky plain toward them. The gleaming, faceted crystalline things advanced inexorably, motivated by an electric force in their strange inorganic bodies that gave them the power of attraction and repulsion to each other.

With a clicking, murmuring, rustling sound, the brilliant flood moved at the rate of a few feet a moment, each separate gleaming crystal jerking a few inches forward by exerting repulsion upon those behind it. They were but a hundred feet away.

'Grag, wreck the cyclotrons of this ship!' Captain Future ordered. 'Then we'll be off.'

As the big robot sprang into the black craft to obey, Orris and Skeel voiced wild protest.

'You're not going to leave us here to be killed by those things!' they cried.

Curt bent over the two helpless men and touched their nerve-centers, lifting the paralysis that held them. As they staggered up, Grag came out of the ship.

'It is wrecked, master,' boomed the robot. 'That ship will not fly space again.'

'You two men can run now, and you can easily keep away from the crystals here,' Curt told Orris and Skeel. 'I'll notify the Planet Police at Jovopolis and they'll send a ship out to pick you up.'

His eyes flamed.

'If I did what I'd like to, I'd let the crystals have you! You've helped to spread a horror that's blacker than murder!'

The two criminals stared wildly at the clicking, advancing flood of crystals now only fifty feet away, and then broke into a crazy run in an opposite direction, stumbling frantically away across the drab gray desert.

'Quick, to the *Comet* before those things cut us off!' Curt cried.

Grag snatched up the handle of Simon Wright's square brain-case. He and the disguised Otho and Captain Future ran hastily toward their ship.

The clicking crystals were only yards from them as they passed the head of their cataract. Tumbling inside the *Comet*, Curt leaped to the control-room, and in a moment had the little teardrop ship zooming upward with a muffled roar of tubes.

He looked back down and saw the baffled crystals flowing over the disabled black ship, smothering it until it seemed encrusted with blazing diamonds, searching its interior for any living thing. The two criminals who had fled were already far away across the rocky surface of Callisto, and would be safe until the Planet Police came for them.

Captain Future had an eager gleam in his gray eyes as he steered upward.

'Now for Jovopolis,' he said tautly, 'and the Space Emperor!'

CHAPTER V

Power of the Space Emperor

Jupiter, like all the other outer planets, had once been considered impossible as a habitation for Earthmen. Before interplanetary exploration actually began, it had been thought that the giant world would be too cold, its atmosphere too poisonous with methane and ammonia, its gravitation too great for human life.

But the first Earthmen who visited Jupiter found that the great planet's interior radioactive heat kept it at tropical warmth. The methane and ammonia, they discovered, existed only in the upper atmospheric layers. The lower layers were quite breathable. And the invention of the gravity equalizers had solved the problem of the powerful gravitation.

Down through the darkness toward the night side of this great world, splitting the deep atmosphere with a shrill, knife-edged sound, plunged the *Comet*.

Captain Future held the controls, with Grag and the disguised Otho and Simon Wright beside him. And the red-haired adventurer was tense with fierce hope as he peered downward.

'Here we are,' Curt muttered finally, easing back a throttle. 'We're west of South Equatoria.'

'Not far west, I think,' rasped Simon Wright, from the special pedestal upon which his brain-case rested.

Beneath them lay a vast, heaving sea, bathed in silvery light by the three moons now in the sky. It was one of the thirty tremendous oceans of the monarch planet, and endless watery plain whose moonlit surface heaved in great billows toward the sky.

Curt had leveled off, and now the *Comet* screamed eastward low above the tossing silver ocean. Under the brilliant rays of Ganymede and Europa and Io, the waste of waters stretched to the far horizons in magnificent splendor.

Moon-bats, those weird Jovian birds that for some mysterious reason never fly except when the moons shine, were circling high above the waters. Their broad wings shone in the silver light with uncanny iridescence, due to some strange photochemical effect.

Schools of flame-fish, small fish that glowed with light because of their habit of feeding on radioactive sea-salts, swam just under the surface. The triple head of hydra, a species of big sea-snake always found twined in curious partnerships of three, reared above the waves. Far northward a 'stunner,' like an enormous flat white disc of flesh, shot up out of the moonlit sea and came down with a thunderous shock that would stun all fish immediately beneath and make them easy prey.

The *Comet* drove on low above the silver-lit ocean teeming with strange life. Under the three big, bright moons, the teardrop ship cleaved the atmosphere like a meteor, hurrying toward the perilous rendezvous with mystery that Curt Newton was determined to keep.

'Lights ahead, master,' boomed Grag, the robot's photoelectric eyes peering keenly.

'Yes, it's South Equatoria,' Curt said. 'Those are the lights of Jovopolis.'

Far ahead a low black coast rose from the moon-lit ocean. A little inland lay a big bunch of lights, dominated by the red-and-green lamps of the lofty spaceport tower.

Beyond the city lights stretched the black obscurity of the big plantations and the deep jungles beyond. And in the horizon the sky was painted by a dazzling aurora of twitching, quivering red rays – the crimson glare flung up by the distant Fire Sea.

'Only Saturn has more wonderful nights than this,' Curt said, feeling even in his tensity the weird beauty of it.

'You're not going to land openly in Jovopolis?' Simon Wright questioned Curt.

Captain Future shook his red head at the question.

'No, we'll drop down secretly at the edge of the spaceport.'

The *Comet* glided with muffled rocket-tubes over the moonlit mud flats along the shore, against which the great lunar tide of the Jovian ocean was hurling itself in mighty combers. Silent as a shadow, the little teardrop ship approached the spaceport, avoiding the docks and sinking down at the unlighted edge of the field.

Curt Newton cut the cyclotrons and stood up. He had already set his gravity equalizer, so that he did not feel the full power of the crushing Jovian gravitation.

'Otho and I must hurry,' he said tensely. 'We must be at Orris' hut when the Space Emperor comes there.'

'Can't I come too, master?' asked big Grag.

'You could never pass as a man,' jeered Otho. 'One glimpse of your metal face would give us away.'

Grag turned angrily toward the android, but Captain Future intervened hastily between the two.

'You must stay with Simon and guard the *Comet*, Grag,' he said. 'We'll be back soon if we catch the one we're after.'

'Be careful, lad,' muttered the Brain. 'This Space Emperor is the most dangerous antagonist we're ever encountered.'

Curt smiled pleasantly.

'A foeman worthy of our steel, eh? Don't worry, Simon. I'm not underestimating him!'

Curt and Otho emerged from the *Comet* and started toward the bright-lit Street of Space Sailors that ran eastward from the spaceport. The Jovian night lay soft and heavy upon them, the warm air laden with fetid scents of strange vegetation. The three bright moons cast queer multiple shifting shadows around them.

Curt knew the Street of Space Sailors well. It was usually roaring with lusty life, for in its dubious taverns gathered Earthmen who knew swampy Venus and desert Mars and icy Pluto, men who would be here for only a few days and who made the most of them before they went back.

But now the street was less crowded than usual. A pall seemed to lie over the motley interplanetary throng, and fewer rocket-cars came and went than was usual. There were many space-bronzed Earthmen drinking in the disreputable taverns, but they drank in unnatural silence. It was evident to Curt's keen eyes that the dark shadow of the plague lay over this city.

In the street were many Jovians, the planetary natives of this world. They were manlike, man-size creatures, but their green-skinned bodies were squatter than the human, their heads were small, round and hairless, with large, circular dark eyes, and their arms and legs ended in queer flippers instead of hands or feet.

Their clothing was a scanty black leather harness. They seemed to watch the passing Earthmen with unfriendliness and distrust.

'The Jovians don't seem to care much for Earthmen any more,' muttered Otho.

Curt's gray eyes narrowed slightly.

'According to what Orris told us, it's the Space Emperor who's stirred them into unrest.'

'Look out!' yelled a wild voice suddenly from somewhere in the throng ahead. 'He's got it!'

'Atavism – get away!' roared other voices.

Curt saw men darting away from an Earthman who had been wandering dazedly along the street, but who now was beating his breast, frothing at the lips, his glazed eyes glaring bestially around.

All shrank from the man thus suddenly stricken by the dread evolutionary blight. For a moment there was a frozen silence except for his growling cries. Then whistles shrilled and a rocket-car dashed along the street.

Haggard-faced hospital orderlies grabbed the struggling man who had just been stricken, pulled him into the car, and dashed away.

The tense silence lasted for an eternal moment, in which men stared sickly at each other. Then, as though desirous to get away from the spot, the motley throng moved rapidly on.

'So *that* is what it is like to be stricken by the horror!' hissed Otho.

A dangerous light flared in Captain Future's gray eyes, and his big form tensed.

'I think I'm going to enjoy meeting the black devil who's causing this,' he said between his teeth.

They moved on along the Street of Space Sailors, out of the lighted section of the dark end of the avenue. Before them lay the black, vague fields beyond the city. Curt's keen eyes glimpsed a dark little metalloy cabin, that stood a little beyond the street end, beside a clump of towering, moonlit tree-ferns.

'Orris' cabin,' he muttered, his hand dropping to his proton pistol. 'Come on, Otho.'

He listened at the door of the cabin, then pushed it open and entered the dark interior. The place was deserted.

Curt pulled the cord that uncovered the glowing uranite bulb in the ceiling. The illumination revealed a slovenly metal room, with a bunk in one corner, some zipper-suits and a couple of Jovian leather harnesses on hooks. The wide windows were screened against those pests of the planet, sucker-flies and brain-ticks.

Captain Future slipped his pistol inside his jacket. Then he stretched himself out on the bunk in the corner.

'The Space Emperor should be here soon,' he told the android crisply. 'When he comes, tell him you captured me, drugged me, and brought me here. Maneuver to get between him and the door.'

Otho nodded his disguised head in understanding. There was a fierce, throbbing glitter in his eyes.

'No more talk now,' Curt ordered tensely.

Lying sprawled stiffly on the bunk in perfect simulation of a drugged stupor, Curt watched through half-closed eyes. The android walked nervously back and forth, as though awaiting someone.

Eager suspense gripped Curt's mind. He, Captain Future, who had met and conquered so many evil ones in the past, was about to confront the most formidable adversary he had yet faced. His reckless soul almost exulted in the prospect.

Curt heard a sudden, low exclamation of astonishment from Otho. He opened his eyelids a trifle more, and received a surprise that was like an electric shock.

A black, weird figure now stood inside the cabin with them. The door had not opened, for Curt had been watching it. It was as though this dark visitant had come silently through the *walls*.

The Space Emperor! The mysterious figure who was turning Jupiter into a planetary hell! Curt knew that he looked upon his unknown antagonist.

The Space Emperor wore a grotesque, puffy black suit and helmet of mineraline, flexible material. The helmet had small eye-holes, but the eyes inside could not be seen. His real appearance was perfectly concealed by that puffy suit. It was impossible even to tell whether he was an Earthman or Jovian.

'You – you're here!' stammered Otho, in Orris' voice, putting into it and into the expression of his disguised face the same dread that Orris had shown in speaking of the Space Emperor.

Out of that helmet came a voice that rasped the fibers of Captain Future's spine. It was not a human-sounding voice. It was more like the deep voice of a Jovian, yet instead of being soft and slurred it was heavy, strong, vibrating with power.

'I'm here, yes,' the Space Emperor said. 'Did you and Skeel succeed in killing Captain Future?'

'We did better than that,' Otho said, with assumed pride. 'We captured him and I brought him here – see!'

Otho pointed toward the bunk upon which Curt Newton lay sprawled in apparent coma.

'Skeel was killed in the fight,' Otho went on, 'but I got Captain Future, all right. I gave him a shot of *somnal* to keep him quiet, and brought him here for you.'

'You fool!' came the deep voice of the Space Emperor, shaking now with rage. 'Why did you not kill him out there at once? Don't you know that this Captain Future is deadly dangerous as long as he is alive?'

The Space Emperor advanced a little in his rage, his dark figure not walking but moving with a queer, smooth glide across the metal floor.

Otho, pretending to shrink aside in fear, edged slowly to get between the dark visitant and the door.

'I thought you'd want him alive,' Otho was apologizing abjectly. 'I can kill him now, if you want me to.'

'Kill him, at once!' throbbed the Space Emperor's voice. 'This man has spoiled great plans before. He is not going to spoil mine!'

Curt Newton had been gathering his muscles for action. Now, as the last word vibrated, the red-haired adventurer launched himself upward in a flying spring at his enemy.

Straight at that dark, erect figure plunged Curt. He expected to knock the mysterious plotter to the floor, overcome him. But Curt received the greatest surprise of his life.

For Captain Future felt himself plunge *through* the Space Emperor as though the latter did not exist! Just as though the Space Emperor were but an immaterial phantom, Curt hurtled through his solid-seeming body and crashed against the wall with stunning force.

'So!' cried the criminal's deep voice. 'One of Captain Future's traps!'

Otho had charged in almost the same instant as Curt. And the disguised android also had plunged *through* the dark figure.

Curt had his proton pistol out, as the black form started to glide swiftly across the room. Astounded, dazed as he was by the incredible thing that had happened, Captain Future did not lose his presence of mind for a moment.

He pulled trigger, and a pale thin beam lanced from the slender pistol toward the gliding dark figure.

Curt's proton pistol was more deadly than any of the atomic flare-guns used by other men. It could be set either to stun or kill, and it was set to kill now. But its concentrated jet of protons merely drove through the Space Emperor without harming him in the least.

'At last you meet someone with powers greater than your own, Captain Future!' the hidden voice taunted.

The dark figure glided away. The solid-seeming shape passed through the solid metal wall. Then it was gone.

Otho stood still, numbed by the incredible sight. But Captain Future leaped toward the door, galvanized into action.

He burst out into the moon-shot darkness and swept the obscurity with his eyes. There was no sign of the Space Emperor. He had disappeared completely.

'He got away, that devil!' Curt cried, anger and self-reproach flaring in his voice.

'He wasn't real at all!' Otho exclaimed dazedly. 'He was only a shadow, a phantom!'

'A phantom couldn't talk and be heard!' Curt snapped. 'He's as real as you or I.'

'But he came and went through the wall –' the android muttered bewilderedly.

Captain Future's tanned face frowned in thought, as he tried to comprehend his enemy's secret.

'I believe,' he announced, 'that the Space Emperor is using some secret of vibration to make himself effectively immaterial whenever he wishes.'

Otho stared.

'Immaterial?'

Curt nodded his red head slowly.

'It's always been considered theoretically possible that if the frequency of atomic vibration of an object or man were stepped up higher than the frequency of ordinary matter, that object or man could pass *through* ordinary matter, just as two electric signals of different frequency can pass through the same wire at the same time.'

'But if that were the case, he would sink right down through the ground to the center of gravity of the planet!' Otho objected.

Impatiently, Captain Future shook his head.

'Not if he set his gravity equalizer at zero. And he could use reactive force-push of some kind to achieve that gliding lateral motion. Of course, he couldn't breathe ordinary air, but inside that suit would be an air-supply whose atomic frequency would be changed along with his body.'

'But how could he talk, and see, and hear us?' Otho wanted to know.

'That I can't understand yet myself,' Captain Future admitted ruefully. 'The whole thing embodies a science that is not human science. No Earthman scientist has ever yet achieved such a vibration set-up.'

'Then where did he get the secret, and the secret of the evolutionary horror?' the android demanded. 'There's supposed to have been a great civilization on Jupiter in the dim past. Now there's nothing here now but these half-civilized Jovians who have no science. Do you think the Space Emperor could be a Jovian?'

Curt shook his head. He felt baffled, for the moment. The sinister mystery around the dark plotter had deepened.

And his pride in his scientific knowledge had received a bad blow. He had run up against someone who apparently possessed scientific secrets beyond even his own attainments.

'We've got to find out *who* the Space Emperor is before we can even hope to get him,' he declared. He looked at Otho. 'You can make up as a Jovian, can't you?'

Otho stiffened.

'You know there isn't a planetary being in the System I can't disguise myself as, when I want to,' he boasted.

'Then go ahead and assume Jovian disguise,' Curt said quickly, 'and go back into the crowded quarter. Mingle with the Jovians there. Try to find out what they know about the Space Emperor, and above all, if he is a Jovian or an Earthman.'

Otho nodded understandingly.

'Shall I come back here if I learn anything?'

'No, report back to the *Comet*,' Curt ordered. 'I'm going to the Governor. There's a lead there somewhere to the Space Emperor. For the Governor, remember, would be the only person here notified that we were coming to Jupiter – and yet the Space Emperor knew of our coming and set an ambush for us!'

In surprisingly few minutes, Otho had shed the disguise of Orris and had assumed the likeness of a native Jovian.

The android had used the oily chemical spray to soften the synthetic flesh of his face, hands and feet. Then he had molded his head and features into the round head and flat, circular-eyed face of a Jovian, and his hands, and feet into the flipper-like extremities of the planetary natives.

He smeared green pigment from his make-up pouch smoothly over all his body. A skillful hunching of his rubbery figure gave him the squat appearance of a Jovian. And finally, he donned one of the black leather harnesses hanging beside the zipper-suits on the wall of the cabin. Earthmen often wore those scanty harnesses in the damp, hot jungles of Jupiter, for the sake of coolness and freedom.

When Otho spoke, it was in the soft, slurred bass voice of a Jovian.

'Will I pass?' he asked Curt.

Captain Future smiled.

'I wouldn't recognize you myself,' he said. 'Get going, and watch yourself.'

Otho slipped out of the cabin, and was gone. In a moment, Curt emerged also into the moonlit night.

The red-headed space-farer strode rapidly toward the silvered metal mass of buildings of the city, heading toward the central section where was located the seat of colonial government.

Somewhere there, he was certain, was a key to the mystery that had shrouded this planet in a spell of dark horror.

CHAPTER VI

Monsters That Were Men

The governor's mansion stood in parklike grounds of big tree-ferns and banked shrubbery. It was a large rectangular structure, built of gleaming metalloy like all the rest of the Earthman city. Tonight, its many wide windows were glowing with light.

Curt approached it silently through the dark grove. Brilliant rays of the three big moons struck down between the fronds of the towering tree-ferns and glistened on his determined face. Perfume of beautiful but forbidding 'shock flowers' was heavy in his nostrils. High above glided moon-bats, those weird, iridescent winged creatures of Jupiter that appear only when one or more moons are in the sky.

He reached a terrace on the west side of the big metal mansion. Soundlessly, Captain Future advanced to an open window that spilled forth the bright white glow of powerful uranite bulbs. He peered keenly into the office inside, and at once recognized the governor of the Earth colony, from the President's description.

Sylvanus Quale, the colonial governor, sat behind a metal desk. Quale was a man of fifty, with a stocky, powerful figure, iron-gray hair, and a square face that had a stony impassivity. He looked as inscrutable as a statue, his colorless eyes expressionless.

Captain Future saw that Quale was talking to a girl in white nurse's uniform.

'Why didn't Doctor Britt bring the report from Emergency Hospital himself, Miss Randall?' Quale was asking.

'He's worn out and on the verge of collapse,' she replied. Her eyes were shadowed as she added, 'This terrible thing is getting too much for us.'

Curt saw that the girl was strikingly pretty, even in the severe white uniform. Her dark, wavy, uncovered hair framed a small face whose brown eyes and firm lips gave an impression of cool steadiness and efficiency. Yet deep horror lurked in her eyes.

'Mr Quale, what are we going to do?' Curt heard her appeal to the governor. 'There are over three hundred cases of the blight in Emergency Hospital now. And some of them are getting – ghastly.'

'You mean they're still changing, Joan?' Quale asked, forgetting official formality in his deep thoughtfulness.

The girl nodded, her face pale.

'Yes. I can't describe what hideous monsters some of them have become. And only days ago they were men! You must do something to stop it!'

Curt stepped into the office through the open window, silently as a shadow.

'I hope there is something that *I* can do to stop it,' he said quietly.

Joan Randall turned with a little startled cry, and Sylvanus Quale half rose to his feet as he saw the big, red-haired, gray-eyed young man who stood inside the room, gravely facing them.

'Who – what –' the governor stammered, reaching toward a button on his desk.

'You needn't call guards,' Curt told him impatiently. 'This ring will identify me.'

Curt Newton held out his left hand. On that hand he wore a ring with a curious, large bezel. At its center was a little glowing sphere of radioactive metal, representing the sun. This was surrounded by nine concentric circular grooves, in each of which was a small jewel.

The jewels represented the nine planets. There was a tiny brown one for Mercury, a larger pearly gem for Venus, and so on. And the jewels *moved* slowly, circling the little glowing sun. Motivated by a tiny atomic power plant, they moved exactly in accordance with the planets they represented. This unique ring was known from Mercury to Pluto as the identifying emblem of Captain Future.

'Why, you're Captain Future!' Sylvanus Quale exclaimed startledly.

'Captain Future?' echoed Joan Randall, staring with sudden eagerness at this big, red-haired adventurer.

'President Carthew notified you that I was coming here?' Curt asked the governor.

Quale nodded quickly. 'He televised me when you started.'

'Did you tell anyone else I was coming?' Curt asked keenly.

He watched Quale narrowly as he awaited an answer. If the governor admitted having told no one, it meant—

But Quale was nodding.

'I told Eldred Kells, the vice-governor, and Doctor Britt, chief planetary physician, and some others here. I wanted to reassure them – they're all so panicky.'

Curt felt momentarily thwarted. It looked as though his possible lead to the Space Emperor had faded out.

Disguising his disappointment, he told Quale briefly about the ambush and the two criminals now marooned on Callisto.

'I'll send a Planet Police cruiser out to pick them up,' Quale promised quickly.

At that moment a door opened. A tall, blond man of thirty in a white zipper-suit entered the office. His strong face was worn and lined by too-great strain.

'What is it, Kells?' Sylvanus Quale demanded.

Eldred Kells, the vice-governor, was staring wonderingly at Curt. Then, as he glimpsed the red-haired man's ring, Kells' worn face lighted with hope.

'Captain Future – you're here!' he cried. 'Thank God! Maybe you can do something to end this horror.'

Kells turned quickly back to his superior.

'Lucas Brewer and young Mark Cannig are here, sir. They just flew down from Jungletown. I gather that things are getting pretty horrible up there.'

Quale turned to Captain Future.

'Brewer is president of Jovian Mines, a small company that owns a radium mine north of Jungletown,' he explained. 'Mark Cannig is his mine-superintendent.'

'I remember hearing of this Brewer before,' Curt said, frowning. 'On Saturn, three years ago.'

Kells returned in a moment with the two men he had named.

Lucas Brewer, the mine owner, was a grossly fat man of forty, with dark, shrewd little eyes and a puffy face that wore the pitiless look of those who live too well.

Mark Cannig, his mine-superintendent, was a dark, handsome young fellow with a rather nervous look. He glanced eagerly at Joan Randall but the pretty nurse avoided his gaze.

'Quale, you've got to do something!' Lucas Brewer said emphatically as he entered. 'This thing is getting—'

He stopped suddenly, as his eyes rested on Captain Future. An expression of recognition came into his eyes.

'Why, is that—' he started to say.

'It's Captain Future, yes,' Quale said. 'I told you he was coming, remember.'

Curt saw something of apprehension creep into Brewer's small eyes. And it seemed to him that there was a sudden uneasiness also in the face of young Mark Cannig.

Curt hated promoters of Brewer's type. He had met them before on many planets. They were ruthless tricksters whose greed brought misery to colonizing Earthmen and planetary natives alike.

'I've heard a lot about you, of course, Captain Future,' Brewer was saying hesitantly.

'And I heard something about you and your business activities on Saturn a few years ago,' Curt said disgustedly.

He asked suddenly, 'Why did you come here from Jungletown tonight?'

'Because things are getting so bad up at Jungletown!' Brewer declared. 'We've got over five hundred cases of the blight there. The hospital's hopelessly overcrowded, and I wanted to urge Quale to do something to stop this horrible thing. Anyone up there may be the next stricken by that horror. Why, I might be next!'

Captain Future stared contemptuously at the fat promoter. But Eldred Kells immediately answered him indignantly.

'We can't stop the plague until we know what's causing it,' defended the haggard vice-governor.

'Where did the thing start?' Curt asked him.

Quale answered.

'Up at Jungletown, several hundred miles north of here. It's a new boom town. Sprang up after radium and uranium deposits were located nearby. The place is pretty close to the southern shore of the Fire Sea, and there are some thousands of Earthmen engineers, prospectors and the like who make it their base.

'The first cases were of a few radium prospectors,' Quale went on. 'They stumbled out of the jungle, already horribly transformed into ape-like creatures. Since then, more people have been stricken every day. Most of the cases have been at Jungletown, but there have been a large number down here at Jovopolis, and others elsewhere.'

'We're completely in the dark about the cause of this awful disease,' Eldred Kells added hopelessly.

'It's not a disease,' Curt told them forcefully. 'It's being deliberately caused.'

'Impossible!' exclaimed Lucas Brewer. 'What man would do such a fiendish thing?'

'I didn't say it was a man doing it,' Captain Future retorted. 'The one who is causing it calls himself – the Space Emperor.'

He watched their faces closely as he spoke the name. Brewer looked blank. Young Mark Cannig shifted uneasily. But Kells and the governor only started wonderingly.

'Have any of you ever heard that name?' Curt demanded.

All of them shook their heads negatively. Curt came quickly to a decision.

'I want to see the victims you have here in Jovopolis,' he declared. 'I'd like to study them. You spoke of an Emergency Hospital you're keeping them in?'

Sylvanus Quale nodded.

'We converted our Colony Prison into an emergency hospital. It alone could hold those – creatures. Miss Randall and I can take you there.'

Curt's big figure strode with the governor and the nurse out of the office and through the halls of the mansion. They emerged into the soft, heavy night, which was now illuminated by only Europa and Io.

The two bright moons cast queer forked shadows down among the tall, solemn tree-ferns as they went through the grounds. The buildings housing the colonial government bordered the square around the governor's mansion.

The Emergency Hospital, formerly a prison, was a massive structure with heavy blank walls of synthetic metal.

As they entered the vestibule, in which nervous-looking orderlies were on guard, an aide rushed in after the governor.

'There's an urgent televisor call for you from Jungletown, sir,' he told Sylvanus Quale breathlessly.

'I'll have to go back and answer it,' Quale said to Captain Future. 'Miss Randall will show you the atavism cases.'

The girl led the way from the vestibule into a long, lighted main hall of the prison. She went to the heavy, solid metal door of the first cell-block. There she touched a switch outside the door, and they heard its bolt shoot back.

They stepped into the cell-block. It was a windowless barracks with solid metal walls, lighted by a half-dozen glowing uranite bulbs in the ceiling. Cell doors were ranged along either side of the corridor which they had entered.

'These are cases of varying dates,' the pale girl told Curt. 'Some of them are recent and are only apelike, but others are – you can see for yourself.'

Curt went down the row of doors, peering through the gratings into the cells.

The cells contained a nightmare assortment of ghastly horrors. In some were huge ape-like creatures standing erect and beating with hairy fists at their doors, roars of rage coming from their throats.

In others were creatures that were even more bestial, quadrupedal hairy brutes with pouched bodies and blazing feral eyes and wide jaws bristling with fangs. Still other cells held scaled green reptilian monsters shuffling forward on four limbs and crawling with their talons to reach Curt and Joan Randall.

Captain Future was shaken by a storm of fierce wrath such as he had never felt before. Never before, on any of the nine worlds, had he encountered a horror like this. He felt in the presence of something utterly unclean and monstrous.

'God help the devil who did this if I get my hands on him,' he gritted.

Joan Randall, who had followed him down the corridor, looked up into his face.

'If it was an Earthman who caused this, I have a suspicion as to his identity, Captain Future,' she said.

She had taken from a pocket a little badge which she showed him. It bore the initials 'P.P.'

'I'm a Planet Police secret agent,' the girl explained. 'There have been several of us here since this horror began.'

'Whom do you suspect?' Curt demanded quickly.

Before the girl could answer, there came a startling interruption. It was the click of the cell-block door bolt.

'Someone has locked us in!' Joan cried.

Curt sprang toward the door. It was immovable, the bolt having been shot home by the electric control outside.

'It's a trap!' he declared.

He drew his proton pistol, aimed it at the door, and released a lightninglike lance of force. But the heavy slab of artificial metal resisted the flash of force. It was scorched but unharmed.

'Is there any other way out of here?' Captain Future demanded.

'No. This was a prison, remember,' Joan answered. 'Ventilation is indirect, and the whole place is soundproofed and rayproofed.'

'What the devil is that?' Curt exclaimed.

A loud, simultaneous clicking had sounded, and every cell-door along the corridor had suddenly slid open.

Joan went deathly white.

'The cells have been unlocked!' she cried. 'They are controlled from a switch out there, and someone has opened that switch!'

She uttered a little scream.

'Look, they're coming out—'

With the opening of the cell-doors, the hideous creatures inside the cells were beginning to emerge.

Out into the corridor shuffled a great, hairy ape-thing, then another, then a shambling, blazing-eyed quadrupedal beast, and then one of the shuffling, taloned reptilian monstrosities.

Captain Future felt Joan Randall shrink against him, terrified. The monsters emerging into the corridor, monsters that had once been men, had sensed the presence of the man and girl and were starting down the hall toward them.

CHAPTER VII

Otho Takes the Trail

Back at the Street of Space Sailors, Otho the android moved slowly through the crowded, noisy quarter. Perfectly disguised as one of the green, squat Jovians, the synthetic man walked with the shuffling movement characteristic of the planetary natives. He concentrated upon maintaining an appearance of sulky silence.

Inwardly, Otho was intensely alert to everyone about him. The android was absolutely loyal to Captain Future. His devotion to the laughing, red-headed adventurer was the strongest trait of his fierce, unhuman nature, stronger even than his love of action and combat. He was determined to find out what he could for Curt, no matter what the cost.

He kept an eye out for other Jovians. His task was to mix with the planetary natives and find out what they knew about the Space Emperor. Otho had no doubt of success. His supreme, cocky self-confidence was bolstered by his knowledge of the Jovian language and customs, gained on former trips to this planet with Captain Future.

So intently was the android looking out for other Jovians with whom he might strike up acquaintance, that he bumped into a big, hulking Earthman prospector in the crowd.

'Git outa my way, greenie!' roared the angry Earthman, and gave Otho a cuff that sent him spinning aside.

The fierce-natured android's body tensed for a spring at the other. Then he realized that for a Jovian to attack an Earthman would cause a riot and give him away.

'I did not mean to bump you, Earthman,' Otho said humbly, in the Jovian language.

'Why don't you greenies stay out in your jungles and keep out of this colony?' the prospector demanded roughly, and then moved on.

Otho had noticed that three Jovians stood at the side of the street, and that they had been watching the incident. In a flash, the android saw how he could make capital of it.

He moved over to the three squat planetary natives, and spoke to them in a voice whose slurred bass tones he kept throbbing with resentment.

'I am only trying to find the way out of here,' Otho told them, 'yet these Earthmen will not even allow me to walk freely through the city.'

The Jovians looked at him. One of them was a very large individual, with strong intelligence in the stamp of his unhuman green face and his dark, round eyes.

'Are you a stranger in this country?' he asked Otho. 'I have never seen you in our northern villages.'

'I am not from the north,' Otho answered quickly. 'I come from a village which lies far east of here in the jungle. My name is Zhil.'

'And I am Guro, chief of my people,' the big Jovian told Otho, pride in his deep, bass tones.

At that moment there was an interruption to their talk. Out of a doorway farther down the street burst another Earthman who had suddenly fallen victim to the dreaded blight.

'Atavism!' went up the familiar, dreaded cry from scores of voices. 'Call the police!'

'Keep away from him or you'll catch it!' yelled others in horror.

In very few moments, a rocket-car had come and the growling, frothing Earthman had been overcome and taken away. And, as Otho had noticed before, the throng in the street hastened fearfully away from the place as though hoping to escape possible contagion.

'The curse of the Ancients spread fast,' said Guro solemnly to his two Jovian companions and Otho.

'Yes, the time grows near,' one of the other two green natives declared.

Otho felt a dawning surprise. What did they mean by the curse of the Ancients?

He knew that the Jovians believed the mighty, mysterious ruins in the jungle had once been the cities of a race of demigods they called the Ancients. But what had that legend to do with this avatism terror?

Otho decided upon a bold attempt. He had to find out what these Jovians knew about the Space Emperor, and for that reason he risked exposure by his next words.

'Our dark leader told us the truth,' Otho said solemnly, looking at the others.

Guro's round eyes expressed surprise.

'Then you of the eastern villages have seen and heard the Living Ancient also? He has appeared to you as he has to us?'

The Living Ancient? So that was what the Jovians called the Space Emperor? Otho wondered what the name could mean.

'Yes, he has appeared to us,' he told Guro. 'He brought his message to us also.'

That could cover almost anything, Otho thought. Yet he was puzzled over the calling of the Space Emperor the *living* Ancient. Was it possible their enemy was a Jovian?

'Then you will also be ready to rise and sweep away the Earthmen when the Living Ancient gives the word?' Guro asked.

So his guess had been right! Otho almost gave himself away by a slight start of surprise which he could not wholly suppress.

A rising of the Jovians against the Earthmen? Was that the mainspring of the mysterious Space Emperor's gigantic plot? But how could such an attack of the natives hope to succeed? Their weapons were very primitive. And how was the spread of the atavism terror connected with it?

The thoughts flashed swiftly through the android's mind in a moment. But he did not hesitate in answering Guro.

'Yes, we too are ready when the word comes,' he told Guro fervently.

'Good!' muttered the big Jovian. 'And the word will come soon. The wrath of the mighty Ancients grows ever greater against the Earthmen, making more and more of them into brute beasts. Soon the Living Ancient will give us the word.'

Otho thought quickly, and then spoke in the same fervent tones.

'I was to bring word to the Living Ancient of our preparations,' he told Guro. 'He commanded us to send such word when we were ready. But I do not know where to find our mighty leader.'

'The Living Ancient is to appear to us tomorrow night in a spot near my own village,' Guro told him in a bass whisper. 'That spot is the Place of the Dead.'

'I know that,' lied Otho. 'But how shall I hope to find it, when I do not know the land here in the north?' Otho asked doubtfully. 'I have never been this far toward the Fire Sea before.'

Guro reassured him.

'You will have no trouble finding it, for we shall take you there ourselves. We are returning northward now, and you can come with us. Two nights hence you can go with us to the Place of the Dead, and deliver your message to our leader when he appears.'

Otho thanked him quickly. It was apparent that Guro and the other two Jovians had completely accepted him.

'We leave now,' Guro told him. 'The mission that brought us here is finished. Our lopers wait in the jungle beyond this city.'

Otho shuffled with the three Jovians, following Guro's lead through the rowdy, noisy streets of the interplanetary colonial city. They were not molested, and presently they were out of the metalloy streets of Jovopolis, and moving along the road that led between the great grain fields of the Earthmen.

The android's mind was racing. He must notify Curt Newton of what he had learned and where he was going. But though he had his pocket televisor concealed inside his leather harness, he dared not try to use it while Guro and the others were so close to him.

The three Jovians and the disguised android shuffled on along the road between the mingled brilliance of the two moons now in the sky. Soon they reached the end of the grain fields, and entered the moon-drenched jungle whose wilderness stretched unbroken toward the Fire Sea.

Just inside the jungle waited another Jovian, with four 'lopers,' as the Jovians called their queer steeds. The lopers were large, lizardlike creatures, with scaled, barreled bodies supported by four bowed legs that gave them incredible speed. Their necks were long and snaky, ending in reptilian heads from whose fangless mouths ran the leather reins by which the rider controlled his mount.

'We need your loper for this stranger. You will stay here until we send back another,' Guro told the Jovian who had waited with the animals. Then he told Otho, 'Mount, Zhil.'

Otho had never ridden one of the lizardlike creatures before, but the android, afraid neither of man nor devil, swung up unhesitatingly into the rude leather saddle.

The creature turned and hissed angrily at him, its small eyes flaring red. Otho saw the other Jovians kick their mounts to quiet them, and he did the same. The creature calmed down.

'Now, northward!' Guro called in his deep bass voice, and uttered a loud cry to their mounts.

Next moment, Otho was clinging for his life. It was as though the creature had exploded forward.

All four of the lopers were rushing at a nightmare pace along a dim trail through the moonlit jungle. Their speed was incredible, yet the motion was so gliding that Otho soon adjusted himself to it.

Guro and the other Jovians were riding around him. There was still no chance to call Captain Future on the pocket televisor, so the android gave up the idea for the time.

'It is a long ride,' Guro called to him over the rush of wind, 'but we shall be with my people by tomorrow night, and you will go with us to the Place of the Dead.'

'I am eager to see the Living Ancient again,' Otho called back, and reflected that he was not lying about that.

The moonlit jungle through which they rode along narrow, dim trails was dense and wild. Huge tree-ferns reared their glossy pillared trunks nearly a hundred feet. Big stiff brush-trees towered almost as high. Slender 'copper trees' whose fibers contained a high copper content gleamed metallically in the light of the moons.

Snake-vines hanging from the tall trunks swayed blindly toward the quartet as they sped past. Sucker-flies swarmed around them, and deadly brain-ticks were visible on leaves. Somewhere off in the jungle, a siren-bird was charming its prey with weird song. Now and then a tree-octopus flitted hastily through the fronds above like a white ghost.

Otho was enjoying this wild, rushing ride through the moon-shot Jovian jungle. The android had, more than any human could have, the capacity for taking things as they came.

Whether he was battling through blinding red sandstorms on desert Mars or wading poisonous Venusian swamps, climbing down into the awful chasms of mighty-mountained Uranus or braving the terrible ice-fields of Pluto, he did not usually bother to look far ahead.

But now the necessity of getting word to Captain Future weighed upon his mind. Several hours of unceasing riding passed without his getting a chance to use his pocket televisor. One or other of the three Jovians was always near him.

Finally Guro pulled in on his reins and their lopers came gradually to a halt, as the others did likewise.

'We stop here to eat,' Guro announced. 'The lopers must have a little rest. We start again at dawn.'

They dismounted, and the four lizardlike creatures stretched out upon the soft black ground of the little clearing in which they had halted.

'I will get food,' Guro declared, and strode out of the clearing into the brush.

The other two Jovians were seeing to the girths of their saddles. Otho saw his opportunity, and crouched down quickly as though relaxing, drawing out his watchlike pocket televisor.

He touched its call-button hastily. He was not sure that the little instrument, designed for short distances, could reach as far back as Jovopolis. Tensely he waited for an answering buzz.

There was no answer. Otho felt something as near despair as his fierce, resolute nature could experience. Again he jabbed the call-button, and again.

Then came a faint answering whirr from the little instrument, an indication that his call-signal had been heard.

'This is Otho speaking,' he whispered tensely into the tiny thing, not turning on its visi-wave. 'I am going with Jovians northward. The Space Emperor is to be—'

A shadow fell across the moonlit ground in front of him. And a deep voice sounded.

'What are you doing?' it demanded.

The android turned swiftly. Behind him stood Guro, a bunch of brilliant flame-fruit in his hand. He stared down at Otho with suspicious eyes.

CHAPTER VIII

The Trail

Inside Jovopolis' former prison, Captain Future rapidly set his proton pistol, then triggered quickly at the horde of monsters advancing down the corridor of the cell-block toward Joan and himself.

The thin white beam from his weapon struck some of the creatures in the front of the savage mob. They collapsed as though struck by lightning, stunned by the potent beams.

The others hesitated. But as more and more of them emerged from the unlocked cells, they came forward again.

'Captain Future, it must have been the Space Emperor you spoke of who trapped us like this!' cried Joan Randall.

'Yes,' gritted Curt, 'and that means that the Space Emperor is one of those men who were with us in Quale's office. Only they knew we had come here!'

His mind was seething. Which of those men had followed them here and trapped them? Which one was the Space Emperor?

Could it be Quale himself, he wondered? Or Lucas Brewer, or Kells, or young Cannig?

As his mind grappled with that problem, he was firing again at the advancing monsters. Again the creatures retreated from the beam that had stunned a dozen of their number.

A fight started between an ape-thing and a scaly green reptilian creature. Snarling, hissing, clawing each other, the two nightmare brutes soon had involved others in the battle. Their ferocity was bestial, terrifying.

'What are we going to do?' cried Joan Randall. The girl's face was deathly pale.

Curt smiled grimly.

'Don't worry, we'll get out somehow. I've been in worse spots than this.'

Somehow the confidence of this tall, red-haired young man was reassuring to Joan, even in the face of inevitable death.

'If these walls are rayproof, there's no chance to call Grag and Simon on my pocket televisor,' he was muttering. 'I could make us invisible, but it wouldn't last long and wouldn't do us any good.'

'Invisible?' cried the girl, astounded even in this moment of terror.

'Yes, I could do it,' Curt smiled. 'But it only lasts ten minutes or so. We've got to think of something else.'

'Captain Future, they're coming again!' Joan exclaimed fearfully.

The evolutionary monsters had broken off their battle, and now were once more beginning to shuffle down the white-lit corridor toward the man and girl.

Captain Future's beam licked forth hungrily. Again, the creatures hesitated as some of them fell stunned. Curt had not set the beam at full strength. He didn't want to kill these creatures who had been men once and might become normal if a cure were found for them.

Curt's clear gray eyes swept the interior of the cell-block again, in search of some way out. It seemed hopeless to think that they could escape or get any call for help through these soundproofed, rayproofed walls.

Then his gaze fastened on the glowing uranite bulbs in the ceiling of the corridor. At once, his eyes lit up.

'I've got it!' he exclaimed. 'The only way for us to get out is to destroy the lock of the door. And there's a chance that we can do that.'

'Your pistol's ray can't get at the lock,' the girl reminded him, her voice hopeless. 'The electric mechanism is encased in the wall beside the door.'

A quadrupedal monster hurtled through the air at that moment. Curt's beam caught him and he fell unconscious in a mass at their feet.

'My pistol won't reach the lock,' Captain Future admitted, as coolly as though nothing had happened, 'but maybe I can get at it with something else. Here, take my pistol and hold those creatures off while I work.'

He did not ask the girl whether she could do it. He calmly assumed her courage, and this trust on the part of the red-haired adventurer steadied Joan's nerve.

She took the proton pistol, and each time one of the growling, roaring monsters moved forward, she pulled the trigger.

Meanwhile, Curt was bunching himself for a spring. He might have used his gravity equalizer, he thought fleetingly, but there was no time. With all his force, he leaped upward. The metal ceiling was only a few feet above his head. His superb muscles shot him up toward it, and his hand grasped one of the glowing uranite bulbs.

He fell back to the floor, sliding the glowing bulb out of its socket. The thing was merely a glass bulb containing a few ounces of the glowing, powerful white radioactive powder called uranite.

Hastily, Curt took from his tungstite belt-kit a thin little glass tube. It contained a restorative gas he always carried with him. Deliberately, he broke both ends of the sealed tube, allowing the gas to escape. This left him a tiny glass pipette.

He broke the uranite bulb, then deftly filled the little pipette with the glowing radioactive powder. As he worked, he glanced up every few moments to make sure that Joan Randall was managing to hold off the monstrous mob, smiling at her encouragingly.

'Now I'll try it,' he told her, when the pipette was full of the uranite powder. 'Hope it works. If it doesn't we're stuck here.'

Quickly Captain Future went to the door of the cell-block.

He applied one open end of the pipette of uranite to the crack between door and wall, just where the lock was located.

Then, with extreme care to make sure that he did not inhale any of the super-powerful radioactive powder, he applied his lips to the other end of the pipette and blew.

The radioactive powder was blown in a little jet into the crack between the door and frame. Wherever a grain of the glowing stuff struck the metal, it sizzled and hissed, eating into the surface like a red-hot poker applied to an ice-cube.

'If I was able to blow any of the powder into the lock, it ought to eat away the delicate mechanism there and the magnetic control of the bolt will be released,' he told the girl.

'I – I don't think I can hold them back much longer,' came Joan's shaken voice heard over the babel of growls.

Captain Future could hear the powerful uranite eating into the metal between door and wall. Had he got any of the grains into the lock? He waited, his nerves taut.

Suddenly he heard a sharp click. The bolt of the door shot back, released when the magnetic pull of the lock was ended by destruction of the electric lock-circuit.

'Come on, Joan!' cried the space-farer, seizing the girl by the arm.

They burst out into the main hall of the prison and raced down it, monsters emerging after them.

In a moment they were safe in the vestibule.

'That was too close for comfort!' Captain Future declared. His big figure swung toward the startled orderlies. 'Has anyone come through this vestibule in the last half hour?'

They shook their heads. Curt's tanned face frowned, but in a moment he spoke again to the orderlies.

'You'd better use sleep-gas to get those creatures back into the cell-block,' he said. 'And you'll have to fix the lock.'

As the orderlies hastened to restore order, Curt turned to the pale girl.

'Joan, tell me – is there any way someone from outside could have got to that door-switch without coming through this vestibule?'

Joan nodded quickly.

'Someone who knew the building could come into the main hall through the Prison Warden's offices, which are unoccupied since this was made into a hospital.'

'Then that's how the Space Emperor, whoever the devil is, came and trapped us!' Captain Future said.

He asked the girl another question.

'Just before we were locked in there, you were saying that you suspected some Earthman here as possibly being the one behind this terrible blight?'

'Yes, Lucas Brewer,' said the girl. 'Brewer seems to have some queer, mysterious influence over the Jovians. They work in his radium mine as laborers, and they won't work for any other Earthman, no matter what pay is offered them.'

The girl continued.

'You said that the Space Emperor, the one who is causing the horror, is worshiped by the Jovians. That's what makes me suspect it is Brewer.'

Curt frowned in deep thought.

'That's certainly grounds for suspecting Brewer. And also, we *know* now that the Space Emperor is one of the four men who were in Quale's office when we left it, and Brewer is one of those four.'

His chin hardened.

'I think I have some questions to ask Mr Brewer. Come along!'

CHAPTER IX

Laboratory Magic

They hastened back beneath the two brilliant Jovian moons toward the metalloy mansion of the governor.

Sylvanus Quale and Eldred Kells were bending over a map when Curt and the girl entered the white-lit office.

'Why – what's happened?' exclaimed Quale, his colorless face startled as he looked inquiringly at the disheveled two.

'The Space Emperor tried to scrag us and nearly succeeded, that's what happened,' rasped Captain Future. His gray eyes were searching their faces as he told what had occurred.

'Where are Brewer and young Cannig?' he demanded.

'They've left – gone back to Jungletown in their rocket-flier,' Quale replied.

'Why did they go?' Curt demanded, his big figure stiffening.

'That message that called me back here to my office was from Captain Gurney, the police marshal up there at Jungletown,' Quale explained. 'He reported that the atavism cases are getting out of control up there, and also that the unrest of the Jovians up there seems to be increasing.'

The governor paused.

'Brewer said that he and Cannig ought to return to look after his company's mine,' he continued. 'He insisted on going.'

'That's right,' confirmed Eldred Kells, the blond vice-governor. 'I tried to get them to stay, but couldn't.'

Curt was thinking. Either Brewer or Cannig could have slipped into the Emergency Hospital to spring that death-trap, before leaving.

'Kells is going up to Jungletown at once, to see how bad conditions are there,' Quale told Curt.

'I'll go too,' Joan Randall said quickly. 'If the number of victims is increasing so, I'll be needed at the hospital there.'

The girl secret agent flashed Captain Future a glance as she spoke. Curt realized she intended to continue her observation of Brewer and Cannig, if possible.

Kells hesitated at her going along.

'Jungletown is rather a tough, wild town for a girl to go into,' he declared. 'But it's true you'll be needed up there. Come along, and we'll start at once.'

Captain Future made no comment as the man and girl left the office. A few moments later, the roar of their rocket-flier was heard as they took off from the nearby hangar.

Curt turned toward the governor.

'Quale, as governor here you know something about these legends of a mighty Jovian civilization that is supposed to have existed on this planet in the remote past?'

The governor looked surprised.

'Why, yes, I've heard the superstitious stories the Jovians tell,' he admitted. 'And the few archaeologists who have looked at those queer ruins in the jungle say that they really were once the cities of a highly civilized race. But why do you ask, Captain Future?'

'Has anyone ever unearthed any of the scientific secrets of that vanished Jovian race?' Curt demanded.

Quale was a little startled. 'Why, no. It's true that some have hoped to find the hidden secrets of that mysterious race. One young archaeologist who was through here some weeks ago was sure he could. But no one has ever done so.'

'What was the name of that young archaeologist?' Curt asked quickly.

'His name was Kenneth Lester,' Quale replied. 'He told me he'd been studying the Jovian legends and believed he was on the trail of solving the whole mystery of the vanished race. He went from here up to Jungletown, and then on northward into the jungles toward the Fire Sea.'

Captain Future's eyes narrowed.

'Where's Lester now? What did he say he'd found when he came back?'

The governor shook his head.

'Lester never came back. Nothing more was ever heard from him, though he'd promised to notify me of any discoveries he made. He had no experience with those jungles, and undoubtedly he perished up there in them.'

Captain Future remained silent for a moment, wrapped in thought. The governor looked attentively at the big, red-haired young man.

'That's all I wanted to know,' Curt said finally. 'One more thing, though – I would like to have one of the most recent atavism cases from your hospital, for study by Simon Wright and myself, in order that we can try to find a cure for this thing.'

A quarter hour later, in a borrowed police rocket-car, Captain Future reached the edge of the dark Jovopolis spaceport where the *Comet* waited. He carried out of the car an unconscious Earthman with a brutalized, flushed face – the atavism victim the governor had allowed him to bring from the hospital.

Inside the little ship, Grag the robot greeted him with noisy, booming relief. Simon Wright's lens-eyes focused at once on the big young adventurer's taut face.

'Did you succeed in trapping the Space Emperor, lad?' the Brain asked quickly.

'He nearly trapped me, damn him!' Curt exclaimed ruefully. 'Isn't Otho back yet?'

'No, he hasn't been here,' Wright declared.

Curt uttered an impatient exclamation.

'I wanted to get on up to Jungletown at once. Now we'll have to wait for that crazy android who's probably busy getting himself into trouble.'

Concisely, he told Simon Wright all that had happened, while Grag listened also.

'So I believe,' Curt finished, 'that the Space Emperor has actually discovered the secret of making matter temporarily immaterial, by a step-up in frequency of its atomic vibration. The thing's possible, isn't it, Simon?'

'It's possible theoretically, though no known scientist has ever done it,' rasped the Brain. 'Furthermore, not one of your four suspects is a scientist.'

'I know!' Curt exclaimed. 'And that's what makes me think the Space Emperor has discovered the scientific secrets of the vanished race of this world. The secret of vibration-step-up is probably one of them, and the atavism weapon another.

'And what's more,' Curt declared, 'I believe this Kenneth Lester, the missing archaeologist, ties into it somewhere. This Lester was highly certain, according to Quale, that he could find the secrets of the vanished race. Then he disappeared.'

Grag had listened with attention, trying to follow Curt's explanation. Now the big robot asked a question.

'If the Space Emperor can make himself immaterial whenever he wants to, how can we catch him, master?'

'We can't catch him if he's immaterial, that's the devil of it,' Captain Future told the robot. 'Our only chance is to grab him while he's in his normal state.'

He turned to the Brain.

'I want to investigate this Lucas Brewer first. As soon as Otho comes, we'll go up to Jungletown and I'll see what I can find out about that fat swindler. While we're waiting for Otho,' he went on, 'we can start study of this atavism victim I brought with me. It's urgent that some cure for the blight be found as soon as possible, or this whole colony will be wiped out.'

Grag unfolded the metal table from the wall of the little compact laboratory that occupied the whole midship of the *Comet*. The robot laid the stricken, drugged man upon it.

Captain Future hung a curious lamp over the unconscious man. It was a long cylindrical glass tube that could project 'tuned' X-rays which made either bone, blood or solid flesh tissue or nerve-tissue almost invisible, at will.

Curt set the rays to block out the whole skin, skull, and outer tissues of the victim's head. Then he donned the fluoroscopic spectacles that were part of the equipment, and slipped similar spectacles over the eye-lenses of Simon Wright.

They could now look deep into the head of the victim as though he were semi-transparent.

'I believe,' Curt said tersely, 'that this evolutionary blight is caused by a deep change in the ductless glands. We know that slight malfunctioning of the pituitary gland will produce acromegaly, in which the victim becomes brutish of body and mind. Suppose that the pituitary is really the secret control of physical evolution?'

'I understand,' said Simon, his lenses glittering. 'You think that acromegaly, which has always been considered a mere disease, is really a case of mild atavism?'

Curt nodded his red head keenly.

'That's it, Simon. And if a man found a way to paralyze the pituitary gland completely, then the resulting atavism would not be just mild but would become worse each day, the victim reverting farther each day to the brute!'

'Let's look at the pituitary gland and see,' said Simon Wright.

Intently, they scrutinized the big gland that was attached to the base of the victim's brain by a thin stalk.

'See the dark color of the gland!' Captain Future exclaimed. 'That's abnormal – the pituitary of this man has been subjected to some freezing or paralyzing radiation!'

He straightened his big figure, and there was a gleam in his gray eyes as he took off the fluoroscopic glasses.

'What we've got to do is to devise some way of starting the paralyzed pituitaries of the stricken man,' he said. 'Do you think we could find a counter-radiation that would do it?'

'I doubt it, lad,' muttered Simon Wright. 'It seems to me that our best chance would be to devise a chemical formula that could be injected directly into the victims' bloodstream and which would reach their glands in that way.'

'Then we'll try out different formulae on this victim—' Curt started to say. He suddenly stopped.

His keen ears had just caught the faint whir of the buzzer in his pocket-televisor. He snatched out the little instrument and touched the call-button to signal that he had heard.

'This is Otho speaking!' came a rapid whisper from it. 'I am going with Jovians northward. The Space Emperor is to be—'

Suddenly the android's whisper broke off. Curt waited, his tanned face a little alarmed in expression.

He dared not call the android back, without knowing what had happened. Minutes passed in silence. After a quarter-hour, Otho's whisper came again, a little louder.

'One of these Jovians nearly caught me calling you, but I convinced him I was just talking to myself,' Otho chuckled.

'You crazy fool, be careful!' Captain Future spoke angrily into the instrument. 'Do you want to get yourself killed? What the devil are you up to, anyway?'

'I'm going to stay with these Jovians until I find out where the Space Emperor is to appear before them,' Otho's answer came back. 'It's to be tomorrow night, at some spot called the Place of the Dead, in the north jungles. As soon as I find out where the place is, I'll come back and tell you.'

'We'll have the *Comet* at Jungletown,' Curt told the android quickly through the instrument. 'We're going there now.'

'Give my regards to Grag and tell him that I am sorry he is sitting in the ship and doing nothing,' Otho's voice teased, before he was silent.

Grag moved his metal head furiously.

'Is it my fault that I have been sitting here?' boomed the robot. 'I wanted to go with you, and you took him instead!'

Curt gave the massive robot a powerful shove toward the control-room.

'Get in there and start the ship without more grumbling or I'll disconnect your speech-apparatus!' he warned Grag. 'We're flying north to Jungletown, in a hurry.'

'What about our patient – do we take him too?' asked the robot.

Curt nodded.

'Simon can keep hunting for a cure and test his formulae on that poor fellow. I've got to attend to more urgent business.'

As Captain Future turned back to the Brain, his gray eyes had an expectant gleam.

'So the Space Emperor is to appear up in those northern jungles tomorrow night? And Lucas Brewer had to fly north tonight. The trail leads to Brewer, Simon!'

CHAPTER X

Beneath Jovian Moons

Jungletown throbbed with roaring life tonight, under the two bright moons. Even the dreadful shadow of the horror that had stricken down hundreds, even the knowledge that the Jovian aborigine hordes were ominously restless could not slacken the gusty, lusty tempo of life in this wild new town.

This was a typical planetary boom town, such as sprang up wherever a great new strike was made, be it on desert Mars or mountainous Uranus or Arctic Pluto. To these boom towns thronged adventurous Earthmen from all over the System, prospectors and gamblers, merchants and criminals, engineers and drug-peddlers, dreamers and knaves and fools.

The great strike of uranium and radium northward had been responsible for the birth of Jungletown. It had grown with mushroom speed, till now it was a straggling mass of some thousands of metalloy houses, huddled together in the big clearing that had been blasted out of the mighty fern-jungles.

Captain Future peered keenly toward the town from where he stood with his comrades beside the *Comet*. They had landed the ship near the dark edge of the jungle, unobserved.

'The atavism cases haven't slowed this place down much,' Curt muttered as he stared.

'These boom towns aren't afraid of man or God or devil,' rasped Simon Wright dourly. 'Murder and robbery walk in them hand and hand. Remember the one on Neptune's moon?'

'That town where those criminals laid the atomic trap for us?' said Curt. He chuckled softly. 'I remember!'

'Hear that queer throbbing, master?' Grag boomed suddenly to Curt.

Captain Future and his companions stood with the solemn, murmurous black jungle towering at their backs. Out of it came heavy exhalations of rotting vegetation and the spicy scent of flowers.

The heavy tread of 'stampers' was audible from its depths, and the rustle of a tree-octopus. Balloon-beasts floated overhead in the moonlight, the membranous gas-sac that held them aloft glimmering. And little sucker-flies hummed viciously around, while big death-moths fluttered in their strange dying flight that lasts for days.

In front of them, beyond the black, raw fields, lay the moonlit metal roofs and blazing, noisy streets of the town. Even from here the vibration of brassy music could be heard. And above the town, the whole northern sky flamed brilliant, quaking crimson from the great glare of the mighty Fire Sea beyond.

Curt was listening tensely. Then he heard the sound the robot's artificial hearing had detected. It was a dim, deep throbbing that came from the dark jungles northwest of the town, and that he felt rather than heard. It seemed to roll up from the ground on which they stood, in a steady, heavy rhythm.

'It's Jovian ground-drums,' Simon Wright rasped.

Curt nodded tightly.

'There's no doubt about it. They're out there somewhere northwest of the town.'

Captain Future had heard the 'ground-drums' before – unknown instruments by which Jovian aborigines caused a percussive vibration in the ground which could be heard for far.

'That means trouble, lad,' the Brain said harshly. 'The Jovians ordinarily never do any ground-drumming where Earthmen can hear them.'

'I'm going into the town and hunt up Ezra Gurney, the Planet Police marshal here,' he told the Brain. 'You can stay here and work on the atavism cure, Simon.'

'Yes, of course,' rasped the Brain.

'I go with you this time, master?' Grag asked anxiously.

'No, Grag, you'd attract too much attention in the town,' Captain Future told the big robot. 'I'll call you if I need you.'

Then Curt strode across the dark fields toward the town. The two moons looked down on his big figure, and the shaking glare of crimson in the sky tinged his keen face redly.

Curt entered the chief street of Jungletown, a narrow, unpaved one bordered on both sides by metalloy structures of hasty construction. Gambling places, drinking shops, lodging houses of ill appearance, all stood out under a blaze of uranite bulbs. Music blared from many places, and a babel of voices dazed the ears.

He shouldered through a motley, noisy crowd that jammed the street. Here were husky prospectors in stained zipper-suits, furtive, unshaven space-bums begging, cool-eyed interplanetary gamblers, gaunt engineers in high boots with flare-pistols at their belts, bronzed space-sailors up from Jovopolis for a carousal in the wildest new frontier-town in the System.

Curt noticed that only a few of the green Jovians were in the streets. The flipper-men made no remonstrance when drunken Earthmen cuffed them out of the way, but their silence was queerly ominous.

'Anybody want to buy a Saturnian "talker"?' a big space-sailor with an owl-like bird on his shoulder was shouting.

'Anybody want to buy a Saturnian "talker"?' the bird repeated, exactly mimicking its master's voice.

'Biggest bar on Jupiter!' a telespeaker outside the roaring drinking place was calling. 'Martian gold-wine, Mercurian dream-water – any drink from any planet!'

As Curt passed a big gambling-hall noisy with the click of 'quantum wheels,' a hand grasped his hand. It was a thin-bodied, red-skinned native Martian, whose breath was strong with Jovian brandy as he appealed to Curt in his shrill, high voice.

'Help me out, Earthman!' he begged. 'I've been stranded here a year and I've got to get back to Mars to my family.'

Curt chuckled.

'You've not been on Jupiter more than a month or your skin would have bleached out. You've no family for you belong to the Syrtis people of Mars, where the children are raised communally. But here's something for a drink.'

The Martian, startled, took the coin and stumbled hastily away from the big red-head.

Then as Curt passed a tavern from which came wild, whirling music with the pulsing Venusian double-rhythm in it, he heard a sudden uproar break loose inside.

'Marshal or no marshal, you can't tell Jon Daumer what to do!' roared an Earthman's bellowing voice.

'I'm telling you, and I'm not telling you again,' answered a steely voice. 'You and your friends get out of town and get out now.'

Captain Future recognized that hard second voice. He pushed quickly into the tavern.

It was a big, bright-lit metal hall, hazy with the acrid smoke of Venusian swamp-leaf tobacco. A mixed throng jammed the place. There were prospectors, gamblers and engineers, some of whom had been drinking at the long glassite bar, others of whom had been dancing with hard-faced, painted girls.

All eyes were now watching the tense drama taking place. A big, heavy-faced Earthman in white zipper-suit, with three other mean-eyed men behind him, confronted a grizzled, iron-haired man who wore the black uniform of the Planet Police and a marshal's badge.

Ezra Gurney, the gray-haired marshal, was looking grimly at the quartet who faced him.

'I'm giving you and your three fellow-crooks just one hour to leave Jungletown, Daumer,' he warned.

Curt saw Daumer crimson with rage.

'You've not proved that we have broken any laws!' the man bellowed at Gurney.

'I don't need any more proof than what I've got,' said Ezra Gurney. 'I know you four have been getting prospectors drunk and robbing them of their radium. You're leaving!'

Daumer's face stiffened. He and his companions dropped their hands toward the hilts of their flare-guns.

'We're not going, Gurney,' he said ominously.

Curt Newton stepped suddenly from behind Gurney. His tall, red-headed figure confronted Daumer and his companions.

'Take your hands off those guns and get out of town as Marshal Gurney says,' Curt ordered the four men coldly.

Daumer was first amazed at the stranger's audacity. Then he uttered a guffaw of laughter that was echoed by the motley crowd.

'Listen to this Mr Nobody that's telling me what to do!' he exclaimed. The crowd roared in appreciative mirth.

'Captain Future!' cried Ezra Gurney suddenly as he glimpsed Curt's face.

'Captain Future?' echoed Daumer blankly. His eyes dropped frozenly to the big ring on Curt's finger.

'It's him!' he whispered through stiff lips.

The laughter of the crowd was struck to silence as by a blow. In frozen, unbelieving stillness, they stared at Curt.

The greatest adventurer in the Solar System's history, the mysterious, awesome figure whose legend dominated the nine worlds, stood in their midst. As they realized it, they could only stare rigidly at this big, red-haired, gray-eyed man whose name and fame had rung around the System.

'We're – going, Captain Future,' Daumer said hoarsely, his brutal face pallid.

'See that you take the first ship off Jupiter,' Curt lashed, his bleak gray eyes boring into the faces of the four men.

Daumer and his companions were out of the place in a moment. Curt and Ezra Gurney followed them.

No man or woman in the crowded hall moved, as Captain Future and the grizzled marshal walked out to the street. But as they reached the noisy, thronged thoroughfare, they heard a great babel of excited voices from behind them blast forth in the tavern.

'Thanks for steppin' in to help me out, Captain Future, but you spoiled a swell fight,' said Ezra Gurney testily.

Curt grinned.

'I see you're as bloodthirsty as ever, Marshal. I thought maybe that fracas in the Swampmen's Quarter on Venus two years ago would have quieted you down.'

Gurney looked at him with shrewd old eyes.

'What brings you to Jupiter is this atavism business, isn't it?'

Curt nodded grimly.

'That's it. What do you know about it, Ezra?'

'I know it's hell's blackest masterpiece,' said Ezra Gurney somberly. 'Captain Future, I've been out on the planetary frontiers for forty years. I've seen some evil things on the nine worlds in that time. But I never saw anything like this before.'

His weatherbeaten face tightened.

'This town is sitting on top of hell, and no one knows when it'll bust loose. The atavism cases are increasing daily, and the Jovians are acting queer.'

'You called Quale tonight about the Jovian unrest increasing?' Curt said, and Ezra Gurney nodded emphatically.

'Yes, I told Quale the truth, that the Jovians are working up to something big. You can hear their ground-drums out in the jungle all the time now.'

They had turned off the crowded street into the small metalloy structure that housed Planet Police Headquarters.

'Ezra, what do you know about Lucas Brewer's radium mine?' Captain Future asked.

Gurney looked at him keenly.

'There's something queer about it. Brewer is able to get the Jovians to work for him as laborers, something nobody else can do. That gives him a big advantage, with labor as scarce as it is here. He's getting rich producing radium up there.'

'How does he explain the fact that the Jovians work for him and no one else?' Curt demanded.

'He says he treats 'em right,' Gurney answered skeptically. 'I know he pays 'em a lot of trade-goods – shipments go up to his mine all the time. But the green critters won't work for nobody else, no matter what pay is offered them.'

The big red-haired man considered that, his tanned face thoughtful. He asked another question.

'Do you know anything about the disappearance of Kenneth Lester, a young planetary archaeologist, up here?'

'Not a thing,' Ezra confessed. 'He went up into the jungles weeks ago. Then he flew back down here to send a letter off, and went back north. No more word ever came back from him and he's never been found.'

'I'm going out and make a secret investigation of Lucas Brewer's mine,' Captain Future declared, getting up. 'Lend me a rocket-flier?'

Gurney's face grew anxious.

'That's a dangerous place to monkey around. Brewer's got guards all around the mine. Says he's afraid of radium-bandits.'

Curt grinned, and there was no trace of alarm in the big young adventurer's cheerful face.

'I'll take my chances, Ezra. What about that rocket-flier?'

Ten minutes later, in a small, torpedolike Planet Police flier, Curt flew up above the blazing, turbulent streets of Jungletown and headed northward.

Black, brooding jungle unreeled beneath an endless blanket of dark obscurity. Ahead, the whole northern sky flamed shaking scarlet from the glare of the Fire Sea.

Dark, low ranges of hills showed far ahead, standing out blackly against the quivering red aurora.

Curt hummed a haunting Venusian tune as he flew on, keenly eyeing the blank blackness of jungle. He sensed himself closer on the trail of the Space Emperor, and the thought of coming to grips with his unknown adversary brought a cheerful gleam to his eyes.

At last he saw what he was looking for – a little cluster of lights far ahead and below. At once, he swooped downward in the flier, hovered hummingly above the dense dark tangle of jungle, and then landed expertly in a small clearing.

In a few minutes, Curt was slogging steadily through the moon-drenched jungle of tree-ferns toward the lights.

Tree-octopi flitted overhead. Bulbous balloon-beasts sailed slowly by high above the ceiling of foliage. Once Captain Future's foot crashed down into the mouth of an underground tunnel made by 'diggers.' They were big, bloodthirsty burrowers who seldom appeared above ground.

Sucker-flies swarmed around him, cunningly injecting a tiny drop of anaesthetic to deaden their sting. And once Curt fancied he heard the distant, flowing passage of a 'crawler,' one of the most weird and dreaded of Jovian beasts.

He came finally to the edge of a mile-wide blasted clearing in which lay the mine. Out there in rock quarries scores of Jovians clad in protective lead suits were digging radium ores, working by the brilliant light of uranite bulbs, and superintended by Earthmen overseers.

Further away lay the field-office of the mine, and the warehouses, smelters and other buildings. Their windows glowed with light.

'Looks innocent enough,' Captain Future muttered, 'but there's something damned queer about it. Who ever heard of Jovians doing dangerous labor like that, for any Earthman?'

He loosed his proton pistol in its holster.

'I think we'll see whether the corpulent Mr Brewer is here or not. And first, a look inside those warehouses—'

Curt started along the edge of the clearing, keeping inside the shadow of the jungle. He had gone but a few rods when a faint sound behind him made him whirl quickly.

A dark Earthman guard stepped out of the shrubbery, his flare-pistol leveled menacingly at Curt's head.

'Spy, eh?' rasped the guard. 'You get it now!'

And he loosed a blazing flare from his gun that shot straight toward Curt's face.

CHAPTER XI

Brain and Robot

Grag was worried. The big robot paced restlessly, back and forth inside the *Comet*, in ponderous stride. Every few minutes he went to the door and peered out.

He had run the ship into the jungle outside Jungletown. The boom town lay out there, beneath the thin wash of red light from the setting sun. The lights were coming on in its streets, the uproar commencing as night came once more.

'Something has happened to our master,' the robot boomed as he came back from the door to the midship laboratory. 'He said he would be back soon. That was last night. A whole day has passed, and he has not come back.'

Simon Wright's eye-stalks turned irritatedly toward the robot.

'Will you quit worrying?' the Brain demanded. 'Curtis isn't a boy any more. He can take care of himself, better than any man in the System. You seem to think you're still his guardian and nursemaid.'

Grag answered.

'I think you worry about him as much as I do.'

From the Brain's vocal opening came something that might have been a rasping chuckle.

'You are right, Grag. We all three worry about him, you and I and Otho. We cannot forget the long years of his babyhood and boyhood on the moon, when we alone protected him.'

'But there is no need to worry, really,' Simon went on. 'He'll be back soon now surely. And in the meantime I can't go on with the synthesizing of this new formula without your help.'

'I am sorry, I will help now,' Grag said simply.

Simon was about to prepare still another chemical formula which he hoped would prove capable of reviving the paralyzed pituitary glands of the blight's victims, and bring about their recovery. He had tested several such formulae already on the stricken Earthman who still lay here in drugged sleep, but without success.

Now, from the pedestal upon which his chromium case rested, Simon called out the exact measures and actions which must be combined, and Grag performed them with an exactitude of which only a robot was capable, pouring, mixing, weighing and heating as the Brain directed.

Simon and Grag had worked thus together for many years. Otho was too restless and impatient to make a perfect partner for the Brain. But Grag, with his superhuman patience and precision, was an ideal partner.

The formula was finally finished. Darkness had come, by then. Simon directed the robot as he injected the pinkish fluid into the drugged Earthman's veins.

Then, after some minutes, the Brain had Grag turn on the X-ray lamp, and peered into the drugged man's skull for long minutes through the fluoroscopic glasses.

'It works!' he rasped finally. 'We've found a cure, Grag!'

'But the man looks just the same,' objected the robot, staring down dubiously at the drugged, brutish victim.

'Of course – he won't recover all in a minute,' Simon snapped. 'But now that his pituitary gland is functioning again, his body and mind will again come back to human semblance in a period of days.'

Grag stalked to the door and looked out. The flare of light and noise from rioting Jungletown rose against the red, distant glare of the Fire Sea.

Three moons were in the sky, and the fourth was rising. But the anxious robot did not see by their light the big, red-haired figure he yearned to see.

'Still master has not come back,' he boomed. 'And neither has Otho come. Something has happened.'

'You may be right, at that,' Simon muttered. 'It shouldn't have taken Curtis all this time to go out to that mine and back.'

'Perhaps he did not go there?' Grag suggested. 'Perhaps he went somewhere else?'

Simon thought.

'We'd better find out,' the Brain finally declared. 'Curtis went into the town to see Marshal Ezra Gurney, so Gurney ought to know just where he went.'

'Pick me up, Grag,' the Brain continued. 'We're going to find the marshal.'

Quickly, the robot grasped the handle of the Brain's transparent case in his metal fingers. Then he strode out of the *Comet* and stalked with mighty strides across the moonlit fields toward the flaring, noisy town.

They could hear the chatter of deep and shrill voices from the streets. The heavy throb of the Jovian ground-drums seemed louder tonight.

'Avoid the streets,' Simon ordered the robot who carried him. 'Keep behind the buildings, in the shadows, until we see Gurney.'

Grag obeyed, stalking behind the rows of metalloy structures, pausing at breaks between them so that he and Simon could peer into the bright, crowded streets in search of the marshal.

But neither the Brain nor the robot could spot the veteran peace-officer. As they continued their search an intoxicated Earthman came staggering back from the street toward the shadows from which Grag and Simon were watching. He stopped suddenly as he glimpsed them in front of him.

The drunken man tipped his head back and looked up unbelievingly with bleared eyes at the blank metal face and gleaming photoelectric eyes of the huge robot.

'Go 'way,' he muttered thickly. 'I know you're not real.'

'Shall I silence him, Simon?' asked Grag in his deep voice.

'No, he is only a drunken fool,' rasped the Brain.

As the intoxicated one heard the voices from the robot and the transparent brain-case he carried, he uttered a wild shriek.

'They're *real!*'

And with the cry, he stumbled wildly back out into the street.

'Police!' he yelled. 'Where's the Planet Police?'

Ezra Gurney came along the street quickly in answer to that cry, and the drunken one grabbed his arm.

'There's a couple of – monsters – back there,' he babbled wildly, pointing.

Gurney was about to reply in disgust, when Simon Wright's rasping voice reached him.

'Marshal Gurney! This way!'

Gurney started at the sound of the metallic voice, then pushed the drunk away and hastened back into the shadows. He uttered an exclamation as he glimpsed the big robot and the Brain he carried. He knew Captain Future's aides well.

'Simon Wright! And Grag!' he exclaimed. 'What's wrong now?'

'Curtis hasn't come back,' Simon told him quickly. 'Did he go to the Brewer mine last night?'

'That's where he said he was goin',' Gurney declared. 'An' he's not back yet? That don't look so good.'

'Is Brewer in town now, or out at the mine?' Simon demanded keenly.

'I don't know but we can soon find out,' the marshal answered. 'His company office is over in the next street, and if he's in town he'll be there.'

They started through the shadows, keeping out of the moonlight of the four silver satellites, toward the next street.

It was a sober business thoroughfare rather than a carnival street, bordered by small metalloy offices. Gurney led the way to the door of one whose windows glowed with light.

As Gurney walked in, followed by the huge robot with the glittering-eyed Brain, a man alone in the room uttered a startled cry.

'Good God, what are those creatures?'

It was Mark Cannig. His eyes bulged as he stared at Grag and Simon Wright.

'They're Captain Future's pals,' Gurney replied sharply. 'Is Brewer here?'

'No – I don't know where he is,' Cannig answered uneasily.

The nervousness of the young mine superintendent did not miss Simon Wright's keen lens-eyes. Then the Brain glimpsed something lying on the floor near the wall.

'Pick that up, Grag,' he directed sharply, looking toward it.

Grag obeyed, and held the little object so the Brain could inspect it closely.

It was a small badge with the letters 'P.P.' on it, and a number on its back.

'That's a Planet Police secret-agent emblem,' Gurney said sharply. 'And the number is Joan Randall's number.'

He turned on Cannig.

'When was she here?'

Cannig flushed uneasily.

'I don't know if she was here or not. I just came myself.'

'Call the hospital and find out if she's there, Marshal,' Simon Wright suggested raspingly.

Gurney went to the televisor on the desk and made the call. His face was grim as he straightened.

'She left the hospital an hour ago and didn't come back. They don't know why she hasn't, either.'

'I don't know where she is!' Cannig exclaimed. 'I don't know anything about that badge.'

'In other words, you just don't know nothin',' Ezra Gurney said sarcastically.

There was a rush of feet, and into the room came a flying figure. It was a green Jovian, moving with amazing speed, his round, dark eyes blazing.

'Get out of here, greenie,' ordered the Marshal. 'We're busy.'

'You're no busier than I've been,' answered the Jovian in a hissing, familiar voice. 'And I've got news.'

'Otho!' exclaimed Simon instantly, as he recognized the android's voice through his disguise. 'What have you learned?'

'I've learned the exact spot where the Space Emperor will appear to these benighted Jovians tonight, an hour from now!' Otho declared, 'I was supposed to be there with them, but I slipped away to bring Captain Future the news.'

His eyes swept the room. 'But where is Captain Future?'

'We don't know!' Simon Wright exclaimed. 'It's beginning to look as though something has happened to him, and to Joan Randall too!'

CHAPTER XII

Secret of the Mine

Curt Newton's physical and mental reflexes were a shade faster than those of any other man in the System. He could not quite match the blurring speed of the android who had taught him quickness, but his reactions were almost as instantaneous. As the Earthman guard fired his flare-gun at Captain Future, the big red-head was already diving beneath the whizzing flare in a low, swift tackle. Curt had started moving in the second before the guard could pull his trigger.

He knocked the man crashing from his feet. Before the fellow could utter a cry, Curt smashed his fist hard upward to the chin. The guard's head snapped back and he went limp and senseless.

Captain Future straightened, tensely listening. The scuffle and the whizzing shot had not aroused alarm among the laboring Jovians and alert overseers out in the radium diggings.

But dawn was coming. Already the sky was reddening. Hastily, Curt dragged the senseless guard into the jungle and tightly bound his hands and feet with strips from his jacket.

'You shouldn't be so free with your little flare-gun,' Captain Future told the man pleasantly as he groggily opened his eyes. 'You might hurt somebody one of these days.'

The guard looked up at this big red-haired young man grinning down at him, and uttered a vicious curse.

'Such language!' Curt deprecated. 'By the way, don't attempt to cry out, or I'll have to knock you out again.'

'What do you want here?' the guard snarled to him.

'I want to know just what the estimable Mr Brewer is carrying on at this mine,' Captain Future told him. 'There's something funny about this place, and you can tell me what it is.'

'I can, but I won't,' the guard declared. 'What are you, anyway, a Planet Police agent?'

Curt held up his left hand so that the man could see the big, odd ring he wore.

'Captain Future!' muttered the man appalledly. He looked up at the big red-head in sudden fear. Then his lips compressed. 'You're not getting anything out of me, anyway.'

'So you don't want to talk?' Curt said mildly. 'Very well, then I shall make very sure that you don't talk, or shout either.'

And coolly, he efficiently gagged the bound guard with more strips that he tore from the man's own zipper-jacket.

By this time, the Jovian day had fully dawned, the sun throwing a pale flood of light across the clearing of the mine. From his hiding place in the dense jungle, Curt studied the place.

He saw at once that he could not hope to venture out during the daylight. The scores of Jovians were still working out there, and with them were the half-dozen or more armed overseers.

'Have to wait for night,' Curt muttered to himself. 'Lucky the days are so short here on Jupiter.'

Curt settled down to wait. The big red-haired man had learned patience from Grag, and he exercised it now. As he waited through the five hours of the Jovian day, he watched every move out in the mine.

He saw nothing of either Lucas Brewer or Mark Cannig. But the work went on steadily under the direction of the overseers. Hour after hour, the Jovians labored at digging the radium-bearing rock and hauling it in hand-trucks to the smelter.

Curt would have liked to call Simon Wright by his pocket-televisor, to tell them where he was and what he was doing. But he feared that his call might happen to be picked up if someone in those mine-offices was using a televisor, and decided not to risk it.

Night finally came down, the dramatically sudden Jovian night that clapped down after only a few moments of twilight. Callisto and Europa and Ganymede were in the heavens, moving toward conjunction, while Io hurtled up to join them.

Curt made sure of the bound guard's safety, then rose to his feet to venture out into the clearing. But he stopped a moment, peering.

'Now what goes on?' he muttered to himself. 'Are they quitting for good?'

The Jovians who had worked through a shift of ten hours during night and day were now dropping their tools, and streaming with the overseers toward the mine-office.

The green natives discarded their protective lead suits as they left the radium diggings. They clustered in the moonlight outside the office.

Captain Future moved hastily around the edge of the clearing until he had the smelter-structure between him and the office-building. Then he moved out, silently as a shadow.

From behind the smelter, he watched. And he saw that the overseers were now distributing some objects from big boxes to the Jovians who crowded eagerly forward.

'Paying them off in trade goods,' Curt muttered to himself. 'But what—'

Then his keen eyes made out what the Earthmen were passing out to the Jovians. And his big crouching figure stiffened as though he had received an electric shock.

'So *that* is how Brewer induces the Jovians to work for him!' he muttered, his eyes suddenly blazing.

The things that the overseers were passing out to the green natives as reward for their labor were – flare-guns.

Guns! The one thing that Earthmen were utterly forbidden to sell or give to the planetary natives! The strictest laws forbade it on every world in the System.

Captain Future felt like rushing out to stop the distributing of the weapons. But he knew well that it would be suicide to try it. Those Jovians, armed with the deadly flare-guns, would destroy any man who tried to take the weapons from them.

'Have to wait,' Curt told himself fiercely. 'But by Heaven, Brewer will have to account for plenty!'

As the Jovians received the weapons, they streamed away from the mine into the jungles eastward. From those moonlit jungles, the ground-drums had begun to throb. The deep, pulsing rhythm was now loud to Curt's ears, as though it came from nearby.

Finally all the Jovians had received weapons and hurried away into the moon-shot fern-forest. The overseers went into the office-building.

Curt drew his proton pistol and crept forward. He gained the screened door of the lighted offices, then poised there, listening.

'Don't like giving those damned greenies guns,' one of the Earthmen inside was saying. 'They're too cursed eager to get them.'

'What difference does it make to us?' another demanded. 'They're only going to use the guns in a war with another tribe, Brewer says.'

'That's what Brewer says,' the first man muttered, 'but I'm not so sure about it.'

'Neither am I, gentlemen,' spoke a throbbing voice from the doorway.

The six Earthmen whirled, astonished. In the door bulked Curt Newton's big, broad-shouldered figure and red head, a little grim smile playing on his lips, and his slender proton pistol leveled at them.

With an oath, one Earthman reached for the flare-gun at his belt. Captain Future's proton beam licked forth, and the man fell stunned.

'I could kill you with this beam as easily as stun you,' Curt said pleasantly. 'Don't make me do it.'

'It's Captain Future!' exclaimed one of the men, going pale as he recognized the unique ring on Curt's finger.

'You men,' Curt told them, 'are going to spend a long time out on the prison moon of Pluto for violating interplanetary law! Supplying natives with guns is risky business.'

'I didn't want to do it!' the first overseer defended desperately. 'Brewer made us. He's been getting rich that way, for the greenies will labor for guns when they won't for anything else.'

'How did you get the guns up here from Jovopolis without detection?' Captain Future demanded.

'They were shipped in as trade-goods,' the man explained hastily. 'But each box had a false bottom, under which were the guns.'

'You'll have a chance to testify to all that when the time comes,' Curt said grimly. 'In the meantime, I must ask you to sit down in those chairs and keep your hands up. I am going to make sure that you remain here while I am busy elsewhere.'

Helplessly, the men sat down, their hands raised. Curt tore flexible metal cords from the shutters at the windows. Swiftly, he went about using them to bind the men to the chairs.

He worked with his pistol in one hand, keeping behind the seated men. In a few minutes, he had all of them securely lashed.

'Be sure and wait till I come back, gentlemen,' he grinned at them, and then started a rapid search of the office and other buildings.

He was hoping to find some evidence that would definitely establish whether or not Lucas Brewer was the Space Emperor. But he could find nothing.

Time was flying. The throb of ground-drums from the moonlit jungles westward seemed louder. Curt rapidly made up his mind.

'The Space Emperor was to appear to the Jovians tonight in these jungles, according to Otho,' he muttered to himself. 'So that's where all those Jovians who left here must have gone.'

He hastened out into the moonlight, and hurried across the clearing toward the jungle.

'If I can be there when the Space Emperor shows up, and if I can get him when he isn't in an immaterial state—'

He plunged into the jungle, following the Jovians westward along dim trails, able to hear their excited voices as they pressed on.

Somewhere ahead, he knew, lay the meeting place Otho had spoken of, the locale that the Jovians called the Place of the Dead. From there, the ground-drums were throbbing. And there, if he was lucky, he would come to grips with the dark super-criminal who was terrorizing a world.

CHAPTER XIII

Place of the Dead

Boom! Boom! Through the moonlit Jovian jungles throbbed the heavy, rhythmic vibration, one that was felt rather than heard.

Ground-drums of the flipper-men, beating in the night like the dark heart of the savage Jupiter! *Boom! Boom! Boom!*

Captain Future looked up tensely through the canopy of tree-fern fronds high above. Callisto, Ganymede, Europa and Io were converging near the zenith, four brilliant moons nearing wonderful conjunction.

'The hour of the four moons meeting must have been the appointed time,' he muttered to himself.

A moment later, his big figure tensed as he hurried on along the dim trail he was following through the forest.

'What's that?'

A dim, deep chanting sound came through the jungle in a murmurous wave, rising and swelling strangely in the night and then dying away.

For more than an hour, Curt had followed the Jovians through the unearthly wilderness. The green natives had pressed on at high speed, as though afraid that they would be late for the great gathering.

They had unerringly followed narrow trails that wound tortuously through the ferns. And they had kept the angry red glow of the Fire Sea always on their right.

The jungle was weird tonight! The drenching radiance of the four moons made it a fantastic fairyland of deep black shadows and dappled silver light. High overhead stretched the great tree-ferns' masses of feathery fronds, tipped with spore-pods. Gleaming bright in the moons towered the metallic copper-trees. The blindly swaying snake-vines hung like dark pendulous serpents from the branches.

In the choked spaces between the great fern-trunks bloomed supernally lovely shock-flowers, tempting, wonderful blossoms ready to give the unwary toucher a stinging electric shock from the biochemical 'battery' inside their calyxes. Giant night-lilies flourished in the shadows, their yard-wide white petals slowly closing and unclosing. Down from the upper canopy when it was stirred by the breeze floated shining clouds of spore-dust, silvering all things below.

Curt could glimpse iridescent moon-bats gliding on motionless wings above the fern-tops, and bulbous balloon-beasts floating slowly by. From beneath his feet more than once came the queer rasping sound of 'diggers' burrowing. There was no sign of the dreaded 'crawlers' about, and for that the big red-head felt thankful.

'Must be almost there,' he told himself as the throbbing and chanting from ahead grew louder.

A tension such as he had seldom felt was mounting inside Captain Future as he hurried on. He felt himself on the verge of a second encounter with the Space Emperor.

But what would be its result? Would he be able to catch the Space Emperor off guard in his normal material state, or was there no chance of that?

'Getting close,' Curt muttered. 'Take it easy, my boy—'

Boom! Boom! The ground-drums were throbbing so near now that he could feel the vibration strongly beneath his feet. Tensely, he crept on.

The jungle was thinning ahead. He stopped a moment later, sank down behind a clump of shock-flowers.

Captain Future looked out upon an uncanny scene. It was a mile-wide circular clearing in the jungle, in which only scattered tree-ferns and shrubs and vines grew.

In this clearing, bathed in the wonderful silver radiance of the four moons, lay the crumbling ruins of what had once been a great city.

City of Jupiter's unguessable past, mystery metropolis that long and long ago had fallen to wreck and had been swallowed by the jungle! Cyclopean masses of crumbled black masonry of grotesque architecture, towering solemnly out of the shrubs and clinging vines.

There had been paved streets and courts, Curt saw, but they were broken and covered by creeping moulds and fungi. There had been curving colonnades, but of them there remained nothing but a few broken, lonely black stone pillars.

'Place of the Dead,' he whispered to himself. 'It's well-named.'

Captain Future had looked upon dead planetary cities before. He had seen the wonderful lost city on Tethys, moon of Saturn, whose history no man knows. He was familiar with those mysterious wrecks which are found everywhere in the deserts of Mars.

But he had, he felt, never looked upon a place more somber and darkly sentient than this ruined and forgotten metropolis that brooded beneath Jupiter's brilliant moons. The spirit of a mighty past reached out from it to lay cold fingers on the heart.

Captain Future glimpsed, far toward the center of the ruined city, a large circular plaza in which thousands of the Jovians were gathered in a tightly packed mass. Almost all seemed to possess flare-guns. They were facing toward a low, half-preserved black structure which partly hid them from Curt's view. It was from there that emanated the deep, rumbling throb of the booming ground-drums.

'Have to get closer,' Curt muttered tensely. 'If the Space Emperor's already there—'

Stealthily, he slipped out of the jungle into the vast circle of ruins. Like a shadow, he worked toward the low and half-ruined stone structure that lay between him and the plaza of the gathered Jovians.

Keeping always within the shadows of brooding masonry masses, moving soundlessly over the broken paving, the big adventurer advanced. He breathed more easily when he reached the deep shadow of the low building. From the plaza on the other side of it came loudly the deep throb of the ground-drums and the steady, swelling chanting of thousands of bass Jovian voices.

Boom! Boom! Boom! quivered the deep vibrations, shaking the ground under him.

Full of deep fanaticism, laden with a strange note of overwhelming sadness and despair, the chanting of the natives swelled frenziedly.

Curt knew the Jovian tongue well, but this chant was apparently in an archaic form that he could not understand.

He flattened himself on the broken paving and inched forward until he could peer out into the moonlit plaza from behind the corner of the crumbling building. His eyes photographed the strange scene before him in a second.

Directly in front of the ruin behind which he crouched were the two great ground-drums. They consisted of deep pits that had been dug by the Jovians in the black ground, thirty feet deep and shaped like hollow cones with the apex at the surface.

A group of Jovians at each pit held a heavy fern-trunk with a flattened end, which they raised a little and then allowed to fall heavily, producing by the concussion the throbbing vibrations in the ground.

Captain Future saw between the ground-drum pits a great black stone globe carved with the outlines of continents and seas. It was set with scattered silver stars that he guessed immediately marked the location of other cities of the Ancients. He saw something else on the surface of the globe that made him start. He peered closer.

'If that's what it is –' he whispered tautly to himself, and then forgot his discovery as he heard a sound.

It was the distant, almost inaudible sound of a rocket-flier landing. The Jovians appeared not to have heard it through the boom of ground-drums and the chanting, but Curt's super-keen ears had detected it.

He waited, his pistol in his hand. After a few minutes, as the four moons overhead gathered together in a dazzling cluster, the chant of the Jovians ceased and the fern-trunks were withdrawn from the ground-drum pits. An air of tense expectancy seemed to grip the thousands of green men.

'Zero hour,' Curt thought. 'The four moons have – met!'

CHAPTER XIV

The Living Ancient

A stir ran through the crowd of Jovians, and there was a movement near the far edge of the grotesque, moonlit crowd.

'He comes! The Living Ancient comes!' sped the rustling Jovian cry.

'The Living Ancient?' Curt wondered. 'So that's what he calls himself?'

Into the packed plaza from the jungle on the far side of the city was coming a dark shape.

Curt raised his proton pistol. If he could blast the Space Emperor before he became immaterial—

He saw that it was indeed the Space Emperor, the same figure he had battled in Orris' cabin in Jovopolis. A grotesque shape in his dark suit with its tiny eye-holes.

The Space Emperor was material, Curt saw at once. For he was *carrying* someone – the bound figure of a girl in a white synthe-silk uniform, whose dark, wavy hair fell back from her moonlit white face.

'Joan Randall!' Captain Future gasped. 'That devil has seized her and brought her here for some reason!'

Curt's whole plan of action was upset by the disastrous surprise. He knew the Space Emperor was now material and vulnerable. But he could not blast him down while he held Joan.

The Space Emperor uttered a few words in his deep voice. Out of the worshipful Jovian crowd, two green natives sprang in obedience. They took the bound girl from their sinister ruler's arms.

As the Jovians stepped back with Joan, Curt's pistol was poised to blast the super-criminal. But the Space Emperor had touched something at his belt as the Jovians stepped back. And now the Space Emperor moved glidingly forward, *through* the two Jovians.

'Too late!' Captain Future hissed, with a feeling of blind anger.

Too late! The Space Emperor had made himself immaterial, and no proton-beam could harm him.

A great cry arose from the Jovian horde as they saw the dark figure glide forward through their comrades, like an unreal phantom. It was a cry of fanatic worship.

The Space Emperor glided forward, until he reached the paving between the ground-drum pits. There he turned to face the Jovian throng, his back toward Captain Future.

Curt could see now that the dark criminal moved, in his immaterial state, by the reactive push of a force-tube attached to his belt. There was a small switch beside it, that he guessed was the control of the Space Emperor's dematerializing apparatus. Apparently, the device that would return him to a normal state had also been changed into an immaterial state.

The two Jovians laid down Joan Randall's helpless form a little to one side of and behind the Space Emperor. Then they stepped back into the throng.

The deep, heavy voice of the black figure rolled out, speaking to the masses of Jovians in their own language.

'I bring to you again the command of the great Ancients, of whom I am the last living one,' vibrated his voice.

A sigh of awe swept through the horde of green natives as they heard.

'You know that the spirits of the Ancients are wroth with the Earthmen who have come to this world,' the black figure continued. 'You have seen our curse fall upon many of them and change them into beasts.'

'We have seen, lord,' came a great responding cry from the Jovians.

'It is the curse of our anger that has made them change so,' went on the Space Emperor. 'Before you leave here, you shall see me put that curse upon this Earth girl.'

Captain Future's big body went rigid. The super-plotter was going to use the dread atavism weapon on Joan—

'The time is almost here,' the dark criminal was saying loudly, 'when you must gather and sweep the Earthmen from this world to appease the anger of the Ancients. Are you ready for that?'

'We are ready, lord,' answered a big Jovian fervently from the throng. 'We have obtained many of the Earth guns from the Earthman at the radium mine, in exchange for our labor. All through the jungles now, the villages of our people only await the great signal of the ground-drums to attack the Earthmen.'

'That signal will be given to you soon, perhaps within hours!' the Space Emperor declared. 'I will lead you when the moment comes and we will sweep first upon the Earthman town they call Jungletown, and then upon the other Earthman cities until all are taken. Then *I*, the last of the Ancients, shall rule this world for your good.'

'You shall rule, lord,' answered the Jovians in a reverent, humble chorus.

Captain Future was clawing in his belt, working to extract something from that flat, capacious tungstite container.

'There's only one chance to get Joan away before that devil inflicts the blight upon her,' he whispered fiercely to himself. 'The invisibility charge—'

Captain Future extracted from his belt the little mechanism he wanted. It was a disclike instrument that was one of the greatest secrets of Curt and Simon Wright.

He took it, pressed a stud upon it, holding it above his head. He felt the unseen force that streamed down from it flood through every fiber of his body with stinging shock.

Quickly, Captain Future saw his own body becoming a little misty and translucent. For Curt was disappearing!

The little instrument was one which could give any matter a charge of force that caused all light to be refracted around it, thus making it invisible. But the charge only lasted temporarily, for ten minutes. Then the charge dissipated, and such matter became visible again.

Captain Future, as he became slowly invisible, felt an utter darkness close in around him. With all light refracted around him, he was now in complete darkness. He could see nothing whatever! For no light could reach his eyes. By that he knew finally that he had become completely invisible.

Curt started soundlessly around the corner of the ruined building, moving in an absolute and rayless blackness.

Captain Future could move in this darkness that now encompassed him, almost as well as by sight. His super-keen senses of hearing and touch, and his long practice in this, enabled him to do what no other man could have done.

He crept around the crumbling ruin. He knew that, had he been visible, he would be standing in full view of the Jovian thousands. He could hear the Space Emperor, still speaking in his heavy, disguised voice, exhorting the green natives.

Curt crept toward that voice. Moving with utter care, he crept on until he neared Joan. He could hear her frightened breathing. He clapped his invisible hand over her mouth and felt her body quiver in wild alarm.

'It's me – Captain Future,' he murmured in the faintest of whispers in her ear. 'Lie still, and I'll untie you.'

He felt Joan stiffen, then relax. He groped at her bonds, which he discovered were tough metal cords.

Curt could not untie the cords, nor break them. Frantically he clawed in his belt, and brought out a sharp little tool. Slowly, so as to make no twanging sound, he cut the cords.

'Don't get up,' he murmured to the girl. 'I'll drag you slowly back around the ruin. If the Jovians notice you, we'll have to run for it.'

He gripped Joan's shoulders firmly. Then, with infinite care to make no sound, he drew the girl back from the loudly declaiming Space Emperor.

In the darkness, Curt was tensely listening for signs of discovery. But he heard no sound of alarm from the Jovian throng. Intently listening to their leader, Curt guessed that they were not watching the half-hidden shape of the girl.

Captain Future's hopes were soaring when he heard a wild cry from a Jovian in the throng.

'See! A spirit of the Ancients appears to us now!'

At the same moment, faint light began to penetrate the rayless blackness in which Curt moved.

He looked down at himself. His ten minutes of invisibility had expired. He was becoming visible again!

CHAPTER XV

Doom of An Earthman

There was a taut silence in the little office of Jovian Mines in Jungletown, as Simon Wright and Grag and the disguised Otho realized the situation.

Mark Cannig stood before the incredible trio of comrades, fear evident in his eyes. The young mine superintendent's face was flushed and queer, as though he labored under strong emotion.

'You know what happened to Joan, Cannig,' rasped the Brain. 'You'd better talk, quickly.'

'I tell you I don't know anything,' asserted Cannig desperately, his voice thick and hoarse.

'We can make you talk, you know!' hissed Otho ominously, his eyes blazing. 'Where is the girl? And where is Captain Future?'

Grag took a ponderous step forward toward the young man, and half-raised his enormous metal hands.

'Shall I squeeze the truth out of him, Simon?' boomed the great robot questioningly.

Mark Cannig appealed wildly to Ezra Gurney who stood beside the unhuman trio.

'Marshal Gurney, you can't let them harm me!' cried the young man hoarsely.

Ezra Gurney's weatherbeaten face was grim and his blue eyes cold.

'I'm with them on this, Cannig,' he said uncompromisingly. 'You've done something to that girl, and you're going to tell what.'

Cannig made a bolt for the door. But before he reached it, Otho had moved with blurring speed to intercept him.

The android hauled him back despite his struggles and yells.

'He's guilty as hell or he wouldn't have tried to get away!' cried Ezra Gurney.

'What's going on in here?' demanded a startled voice from the door.

Sylvanus Quale stood there, and behind him was the vice-governor, Eldred Kells. The governor's colorless face was amazed as he looked in at the strange tableau presented by the brain and robot and android, and to the two Earthmen.

Quale and Kells strode inside. And at once Cannig appealed hoarsely to the governor.

'Captain Future's comrades are planning to torture me!' he cried.

'It wouldn't be a bad idea, at that,' Gurney said.

The marshal told the governor what had happened and showed him the Planet Police badge they had found upon the floor.

'Captain Future and Joan both missing?' Quale exclaimed. His face grew strange. 'I was afraid things were going wrong up here at Jungletown. That's why I just flew up here to check.'

'Do you suppose that Cannig could be the Space Emperor?' Eldred Kells exclaimed excitedly.

'I'm not – I'm not!' howled Cannig, his face distorted and his cry almost unrecognizable.

'Where's Lucas Brewer?' Quale demanded of him, but he did not answer.

'Brewer may be out at the mine, or he may be lying low somewhere here in Jungletown,' Gurney answered. 'I've an idea hell is going to pop tonight.'

'And meanwhile we're wasting time here!' Otho hissed fiercely.

'You'd better talk fast, Cannig,' rasped Simon Wright to the young superintendent. 'Grag and Otho will do some unpleasant things to you if you don't.'

Cannig's nerve seemed to break. His voice babbled hoarsely of a sudden.

'I'll tell you what I know! I don't know anything about where Captain Future is, but Joan was taken from here tonight by the Space Emperor, because she saw us together.'

'You've been an accomplice of that criminal, then?' Simon rasped instantly.

Mark Cannig nodded, slowly and dazedly.

'Yes,' he muttered. 'There's no use denying it now.'

'Who is the Space Emperor, Cannig?' the Brain demanded quickly.

'I don't know,' Cannig choked. 'I never knew who he was.'

'Tell the truth!' Otho hissed, his voice threatening.

'I'm telling the truth!' choked Cannig dazedly. 'I was just a pawn of the Space Emperor, like Orris and Skeel and a few others. The Space Emperor never appeared to me except inside that concealing suit. And he was almost always immaterial. He didn't take any chances.'

Cannig seemed struggling for words, his glazed eyes wild and his voice thick and stumbling.

'He told me he would soon hold supreme power on Jupiter, and that I would share that power if I helped him. I agreed, like a fool. Then when the atavism cases began, I realized that he was causing that horror.

'He said he'd found powers beyond any Earth science, and that one of them was the atavism force. He was using it on Earthmen at random, to create a demoralization of horror and influence the superstitious Jovians, through whom he meant to win power over the whole planet. He inflicted the blight with an invisible beam. Victims didn't feel it at the time, but a few days later the horrible change began.'

'And you were helping him?' cried Eldred Kells, looking at the young man in utter loathing.

'I had to obey him. I was afraid of him!' Cannig cried hoarsely. 'That black devil has been more and more menacing to me of late, because of the protests I made to him against the horror he was causing.'

'Did he say just when he intended to lead the Jovians against the Earthman towns?' Simon Wright demanded.

Mark Cannig nodded dazedly.

'Yes, he said that—'

Cannig stopped, the words trailing from his lips, his eyes glazed and strange. He passed a hand unsteadily over his face.

'He said that –' he started to continue, in the same stumbling voice.

But again, his thick voice trailed off. He looked from one to another of them with blank, empty eyes.

'Why,' he said hoarsely. 'I feel—'

'Look out!' yelled Ezra Gurney an instant later.

Mark Cannig's flushed, strange face had suddenly stiffened into an animal-like snarl, his lips writhing back in a bestial grin from his teeth, his eyes blazing with new feral light.

Growling like a suddenly enraged beast, he wrenched himself from Otho's grasp with a superhuman surge of strength, and launched himself at the throat of Sylvanus Quale.

'Grag – get him!' cried Simon Wright.

The robot seized the maddened Cannig, and tore him from Quale. The stricken man struggled ferociously, frothing at the lips, until Grag's metal fist knocked him senseless.

Cannig went down, unconscious. Yet even in unconsciousness there were bestial lines in his flushed face.

'Good God!' muttered Ezra Gurney. 'The blight has got *him!*'

For a moment there was a strained silence. And in that silence there came to them from northward the distant, persistent throbbing of the Jovian ground-drums.

Boom! Boom! They throbbed, in faraway, ominous quivering vibration that was felt rather than heard.

'Cannig said that he'd been afraid of the Space Emperor lately,' Simon rasped. 'He had reason to be. His protests against the atavism horror had made the black devil suspicious of him, and the thing was turned on *him*.'

'And he didn't know that poison was working in him till it hit him just now!' exclaimed Ezra Gurney, aghast.

'But what of master, Simon?' asked Grag anxiously of the Brain.

The robot's unswerving devotion to Captain Future ruled him now as always.

'We're going to find Curtis,' Simon declared. 'We'll go first to Brewer's mine, where you said he'd gone, Ezra.'

'I'll go with you!' Ezra Gurney declared instantly.

'You can take Cannig up to the hospital,' the Brain rasped to the staring Quale and Kells. 'And tell them up there I now have a cure for the atavism horror which I'll use on the victims when we get back.'

'A cure?' echoed Quale unbelievingly.

'Come on – what are we waiting for?' Otho interrupted. 'Let's go.'

The three unhuman comrades and Ezra Gurney hastened out into the night. By dark back-streets they hurried to the jungle-edge where the *Comet* waited.

Presently, with Grag at the controls, the little teardrop ship was hurtling northward over the moonlit jungles. Otho removed his Jovian disguise as they flew on.

Gurney directed their course. Presently the little cluster of lights at the Brewer mine came into view, and with a rush, the *Comet* landed beside the lighted offices.

A half-dozen men bound in chairs met their eyes as they entered the office. The men, now thoroughly surrendering to the inevitable and hoping for judicial mercy, told them of Captain Future's visit and the flare-gun traffic with the natives.

'Giving the Jovians guns!' Ezra Gurney cried wrathfully. 'By heaven, Brewer will spend the rest of his life in prison out on Cerberus for this.'

He went to the televisor and called Planet Police Headquarters in Jungletown.

'Send a flier up here to pick up some prisoners. I'll wait until you come,' the marshal said. 'And if you see Lucas Brewer anywhere, arrest him at once!'

'We're not going to wait here,' Simon told the marshal. 'Curtis isn't here. That means he's gone to the Jovian meeting where the Space Emperor was to appear, the meeting of which Otho brought us news.'

'The place is only a little west of here!' Otho cried. 'It's a ruin the Jovians call the Place of the Dead.'

'Let us go, then,' boomed Grag anxiously.

'Go ahead – I'll see you when I've taken these men back to Jungletown,' Gurney told them. 'And save that girl, if you can!'

The *Comet*, with only the three weird comrades aboard it now, split the night like a shooting star, plunging westward over the moon-drenched jungle.

The throb of the ground-drums had ceased for the time being, and that fact was like an ominous warning to the three.

'There's the place!' Otho cried, his green eyes peering intently ahead. 'That big clearing—'

'There's a fight going on there!' boomed Grag suddenly. 'Look!'

The sinister flash of a deadly beam was visible amid a group of struggling figures in the moonlit ruins.

CHAPTER XVI

Prison Pit

Captain Future realized that his concealment was gone. The invisibility-charge was now dissipating by the second, and he was already almost solidly visible.

The Jovian throng was uttering a chorus of cries and surging toward him. The dark shape of the Space Emperor had turned, and from the mysterious plotter came a low cry.

'Captain Future – here!'

Then the Space Emperor uttered a deep shout to the Jovians.

'Seize the Earthman spy!'

The green natives surged forward with wild bass yells of rage, incited by that shout.

Curt sprang erect, drew his pistol and triggered at the sinister black figure. Now that he was discovered, he would at least make one more attempt to destroy the dark plotter.

The attempt was as futile as he had known it must be. The proton beam splashed through the immaterialized form of the Space Emperor without harming him.

'Run!' Curt was calling fiercely to Joan Randall as he fired. 'I'll hold them off—'

The pale ray of his pistol leaped like a thing alive, and knocked down Jovians in their tracks. The weapon was only set at stunning force now. Even in this desperate moment, Curt could not bring himself to kill these misguided natives.

Joan had gained her feet. But the girl had not tried to make an escape.

'I'll not leave you, Captain Future!' she cried pluckily.

'Don't be a fool!' Curt cried, his gray eyes blazing. 'You can't—'

'Captain Future!' screamed the girl. 'Behind you—'

Curt whirled. But too late. Jovians who had rushed around to get at him from behind now leaped up upon him.

For moments Curt stood erect, struggling with superhuman strength, his red head and straining face towering out of the mass of green flipper-men who sought to pull him down. The proton pistol had been torn from his hands but his big fists beat a devil's tattoo on the faces of the natives.

But the struggle was hopeless. He felt himself pulled down by the smothering mass of enemies. His belt, too, was torn from him and flung aside like the pistol.

Then he was hauled to his feet, held by the flipper-hands of so many Jovians that escape was impossible. He saw Joan, similarly held, nearby.

'Why the devil didn't you get away when there was a chance!' Curt panted to the girl. 'Now we're both in for it.'

The Space Emperor, a dark, erect shape of mystery, glided forward until he towered in front of Curt and Joan.

'So the famous Captain Future meets defeat at last,' mocked the mysterious criminal.

Curt felt an emotion as near despair as he ever could feel. Yet the big redhead let no trace of it enter his voice as he stared contemptuously at the black figure.

'Just who are you inside that suit?' he demanded. 'Quale? Kells? Lucas Brewer?'

The Space Emperor jerked, as though startled by Curt Newton's guesses.

'You'll never know, Captain Future!' he declared. 'You're going to die. Not a quick, easy death, but the most horrible one that any man could die.'

The uncanny plotter raised his voice in a command to the Jovians who held the man and girl.

'Drop them into one of the ground-drum pits!' he ordered.

Captain Future struggled suddenly, used every trick of super ju-jitsu that Otho the android had taught him. But it was futile.

He and Joan were dragged to one of the deep pits that had been used for the ground-drums. They were lowered into the big dirt pit by the Jovians, and then released.

Curt dropped over twenty feet, and struck the dirt floor of the pit. Joan was crumpled beside him.

'I'm not hurt,' she gasped. Then horror came into her eyes. 'Is he going to leave us in here to starve to death?'

'I'm afraid it's something a devil of a lot worse than starvation,' the big redhead answered tightly.

He looked up. The dirt walls of the pit sloped upward toward each other, and at the small opening at the top he could see Jovians armed with flare-guns looking down at them.

The dark, helmeted head of the Black One became visible at the top, against the brilliant moonlight. The super-criminal leaned down toward them.

Curt saw that the Space Emperor was again material, since in his hand he carried a small, flat metal lanternlike thing, with a big translucent lens in its face.

'You wanted to find out how I produce the atavism effect, Captain Future,' mocked the plotter. 'Now you are going to have your curiosity gratified.'

He held out the little lanternlike apparatus as he spoke.

'This apparatus produces a super-hard vibration that paralyzes the pituitary gland of any living creature and allows atavism to occur,' rumbled the black figure. 'Allow me to demonstrate it for you.'

'Back, Joan!' yelled Captain Future, sweeping the girl behind the shelter of his own big form, against the wall.

It was too late. The lens in the thing the Space Emperor held had glowed palely for an instant, and a dim, almost wholly invisible ray had flickered from it and bathed the heads of Curt and Joan. They felt a momentary sensation of shivering cold.

Joan screamed in horror. Curt felt a blind, raging fury. He had not felt anything but that momentary sensation of cold, but he knew that the deadly work had been done. The pituitaries of Joan and himself were paralyzed, and inevitably the atavism would begin in them—

'*You* will suffer the change now, Captain Future!' mocked the sinister black shape. 'Down in that pit, you and the girl will become hideous creatures within a few days. And I am leaving a few of my faithful Jovians here to watch and make sure that you stay in the pit to suffer.'

Curt kept his voice steady, by a supreme effort, as he looked up at the mocking figure.

'I have never promised death to a man without keeping my promise,' he said in chill, even voice. 'I am promising it to you now.'

He said nothing more. But something deadly in his tones made the Space Emperor stiffen.

'Not you or any other Earthman can harm me, protected as I am by immateriality,' the criminal retorted. 'And you forget that *you*, and the girl too, will soon be raving, hideous brutes!'

The Space Emperor withdrew. They could hear the Jovians above being dismissed by the plotter. A number of Jovians remained on guard above the pit, however. They could hear the excited bass voices overhead.

Joan Randall was staring at Captain Future with dark eyes wide with dazed horror. It was as though the girl could not yet realize what had happened.

'We – becoming beasts down here,' she choked hoarsely. 'Changing more horribly, day by day—'

Curt's big figure strode to her, and he grasped her shoulders in strong hands and shook her.

'Joan, get a grip on yourself!' he commanded harshly. 'This is no time to get hysterical. We're in a devil of a bad jam and it will take all our brains and nerves to get us out.'

'But we *can't* get out!' sobbed the girl. 'Those Jovians above would kill us if we could manage even to get out of this pit. And even if we did, we'd still change and change – like those horrors in the hospital—'

She buried her face in her hands. Curt soothed her and spoke encouragingly.

'There's a strong chance we can escape the atavism if we can escape from here and get back to Jungletown quickly,' he told her. 'Simon Wright should have found a cure by now. He was working on it when I left.'

She raised a tear-smeared face.

'I'm – sorry,' she said unsteadily. 'It isn't just dying that I'm afraid of, but changing—'

'We're not going to die or change either!' Curt declared forcefully. 'It will take hours, perhaps days, before the paralysis of the pituitaries begins to affect us in the slightest. That gives us a reasonable time to try to get away.'

His gray eyes flashed as he added, 'And we've got to do that, not for our own sakes alone, but to prevent a terrible thing from happening. That black devil is inciting the Jovians to attack all the Earthman settlements, and that attack may take place within hours!'

His big fists clenched.

'I've an idea now of a way in which the Space Emperor could be conquered – the only way. But it'll do no good as long as we're trapped down here.'

'You wouldn't be here if you hadn't tried to rescue me,' Joan said in self-reproach.

'Joan, how did it happen that the Space Emperor kidnaped you?' Captain Future asked. 'Did you see who he really is?'

'I don't know who he is,' the shaken girl replied, 'but I know someone whom I think does know.'

She explained unsteadily.

'Earlier tonight I slipped out of the hospital in Jungletown and went down to spy on Lucas Brewer and Mark Cannig in their offices. I peered in through a window.

'I saw Mark Cannig, in the offices, talking to the Space Emperor! He was, just as you had described him, concealed in that dark suit. Then as I watched, Cannig glimpsed me at the window and rushed out. I tried to escape but someone struck me a blow that knocked me unconscious. When I awoke I was bound, on my way here in the Space Emperor's rocket-flier.'

Curt Newton's red head jerked up.

'So Mark Cannig is an accomplice of the Space Emperor!'

His eyes narrowed.

'That eliminates Cannig of my four suspects, at least. But of the other three—'

'Captain Future, do you think there's any hope at all of our getting out of here?' Joan interrupted. 'Can we dig steps and climb out of this place?'

'Wouldn't do us any good with those Jovians watching the mouth of the pit,' Curt told her. His eyes swept the dark dirt walls of the pit. 'But there must be some way.'

Curt was reduced to his bare hands. Deprived of his belt and pistol, he was robbed of all the instruments he might have used to escape. Even his pocket-televisor was gone.

Joan had sunk to the dirt floor.

'We'll never get out,' she said in dull hopelessness. 'We'll change into awful creatures and die, down in this pit.'

'Like the devil we will!' Captain Future declared. 'I was chained to a rock on the Hot Side of Mercury once and left there to die. But I didn't die.'

His powerful mind was working at top speed to find a way out of this trap. He went around the dark pit, his keen eyes inspecting the dirt walls.

Suddenly Curt stopped and listened. His ears had detected a faint rasping sound that was barely audible. Quickly he pressed his ear against the dirt wall. And now he heard it much more plainly, a chewing, grinding rasp.

'It's a digger!' he exclaimed in a low voice to the girl. 'I don't think it's many yards away from this pit in the soil.'

Joan shivered at the mention of the bloodthirsty subterranean burrowers which inhabit the soil beneath the Jovian jungles.

'I hope it doesn't come this way,' she said fearfully.

'On the contrary, I want it to come this way!' Captain Future said. 'Don't you understand? The tunnels those diggers make connect with each other, and open at many places to the surface. It would be a way out for us!'

'But if the creature came into the pit here and attacked us –' the girl began terrifiedly.

'I can take care of that,' Curt told her. 'The thing I've got to do now is to attract the beast to come here.'

The ingenious fastener of Curt's zipper-suit was made of woven gray wire. He quickly broke a bit of this wire away, and with it he gashed his wrist.

As blood spurted, Curt smeared it onto the wall of the pit. Then he rapidly bound his wrist with a strip torn from his jacket.

'Those creatures can sense blood for hundreds of yards through the solid soil,' he told the girl. 'I think that will bring it here.'

In a moment he heard the rasping, chewing sound definitely louder and nearer.

'It's coming!' he exclaimed.

Joan shrank back against the opposite wall of the pit.

Captain Future was rapidly unraveling more of the tough gray wire from his woven suit-fastenings. When he had a doubled length of twelve feet, he fashioned a running noose and loop.

By that time the rasping, grinding sound of the advancing digger was very audible, and little flakes of dirt were falling from a spot on the dirt wall. Curt waited beside that point, his wire loop ready in his hand.

'Here it comes – make no sound!' he muttered.

Joan uttered a gasp of horror a moment later. Dirt had fallen from the wall, and through an opening its own jaws had made protruded the snout of a weird and menacing creature.

The digger was like a giant six-foot rat, with a broad, flat face opening in tremendous jaws armed with the big, flat grinding fangs with which it burrowed its way.

Its small red eyes glimpsed Joan Randall and it sprang out into the pit toward her. Curt cast his loop swiftly.

The loop settled around the leaping brown beast's head, tightened cruelly about its neck as Curt pulled hard. With a muffled squeal, the creature turned on its short legs. But Captain Future leaped aside, tightening the noose.

There was a brief, almost soundless flurry of struggle as the choking creature sought to reach the man. Soon its movements became weaker and it fell on its side, motionless.

'It's done for!' Curt exclaimed. 'Come on – we're going out of here through the tunnel it burrowed.'

He scrambled into the raw new passageway that the bloodthirsty beast had excavated. It was full of loose dirt, but Captain Future squeezed blindly on through the darkness, with Joan bravely crawling after him.

Presently this raw, stifling passage opened into a larger tunnel, within which they could stand by stooping.

'This is a regular digger run,' Curt told the girl. 'It may lead to the surface.'

They followed it forward, almost suffocated by the heavy, dirt-smelling air. Captain Future's hopes rose as the tunnel slanted slightly upward. The darkness was absolute.

In some minutes they emerged suddenly from the low tunnel into a much larger space. They could stand erect here. But here too the air was heavy, and foul with the odor of old bones and animals.

'Where are we?' Joan asked bewilderedly. 'I thought—'

'Quiet!' Captain Future hissed. 'See – those eyes!'

In the utter darkness, a dozen pairs of red eyes that glowed with uncanny phosphorescence were watching them.

'We've blundered into a nest of the diggers!' Curt whispered. 'And they see us!'

CHAPTER XVII

Chamber of Horrors

Joan uttered a little cry of horror. At the sound, the phosphorescent red eyes of the watching beasts began moving toward them.

Captain Future swept the girl behind him, against the dirt wall of this underground dirt cave, and awaited the attack of the ravenous beasts.

'Can't we escape back through the tunnel?' Joan whispered frantically in the darkness.

'They'd run us down in a minute, and we couldn't turn to fight in that narrow passage,' Curt gritted. 'Here we can at least put up a fight.'

The scene was enough to affect even the iron nerves of Captain Future. The utter blackness, the stifling atmosphere of ominous odors, and the red eyes that warily advanced.

He clenched his fists, knowing full well that they were useless against the fangs of these gathered beasts. Yet he would go down fighting, he knew – fighting as he had fought against hopeless odds from Mercury to Pluto.

Queerly enough, in that moment the paramount emotion of Curt was rage. Rage at the thought of the Space Emperor continuing his nefarious plot unchecked, of Jupiter turned into a hell of horror and struggle to further one man's mad ambitions.

'Look!' cried Joan suddenly. 'What's that?'

Captain Future saw it, at the same instant. It was something flowing down into the digger nest from one of the tunnels, something vaguely shining and liquid.

It looked like a viscous tide of strangely shining jelly, gliding smoothly down into the dirt chamber. The sight of it startled Curt with a cold shock.

'It's a crawler!' he exclaimed, hoarsely.

'A crawler?' Joan's voice shook at the mention of the most dreaded of all Jovian beasts.

For the crawlers were almost the most deadly life-form on Jupiter. They were like great viscous masses of protoplasm, moving by flowing over the ground, seizing prey by protruding pseudopods. At first, Earthmen explorers had considered them a very low form of life.

But now it was known that the crawlers possessed a mysterious, high intelligence. Every other creature on Jupiter was in terror of them. And now Curt had visual evidence that they would descend even among the tunnels of the 'diggers' in search of prey.

The diggers advancing toward Curt and Joan had not seen the flowing menace entering behind them, for their red eyes were still facing the man and girl. Then Curt saw a pseudopod of the shining viscous creature lick forth and seize a dark digger.

Squeals rent the air, and the diggers dashed in all directions in a wild effort to escape by the tunnels.

And the crawler, its two huge eyes coldly blazing in the midst of its formless body, towered up and sent one shooting pseudopod after another forth to seize the ratlike beasts.

'Out of here before the thing seizes us too!' Captain Future cried to the girl. 'Quick, the tunnel it came from—'

He seized Joan's hand and leaped around the rim of the dirt cavern that had now become a chamber of horror.

The crawler, intent on seizing as many of the bolting beasts as possible, did not notice the man and girl until they were entering the tunnel down through which it itself had come.

Then, as Curt pushed the girl up the cramped tunnel before him, he saw the crawler's huge eyes turn on its viscous mass toward him, and a big pseudopod shoot swiftly out.

By main force, Captain Future thrust the girl secret agent up the tunnel, in a tremendous thrust. The pseudopod of shining liquid darted up the tunnel after them.

But they were beyond its reach. The viscous arm retreated. They could hear the squeals of the diggers from below as the monster down there seized and ingested them.

'Hurry!' Curt urged the girl. 'The thing may follow us! This tunnel must lead to the surface, since it came down this way.'

After a few moments more of climbing up the cramped dirt passageway, a circle of brilliant moonlight showed above.

In a moment they were climbing out into the brilliant radiance of the four moons. Joan staggered, and Curt supported her.

He looked swiftly around. They were in the jungle, but he could glimpse the cyclopean masses of brooding masonry of the Place of the Dead, some hundreds of yards away.

'I've got to go back there,' Captain Future told the girl rapidly. 'I'll have to find my belt and gun.'

'But the Jovians guarding the pit we were imprisoned in –' the girl began fearfully.

'I can take care of them, I think,' he said. 'Keep behind me, and make no sound.'

Silently, stealthily, he advanced through the jungle toward the edge of the great circle of ancient ruins.

Crouching down on the edge of that wrecked city, he peered forth.

The moonlit ruins were now deserted except for six Jovians armed with flare-guns who sat around the ground-drum pit in which they supposed Captain Future and Joan to be still confined.

Curt's eyes searched the ground all around and finally fixed on what he was hunting for. His tungstite belt and pistol! They lay near the pit, where they had been flung by the Jovian who had ripped them from him at the Space Emperor's orders.

Curt motioned for the girl to remain hidden, and inched silently forward in a wriggling crawl. He was only a few yards from the belt and pistol when a Jovian saw him. The green man cried out and jumped up. Captain Future dived desperately toward the weapon.

He scooped it up and pulled trigger in the same swift movement. The pale beam that lanced from it hit the Jovians as they were leveling their own guns, and sent them tumbling into a stunned heap.

'Captain Future, someone's coming!' cried Joan Randall, running wildly out into the clearing toward him.

A dark, humming bulk was diving toward them out of the moonlight. Curt raised his pistol swiftly, then lowered it with a throb of gladness and relief.

'It's the *Comet!*' he cried.

He ran forward. Out of the little teardrop ship burst Grag and Otho.

The big robot boomed noisily as he patted Curt with heavy metal hands. Otho held Simon Wright's square brain-case.

'Simon, have you perfected the atavism-cure formula yet?' Curt asked the Brain tensely.

'Yes, lad – why do you ask?' the Brain countered quickly.

Curt explained. And a cry of heart-checking rage went up from Otho as he heard.

'He dared turn the thing on you!' hissed the android furiously.

Grag spoke solemnly.

'For daring to do that, I will kill the Space Emperor myself.'

'Bring the girl inside,' Simon told Curt quickly. 'I can give you both an injection at once. Hurry inside!'

In the laboratory of the *Comet*, the Brain gave Curt directions. Rapidly, an injection of the pink formula was made into the veins of Captain Future and the girl.

'I don't feel any differently,' Joan said doubtfully.

'No, but you are both safe now from the atavism,' Simon told them. 'The paralysis of your glands had been ended, before it could have any effect upon you.'

'What now, lad?' the Brain asked Curt.

'Simon, things are rushing toward a climax,' Curt said earnestly. 'The Space Emperor plans to lead the Jovian hordes onto the Earthman towns, perhaps this very night. The only thing that will stop the Jovians is the destroying of that black devil whom they worship and follow.

'There's not a chance in the world of our harming the Space Emperor while he can take refuge in immateriality through that vibration step-up. We've got to master that power ourselves before we can come to grips with him.'

'You have a plan?' the Brain asked him keenly.

'The only plan possible, and its possibility depends on something I glimpsed in these ruins,' Curt answered. 'Come with me.'

He led the way back out into the moonlight, and hastened toward the great black stone globe that towered between the two ground-drum pits.

Upon its surface, as he had noticed before, were carved outlines of the continents and seas of Jupiter. Set in it were the silver stars that he had guessed marked the location of the long-perished cities of the Ancients. He had formed that guess because one star marked this exact location he stood in now.

Captain Future located the thing about the globe which had aroused his attention when he had glimpsed it from his hiding-place previously. From the star that marked this dead city he stood in, a line had been drawn due northward on the globe in white *pencil*.

'An Earthman drew that line while plotting directions,' Curt told the others rapidly. 'And the only one who was likely to have done that was Kenneth Lester, the young archaeologist who disappeared up here weeks ago.'

The penciled line ran straight northward toward another silver star, enclosed in a circle, which was set on the southern edge of the big red oval that marked the precise location of the Fire Sea.

'Lester was plotting the direction from this ruined city to some other city or ruin of the Ancients that lies up there on the shore of the Fire Sea,' Curt declared. 'So that is where Lester must have gone.'

'But there couldn't have ever been any city up there by the Fire Sea!' objected Joan. 'Why, no one or no thing can live that close to that terrible flaming ocean!'

'The Ancients had a city of some kind there,' Captain Future insisted, 'but it was different somehow from their other cities, for it is distinguished by a silver circle around the star that marks its location.'

'You think then that up there is the storehouse of knowledge from which the Space Emperor got the scientific secrets of the Ancients?' Simon Wright asked thoughtfully.

Curt nodded his red head quickly.

'Yes, I do think so. And I think that there I could secure that power of immaterialization for myself, and be able at last to come to grips with that black devil before he can loose an uprising.'

'It's a long chance, lad,' muttered the Brain. 'It's hard, as Joan says, to believe that any city could ever have been located on the shore of that awful sea of flame.'

'It's the only real chance we've got of stopping the Space Emperor,' Curt warned. 'I've got to take it. I'm going up there now, and I'll take Grag with me. We can go in the rocket-flier I left over at the radium mine.

'Otho will fly you and Joan back to Jungletown, Simon,' he went on. 'It's important that you get that atavism cure working on the victims that crowd the hospital there.'

'But I should go with you instead of Grag!' Otho objected loudly.

Curt silenced him peremptorily.

'Someone has to fly Simon and Joan back. And Grag's strength may be more useful to me up there than anything else. Do as you're told, Otho!'

Grumbling, the android gave in. They entered the *Comet*.

'You can drop Grag and me at the mine, and we'll pick up our flier,' Curt ordered.

As they flew eastward over the moonlit ferns again, Curt's mind was worked up to a fever pitch of excitement. He felt that at last there was a chance of getting to grips with the sinister criminal who had thus far slipped through his hands like a shadow.

The little teardrop ship landed in the mine-clearing within minutes. The prisoners and Ezra Gurney were gone. Evidently, a police flier had already taken them back to Jungletown.

'Be careful up there, lad,' begged Simon Wright as they parted. 'You know that it's death to meddle with that hellish ocean.'

'I will take care of master,' Grag announced, joyful with pride at being chosen to accompany Captain Future.

The *Comet* shot away, hurtling southward toward Jungletown. Curt and the robot hastened toward the rocket-flier he had left inside the jungle.

In a few moments the little torpedo-like craft rose sharply out of the jungle, and headed northward at its highest possible speed.

Ahead of them the whole night sky was a vivid glare of scarlet, a shaking splendor of wild red rays. Black against the glare stood out the dark, jagged hills that rimmed the southern shore of the Fire Sea.

As they neared the hills, the glare became so intense that their eyes could hardly look into it. Grag turned a little uneasily from the controls toward Captain Future.

'Shall I keep straight on over the hills and above the Fire Sea, master?' he asked.

'Keep on over the hills – we're going to reconnoiter the coast of the sea,' Curt told him. He added with a quick grin, 'You're not afraid of a little molten lava, Grag?'

'I would not be afraid of a little,' Grag answered seriously, 'but there is a great deal of it in that ocean, master.'

Curt chuckled. 'A great deal is right. But it won't hurt us – I hope!'

The flier was now pitching and tossing slightly despite its powerful drive, as it encountered great winds and blasts of superheated air rushing up from the vast, flaming ocean that lay ahead. The whole sky was an unthinkable flare of scarlet from the molten sea.

Curt felt his muscles tightening. They were, he knew, rushing toward one of the most stupendous and perilous natural wonders in the Solar System – one that had claimed the lives of almost all the Earthmen who had ever dared attempt the exploration of its shores.

Whirling blasts of smoke and fumes engulfed the speeding flier, as it raced on over the rocky hills toward the dreaded ocean of fire. Would they be able to survive the fiery sea's perils? Captain Future wondered.

CHAPTER XVIII

The Sleeper in the Cavern

Fire Sea of Jupiter! Most dangerous and stupendous feature of the mightiest planet, which was spoken of with awe by men from Mercury to Pluto!

It stretched before them now, a vast ocean of crimson, molten lava that extended to the dim horizons and beyond for eight thousand unthinkable miles, and that extended east and west for three times that distance. A flaming sea that was constantly kept liquid by the interior radioactive heat.

The surface of that evilly glowing red-hot ocean was rippled by little, heavy waves and boiling maelstroms. Upon it like genies danced lurid flames, and whirls of sulfurous smoke. Its radiated heat was overpowering, even through the filter-windows of the rocket-flier.

Captain Future felt awe as he looked, not for the first time, on this incredibly fiery gulf into which all Earth could have been plunged.

'Don't go out over it, Grag,' he told the robot. 'The air-currents above it would capsize the flier. Follow along the shore-line.'

'Yes, master,' boomed the robot, turning the ship to move eastward. He added naively, 'I do not like this place.'

'I prefer even the ice-fields of Pluto to this myself,' Curt admitted ruefully.

'I see nothing along the shore, master,' Grag said.

'Neither do I,' Curt admitted. 'But there must be something here.'

Below them lay the southern shore of the Fire Sea. The flaming ocean's molten waves lapped directly against the great range of black rock hills which acted as a dike to dam them back.

The rock slopes of the hills were heavily encrusted with solidified lava that showed the tide-marks to which the molten flood reached. But there was nothing else to be seen upon that incredible shore, and indeed, it seemed impossible that ever any living beings could have set foot there.

Captain Future watched with close attention as the flier throbbed eastward along the shore-line. He believed that there must be some ruin or other vestige that would mark the spot which had once been frequented by the ancients.

Doubt grew in Curt's mind, as the miles unreeled beneath without yielding any sign. After all, he told himself, he had only the evidence of that ancient world-globe in the Place of the Dead to guide him.

An hour passed, in which they had flown steadily east along the flaming coast. Curt made a sudden decision.

'Turn back and fly westward down the coast, Grag,' he ordered. 'It may be in that direction.'

The robot obeyed, and the flier raced back at top speed over the ground they had covered, then moved on westward along the shore.

Again they watched with closest attention. Yet still there was nothing to see but the lava-crusted rock slopes, and the evilly glowing red ocean of molten lava that stretched away on their right.

Blasts of sulfurous air, and howling currents of superheated gases shrieked like fiends around them. The small rocket-flier pitched uneasily, yet Grag held it steadily above the fiery coast.

'Slow down!' Captain Future cried suddenly to the robot, his big figure tensing.

He had glimpsed something ahead – a queer opening in the rock shore at the edge of the lava sea.

They glided closer, hovered above the spot. From Curt Newton came an exclamation.

'This may be the place we're looking for, Grag!' he declared.

'But I see nothing, master – nothing but a big round hole in the shore, into which the lava is pouring,' boomed the robot puzzledly.

Below them, there was a large, jagged circular opening in the rock slope of the hills, just where the fire ocean lapped against it.

As a result, a stream of the molten lava was pouring ceaselessly down over the lip of that opening, with a dull, reverberating thunder.

'There's a big cavernous space of some kind down there in the rock,' Captain Future declared. 'And that round opening leading down into it is too round to be natural. It looks as though it had been artificially enlarged at some time in the past.'

'Do you think then that the place of the Ancients we are hunting is down in that hole?' Grag asked incredulously.

'It's a chance,' Curt said. 'We've seen no place else that could be what we're looking for. We'll investigate this.'

'But how do we get down in there?' Grag boomed puzzledly. 'There does not seem to be any opening except this one through which the lava falls, master.'

Curt grinned at the big robot.

'When there's only one door to go through, you can't take the wrong one, Grag. That's our way in.'

Grag stared.

'Down through that opening alongside the falling lava? There is barely enough room for the flier to make it without being caught in the fire-fall.'

'Enough room is as good as a light-year,' Curt shrugged. 'Take her on down, Grag.'

Curt gave the order coolly, yet he knew the perilous nature of the descent they were about to attempt.

He would have taken the controls himself, but knew that the robot would take that as a lack of confidence on his part. And he had perfect faith in Grag's abilities.

Grag moved the controls slightly, the robot's photoelectric eyes peering downward. The little rocket-flier sank gently toward the dark, jagged opening through which the fire-fall plunged into unguessable depths.

Down sank the little craft, on an even keel, supported by its keel-tubes. The cataract of falling lava was only a yard away on their one side, and its thunder was deafening.

Wild air-currents screaming upward shook the flier as it sank lower. Its stern rasped ominously against the rock side of the opening, threatening to send the ship lurching into the falling lava.

But Grag steadied the craft, kept it sinking directly downward. In a moment they had descended through the opening into a vast, dim subterranean space weirdly illuminated by the red glow of the falling lava.

'Run into the cavern a little and then land, Grag,' Captain Future ordered excitedly.

They were hovering near the northern end of the enormous underground space. It extended shadowly southward, a cavern a thousand feet wide and of unguessable length.

The molten red lava of the fire-fall thundered down into a flaming pool, and then ran down the center of the cavern in a sunken channel or canal, a flaming, sluggish river.

Grag landed the flier on the rock floor of the dim cavern, near that fiery river. In a moment, Curt and his companion were emerging.

'This place is incredible,' declared Curt, raising his voice above the deafening thunder of the cataract.

'Even the caverns of Uranus are not as uncanny as *this!*' Grag agreed, staring in awe.

Captain Future felt a throb of leaping excitement that kindled higher each moment.

'It's the place of the Ancients we were hunting!' he cried. 'See!'

A little farther along the cavern from them, upon either side of the flaming lava river, rose two strange statues of silvery metal.

They represented creatures almost exactly like the Jovians, erect bipeds with round heads, unhuman but strangely noble features, and limbs that ended in flipperlike hands and feet.

The metal figures stood, each with a slender arm upraised, as though to warn Captain Future and the robot back. And upon the pedestal of each statue was a lengthy inscription in queer, wedge-shaped characters.

'The Ancients?' Grag said wonderingly as they paused beneath one of the statues. 'But they look just like the Jovians.'

'Yes,' Captain Future nodded, his gray eyes gleaming. 'I believe that the great Ancients *were* nothing but Jovians such as inhabit this world today.'

The big robot stared at Curt, his simple mind trying to comprehend the statement.

'But the Jovians today do not build great cities and statues and machines,' Grag objected. 'They cannot do the things the Ancients are supposed to have done.'

'I know,' Curt said thoughtfully, more to himself than to the robot. 'Yet, I've felt all along that the Jovians are simply the descendants of the mysterious Ancients of whom they tell legends – that the great race of the Ancients had its civilization swept away by some catastrophe.

'If I'm right,' Curt added, 'the present Jovians have not even a suspicion that the Ancients they revere were their own forefathers. All they have are vague legends, distorted by ages.'

'They look as though they were warning us to stay out of here,' said Grag, peering up at the solemn statues.

'We're going on,' Captain Future said, striding forward, his big figure animated by driving determination.

They passed the silvery figures, and moved on along the edge of the fiery lava river whose dancing flames eerily illuminated the cavern.

Sulfurous smoke from the lava drifted about them, and the heat from it was fierce on their faces. From behind them came the perpetual booming thunder of the awful fire-cataract.

'See, master!' called Grag, pointing ahead with his metal arm. 'Machines!'

Vague, towering metal shapes loomed up out of the dim shadows ahead. They were big mechanisms of so alien and unfamiliar a design that their purpose was unfathomable.

One was a complexity of cogged wheels of silver metal, geared to a sliding arm whose end suggested the muzzle of a gun. Another was a huge upright metal bulb that suggested a cyclotron in appearance.

Upon the base of each machine was a lengthy inscription in the queer, wedge-shaped characters of the Ancients.

'If I could only read those!' Captain Future exclaimed tensely. 'Here, for some mysterious reason, were gathered all the powers and weapons of that perished race. And I can't translate the key to this riddle, discover those powers!'

'Maybe you can decipher those characters in time, master,' Grag suggested.

'Time? There is no time, now!' Curt exclaimed. 'Unless we find in here the powers we need to crush the Space Emperor, and return to do that at once, the Jovians will have trampled Jungletown and the other Earthmen towns out of existence!'

Curt was feeling the strain of agonizing apprehension. The knowledge that somewhere southward the Black One was spurring the Jovian hordes on to the attack was like a prodding goad in his mind.

'But we can't decipher these inscriptions at once. Nobody could,' he muttered hopelessly.

'I hear someone in here,' Grag suddenly said uneasily. 'Someone living!'

'Be quiet and listen,' Captain Future commanded. 'Your ears are keener than mine, Grag.'

Curt's hand had dropped to the hilt of his proton pistol. Standing motionless, listening intently, he cast his glance quickly around.

He could see nothing but the mysterious, silent mechanisms towering about him in the red-lit shadows, the dim spaces of the cavern stretching southward. And he could hear nothing but the thunderous reverberation of the fire-fall.

'I hear it again,' Grag asserted in a moment. 'Someone moving—'

'I hear too, now!' Curt exclaimed, his keen ears catching the slight, shuffling sound above the thunderous roar. 'It's from farther along the cavern.'

He drew his pistol swiftly, and Grag imitated him.

'Come on,' Curt muttered. 'There's someone else in here. If it's the Space Emperor—'

His pulses leaped at the thought, even though he knew that his next encounter with the mysterious plotter might be his last.

They crept forward, big Grag moving soundlessly on his padded feet. They moved around towering, dusty machines, on along the flaming river, deeper into the great cavern.

'There – an Earthman!' Grag boomed, pointing his metal arm.

Curt had seen the man at the same moment. He was not a hundred yards ahead.

A slight-looking figure in a worn brown zipper-suit, the man lay sprawled on his face on the rock floor of the cavern. Near him stood a table which bore an extinguished argon-lamp, and many papers covered with wedge-shaped characters.

'He's either unconscious or sleeping, master,' said the robot.

Captain Future saw that the man's limbs were moving restlessly, as though in sleep. It was the sound Grag had heard.

Curt bent over the man, and as he did so he smelled an acrid, unforgettable odor.

'This man's been drugged,' he declared. 'He's been given a shot of *somnal*, the Mercurian sleep-drug.'

He turned the man over on his back. The face of the drugged sleeper was exposed to the red glow of the fire-river.

It was a serious, spectacled, haggard young face that Curt had never seen before. The red-haired adventurer stared down at the man, utterly perplexed.

Then he noticed a monogram on the sleeper's synthesilk jacket. The letters were 'KL.'

'Kenneth Lester!' Curt cried. 'That's who this is – the missing archaeologist!'

CHAPTER XIX

The Epic of Ages

Captain Future's pulses throbbed with excitement as he raised the drugged man to a sitting position.

He had felt all along that Kenneth Lester was somehow the key to this whole great planetary plot. And now at last he had found the young archaeologist.

'He's been drugged more than once,' boomed the robot. 'See the needle-scars on his wrist.'

'I can bring him around, I think,' Curt muttered.

He fished in his belt for his medicine-kit. It was hardly larger than his finger, but inside it were minute vials of the most powerful drugs known in the Solar System.

Captain Future dipped a sterile needle into one of those vials, and then pressed its wet point into Kenneth Lester's veins.

As the tiny drop of super-powerful anti-narcotic raced through the young archaeologist's bloodstream, he began to stir. In a moment he opened dazed, dark eyes. He looked haggard, worn.

'Why don't you kill me, and get it over with?' he asked hoarsely, looking up unseeingly. 'This horrible existence—'

Then as Lester's vision cleared and he saw Captain Future and the towering metal robot bending over him, he uttered a startled cry.

'Who – what—'

'I'm Captain Future,' Curt told him rapidly. 'You may have heard of me.'

'Captain Future?' Lester cried incredulously.

The young archaeologist knew that name, as did everyone in the Solar System. As it sank into his fogged mind, a wild relief showed on his haggard face.

'Thank God you're here!' he sobbed. 'It's been a hellish death-in-life for me here, these last weeks. The Space Emperor—'

'Who is the Space Emperor?' Curt asked swiftly, hanging on the answer.

But again he was doomed to disappointment.

'I don't know!' cried young Lester. Then he raged feebly, 'Whoever he is, he's a fiend from hell! He's kept me here, for how many weeks I can't guess – forcing me to decipher these ancient Jovian inscriptions for him, and leaving me drugged whenever he went away.'

'You were the one who found this place originally, weren't you?' Curt asked.

He had been sure of that, from the first. And he found now that his reasoning had been correct.

'Yes,' nodded Lester weakly. 'I found it, and I thought I had made the greatest archaeological discovery in the history of the Solar System.'

He was sitting up, now, talking with feverish rapidity as he looked up into Captain Future's tanned, set face.

'I came to Jupiter because I had heard of Jovian legends that spoke of a great, ancient race who had once inhabited this planet. I believed that there must be some basis to those legends, and resolved to track it down.

'From Jungletown, I went northward into the fern-jungles and there I tried to learn more from the Jovians, but those primitive creatures became sullenly silent and suspicious when I mentioned the legends of the Ancients. I did learn that they gathered now and then for strange ceremonies at a spot they called the Place of the Dead, so I trailed them there and found it to be a ruined city of the Ancients.

'There was a world-globe map of Jupiter made by the Ancients there. It showed the sites of their cities. But one site was marked differently than the rest, and I guessed it was more important. It was situated on the shore of the Fire Sea, where no city could ordinarily have been.

'So I came north alone in my little rocket-flier and searched along the shore of the flaming sea until I found the opening down into this place. I got down into it with my flier – and found it to be a wonderful storehouse of the powers and knowledge of the Ancients.'

Kenneth Lester's haggard face lit for a moment with scientific passion as he continued.

'I succeeded in deciphering some inscriptions here, and learned something of the history of those great Ancients. I learned that ages ago they had had a mighty civilization, as high if not higher than that of Earth today. Along certain scientific lines, they had gone farther than we have.

'They had succeeded in solving many a problem that has baffled Earth physicists. They had achieved intra-atomic means of power. They had even been able to perfect a means of making matter effectively immaterial, by causing a step-up of the frequency of atomic vibration which allowed such matter to interpenetrate other matter freely as though it did not exist. They had used this immaterialization process to explore even the bowels of the planet.

'Also their biologists had found a method of causing atavism at will, which allowed them to study the past evolution of their own and every other race. The method depended upon the fact that every living organism has a glandular organ which is the real control of its physical and mental characteristics, and which, if it is paralyzed or atrophied, allows the subject to degenerate rapidly into the past forms from which its race evolved.

'The Ancients had done all these things, but apparently they had not risen above the reach of passions and emotions. For an internecine war broke out finally between their cities. It was carried on with unbelievable ferocity, and it laid their great civilization in ruins.

'Finally when only a few of the Ancients retained the former scientific knowledge, and the rest had become half-civilized tribes wandering amid the ruins of former cities, those few remaining enlightened ones sought to preserve the triumphs of their race. Hoping that some day their people might be willing to forget war and again rise to peaceful civilization, those few Ancients gathered in this secret cavern all the scientific powers and instruments they could collect, so that they might not be utterly lost.'

The worn features of young Kenneth Lester showed his deep, bitter emotion as he continued.

'All this, I say, I learned by deciphering some of the inscriptions in this cavern. I realized this was a wonderful storehouse of scientific secrets, which only the proper authorities should know about, lest they fall into the wrong hands.

'So I wrote a report of my find, for Governor Quale. I flew down to Jungletown and mailed it to him, and then flew hastily back here to stand guard over my find. I expected the governor to come here at once.

'But two nights later, as I was sleeping here, I awoke to find myself bound and blindfolded. Someone had learned of my report and had come here to secure the scientific powers of which I had spoken. And that person tortured me into telling all that I had learned so far.

'He learned the secret of immaterialization from me, thus. He used it at once to make himself immaterial, and also he learned the secret of the atavism weapon and took one of the instruments that produce it with him.

'This man whose identity I did not know, the Space Emperor as he called himself, has come here many times since. Each time, he has forced me under threat of instant death to decipher for him more of the secrets of the Ancients. Each time he has left, he has drugged me so that I could not escape while he was gone.'

Lester's eyes flashed with wild fear as he concluded.

'The Space Emperor boasted to me of what he has been doing with these powers, Captain Future! He has said that he has used the atavism beam on Earthmen, to convince the Jovians that the Earthmen are cursed. He intended to use the Jovians to establish his power over this whole planet!'

Captain Future nodded his red head grimly.

'Yes, that black devil has been doing that. And this plot is reaching its climax, for right now the Jovians are gathering to attack the Earthman towns.'

Lester's haggard face went white.

'Can't *you* stop him some way, Captain Future?'

'Not until I too can achieve the immaterialization that protects him from all attack,' Curt replied. 'That's why I came here, looking for the means to do that. Can you tell me the secret of that?' he asked tensely.

Curt hung tautly upon the answer. For upon it, he well knew, depended the success or failure of his effort to halt the chaos threatening Jupiter.

'Yes – there are a number of the immaterialization mechanisms here,' Kenneth Lester answered quickly.

The big adventurer stared at him wonderingly, though his pulses leaped.

'Then why didn't you use one to escape, and walk through the rock?' he demanded.

'You forget. I've been drugged every moment except when the Space Emperor was here!' Lester reminded. 'And when he was here, he stood ready to kill me at my first wrong move. He never allowed me to touch any mechanism. He made me read and translate the inscriptions, and then he operated the things.'

Lester staggered to his feet.

'But at last I'm awake, and that devil not here! Come with me and I'll show you what you want.'

Grag held the staggering young archaeologist to keep him from falling.

'The far end of the cavern,' Lester said weakly. 'This way.'

Curt hastened excitedly with Lester and the robot along the dim length of the cavern, through the towering machines by the edge of the flaming lava river.

Captain Future saw that the end of the cavern was just ahead. There was a jagged aperture in its wall, through which flowed the molten lava stream to empty into unfathomable depths beneath.

Kenneth Lester stumbled toward a big metal rack upon which were ranged dusty rows of the instruments of the Ancients. There were many of the atavism-beam devices, like small flat lanterns with translucent lenses.

And there were a number of belts to which were attached hemispherical metal devices with a simple switch.

'Those are the immaterializers,' Lester said, reaching forward.

'Master, look out!' Grag yelled suddenly and pushed Captain Future aside with a violent push.

Curt spun around, though off balance, in time to see what happened.

The Space Emperor stood in the front part of the cavern, near their own rocket-flier. Curt knew instantly that the dark plotter had come down through the rock in an immaterial state, for he had not come in any flier of his own.

But the Space Emperor was material for the moment, for he had raised a flare gun and had loosed its beam at Curt's back. Grag had knocked the red-haired man aside just in time.

'The Space Emperor!' Kenneth Lester cried wildly as he saw.

Curt wasted no time in words. His pistol was already in his hand and he was triggering.

But as he moved, his enemy moved his hand also, toward his belt. And Curt's proton beam again tore through the dark criminal without harming him in the least.

The Space Emperor had again made himself immaterial, just in time. They saw him glide swiftly back toward their rocket-flier and into it, through its walls.

'Get him!' Curt yelled, plunging wildly forward. 'He's going to take our flier!'

It was too late. Already the rocket-flier was rising swiftly from the cavern floor and darting toward the entrance of the fire-fall.

The Space Emperor had made himself material once more inside the little craft and was stealing it.

Captain Future shot at it, but though the proton beam scorched the side of the darting flier, the craft did not stop. It zoomed up past the thundering cataract of lava, and disappeared up through the vertical shaft.

'He got away!' Grag boomed furiously, coming back from his vain attempt to overtake the flier. 'Master, how could he know that we were here?'

'He must have heard from Joan or the others when they returned to Jungletown of the quest we'd gone on,' Curt exclaimed. 'And he came here to trap us.'

As he spoke, Captain Future was snatching out his pocket-televisor.

'If I can call Simon and Otho, they'll soon be here in the *Comet* to get us out!'

Again and again he pushed the call-button of the little instrument. But no answer came.

'The devil!' Curt exclaimed. 'The rock above us must contain a heavy metal content that screens off our televisor signals. The Space Emperor must have known that, damn him!'

'Then how can we get out?' Grag asked. 'We cannot climb up that shaft down which the fire-fall comes – not even Otho could climb out there.'

'No, we can't climb out there, but we can get out *through* the rock above us!' Captain Future cried. 'We've got those immaterializing mechanisms, and Lester here knows how to use them.'

Kenneth Lester was white as death. He swayed as he stood, and shook his head in dull, hopeless despair.

'We can't do it, Captain Future,' he said heavily. 'We'd die if we tried it.'

'Why would we?' Curt demanded, puzzled.

Lester shrugged hopelessly.

'We have no suit such as the Space Emperor wears. We'd become immaterial, but we would have no air-supply to breathe in that state. We would suffocate long before we could go out through the rock!'

CHAPTER XX

Power of the Ancients

Captain Future was undaunted by the archaeologist's objection. The big red-headed adventurer squared his wide shoulders, and into his tanned face there came a determined fighting-look.

'You forget that Grag doesn't need to breathe!' he exclaimed. 'He can go up through the rock, and then get us out.'

Hope lit in Kenneth Lester's haggard eyes.

'If he could do it—'

Curt hurried back to the rack that held the dusty instruments of the Ancients. He came back with two of the belts to which were attached the hemispherical immaterializers.

He belted one around the big robot, and the other one around his own waist.

'But you won't need one, since you can't go out through the rock,' Lester said puzzledly.

'I'll need one if we do get out, when I meet the Space Emperor,' Curt said meaningly. 'Show me how the things work.'

Lester explained.

'The hemispheres are projectors of a powerful electro-magnetic radiation whose excitation acts to step up the frequency of atomic vibration of any matter. This action is confined to the wearer of the mechanism by means of this control on the side of the hemisphere, which limits the action to the wearer's body and clothing.'

Carefully, with considerable doubt and anxiety, Lester set the control he spoke of on both the instruments.

'The hemispheres also embody a means of projecting speech, even when the wearer is in the immaterial state,' he went on. 'As far as I can comprehend, it is done by translating the sonic vibrations of the immaterialized one's speech into similar sonic waves in the matter around him, by means of a smaller auxiliary step-down transformer inside the hemisphere. A similar principle in reverse, takes care of hearing.'

'I wondered how the Space Emperor was able to speak and be heard when he was immaterial,' Curt muttered.

Kenneth Lester turned.

'It's all ready,' he said anxiously to Captain Future.

'What shall I do, master?' Grag asked, looking toward the big red-head with his gleaming eyes quite calmly.

'First you must set your gravitation equalizer at zero, Grag,' Curt told him.

The robot obeyed, touching the control of the flat equalizer which he wore upon his breast.

As he set the thing at zero, thus nullifying all gravitational attraction upon himself, the great robot hung floating an inch above the floor of the cavern, drifting slightly this way and that with every little movement.

'Take my proton pistol, Grag,' Curt went on tensely, handing the weapon to the robot. 'Now when you touch the switch of this hemisphere at your belt, it will make you immaterial. By firing the pistol downward, the reaction of its force will cause you to float upward.

'You will float up right through the rock above this cavern. You must wait until you have reached the outside surface, and then you must turn off the switch of the hemisphere at once. Is that clear?'

'Yes, master,' Grag said doubtfully. 'But when I have done that, and am outside, how shall I get you two out of here?'

'You will have to get vines from the jungle and make a strong rope and lower it down that shaft through which the fire cataract falls,' Captain Future told him. 'Then you can pull us up.'

'Very well, master,' the robot said docilely. 'Shall I start now?'

Curt nodded.

'The sooner the better, Grag.'

They saw Grag touch the switch of the hemispherical instrument at his belt.

There seemed no immediate change in the robot's appearance. But when Curt thrust forth his hand to touch Grag, it went through the robot as though he did not exist.

'I do not like this much, master,' boomed the big metal creature, uneasily. 'It makes me feel as though I were not real at all, like those Mind Men we found on Saturn.'

Curt made an urgent signal, and the robot pointed the pistol down toward the ground and fired the proton beam.

At once, under the reactive push of the beam, slight as it was, Grag's huge body rose floatingly from the floor.

Curt and young Lester watched tensely. The scene was weird, incredible. The great, gloomy cavern of looming machines and deep shadows, bisected by the river of flaming lava that flowed down its center from the thundering fire-fall; the immaterialized robot, floating up toward the rocky roof.

The scene became even more weird a moment later. For when Grag's slowly rising body reached the rock ceiling, the robot's head disappeared right into the rock. Then his metal shoulders were hidden, and finally his whole body was gone from sight above.

Curt drew a long breath. There had been a thrilling uncanniness to the sight of the robot entering the solid rock. Even though he understood the scientific principle of the process, that did not make it less weird to his eyes.

'He ought to be on the surface in a few minutes,' Curt muttered. 'The rock above this cavern can be no more than a few hundred feet in thickness.'

Kenneth Lester looked at him fearfully.

'But what if he should lose his sense of direction while he's floating blindly through that solid rock? He might move in the wrong direction and get lost in the rock mass of the planet!'

Captain Future had thought of that. His lips tightened, as he waited.

Minutes went by. Each minute seemed abnormally long to the big adventurer. What was going on southward while he was trapped here? What was the Space Emperor doing?

'Come on, Grag,' he whispered under his breath as he waited. 'Hurry!'

Yet still, there came nothing to indicate that the robot had succeeded in escaping.

By the time almost an hour had passed, Kenneth Lester's haggard face had lost all hope. The archaeologist sat down as though he had ceased to struggle against the inevitable.

'He didn't make it,' he muttered. 'We might have known he couldn't.'

Curt did not answer. He paced restlessly to and fro, glancing every few moments toward the fire-fall.

Suddenly he shouted in excitement. Something had dropped down the shaft of the fire cataract – a long rope of tough vines tied together, that now dangled with its end swinging a little above the lava pool.

'Grag made it!' Curt cried.

They ran forward, stopping at the edge of the molten lava pool which lay beneath the shaft.

The vine rope hung out of their reach – more than a dozen feet out above the hissing, bubbling lava.

Blinded by fumes and scorching heat from the thundering cataract of molten rock, Captain Future and Lester stared baffledly at the rope.

'I'll jump for it, and once I get hold of it I can swing over to you,' Curt said rapidly, backing away from the edge of the pool.

'If you miss it when you jump, you'll die in that molten rock!' Lester cried appalledly.

Curt grinned at him.

'Miss an easy little jump like that? Why, Otho would never forgive me if I did.'

Before Lester could protest further, Curt ran forward. All the strength of his superb muscles he put into a springing leap that sent him flying out through the air above the glowing, hissing lava.

His fingers caught the vine rope, and held. There was a nasty slipping of the tough vine, as its knots tightened under his weight. But Grag had fastened carefully, and the improvised rope did not give.

Hanging above the lava, Curt began to swing back and forth like a pendulum, the arc of his swing increasing each time.

Finally, he was swinging widely out over the edge of the lava pool, where Lester stood.

The young archaeologist grabbed the vine rope also. They swung back together out over the lava pool. Curt quickly gave a jerk on the vine to signal Grag.

They began to be pulled up. It was a perilous situation, and the unnerving quality of it was increased by the cataract of molten lava that rushed down close beside them, to thunder into the pool below.

Lester's face was ghastly, as he clung.

He cried chokingly to Captain Future, who barely caught the words.

'Can't – hold on—'

The archaeologist's grip upon the vine was slipping, weak as he was from his long, drugged captivity.

Curt grabbed him just in time with his left arm, hanging onto the vine with his right. The weight put a terrific strain on the red-headed adventurer's muscles. No man less perfect physically could have withstood that strain.

Grag was hauling them up rapidly now. The tremendous strength of the robot was standing him in good stead. Upward they rose, revolving slowly at the end of the vine rope, Lester now an unconscious burden inside Curt's arm.

Curt was nearly overcome by the fumes of the falling lava. Wild air-currents from below screamed and howled around him.

Then he glimpsed the mouth of the shaft above.

At the north side of the opening, the lava sea poured in. At the south edge, upon the rock brink, stood Grag's great metal figure.

In a few moments, Curt stood with the robot upon the rock. It was still night, and they stood beneath the combined light of three moons and the red glare of the Fire Sea.

'Good work, Grag!' Captain Future exclaimed, as he lowered the unconscious archaeologist to the rock.

Grag was pleased.

'It took me a long time to get far enough away from the Fire Sea to find vines growing, or I would not have taken so long,' he explained.

Curt snatched out his pocket-televisor once more. Again he pressed the call-button.

'Ought to be able to get Otho and Simon now that we're out of the cavern,' he muttered.

Presently came the faintest of answering signals from Otho.

'Come in the *Comet* and get us!' Captain Future ordered. 'I'll leave the call-signal of the televisor on as a beam to guide you here.'

He could just hear the faint, distance-dimmed reply from Otho.

'Coming!'

While they waited, Curt hastily examined Lester. The young archaeologist was still unconscious.

'He's in bad shape, but he'll pull through with rest and treatment,' Curt declared.

'Master, the *Comet* comes!' Grag called a little later.

Out of the south like a shooting star drove the little teardrop ship. It dived toward them with a scream of splitting air, and came jarringly to rest on the rock ledge.

Curt shouldered inside, and Grag followed with the senseless archaeologist.

'I've got the immaterializer, Simon!' Curt cried eagerly to the Brain. 'Now I can hunt down the Space Emperor and meet him on even terms.'

'Too late for that, lad!' rasped Simon Wright. 'The Jovians are already on their way to attack Jungletown. They're swarming toward the town from all their villages – thousands of them. By this time, they must be there!'

Captain Future felt the full shock of the Brain's tidings, his big figure stiffening. And Otho was shouting.

'The atavism cases in the Jungletown hospital have broken loose, too!' the android hissed. 'We believe they were purposely released by the Space Emperor, to add to the panic.'

'Head back toward the town at full speed,' Curt's voice flared. 'There may still be time.'

The *Comet* jerked upward, and screamed low above the moonlit jungles toward the south.

The night was wild. The silver radiance of Callistro, Europa and Ganymede was paled by the stupendous red glow of the Fire Sea behind them.

Like a meteor, the teardrop ship knifed the air of Jupiter. Curt watched with superhuman tenseness for the lights of Jungletown. If the Space Emperor's hordes of duped Jovians had already reached it –

Far ahead on the rim of the moonlit jungle appeared the clustered lights if the town. They seemed to leap toward Curt, as Otho recklessly swooped to a landing in one of the blazing-lit streets.

'The Jovians aren't here yet!' Captain Future cried as he tore the door of the ship open. 'There's still time—'

Then a moment later his face froze in incredulous horror, and he uttered a sharp cry.

'This place has become a hell!'

Jungletown, under the light of the three great moons and the shaking, flaring fire-glow northward, had indeed become an inferno.

Men and monsters were battling in its streets. Monsters – that had once been men!

Hairy ape-brutes, four-footed feral creatures, scaled reptiles that fought and tore.

Captain Future's pistol leaped out and his proton beam shot to stun a roaring ape-creature that was rushing toward them.

'Come on – we've got to find Gurney!' he exclaimed.

The big adventurer's red head towered above the wild turmoil as he pushed forward through the streets, Grag and Otho close at his side, the android carrying Simon Wright.

The place was a nightmare of terror.

With chaos of panic reigning and monstrous beasts roaming its streets, Jungletown seemed a city of men reeling back toward the brute.

Boom! Boom! Ground-drums out in the jungles were thundering unceasingly now, in a crescendo of fierce excitement.

'The Jovians must be near here!' Curt exclaimed. Then he yelled, 'Gurney! Ezra Gurney!'

The marshal was forcing down the street, leading a little group of people who fought off the prowling monsters with their flare-guns.

'Captain Future, this looks like the end of us!' cried Gurney, his eyes wild in the moonlight. 'I can't organize any defense, and the Jovians are near now.'

'I'm going out to the Jovians now,' Curt exclaimed. 'The Space Emperor is out there, and destroying him is the only thing that can stop them now.'

Joan Randall, her face deathly white in the moonlight, sprang from behind the marshal to grasp Curt's arm.

'Don't go!' she pleaded. 'Eldred Kells went out to try and talk the Jovians into peace, and he didn't come back. And Governor Quale went after him, and he didn't come back either!'

'We caught Lucas Brewer,' Gurney told Captain Future hoarsely. 'Found him hiding here in town. Not that it makes much difference now, I guess.'

'I'm going,' Curt told them. 'Otho, you and Grag and Simon stay here. This is—'

'Look!' yelled Otho, pointing a finger, his eyes suddenly blazing. 'Here they come now!'

A deep roar of thousands of fierce bass voices rent the air at that instant.

Out of the jungle into the clearing around Jungletown, a solid mass of Jovians, on foot and mounted on lopers, was pouring.

Flare-guns gleamed in their mass, ominously.

And at the head of them moved a dark, gliding figure – the Space Emperor.

CHAPTER XXI

The Unmasking

For a moment the little group around Captain Future seemed frozen by sight of that fierce, advancing horde.

'It's all up!' Ezra Gurney cried. 'There's thousands of those critters.'

'I can still stop those Jovians,' Curt Newton flashed. 'Wait here – all of you!'

'Nothin' can stop them now!' Ezra Gurney exclaimed hoarsely.

But Captain Future's big form was already running out through the moonlight toward the oncoming horde.

The Jovian masses were still pouring solidly out of the jungle. Whipped to fanatic madness by the Space Emperor's playing on their superstitions, convinced that they must destroy the Earthmen, they rolled forward in a solid wave after the dark, gliding figure of their leader.

Captain Future came into full view of the oncoming hordes, his tall figure looming in the moonlight, as he faced the Space Emperor and his followers.

The Space Emperor stopped, in sheer amazement it seemed. And the Jovians behind him stopped also. For a full moment, the horde and its mysterious leader faced Captain Future.

Then Curt Newton cried out in a loud voice to the Jovian masses, in their own language.

'Why do you come here to attack the Earthmen?' he shouted. 'They have never harmed you. You have allowed this Earthman to lead you into a great crime.'

'He is no Earthman!' cried scores of fierce Jovian voices. 'He is the Living Ancient, the last of the great Ancients who has commanded us to sweep away you Earthmen.'

'I'll show you,' Curt cried, and leaped in a flying spring toward the startled black figure.

As Curt sprang through the air, his hands were on the switches of his gravitation equalizer and of the hemispherical mechanism at his belt.

The equalizer he snapped to zero. And as his other hand snicked the switch of the immaterializer, he felt a sickening shock of violent force through every fiber.

There was no other sensation. But he knew that he was immaterial as the Space Emperor now. And then he struck the Space Emperor – *solidly*.

Both Curt and the dark plotter being now immaterial as regarded ordinary matter, they were on a basis of equality. Because their bodies had both received the same atomic vibration step-up, they were real and solid to each other.

But Curt had no air to breathe such as the Space Emperor had inside his suit. He felt a gasping shock of agony in his lungs as he seized the super-criminal.

He and the Space Emperor struggled wildly. And as they struggled, drifting floatingly, they were both floating through the Jovians who had crowded wildly forward. The green natives recoiled in horror.

Curt knew he could last but seconds, without air to breathe. Already his head was roaring. He was trying to reach the switch of the Space Emperor's immaterializer. The other was trying, desperately, to prevent him.

Consciousness seemed draining out of Curt's brain. He vaguely glimpsed Grag and Otho wildly trying to help him, but unable to grasp either himself or his antagonist.

Curt made a savage last effort, putting into it the last of his fading strength. His hand struggled to the switch of the other's mechanism. He snapped it open—

And the Space Emperor became like a phantom in his arms, unreal and tenuous. The dark criminal had been made normal again – and Curt was still in the other, shadowy state.

He glimpsed Grag's great metal fist strike at the Space Emperor. His lungs were on fire, the world dark about him, as he sought to snap open the switch of his own immaterializer. It finally snicked under his fingers – again the sickening shock—

Captain Future found himself staggering on the ground – the solid ground – as he reset his equalizer also.

'The Space Emperor!' he choked. 'Did he get away?'

'No, master!' boomed Grag.

Curt stared. The robot's mighty fist had crushed the whole top of the Space Emperor's helmet.

All this swift struggle had taken but seconds. The Jovian horde had watched, frozen with astonishment. Now, with a wild yell of rage, they surged forward.

'Wait!' yelled Captain Future with all his strength. 'See!'

And with frantic fingers, he tore the black, flexible suit off the prone figure of the plotter.

An Earthman's body was revealed in the bright moonlight! It was the body of a tall man whose blond head had been crushed in by Grag's awful blow. And his face was the face of—

'Eldred Kells!' yelled Gurney wildly.

It was Kells' dead face that lay there in the moonlight. Kells – the Space Emperor!

Curt Newton faced the Jovians. They had again frozen. In their mien was an incredulous horror.

'You see!' Captain Future shouted to them. 'The Living Ancient was a deceiver who duped you. He was not one of the great Ancients, but merely an Earthman like myself.'

'It is true,' said a Jovian to the stunned horde. 'We have been deceived.'

'Return then to your villages and forget this mad folly of war against Earthmen,' Curt said clearly. 'There is room on this great planet for both Earthman and Jovian to live in peace, is there not?'

There was a little, tense silence before the big Jovian who seemed the spokesman answered.

'It is the truth – there is room for both our races,' the Jovian answered slowly. 'We only prepared to war upon you because we thought the spirits of the Ancients wished it.'

Slowly, in a dead silence, the Jovians turned and started to shuffle back into the jungle.

No word was spoken by them. Curt Newton looked after them, pity on his taut face. He knew what a tremendous shock to them had been the discovery that they had been deceived.

Otho and Grag were at his side, and Ezra Gurney and Joan Randall and the others were running forward.

Gurney looked down at the dead face of Eldred Kells as though unable yet to believe his eyes.

'It can't be true!' the marshal muttered.

Joan Randall cried out suddenly.

'Here's Governor Quale!' she announced.

Quale was stumbling out of the jungle. He came toward them, his face pallid.

'The Jovians captured me when I went out to look for Kells,' he said hoarsely. 'They released me just now, and I gathered they'd given up the attack—'

His voice trailed off as he saw the dead body of the vice-governor, in its dark suit. He looked up with a wild question in his eyes.

'Yes,' Captain Future said heavily, 'Kells was the Space Emperor. I've guessed it for some time.'

'How could you know?' Quale cried incredulously.

'I knew the Space Emperor was one of four men who could have trapped Joan and me in that Jovopolis hospital,' Curt replied. 'The four were you, Kells, Brewer and Cannig.'

'You were eliminated, Governor Quale, because you were talking to Marshal Gurney on the televisor when I was trapped. You see, I confirmed the fact from Gurney that you had actually talked to him at that time.

'Brewer,' Curt added, 'seemed the most logical suspect then. He was giving the Jovians guns, as I discovered. But when I found that he was doing it only to get them to dig his radium, I felt he could not be the Space Emperor. He would not stir up a planetary rebellion, when his desire was to get rich from his mine! He'd have everything to lose.

'Cannig,' Captain Future concluded, 'had been seen with the Space Emperor, by Joan, and so he could not be the plotter. That only left Eldred Kells of the four original suspects.'

'I still can't believe it of Kells!' Quale cried. 'He was so capable and efficient and ambitious—'

'He was too ambitious; that was the trouble,' Captain Future said somberly. 'He was chafing here as a mere vice-governor, and when he read the report of his wonderful discovery which Kenneth Lester sent to your office, Kells saw his opportunity to bid for planetary power.

'He saw himself as lord of Jupiter – even as the emperor of other worlds – using the great powers and weapons of the Ancients. He might have done it, too, had he been luckier!'

'Aye,' rasped Simon Wright, his glittering lens-eyes staring at the dead man. 'That is the curse of you humans – lust for power. It has brought a many of you to their deaths, and it will bring many more.'

CHAPTER XXII

The Way of Captain Future

Captain Future stood in the pale sunlight beside the open door of the *Comet*, with Grag and Otho and Simon Wright. The little ship rested on the ground at the edge of the wilderness outside Jungletown.

The big, red-headed adventurer faced three people – Joan Randall and Sylvanus Quale and Ezra Gurney.

'Must you leave Jupiter now?' Quale was asking earnestly.

Curt grinned.

'It's got too tame around here, now that all the excitement is over.'

A brief Jovian week had passed. That week had seen the complete restoration of order in the demoralized colony.

The atavism cases were slowly returning to normal, being treated with the formula Simon Wright had devised. The Jovians were again on friendly terms with the Earthmen, and there seemed no doubt that they would remain so.

A scientific commission was on its way from Earth to consult Kenneth Lester and investigate the secrets of the Ancients stored in that cavern by the Fire Sea. Meanwhile, the place was guarded.

'Everything here's washed up now,' Curt was saying. 'I called President Carthew today and reported so, though of course this whole affair won't be made public.'

Joan Randall spoke impulsively to the big red-head. 'Then the people of the System will never know what you've done for them?'

Curt laughed.

'Why should they know? I've no desire to be a hero.'

'You are a hero, to every man and woman in the nine worlds,' Joan said steadily.

There was a throbbing emotion in the girl's soft face as she looked into the big young adventurer's gray eyes.

'And now you're going back to that lonely home of yours on Earth's moon, to live without another human being near?'

'I'm going back to my home, and my comrades will be with me,' Curt defended.

'Captain Future, are you always going to lead this hard, dangerous life?' the girl cried appealingly.

Curt's face grew somber. His voice was low-pitched, his eyes looking far away, as he answered.

'Long ago, I dedicated my life to a task,' he said. 'Until that task is finished, I must remain – Captain Future.'

He held out his hand, and the cheerful smile came back once more into his gray eyes.

'Good-by, Joan,' he said. 'We'll meet again, somewhere.'

He grinned at Gurney. 'And I'm sure to meet *you* in that part of the System where trouble is the thickest.'

There was a glimmer of tears in the girl's dark eyes as she watched Curt enter his little ship.

The cyclotrons droned, and the *Comet* shot upward into the pale sunlight. Up from Jupiter it roared, out through the dense atmosphere until the mighty planet was a vast white globe behind them, and black, starred space stretched ahead.

Toward the bright gray speck that was Earth, and the smaller white speck that was its moon, the little ship flew.

Curt Newton's eyes were queerly abstracted as he sat at the throttles. He spoke to the Brain, slowly.

'That was a great girl, Simon,' he said. Then he added hastily, 'Not that it can mean anything to me, you understand.'

'Aye, lad, I understand,' the Brain answered. 'I was human once, too, you know.'

'We go back to the moon now, master?' Grag said pleasedly. 'I like it on the moon best.'

'What's good about it?' Otho hissed gloomily. 'There'll be no excitement, no action, nothing else for us to do—'

Curt grinned at the discontented android.

'Sooner or later, there'll be another call from Earth, and then I hope there's action enough for you, you crazy coot.'

Yes, sooner or later dire emergency would arise again to threaten the nine worlds, and set that great signal at the North Pole flashing its summons once more.

And when the summons came, Captain Future would answer!

THE STAR KINGS

1

John Gordon

When John Gordon first heard the voice inside his mind, he thought that he was going crazy.

It came first at night when he was just falling asleep. Through his drowsing thoughts, it spoke sharp and clear.

'Can you hear me, John Gordon? Can you hear me call?'

Gordon sat up, suddenly wide awake and a little startled. There had been something strange and upsetting about it.

Then he shrugged. The brain played strange tricks when a man was half-asleep and the will relaxed. It couldn't mean anything.

He forgot it until the next night. Then, just as he began to slip into the realm of sleep, that clear mental voice came again.

'Can you hear me? If you can hear me, try to answer my call!'

Again Gordon woke up with a start. And this time he was a little worried. Was there something the matter with his mind? He had always heard it was bad if you started to hear voices.

He had come through the war without a scratch. But maybe those years of flying out in the Pacific had done something to his mind. Maybe he was going to be a delayed psychoneurotic casualty.

'What the devil, I'm getting excited about nothing,' Gordon told himself roughly. 'It's just because I'm nervous and restless.'

Restless? Yes, he was that. He had been, ever since the war ended and he returned to New York.

You could take a young accountant clerk out of a New York insurance office and make him into a war pilot who could handle thirty tons of bomber as easily as he handled his fingers. You could do that, for they had done it to Gordon.

But after three years of that, it wasn't so easy to give that pilot a discharge button and a 'thank you' and send him back to his office desk. Gordon knew that, too, by bitter experience.

It was queer. All the time he had sweated and risked his neck out there over the Pacific, he had been thinking how wonderful it would be to get back to his old job and his comfortable little apartment.

He had got back, and they were just the same as before. But he wasn't. The

John Gordon who had come back was used to battle, danger and sudden death, but not used to sitting at a desk and adding up figures.

Gordon didn't know what he wanted, but it wasn't an office job in New York. Yet he'd tried to get these ideas out of his mind. He'd fought to get back into the old routine, and the fight had made him more and more restless.

And now this queer calling voice inside his brain! Did that mean that his nervousness was getting the best of him, that he was cracking up?

He thought of going to a psychiatrist, but shied at the idea. It seemed better to fight down this thing himself.

So the next night, Gordon grimly waited for the voice to call and prepared to prove to himself that it was a delusion.

It did not come that night, nor the next. He supposed it was over. Then the third night, it came more strongly than ever.

'John Gordon, listen to me! You are not having delusions! I am another man, speaking to your mind by means of a science I possess.'

Gordon lay there in semi-sleep, and that voice seemed wonderfully real to him.

'Please try to answer me, John Gordon! Not with speech, but with thought. The channel is open – you can answer if you try.'

Dazedly, Gordon sent an answering thought out into the darkness.

'Who are you?'

The reply came quickly and clearly, with a pulse of eagerness and triumph in it.

'I am Zarth Arn, prince of the Mid-Galactic Empire. I speak to you from two hundred thousand years in your future.'

Gordon felt vaguely aghast. That couldn't be true! Yet that voice was so real and distinct in his mind.

'Two hundred thousand years? That's insane, impossible, to speak across a time like that. I'm dreaming.'

Zarth Arn's reply came quickly. 'I assure you that it is no dream and that I am as real as you are, even though two thousand centuries separate us.'

He went on. 'Time cannot be crossed by any material thing. But thought is not material. Thought can cross time. Your own mind travels a little into the past every time that you remember something.'

'Even if it's true, why should you call me?' Gordon asked numbly.

'Much has changed in two hundred thousand years,' Zarth Arn told him. 'Long ago, the human race to whose first era you belong spread out to the other stars of the galaxy. There are great star-kingdoms now, of which the greatest one is the Mid-Galactic Empire.

'I am high in that Empire, and am a scientist and seeker of truth above all else. For years, I and a colleague have been delving into the past by throwing my mind back across the ages, groping and making contact with minds of men whose spirits are attuned to my own.

'With many of those men of the past, I have temporarily exchanged bodies! The mind is a webwork of electrical energy which inhabits the brain. It can be drawn by suitable forces from the brain, and another electric webwork, another mind, installed in its place. My apparatus can accomplish that by sending my whole mind instead of just a thought-message into the past.

'Thus my mind has occupied the body of a man of past ages, while his mind was simultaneously drawn across time to inhabit my body. In that way, I have lived in and explored the history of many different eras of past human history.

'But I have never gone so far back in time as your own remote era. I want to explore your age, John Gordon. Will you help me? Will you consent to a temporary exchange of bodies with me?'

Gordon's first reaction was a panicky refusal. 'No! It would be ghastly, insane!'

'There would be no danger,' Zarth Arn insisted. 'You would merely spend some weeks in my body in this age, and I in yours. And then Vel Quen, my colleague here, would effect a re-exchange.

'Think, John Gordon! Even as it would give me a chance to explore your long-dead age, so would it give you a chance to see the wonders of my time!

'I know your spirit, restless, eager for the new and unknown. No man of your age has ever been given such a chance to plunge across the great gulf of time into the future. Will you reject it?'

Suddenly Gordon felt caught by the glamor of the idea. It was like a wild bugle-call summoning to adventure hitherto undreamed.

A world and universe two thousand centuries in the future, the glories of a star-conquering civilization – to behold all that with his own eyes?

Was it worth risking life and sanity for? If all this was true, was he not being offered a supreme chance at the adventure for which he had been so restlessly longing?

Yet still he hesitated. 'I wouldn't know anything about your world when I awoke in it!' he told Zarth Arn. 'Not even the language.'

'Vel Quen would be here to teach you everything,' the other answered quickly. 'Of course, your age would be equally strange to me. For that reason, if you agree, I should want you to prepare thought-spools from which I could learn your language and ways.'

'Thought-spools? What are they?' Gordon asked, puzzled.

'They are not yet invented in your age?' said Zarth Arn. 'In that case, leave me some children's picture-books and dictionaries for learning your language and some sound-records of how it is spoken.'

He continued. 'You don't need to decide at once, John Gordon. Tomorrow I'll call you again and you can give me your decision then.'

'Tomorrow I'll think that all this has just been a crazy dream!' Gordon exclaimed.

'You must assure yourself that it is no dream,' Zarth Arn said earnestly. 'I contact your mind when you are partly asleep because then your will is relaxed and the mind is receptive. But it is no dream.'

When Gordon awoke in the morning, the whole incredible thing came back to him with a rush.

'*Was* it a dream?' he asked himself wonderingly. 'Zarth Arn said it would seem like one. Of course, a dream-person would say that.'

Gordon still could not make up his mind whether or not it had been real by the time he went to work.

Never had the insurance office looked so utterly drab and stifling as on that long day. Never had the petty routine of his duties seemed so barren and monotonous.

And all through the day, Gordon found himself dreaming wild visions of the splendor and magic wonder of great star-kingdoms two hundred thousand years in the future, of worlds new, strange, luring.

By the end of the day, his decision was reached. If this incredible thing was really true, he was going to do what Zarth Arn asked.

He felt a little foolish as he stopped on his way home and bought children's picture-books, language texts, and phonograph records intended for the teaching of English.

But that night, Gordon went early to bed. Strung to the highest pitch of feverish excitement, he waited for Zarth Arn's call.

It did not come. For Gordon could not even begin to fall asleep. He was too tautly excited even to doze.

For hours, he tossed and turned. It was nearly dawn by the time he fell into a troubled doze.

Then, at once, the clear mental voice of Zarth Arn came into his mind.

'At last I can contact you! Now tell me, John Gordon, what is your decision?'

'I'll do it, Zarth Arn,' answered Gordon. 'But I must do it at once! For if I spend many more days thinking about the thing, I'll believe myself going crazy over a dream.'

'It can be done at once!' was the eager reply. 'Vel Quen and I have our apparatus ready. You will inhabit my body for six weeks. At the end of that time, I will be ready for the re-exchange.'

Zarth Arn continued rapidly. 'You must first make me one promise. Nobody in this age but Vel Quen will know of this mind-exchange. You must tell *no one* here in my time that you are a stranger in my body. To do so might bring disaster on us both.'

'I promise,' Gordon replied quickly. He added troubledly, 'You'll be careful with my body, won't you?'

'You have my word,' was the answer of Zarth Arn. 'Now relax yourself, so that your mind will offer no resistance to the force that draws it across the time-dimension.'

That was easier to say than to do. Relaxing was not what a man felt like doing when his mind was about to be drawn from his body.

But Gordon tried to obey, to sink deeper into the dozing state.

Suddenly he felt a strange, uncanny turning inside his brain. It was not a physical sensation, but it gave a feeling of magnetic power.

Fear such as John Gordon had never before experienced shrieked in his mind as he felt himself rushing into unplumbed darkness.

2

Future Universe

Consciousness came back slowly to Gordon. He found himself lying on a high table in a room of brilliant sunlight.

For some moments he lay looking up dazedly, feeling a terrible weakness and shakiness. Right over his head, as though just swung back, was a curious apparatus like a silver cap with many wires.

Then a face bent down into his view. It was the wrinkled face of an old, white-haired man. But the excitement he evidently felt made his blue eyes youthfully eager.

He spoke to Gordon in a voice shrill with excitement. But he spoke in a language that was almost entirely unfamiliar.

'I can't understand you,' Gordon said helplessly.

The other pointed to himself and spoke again. 'Vel Quen,' he said.

Vel Quen? Gordon remembered now. Zarth Arn had said that was the name of his scientific colleague in the future.

The future? Then the two scientists *had* effected that incredible exchange of minds and bodies across the abyss of time?

With sudden wild excitement, Gordon tried to sit up. He couldn't do it. He was still too weak, and slipped back.

But he had got a glimpse of his own body as he sat up, and the sight had stunned him.

It wasn't his body. It was not John Gordon's stocky, muscular figure. This was a taller, slimmer body he now inhabited, one dressed in silky white sleeveless shirt and trousers, and sandals.

'Zarth Arn's body!' husked Gordon. 'And back in my own time, Zarth Arn is awaking in mine!'

Old Vel Quen apparently recognized the name he spoke. The old scientist nodded quickly.

'Zarth Arn – John Gordon,' he said, pointing at him.

The exchange had worked! He had crossed two thousand centuries and was now in another man's body!

It didn't feel any different. Gordon tried moving his hands and feet. Every muscle responded perfectly. Yet his hair still bristled from the ghastly strangeness of it. He had an hysterical nostalgia for his own body.

Vel Quen seemed to understand his feelings. The old man patted his shoulder reassuringly, then offered him a crystal beaker filled with foaming red liquid. Gordon drank it, and began to feel stronger.

The old scientist helped him get up from the table, and steadied him as he stood looking wonderingly around the room.

Brilliant sunlight poured through tall windows that filled all eight sides of the octagonal chamber. The light flashed and glittered off machines and instruments and racks of queer metal spools. Gordon was no scientist, and all this science of the future baffled him.

Vel Quen led him toward a corner in which there was a tall mirror. He stood transfixed the moment he caught a glimpse of himself in the glass.

'So this is what I look like now!' Gordon whispered, staring wildly at his own image.

His figure was now that of a tall, black-haired young man of well over six feet. The face was dark, aquiline and rather handsome, with serious dark eyes. It was altogether different from John Gordon's own square, tanned face.

He saw that he was wearing snug-fitting shirt and trousers. Vel Quen threw a long, silky white cloak around his shoulders. The old scientist himself was similarly attired.

He gestured to Gordon that he must rest. But weak as Gordon felt, he couldn't without first looking out at this unknown world of the far future.

He stumbled to one of the windows. He expected to look forth on wondrous vistas of super-modern cities, marvelous metropoli of the star-conquering civilization. But Gordon was disappointed.

Before him lay a scene of wild, forbidding natural grandeur. This octagonal chamber was the upper floor of a massive little cement tower which was perched on a small plateau at the edge of a sheer precipice.

Stupendous mountain peaks crowned with glittering white snow rose in the bright sunlight. From them and from the tower, dark and awesome defiles dropped for thousands of feet. There was not another building in sight. It looked much like the Himalayas of his own time.

Weakness made John Gordon sway dizzily. Vel Quen hastily led him out of the tower-room and down to a small bedroom on the floor below. He stretched on a soft couch and was almost instantly asleep.

When Gordon awoke, it was another day. Vel Quen came in and greeted him, then checked his pulse and respiration. The old scientist smiled reassuringly, and brought him some food.

There was a thick, sweet, chocolate-colored drink, some fruit, some wafers like dry biscuits. It was all evidently charged with nutritional elements, for Gordon's hunger vanished after the slight meal.

Then Vel Quen began to teach him his language. The old man used a box-like little apparatus which produced realistic stereoscopic images, carefully naming each object or scene he exhibited.

Gordon spent a week in his task, not going outside the tower. He picked up the language with astonishing quickness, partly because of Vel Quen's scientific teaching and partly because it was based on his own English. Two thousand centuries had greatly enlarged and changed its vocabulary, but it was not like a completely alien tongue.

At the end of that week Gordon's strength had fully returned, and by that time he was able to speak the language fluently.

'We are on the planet Earth?' was the first eager question he had put to Vel Quen.

The old scientist nodded. 'Yes, this tower is located amid the highest mountains of Earth.'

So it was the Himalayas whose snowy peaks rose around the tower, as Gordon had guessed. They looked as wild and lonely and grand as when he had flown over them in war days long ago.

'But aren't there any cities or people left on Earth?' he cried.

'Certainly there are. Zarth Arn chose this lonely spot on the planet, simply so that his secret experiments would not be disturbed.

'From this tower, he has been exploring the past by going back into the bodies of many men in various epochs of human history. Yours is the remotest period of the past that Zarth Arn has yet tried to explore.'

It was a little overwhelming to John Gordon to realize that other men had found themselves in his own uncanny present position.

'Those others – they were able to return without trouble to their own bodies and times?'

'Of course – I was here to operate the mind-transmitter, and when the time came I effected the re-exchange just as I will do with you later.'

That was reassuring. Gordon was still wildly excited by this unprecedented adventure into a future age, but he hated to think that he might be marooned indefinitely in a stranger's body.

Vel Quen explained to Gordon in detail the amazing scientific method of contacting and exchanging minds across time.

He showed him the operation of the telepathic amplifier that could beam its thought-message back to any selected mind in the past. And then he outlined the operation of the mind-exchange apparatus itself.

'The mind is an electric pattern in the neurones of the brain. The forces of this apparatus detach that pattern and embody it in a network of nonmaterial photons.

'That photon-mind can then be projected along any dimension. And since time is the fourth dimension of matter, the photon-mind can be hurled into past time. The forces operate in a two-way channel, simultaneously detaching and projecting both minds so as to exchange them.'

'Did Zarth Arn himself invent this method of exchanging minds?' Gordon asked wonderingly.

'We invented it together,' Vel Quen said. 'I had already perfected the principle. Zarth Arn, my most devoted scientific pupil, wanted to try it out and he helped me build and test the apparatus.

'It has succeeded beyond our wildest dreams. You see those racks of thought-spools?* In them is the vast mass of information brought back by Zarth Arn from past ages he has explored thus. We've worked secretly because Arn Abbas would forbid his son to take the risk if he knew.'

'Arn Abbas?' repeated Gordon questioningly. 'Who is he, Vel Quen?'

'Arn Abbas is sovereign of the Mid-Galactic Empire, ruling from its capital world at the sun Canopus. He has two sons. The oldest is his heir, Jhal Arn. The second son is Zarth Arn.'

Gordon was astounded. 'You mean that Zarth Arn, the man whose body I now inhabit, is son of the greatest ruler in the galaxy?'

The old scientist nodded. 'Yes, but Zarth is not interested in power or rule. He is a scientist and scholar, and that is why he leaves the court at Throon to carry on his exploration of the past from this lonely tower on Earth.'

Gordon remembered now that Zarth Arn had said he was high in the Empire. But he had had no suspicion of his true exalted position.

'Vel Quen, what exactly is the Mid-Galactic Empire? Does it take in all the galaxy?'

'No, John Gordon. There are many star-kingdoms in the galaxy, warlike rivals at times. But the Mid-Galactic Empire is the largest of them.'

Gordon felt a certain disappointment. 'I had thought the future would be one of democracy, and that war would be banished.'

'The star-kingdoms are really democracies, for the people rule,' Vel Quen explained. 'We simply give titles and royal rank to our leaders, the better to hold together the widely separated star-systems and their human and aboriginal races.'

Gordon could understand that. 'I get it. Like the British democracy in my own day, that kept up the forms of royalty and rank to hold together their realm.'

'And war *was* banished on Earth, long ago,' Vel Quen went on. 'We know that from traditional history. The peace and prosperity that followed were what gave the first great impetus to space-travel.

* Thought-spools were a development of the encephalographic records made as early as 1933 by American psychologists, in which the electric thought-fluctuations of the brain were recorded on moving tape. In this improved model, the encephalographic recording was played back through an electric apparatus and produced pulsations which re-created the recorded thoughts in the listener's brain.

'But there have been wars between the star-kingdoms because they are so widely separated. We are now trying to bring them together in union and peace, as you unified Earth's nations long ago.'

Vel Quen went to the wall and touched a switch beside a bank of lenses. From the lenses was projected a realistic little image of the galaxy, a flat, disk-shaped swarm of shining sparks.

Each of those little sparks represented a star, and their number was dizzying to John Gordon. Nebulae, comets, dark clouds – all were faithfully represented in this galactic map. And the map was divided by zones of colored light into a number of large and small sections.

'Those colored zones represent the boundaries of the great star-kingdoms,' Vel Quen explained. 'As you see, the green zone of the Mid-Galactic Empire is much the largest and includes the whole north* and middle of the galaxy. Here near its northern border is Sol, the sun of Earth, not far from the wild frontier star-systems of the Marches of Outer Space.

'The little purple zone south of the Empire comprises the Baronies of Hercules, whose great Barons rule the independent star-worlds of Hercules Cluster. Northwest lies Fomalhaut Kingdom, and south of it stretch the kingdoms of Lyra, Cygnus, Polaris and others, most of these being allied to the Empire.

'This big black blot southeast of the Empire is the largest dark cloud in the galaxy, and within it lies the League of Dark Worlds, composed of suns and worlds engulfed in the perpetual dimness of that cloud. The League is the most powerful and jealous rival of the Empire.

'The Empire is dominant and has long sought to induce the star-kingdoms to unite and banish all war in the galaxy. But Shorr Kan and his League have intrigued against Arn Abbas' policy of unification, by fomenting the jealousies of the smaller star-kingdoms.'

It was all a little overwhelming for John Gordon, man of the 20th Century. He looked in wonder at that strange map.

Vel Quen added, 'I shall teach you how to use the thought-spools and then you can learn that great story.'

In the following days while he learned the language, Gordon had thus learned also the history of two thousand centuries.

It was an epic tale that the thought-spools unfolded of man's conquest of the stars. There had been great feats of heroism in exploration, disastrous wrecks in cosmic clouds and nebulae, bitter struggles against stellar aborigines too alien for peaceful contact.

Earth had been too small and remote to govern all the vast ever-growing realm of man. Star systems established their own governments, and then

* Six arbitrarily assigned directions were used as axes of reference in galactic travel – north, east, south, west, zenith and nadir.

banded into kingdoms of many stars. From such a beginning had grown the great Mid-Galactic Empire which Arn Abbas now governed.

Vel Quen finally told Gordon, 'I know you want to see much of our civilization before you return to your own body and time. First let me show you what Earth looks like now. Stand upon this plate.'

He referred to one of two round quartz plates set in the floor, which were part of a curious, complex apparatus.

'This is a telestereo, which projects and receives stereoscopic images that can see and hear,' Vel Quen explained. 'It operates almost instantaneously over any distance.'*

Gordon stood gingerly with him on the quartz plate. The old scientist touched a switch.

Abruptly, Gordon seemed to be in another place. He knew he was still in the tower laboratory, but a seeing, hearing image of himself now stood on a stereo-receiver on a terrace high in a great city.

'This is Nyar, largest city of Earth,' said Vel Quen. 'Of course, it cannot compare with the metropoli of the great star-worlds.'

Gordon gasped. He was looking out over a mammoth city of terraced white pyramids.

Far out beyond it he could glimpse a spaceport, with rows of sunken docks and long, fishlike star-ships in them. There were also a few massive, grim-looking warships with the Empire's comet emblem on them.

But it was the great city itself that held his stunned gaze. Its terraces were flowering green gardens with gay awnings and crowds of pleasure-seeking people.

Vel Quen switched them to other stereo-receivers in Nyar. He had glimpses of the interior of the city, of halls and corridors, of apartments and workshops, of giant underground atomic power plants.

The scene suddenly vanished from John Gordon's fascinated eyes as Vel Quen snapped off the telestereo and darted toward a window.

'There is a ship coming!' he exclaimed. 'I can't understand it. No ship ever lands here!'

Gordon heard a droning in the air and glimpsed a long, slim, shining craft dropping out of the sky toward the lonely tower.

Vel Quen looked alarmed. 'It's a warship, a phantom-cruiser, but has no emblem on it. There's something wrong about this!'

The shining ship landed with a rush on the plateau a quarter-mile from the tower. A door in its side instantly slid open.

* The telestereo operated by sub-spectrum rays many times faster than light, the rays that were the foundation of interstellar travel and civilization. Using the fastest of this famous group of rays, it could communicate almost instantly across the galaxy.

From it poured a score of gray-uniformed, helmeted men who carried weapons like long, slim-barrelled pistols, and who advanced in a run toward the tower.

'They wear the uniform of Empire soldiers but they should not have come here,' Vel Quen said. His wrinkled face was puzzled and worried. 'Could it be—'

He broke off, seeming to reach a sudden decision. 'I am going to notify the Nyar naval base at once!'

As the old scientist turned from John Gordon toward the telestereo, there came a sudden loud crash below.

'They have blasted in the door!' cried Vel Quen. 'Quick, John Gordon, take the—'

Gordon never learned what he meant to tell him. For at that moment, the uniformed men came rushing up the stair into the room.

They were strange-looking men. Their faces were white, a pallid, colorless and unnatural white.

'League soldiers!' cried Vel Quen, the instant he saw them thus close. He whirled to turn on the telestereo.

The leader of the invaders raised his long, slim pistol. A tiny pellet flicked from it and buried itself in Vel Quen's back. It instantly exploded in his body. The old scientist dropped in his tracks.

Until that moment, ignorance and bewilderment had held Gordon motionless. But he felt a hot rage burst along his nerves as he saw Vel Quen fall. He had come to like the old scientist, in these days.

With a fierce exclamation, Gordon plunged forward. One of the uniformed men instantly raised his pistol.

'Don't blast him – it's Zarth Arn himself!' yelled the officer who had shot down Vel Quen. 'Grab him!'

Gordon got his fists home on the face of one of them, but that was all. A dozen hands grasped him, his arms were twisted behind his back, and he was held as helpless as a raging child.

The pallid officers spoke swiftly to Gordon. 'Prince Zarth, I regret we had to blast your colleague but he was about to call for help and our presence here must not be detected.'

The officer continued rapidly. 'You yourself will not be harmed in the slightest. We have been sent to bring you to our leader.'

Gordon stared at the man. He felt as though all this was a crazy dream.

But one thing was clear. They didn't doubt he was Zarth Arn. And that was natural, seeing that he *was* Zarth Arn, in body.

'What do you mean?' he demanded furiously of the other. 'Who are you?'

'We come from the Cloud!' answered the pallid officer instantly. 'Yes, we are from the League and have come to take you to Shorr Kan.'

It was still all baffling to John Gordon. Then he remembered some of the things that old Vel Quen had told him.

Shorr Kan was leader of the League of the Dark Worlds which was the greatest foe of the Empire. That meant that these men were enemies of the great star-kingdom to whose ruling house Zarth Arn belonged.

They thought that *he* was Zarth Arn and were kidnapping him! Zarth Arn had never foreseen anything like this happening when he had planned the exchange of bodies!

'I'm not going with you!' Gordon cried! 'I'm not leaving Earth!'

'We'll have to take him by force,' rasped the officer to his men. 'Bring him along.'

3

Mystery Raiders

There was a sudden interruption. Into the tower came running a uniformed soldier, his face livid with excitement.

'The radar officer reports three craft of cruiser size heading in from space toward this quarter of Earth!'

'Empire patrol-cruisers!' yelled the League officer. 'Quick, out of here with him!'

But Gordon had seized the moment of their alarm to bunch himself. Now with a violent effort he broke free of their grasp.

He grabbed up a heavy metal tool as the pallid men rushed him and struck savagely with it at their faces.

They were at a disadvantage for they did not want to kill or injure him, while he had no such reluctance. His savage blows dropped two of the soldiers. Then the others seized him again and wrested his makeshift weapon from him.

'Now to the ship with him!' panted the pallid League officer. 'And hurry!'

Held by four big League soldiers, Gordon was dragged down the stairs and out of the tower into the biting, frosty air.

They were halfway to the shining ship when he saw the grim black gun-muzzles that projected from its side swinging suddenly to point skyward. Volleys of small shells burst upward from them.

The pallid officer yelled as he looked upward. John Gordon glimpsed three massive, fish-shaped warships diving straight down toward them.

There was an immense explosion. It hit Gordon and his captors like a giant hand and hurled them from their feet.

Half stunned, Gordon heard the deafening drone of great ships swooping toward the ground. By the time he stumbled to his feet, it was all over.

The League ship was a wreck of fused metal. The three cruisers that had destroyed it were landing. Even as they touched the ground, their small guns flicked deadly explosive pellets that picked off the dazed League soldiers who still sought to fight.

Gordon found himself standing, his late captors a heap of torn, blasted corpses less than a hundred feet away. The doors of the cruisers were sliding open, and men in gray helmets and uniforms came running toward Gordon.

'Prince Zarth, you're not hurt?' cried their leader to Gordon.

The man was big and burly, with bristling black hair and a craggy, knobby face whose complexion was faintly copper-red. His black eyes were snapping with cheerful excitement.

'I'm Hull Burrel, captain commanding a Sirius-sector patrol,' he told Gordon, saluting. 'Our radar spotted an unauthorized vessel approaching Earth, and we followed it to find it at your laboratory here.'

He glanced at the dead men. 'Cloud-men, by Heaven! Shorr Kan has dared send men to abduct you! This could be cause for war!'

John Gordon thought swiftly. These excited Empire officers also naturally took him for the son of their ruler.

And he couldn't tell them the truth, couldn't tell them he was John Gordon in Zarth Arn's body! For Zarth Arn had made him promise to tell that to no one, had warned that to do so would mean disaster! He'd have to keep up the strange imposture with these men until rid of them.

'I'm not hurt,' Gordon said unsteadily. 'But they shot Vel Quen and I'm afraid he's dead.'

They hurried with him to the tower. He ran hastily up the stairs and bent over the old scientist.

One look was enough. A gaping hole had been blasted in Vel Quen's body by the explosion of the tiny atomic pellet.

Gordon was appalled. The death of the old scientist meant that he was now completely on his own in this unfamiliar future universe.

Could he ever get back to his own body and time? Vel Quen had thoroughly explained the principle and operation of the mind-projecting apparatus. He might be able to operate it if he could get into telepathic contact with the real Zarth Arn.

Gordon quickly made up his mind. It was vital for him to stay here in the tower with the apparatus which alone could restore him to his own body and time.

'I must report this attack at once to your father, Prince Zarth,' the captain named Hull Burrel was saying.

'There is no need,' Gordon said quickly. 'The danger is over. Keep the whole matter confidential.'

He expected his authority as son of the sovereign to overawe the captain. But Hull Burrel, surprise on his craggy copper face, demurred.

'It would be a breach of duty if I failed to report so serious a matter as a League raid like this!' the captain protested.

He went to the telestereo and touched its switches. In a moment on its receiver-plate appeared the image of a uniformed officer.

'Chief of Fleet Operations speaking from Throon,' he said crisply.

'Captain Hull Burrel of the Sirius-sector patrol wishes to report a matter of the utmost importance to his highness, Arn Abbas,' declared the big coppery captain.

The official stared. 'Cannot the matter be submitted to Commander Corbulo?'

'It cannot – its importance and urgency are too great,' Hull Burrel declared. 'I take the responsibility for insisting on this audience.'

There was a little wait. Then on the telestereo the image of a different man flashed into being.

He was a massive giant well past middle age, with shaggy, bristling brows over penetrating, hard gray eyes. He wore a brilliantly embroidered cloak over a dark jacket and trousers, and his great, graying head was bare.

'Since when do mere naval captains insist –' he began angrily, and then as his image looked past Hull Burrel he caught sight of John Gordon. 'So this concerns you, Zarth? What's wrong?'

Gordon realized that this massive, bleak-eyed man was Arn Abbas, sovereign of the Mid-Galactic Empire and Zarth Arn's father – *his* father.

'It's nothing serious,' Gordon began hastily, but Hull Burrel interrupted.

'Your pardon, Prince Zarth, but this *is* serious!' He continued to the emperor. 'A League phantom-cruiser clipped in to Earth and made an attempt to kidnap the prince. By chance my patrol was making an unscheduled stop at Sol, and we detected them by radar and followed them here just in time to destroy them.

Arn Abbas uttered an angry roar. 'A League warship violating Empire space? And trying to kidnap my son? Curse that devil Shorr Kan for his insolence! He's gone too far this time!'

Hull Burrel added, 'We weren't able to take any of the Cloud-men alive but Prince Zarth can give you the details of the attempt.'

Gordon wanted above all else to minimize the whole thing and finish the nerve-racking strain of having to keep up this imposture.

'It must have been just a surprise sneak attempt,' he said hastily to Arn Abbas. 'They won't dare try it again – I'll be in no more danger here.'

'No danger? What are you talking about?' rumbled Arn Abbas angrily. 'You know as well as I do why Shorr Kan was trying to get his hands on you, and what he'd have done if he succeeded!'

The massive ruler continued commandingly to Gordon. 'You're not going to stay there on Earth any longer, Zarth! I've had enough of your slipping away to that remote old planet for your crazy secret scientific studies. This is what comes of it! We'll take no more such chances! You're going to come here to Throon at once!'

John Gordon's heart sank. To Throon, the royal planet of the sun Canopus which lay nearly halfway across the galaxy? He couldn't go there!

He couldn't carry on this masquerade in Zarth Arn's body at the court itself! And if he left the laboratory here, he'd have no chance of contacting Zarth Arn and re-exchanging their bodies.

'I can't come to Throon now,' Gordon protested desperately. 'I have to remain here on Earth for a few days more to carry out my researches.'

Arn Abbas uttered a bellow of anger. 'You do as I say, Zarth! You'll come to Throon and you'll come right now!'

And the emperor swung his angry gaze to Hull Burrel and ordered, 'Captain, bring the prince here at once in your cruiser. And if he refuses, bring him here under guard!'

4
Magic Planet

The big cruiser sped through the interstellar spaces at a velocity already hundreds of times that of light. Earth and Sol had hours before receded astern. Ahead of the ship expanded the heart of the galaxy, thick with glittering star-swarms.

John Gordon stood in the wide, many-windowed bridge of the *Caris* with Hull Burrel and two helmsmen, feeling a quaking inward awe as he looked at that incredible vista ahead. The enormous speed of the warship was evidenced by the fact that the stars ahead grew visibly brighter as he watched.

Gordon felt no acceleration, thanks to the dim, blue-glowing stasis of force that cradled everything in the ship. He tried to remember what he had learned about the motive power of these great ships. They were propelled by an energy drive which utilized the famous sub-spectrum rays that were the basis of galactic civilization.*

* Gordon's study of the history of two hundred thousand years had shown him how the entire structure of galactic civilization was based upon that epochal discovery of sub-spectrum rays.

The era of space-travel had really dawned in 1945 and '46, with the first release of atomic energy and the discovery that radar could function efficiently in space. By the end of the 20th Century, atomic-powered rockets guided by radar had reached the Moon, Mars and Venus.

Interplanetary exploration and exploitation had increased rapidly. But the vast distances to other stars remained unconquerable until late in the 22nd Century, when three great inventions made interstellar travel possible.

The most important of the three was the discovery of sub-spectrum rays. These were hitherto unsuspected octaves of electromagnetic radiation far below even the gamma and cosmic rays in wavelength, and which had velocities vastly greater than the speed of light.

Of these sub-spectrum rays the most useful were the so-called pressure rays in the Minus-30th octave of the spectrum, which could react against the tenuous cosmic dust of space with a powerful pressure. These pressure rays formed the driving power of star-ships. They were produced in generators powered by atomic turbines, and were jetted from the stern of a ship to drive it thousands of times faster than light.

The second vital invention was that of the mass-control. Einstein's equations had shown that if a ship travelled as fast as light, its mass would expand to infinity. This difficulty was overcome by the mass-control, which 'bled' off mass as energy to maintain a constant mass unaltered by velocity. The energy thus obtained was stored in accumulators and fed back automatically whenever speed was reduced.

The final invention concerned the human element. Men's bodies would have been unable ordinarily to withstand those vast accelerations, but this obstacle was conquered by the cradle-stasis. This was a stasis of force which gripped every atom in a ship. The energy-drive jets gave their thrust, not to the ship directly, but to its stasis. Thus everyone and everything in the ship

'It still seems crazy of Shorr Kan to send a League cruiser into our realm on such an errand!' Hull Burrel was saying. 'What good would it do him if he did manage to capture you?'

Gordon had wondered about that himself. He couldn't see the reason for wanting to capture the mere second son of the emperor.

'I suppose,' he ventured, 'that Shorr Kan figured he could use me as a hostage. I'm glad you got the murderous devils, for killing Vel Quen.'

To forestall the strain of further conversation, Gordon turned abruptly. 'I think I'd like to rest, captain.'

With a quick word of apology, Hull Burrel led the way from the bridge and down by narrow corridors and catwalks through the ship.

Gordon pretended to glance only casually about him, but was really devoured by interest in what he saw. There were long, narrow galleries of atomic guns, navigation rooms and radar rooms on this upper deck.

Officers and men whom they met snapped to attention, saluting him with deep respect. These men of the Mid-Galactic Empire differed in complexion, some of them faintly blue of skin, others reddish, others tawny yellow. He

---

remained unaffected by acceleration. Magnetic apparatus furnished artificial gravity on shipboard, similar to that of the tiny gravitation-equalizers worn by all star-travellers.

The fastest of the sub-spectrum rays, those of the Minus-42nd octave, were so speedy that they made light seem to crawl. These super-speed rays were used in telestereo communication and also in the vital function of radar for the star-ships.

Using these inventions to build star-ships, mankind took at once to interstellar space. Alpha Centauri, Sirius and Altair were quickly visited. Colonies were soon established on suitable star-worlds. For some 10,000 years, Sol and Earth remained the center of government of a growing region of colonized stars.

Until then, there had been no serious conflicts. Aboriginal alien races of intelligence had been found at some star-systems and were helped and educated, but there was found no scientific civilization on any star-world. That had been expected, for if such a race existed it would have visited *us* long before we ourselves had conquered space.

But in the year 12,455, a group of star-systems near Polaris complained that Earth was too remote to appreciate their problems, and they set up an independent kingdom. By 39,000, the kingdoms of Lyra, Cygnus, and the Baronies of the great Hercules Cluster had declared independence.

Criminals and fugitives from the law seeking refuge in the Cloud eventually founded the League of Dark Worlds. By 120,000, the star-kingdoms were many. But the biggest was still the Mid-Galactic Empire, and hosts of star-worlds remained loyal to it. For convenience its government had been shifted in 62,339 from Earth to a world of the great sun Canopus.

The Empire took the lead of the star-kingdoms in the year 129,411 when the galaxy was suddenly invaded by alien and powerful creatures from the Magellanic Clusters outside. And after that invasion was repelled the Empire had steadily grown by exploring and colonizing the wild, unmapped star-systems in the frontier regions called the Marches of Outer Space.

Thus when Gordon found himself in the galaxy of this year 202,115, he found its star-kingdoms already old in traditions and history. Many wars had been fought between them, but the Empire had steadily sought to prevent such sanguine galactic struggles and to unify them in peace. But now the ominous growth of the League of Dark Worlds had reached a point where the safety of the Empire itself was challenged.

knew it was because they came from different star-systems, and had learned that Hull Burrel himself was an Antarian.

Hull Burrel slid open the door of an austere little room. 'My own cabin, Prince Zarth. I beg you'll use it till we reach Throon.'

Left alone, John Gordon felt a slight relaxing of the extreme tension under which he had been laboring for hours.

They had left Earth as soon as Vel Quen's burial was over. And every moment of the hours since then had impressed on Gordon the vital necessity of playing a part.

He could not tell the weird truth about himself. Zarth Arn had insisted that to tell anyone would bring disaster on both Gordon and himself. Why was it so dangerous? Gordon couldn't guess, as yet.

But he was sure that he must heed that warning, must let no one suspect that he was the prince only in physical body. Even if he told, they wouldn't believe him! Old Vel Quen had said that Zarth Arn's weird experiments had been wholly secret. Who would credit such a crazy story?

Gordon had determined that his only possible course of action was to play the part of Zarth Arn as best he could at Throon, and return as soon as possible to the tower-laboratory on Earth. Then he could plan a way to re-effect the exchange of minds.

'But it seems that I'm being sucked into some crazy tangle of galactic conflict that'll make it hard to get away,' he thought, dismayed.

Lying on the padded bunk, Gordon wondered wearily if any man since time began had ever found himself in such a situation as this.

'There's nothing for it but to bull ahead and play it out as Zarth Arn, if I can,' he thought. 'If Vel Quen had only lived!'

He felt again a pang of regret for the old scientist. Then, tired and unstrung, he fell asleep.

When Gordon awoke, he unconsciously expected to see the familiar plaster ceiling of his New York apartment overhead. Instead, he looked at a glittering metal ceiling and heard a deep, steady drone.

He realized then it had been no wild dream. He was still in Zarth Arn's body, in this big warship that was racing through the galaxy toward a doubtful reception for himself.

A uniformed man who bowed respectfully when he entered brought him food – an unfamiliar red substance that seemed to be synthetic meat, fruit, and the chocolate-like drink he already knew.

Hull Burrel came in then. 'We're making almost two hundred parsecs an hour and will reach Canopus in three days, highness.'*

* A parsec was the term invented by 20th Century Earth astronomers to measure galactic distances. It equalled a distance of 3.258 light years, or 18,000,000,000,000 miles.

Gordon did not venture any reply other than a nod. He realized how fatally easy it would be to make slips of pure ignorance.

That possibility was a weight on his mind in the hours that followed, adding to the already superhuman strain of his imposture.

He had to go through the big cruiser as though such a ship was familiar to him, he had to accept references to a thousand things which Zarth Arn would know, without betraying his ignorance.

He carried it off, he hoped, by wrapping himself in brooding silence. But could he carry it off at Throon?

On the third day, John Gordon entered the spacious bridge to be dazzled by a blinding flare of light that forced a way even through the heavy filter-screens across the windows.

'Canopus at last,' remarked Hull Burrel. 'We shall dock at Throon in a few hours.'

Again, wild bugle-calls of excitement soared in Gordon's mind as he looked through the windows at a tremendous spectacle.

It was *worth* all risk and danger, it was worth that nightmare traverse from body to body across the gulf of time, for a man of the 20th Century to look on such a sight as this!

The majesty of Canopus was a thundering impact on his senses. The colossal sun revised all his limited ideas of grandeur. It blazed here in white splendor like a firmament aflame, drenching the warship and all space with a glorious, supernal radiance.

Gordon's senses reeled, as he tried to keep his face impassive. He was only a man of the past and his brain was not used to such a shock of wonder as this.

The drone of the great pressure-ray generators dropped in key as the cruiser swung in around an Earth-sized planet that was one of a dozen worlds circling this monster star.

And this was Throon. This world of green continents and silver seas spinning in opalescent white sunshine was the heart and brain of the Empire that stretched half across the galaxy.

'We'll dock at Throon City, of course,' Hull Burrel was saying. 'Commander Corbulo has stereoed me to bring you to Arn Abbas at once.'

Again, Gordon tensed. 'I will be glad to see my father,' he ventured.

His father? A man he had never seen, a ruler who governed the titan expanse of suns and worlds behind him, and who was parent of the man in whose physical body Gordon now lived?

Again, Zarth Arn's remembered warning steadied Gordon. Tell no one the truth – no one! Brazen through this incredible imposture somehow, and get back to Earth for the re-exchange as soon as he could –

The silvery seas and green continents of Throon rushed up toward the

Caris as the warship made planet-fall with massive disregard of preliminary deceleration.

Gordon caught his breath as he looked down. From the edge of a silver ocean rose a lofty range of mountains that flashed and glittered as though of glass. They *were* of glass, he saw a moment later, a towering range formed by extrusion of vast masses of molten silicates from the planet.

And perched on a plateau of these Glass Mountains high above the sea was a fairy, unreal city. Its graceful domes and towers were like bubbles of colored glass themselves. Pinnacles and terraces took the light of Canopus and flashed it back in a glory of quivering effulgence. Throon City, this – the core and capital of the Empire.

The big cruiser sank toward a huge spaceport just north of the fairy city. In its sunken docks and quays brooded scores, hundreds, of the Empire's star-roving warships. Massive, thousand-foot long battleships, heavy cruisers, fast destroyers and slim phantom-cruisers and ponderous, tub-shaped monitors with huge guns – all these craft wore the shining comet-emblem of the Mid-Galactic Empire.

Gordon stepped out of the *Caris* with Hull Burrel and the respectful officers, into sunlight so weirdly white and beautiful that not even the urgency of his situation prevented him looking about in increased wonder.

The brooding bulks of the great battleships loomed up in the docks all around him, their batteries of grim atom-guns silhouetted against the sky. In the distance rose the incredible, shimmering domes and spires of the city.

Hull Burrel's puzzled voice jerked Gordon from his petrification, recalling him to the necessities of the present.

'The car is waiting for us in the tubeway, highness,' reminded the Antarian captain.

'Of course,' Gordon said hastily, forcing himself to move.

He had to watch the trend of Hull Burrel's direction, so as not to go astray. They made their way between the looming ships, past great mobile cranes, respectfully saluting officers, uniformed men standing at rigid attention.

Every minute John Gordon felt more strongly the hopelessness of what he had set out to do. How could he maintain his impersonation, when everything here was so stunningly new and strange?

'Disaster for both of us if you tell!' That warning of Zarth Arn – the real Zarth Arn – rang through his mind again with a chilling, steadying effect.

'Bull it through!' he told himself. 'They can't dream that you're not the prince, no matter what mistakes you make. Watch every moment—'

They reached the opening of a lighted stair that led down beneath the tarmac of the spaceport. Below were round metal tunnels branching off into the darkness. A cylindrical metal car waited.

No sooner had Gordon and Hull Burrel taken their places in its pneumatic-slung chairs, than the car started moving with great speed. Its velocity was so great that to Gordon it seemed barely five minutes before they stopped.

They stepped out into a similar lighted, underground vestibule. But here uniformed guards with slim, rifle-like atom-guns were on duty. They saluted with the weapons to Gordon.

A young officer, saluting likewise, informed Gordon, 'Throon rejoices at your return, highness.'

'There's no time now for civilities,' Hull Burrel broke in impatiently.

Gordon walked with the Antarian captain to an open doorway beyond which lay a corridor with alabaster walls.

The floor of the corridor began to move smoothly as they stepped onto it, almost startling Gordon into an exclamation. As it bore them forward and up long winding ramps, Gordon numbly comprehended that they were already in the lower levels of Arn Abbas' palace.

The very nerve-center of the vast star-empire whose rule swayed suns and worlds across thousands of light-years! He couldn't yet fully grasp and realize it or the coming ordeal.

The moving walk swept them into an antechamber in which another file of guards saluted and stood apart from high bronze doors. Hull Burrel stood back as Gordon went through into the room beyond.

It was a small room wholly without magnificence. Around its walls were many telestereo instruments, and there was a curious low desk with a panel of grids and screens on its face.

Behind the desk a man sat in a metal chair, with two other men standing beside him. All three looked at Gordon as he approached. His heart hammered violently.

The man in the chair was a giant, dominating figure in dull-gold garments. His massive, powerful face, bleak gray eyes and thick black hair graying at the temples gave a leonine impression.

Gordon recognized him as Arn Abbas, ruler of the Empire, Zarth Arn's father. No, *his* father! He had to keep thinking of it that way!

The younger of the two standing men was like Arn Abbas himself, thirty years younger – tall and stalwart but with more friendliness in his face. That would be Jhal Arn, his elder brother, he guessed.

And the third man, grizzled, stocky, square-faced, wearing the uniform of the Empire navy but with golden bars of rank thick on his sleeve – this must be Chan Corbulo, the Commander of the space fleet.

Gordon, his throat tight with tension, stopped in front of the seated man. He nerved himself against those bleak eyes, knowing that he had to speak.

'Father –' he began tightly. Instantly, he was interrupted.

Arn Abbas, glaring at him, uttered an exclamation of wrath.

'Don't call me father! You're not my son!'

5

Weird Masquerade

Gordon felt a staggering shock. Could Arn Abbas suspect the weird impersonation he was carrying on?

But the next words of the giant ruler a little reassured Gordon, even though they were furious in tone.

'No son of mine would go straying off to the edge of the Empire to play scientific hermit for months, when I need him here! Your cursed science-studies have made you utterly forget your duty.'

Gordon breathed a little more easily. 'Duty, father?' he repeated.

'Duty to me and to the Empire!' roared Arn Abbas. 'You know that I need you here. You know the game that's being played across the galaxy, and what it means to all our star-worlds!'

His big fist pounded his knee. 'And see what burying yourself there on Earth nearly brought about! Shorr Kan nearly scooped you up! You know what that would mean?'

'Yes, I know,' Gordon nodded. 'If Shorr Kan had got hold of me, he could use me as a hostage against you.'

Next moment, he realized that he had blundered. Arn Abbas glared at him, and Jhal Arn and Corbulo looked surprised.

'What in the name of all the star-devils are you talking about?' demanded the emperor. 'You should know as well as I why Shorr Kan wanted his hands on you. To get the secret of the Disruptor, of course!'

The Disruptor? What was that? Gordon desperately realized that again his ignorance had betrayed him.

How could he keep going in this mad imposture when he didn't know the vital facts about Zarth Arn's life and background?

Gordon might have blurted out the truth then and there had not remembrance of his promise to Zarth Arn steadied him. He tried to look unruffled.

'Of course – the Disruptor,' he said hastily. 'That's what I was referring to.'

'You certainly did not sound like it!' snapped Arn Abbas. He uttered a fierce exclamation. 'By Heaven, at a time when I need sons to help me, I've got one real son and I've got another who's so cursed dreamy-eyed he doesn't even remember the Disruptor!'

The massive ruler leaned forward, anger dissolving momentarily into an earnestness that betrayed his deep anxiety.

'Zarth, you've got to wake up! Do you realize that the Empire stands on the verge of a terrible crisis? Do you realize just what that devil Shorr Kan is planning?

'He's sent ambassadors to the Hercules Barons, to the kingdoms of Polaris and Cygnus, even to Fomalhaut Kingdom. He's doing everything to detach our allies from us. And he's building every new warship and weapon he can, there inside the Cloud.'

Grizzled Commander Corbulo nodded grimly. 'It's certain vast preparations are going on inside the Cloud. We know that, even though our scanner-beams can't get through the screens that Shorr Kan's scientists have flung around their work.'

'It's the dream of his life to crack the Empire and reduce the galaxy to a ruck of small warring kingdoms that the League could devour one by one!' Arn Abbas went on. 'Where *we* are trying to unify the galaxy in peace, he wants to split and separate it.

'Only one thing holds Shorr Kan back and that is the Disruptor. He knows we have it, but he doesn't know just what it is or what it can do, any more than anyone else does. And because only you and Jhal and I know the secret of the Disruptor, that arch-devil has tried to get his hands on you!'

Light broke upon John Gordon's mystification. So that was what the Disruptor was – some mysterious weapon whose secret was known only to three men of the Empire's ruling house?

Then Zarth Arn knew that secret. But *he* didn't know it, even though he wore Zarth Arn's body! Yet he had to pretend that he did.

'I never thought of it that way, father,' Gordon said hesitatingly. 'I know the situation is critical.'

'So critical that things may well come to a crisis within weeks!' affirmed Arn Abbas. 'It all depends on how many of our allied kingdoms Shorr Kan is able to detach, and whether he will dare to risk the Disruptor.'

He added loudly, 'And because of that, I forbid you to go back to your hideout on Earth any more, Zarth! You'll stay here and do your duty as the second prince of the Empire should.'

Gordon was appalled. 'But father, I've got to go back to Earth for at least a short time—'

The massive ruler cut him off. 'I told you I forbade it, Zarth! Do you dare to argue with me?'

Gordon felt the crash of all his desperate plans. This was disaster.

If he couldn't go back to Earth and the laboratory there, how could he contact Zarth Arn and re-exchange their bodies?

'I'll hear no more objections!' continued the emperor violently as Gordon started to speak. 'Now get out of here! Corbulo and I have things to discuss.'

Blindly, helplessly, Gordon turned back toward the door. More strongly than even before, he felt a dismayed consciousness of being utterly trapped and baffled.

Jhal Arn went with him, and when they had reached the antechamber the tall elder prince put his hand on Gordon's arm.

'Don't take it too hard, Zarth,' he encouraged. 'I know how devoted you are to your scientific studies, and what a blow Vel Quen's death must have been to you. But father is right – you are needed here, in this gathering crisis.'

Gordon, even in his dismay, had to choose his words. 'I want to do my duty. But what help can I give?'

'It's Lianna that father is referring to,' Jhal Arn said seriously. 'You *have* dodged your duty there, Zarth.'

He added, as though anticipating objections from Gordon, 'O, I know why – I know all about Murn. But the Fomalhaut Kingdom is vital to the Empire in this crisis. You'll have to go through with it.'

Lianna? Murn? The names had no meaning to John Gordon. They were mystery, like everything else in this mad imposture.

'You mean that Lianna –' he began, and left the words hanging in hope of provoking further explanation from Jhal Arn.

But Jhal only nodded. 'You've got to do it, Zarth. Father is going to make the announcement at the Feast of Moons tonight.'

He clapped Gordon on the back. 'Buck up, it's not as bad as all that! You look as though you'd been condemned to death. I'll see you at the Feast.'

He turned back into the inner room, leaving Gordon staring blankly after him.

Gordon stood, bewildered and badly worried. What kind of tangled complications was his involuntary impersonation of Zarth Arn getting him into? How long could he hope to carry it through?

Hull Burrel had gone into the inner room when Gordon came out. Now as Gordon stood frozenly, the big Antarian came out too.

'Prince Zarth, I owe you good fortune!' he exclaimed. 'I expected to get reprimanded by Commander Corbulo for putting off my regular patrol course to touch at Sol.'

'And he didn't reprimand you?' Gordon said mechanically.

'Sure he did – gave me the devil with bells on,' Burrel grinned. 'But your father said it turned out so lucky in giving me a chance to rescue you, that he's appointed me aide to the Commander himself!'

Gordon congratulated him. But he spoke perfunctorily, for his mind was upon his own desperately puzzling position.

He couldn't just stand here in the anteroom longer. Zarth Arn must have apartments in this great palace, and he'd be expected to go to them. The devil of it was he had no idea where there were!

He couldn't let his ignorance be suspected, though. So he took leave of

Hull Burrel and walked confidently out of the anteroom by a different door, as though he knew quite well where he was going.

Gordon found himself in a corridor, on a gliding motowalk. The motowalk took him into a great circular room of shining silver. It was brilliantly illuminated by white sunlight pouring through high crystal windows. Around its walls marched black reliefs depicting a wilderness of dark stars, embers of burned out suns and lifeless worlds.

John Gordon felt dwarfed by the majesty and splendor of this great, somber chamber. He crossed it and entered another vast room, this one with walls that flamed with the glowing splendor of a whirling nebula.

'Where the devil are Zarth Arn's quarters in this place?' he wondered.

He realized his helplessness. He couldn't ask anyone where his own quarters were. Neither could he wander aimlessly through this vast palace without arousing wonder, perhaps suspicion.

A gray-skinned servant, a middle-aged man in the black livery of the palace, was already looking at him wonderingly across this Hall of the Nebula. The man bowed deeply as Gordon strode to him.

Gordon had had an idea. 'Come with me to my apartments,' he told the servant brusquely. 'I have a task for you.'

The gray man bowed again. 'Yes, highness.'

But the man remained there, waiting. Waiting for him to walk ahead, of course!

Gordon made an impatient gesture. 'Go ahead! I'll follow.'

If the servant found it strange he let none of that feeling appear in his masklike face. He turned and proceeded softly out of the great nebula room by another door.

Gordon followed him into a corridor and onto a motowalk that glided upward like a sliding ramp. Swiftly and quietly the moving walk took them up through splendid, lofty corridors and stairs.

Twice they confronted groups coming downward by the return walk – two brilliantly-jewelled white girls and a laughing, swarthy naval captain in one, two grave gray officials in the other. All of them bowed in deep respect to Gordon.

The motowalk switched off down a shimmery, pearl-walled passageway. A door ahead slid softly open of its own accord. Gordon followed through it into a high chamber with pure white walls.

The gray servant turned inquiringly toward him. 'Yes, highness?'

How to get rid of the man? Gordon cut that problem short by taking the easiest method.

'I find I won't need you after all,' he said carelessly. 'You may go.'

The man bowed himself out of the room, and Gordon felt a slight relaxing of his tension. Clumsy, his stratagem – but at least it had got him to the temporary refuge of Zarth Arn's apartments.

He found himself breathing heavily as though from exhausting effort. His hands were shaking. He had not realized the nervous effort his impersonation cost him. He mopped his brow.

'My God! Was any man ever in a position like this before?'

His tired mind refused to grapple with the problem now. To evade it, he walked slowly through the rooms of the suite.

Here was less splendor than he had seen elsewhere in the great palace. Apparently, Zarth Arn had not been of luxurious tastes. The rooms were comparatively austere.

The two living rooms had silken hangings and a few pieces of metal furniture of beautiful design. There was a rack of hundreds of thought-spools and one of the thought-spool 'readers.' A side room held much scientific apparatus, was in fact a small laboratory.

He glanced into a small bedroom, then went on toward tall windows that opened on a terrace gay with green verdure and flooded by sunlight. Gordon went out onto the terrace, and then froze.

'Throon City! Good Lord, who ever dreamed of a place like *this*!'

The little garden-terrace of his suite was high in the west wall of the huge, oblong palace. It looked out across the city.

City of the great star-empire's glory, gathering in itself an epitome of the splendor and power of that vast realm of many thousand star-worlds! Metropolis of grandeur so great that it stunned and paralyzed the eyes of John Gordon of little Earth!

The enormous white disk of Canopus was sinking toward the horizon, flashing a supernal brilliance across the scene. In that transfiguring radiance, the peaks and scarps of the Glass Mountains here above the sea flung back the sunset in banners and pennons of wild glory.

And outshining even the stupendous glory of the glassy peaks shone the fairy towers of Throon. Domes, minarets, graceful porticoes, these and the great buildings they adorned were of shimmering glass. Mightiest among the structures loomed the gigantic palace on whose high terrace he stood. Surrounded by wondrous gardens, it looked out royally across the great metropolis and the silver ocean beyond.

In the radiant sunset out there over the glittering peaks and heaving ocean there flitted swarms of fliers like shining fireflies. From the spaceport to the north, a half-dozen mighty battleships rose majestically and took off into the darkening sky.

The full grandeur and vastness of this star-empire hammered into Gordon's mind. For this city was the throbbing heart of those vast glooms and linked stars and worlds across which he had come.

'And *I* am supposed to be one of the ruling house of this realm!' he thought, dazed. 'I can't keep it up. It's too vast, too overpowering—'

The enormous sun sank as Gordon numbly watched. Violet shadows darkened to velvet night across the metropolis.

Lights came on softly all through the glittering streets of Throon, and on the lower terraces of this giant palace.

Two golden moons climbed into the heavens, and hosts of countless stars broke forth in a glory of unfamiliar constellations that rivalled the soft, throbbing lights of the city.

'Highness, it grows late!'

Gordon turned jerkily, startled. A grave servant, a stocky man with bluish skin, was bowing.

One of Zarth Arn's personal servants, he guessed. He would have to be careful with this man!

'Yes, what of that?' he asked, with an assumption of impatience.

'The Feast of Moons will begin within the hour,' reminded the servant. 'You should make ready, highness.'

Gordon suddenly remembered what Jhal Arn had said of a Feast. A royal banquet, he guessed, to be held this night.

What was it Jhal had said of some announcement that Arn Abbas was to make? And what had been the talk of 'Murn' and 'Lianna' and his duty?

Gordon braced himself for the ordeal. A banquet meant exposing himself to the eyes of a host of people – all of whom, no doubt, knew Zarth Arn and would notice his slightest slip. But he had to go.

'Very well, I will dress now,' he told the servant.

It was at least a slight help that the blue-skinned servitor procured and laid out his garments for him. The jacket and trousers were of silky black, with a long black cloak to hang from his shoulders.

When he had dressed, the servant pinned on his breast a comet-emblem worked in wonderfully-blazing green jewels. He guessed it to be the insignia of his royal rank in the Empire.

Gordon felt again the sense of unreality as he surveyed his unfamiliar figure, his dark, aquiline face, in a tall mirror.

'I need a drink,' he told the servant jerkily. 'Something strong.'

The blue servant looked at him in faint surprise, for a moment.

'*Saqua*, highness?' he asked, and Gordon nodded.

The brown liquor the man poured out sent a fiery tingle through Gordon's veins.

Some of the shaky strain left his nerves as he drank another goblet of the *saqua*. He felt a return of reckless self-confidence as he left the apartment.

'What the devil!' Gordon thought. 'I wanted adventure – and I'm getting it!'

More adventure than he had bargained for, truly! He had never dreamed of such an ordeal as was now ahead of him – of appearing before the nobility of this star-flung Empire as its prince!

All the mammoth, softly-lit palace seemed astir with soft sound and laughter and movement, as streams of brilliantly-garbed men and women moved along its motowalks. Gordon, to whom they bowed respectfully, noted their direction and went forward casually.

The gliding walks took him down through the lofty corridors and halls to a broad vestibule with wonderful golden walls. Here councillors, nobles, men and women high in the Empire, drew aside for him.

Gordon nerved himself, strode toward the high doors whose massive golden leaves were now thrown back. A silk-garbed chamberlain bowed and spoke clearly into the vast hall beyond.

'His highness, Prince Zarth Arn!'

6

The Feast of Moons

Gordon stopped stock still, shaken by an inward quaking. He stood on a wide dais at the side of a circular hall that was of cathedral loftiness and splendor.

The vast, round room of black marble held rows of tables which themselves glowed with intrinsic light. They bore a bewildering array of glass and metal dishes, and along them sat some hundreds of brilliantly-dressed men and women.

But not all these banqueters were human! Though humans were dominant, just as they were throughout the galaxy, there were also representatives of the Empire's aboriginal races. Despite their conventional garb, those he could see clearly looked grotesquely alien to Gordon – a frog-like, scaly green man with bulging eyes, a beaked, owl-faced winged individual, two black spidery figures with too many arms and legs.

John Gordon's dazed eyes lifted, and for a moment he thought this whole vast room was open to the sky. High overhead curved the black vault of the night heavens, gemmed with thousands of blazing stars and constellations. Into that sky, two golden moons and one of pale silver hue were climbing toward conjunction.

It took a moment for Gordon to realize that that sky was an artificial planetarium-ceiling, so perfect was the imitation. Then he became aware that the eyes of all these folk had turned upon him. On the dais, there was a table with a score of brilliant people, Jhal Arn's tall figure had risen and was beckoning impatiently to him.

Jhal Arn's first words shocked him back to realization of how badly his caution and self-control had slipped.

'What's the matter, Zarth? You look as though you'd never seen the Hall of Stars before!'

'Nerves, I guess,' Gordon answered huskily. 'I think I need another drink.'

Jhal Arn burst into laughter. 'So you've been fortifying yourself for tonight? Come, Zarth, it isn't that bad.'

Gordon numbly slid into the seat to which Jhal Arn had led him, one separated by two empty chairs from the places where Jhal sat with his lovely wife and little son.

He found grizzled Commander Corbulo on his other side. Across the table sat a thin, nervous-eyed and aging man who he soon learned was Orth Bodmer, Chief Councillor of the Empire.

Corbulo, a stern figure in his plain uniform, bowed to Gordon as did the other people along this raised table.

'You're looking pale and downcast, Zarth,' rumbled the grizzled space-admiral. 'That's what you get, skulking in laboratories on Earth. Space is the place for a young man like you.'

'I begin to think you're right,' muttered Gordon. 'I wish to Heaven I was there now.'

Corbulo grunted. 'So that's it? Tonight's announcement, eh? Well, it's necessary. The help of the Fomalhaut Kingdom will be vital to us if Shorr Kan attacks.'

What the devil were they talking about, John Gordon wondered bitterly? The names 'Murn' and 'Lianna' that Jhal Arn had mentioned, this reference to Fomalhaut star-kingdom again – what did they portend?

Gordon found a servant bending obsequiously over his shoulder, and told the man, '*Saqua*, first.'

The brown liquor spun his brain a little, this time. He was aware, as he drank another goblet, that Corbulo was looking at him in stern disapproval, and that Jhal Arn was grinning.

The brilliant scene before him, the shining tables, the splendid human and unhuman throng, and the wonderful sky-ceiling of stars and climbing moons, held Gordon fascinated. So this was the Feast of Moons?

Music that rippled in long, haunting harmonies of muted strings and woodwinds was background to the gay, buzzing chatter along the glittering tables. Then the music stopped and horns flared a loud silver challenge.

All rose to their feet. Seeing Jhal Arn rising, Gordon hastily followed his example.

'His highness, Arn Abbas, sovereign of the Mid-Galactic Empire, Suzerain of the Lesser Kingdoms, Governor of the stars and worlds of the Marches of Outer Space!

'Her highness, the Princess Lianna, ruler of the Kingdom of Fomalhaut!'

The clear, loud announcements gave John Gordon a shock of astonishment even before the giant, regal figure of Arn Abbas strode onto the dais, with a girl upon his arm.

So 'Lianna' was a girl, a princess – ruler of the little western star-kingdom of Fomalhaut? But what had she to do with him?

Arn Abbas, magnificent in a blue-black cloak upon which blazed the glorious jewels of the royal comet-emblem, stopped and turned his bleak eyes angrily on Gordon.

'Zarth, are you forgetting protocol?' he snapped. 'Come here!'

Gordon stumbled forward. He got only a swift impression of the girl beside the emperor.

She was tall, though she did not look so beside Arn Abbas' giant height. As tall as himself, her slim, rounded figure perfectly outlined by her long, shimmering white gown, she held her ash-golden head proudly high.

Pride, beauty, consciousness of authority – these were what Gordon read in the chiselled white face, the faintly scornful red mouth, the cool, clear gray eyes that rested gravely on him.

Arn Abbas took Gordon's hand in one of his, and Lianna's in the other. The towering sovereign raised his voice.

'Nobles and captains of the Empire and our allied star-kingdoms, I announce to you the coming marriage of my second son, Zarth Arn, and the Princess Lianna of Fomalhaut!'

Marriage? Marriage to this proudly beautiful star-kingdom princess? Gordon felt as though hit by a thunderbolt. So *that* was what Jhal Arn and Corbulo had been referring to? But good God, he couldn't go through with this! He wasn't Zarth Arn –

'Take her hand, you fool!' snarled the emperor. 'Have you lost your wits?'

Numbly, John Gordon managed to grasp the girl's slim, ring-laden fingers.

Arn Abbas, satisfied, stalked forward to take his seat at the table. Gordon remained frozen.

Lianna gave him a sweet, set smile, but her voice was impatient as she said in an undertone, 'Conduct me to our place, so that the others can sit down.'

Gordon became aware that the whole host in the Hall of Stars remained standing, looking at himself and the girl.

He stumbled forward with her, clumsily handed her into her chair, and sat down beside her. There was the rustle of the hosts re-seating themselves, and the rippling music sounded forth again.

Lianna was looking at him with fine brows arched a little, her eyes clouded by impatience and resentment.

'Your attitude toward me will create gossip. You look positively appalled!'

Gordon nerved himself. He had to keep up his imposture for the time being. Zarth Arn was apparently being used as a political pawn, was being shoved into this marriage and had agreed to it.

He had to play the real Zarth's part, for now. He'd find some way of getting back to Earth to exchange places with the real Zarth Arn, before the marriage.

He drained his *saqua* goblet again, and leaned toward Lianna with a sudden recklessness.

She expected him to be an ardent fiance, to be Zarth Arn. All right, blast it, he would be! It was no fault of his if there was deception in it. He hadn't asked to play this role!!

'Lianna, they're so busy admiring you that they don't even look at me,' he told her.

Lianna's clear eyes became puzzled in expression. 'I never saw you like this before, Zarth.'

Gordon laughed. 'Why, then, there's a new Zarth Arn – Zarth Arn is a different man, now!'

Truth enough in that assertion, as only he knew! But the girl looked more perplexed, her fine brows drawing together in a little frown.

The feast went on, in a glow of warmth and color and buzzing voices. And the *saqua* Gordon had drunk swept away his last trace of apprehension and nervousness.

Adventure? He'd wanted it and he'd gotten it, adventure such as no man of his time had ever dreamed. If death itself were the end of all this, would he not still be gainer? Wasn't it worth risking life to sit here in the Hall of Stars at Throon, with the lords of the great star-kingdoms and a princess of far-off suns at his side?

Others beside himself had drunk deeply. The handsome, flushed young man who sat beyond Corbulo and whom Gordon had learned obliquely was Sath Shamar, ruler of the allied kingdom of Polaris, crashed his goblet down to punctuate a declaration.

'Let them come, the sooner the better!' he was exclaiming to Corbulo. 'It's time Shorr Kan was taught a lesson.'

Commander Corbulo looked at him sourly. 'That's true, highness. Just how many first-line battleships will Polaris contribute to our fleet, if it comes to teaching him that lesson?'

Sath Shamar looked a little dashed. 'Only a few hundred, I fear. But they'll make up for it in fighting ability.'

Arn Abbas had been listening, for the emperor's rumbling voice sounded from his throne-like seat on Gordon's right.

'The men of Polaris will prove their fidelity to the Empire, no fear,' declared Arn Abbas. 'Aye, and those of Fomalhaut Kingdom, and of Cygnus and Lyra and our other allies.'

Sath Shamar flushedly added, 'Let the Hercules Barons but do their part and we've nothing to fear from the Cloud.'

Gordon saw all eyes turn to two men further along the table. One was a cold-eyed oldster, the other a tall, rangy man of thirty. Both wore on their cloaks the flaring sun-cluster emblem of Hercules Cluster.

The oldster answered. 'The Confederacy of the Barons will fulfill all its pledges. But we have made no formal pledge in this matter.'

Arn Abbas' massive face darkened a little at that cool declaration. But Orth Bodmer, the thin-faced chief Councillor, spoke quickly and soothingly to the cold-eyed Baron.

'All men know the proud independence of the great Barons, Zu Rizal. And all know you'd never acquiesce in an evil tyranny's victory.'

Arn Abbas, a few moments later, leaned to speak frowningly to Gordon.

'Shorr Kan has been tampering with the Barons! I'm going to find out tonight from Zu Rizal just where they stand.'

Finally Arn Abbas arose, and the feasters all rose with him. The whole company began to stream out of the Hall of Stars into the adjoining halls.

Courtiers and nobles made way for Gordon and Lianna as they went through the throng. The girl smiled and spoke to many, her perfect composure bespeaking a long training in the regal manner.

Gordon nodded carelessly in answer to the congratulations and greetings. He knew he was probably making many blunders, but he didn't care by now. For the first time since leaving Earth, he felt perfectly carefree as that warm glow inside him deepened.

That *saqua* was a cursed good drink! Too bad he couldn't take some of it back with him to his own time. But nothing material could go across time. That was a shame –

He found himself with Lianna on the threshold of a great hall whose fairy-like green illumination came from the flaming comets that crept across its ceiling 'sky.' Hundreds were dancing here to dreamy, waltz-like music from an unseen source.

Gordon was astounded by the dream-like, floating movements of the immeasurably graceful dance. The dancers seemed to hover half-suspended in the air each step. Then he realized that the room was conditioned somehow by antigravity apparatus to reduce their weight.

Lianna looked up at him doubtfully, as he himself realized crestfallenly that he couldn't perform a step of these floating dances.

'Let's not dance,' Lianna said, to his relief. 'You're such a poor dancer as I remember it, that I'd rather go out in the gardens.'

Of course – the retiring, studious real Zarth Arn would be that! Well, so much the better.

'I greatly prefer the gardens,' Gordon laughed. 'For believe it or not, I'm an even poorer dancer than I was before.'

Lianna looked up at him perplexedly as they strolled down a lofty silver corridor. 'You drank a great deal at the Feast. I never saw you touch *saqua* before.'

Gordon shrugged. 'The fact is that I never drank it before tonight.'

He uttered a low exclamation when they emerged into the gardens. He had not expected such a scene of unreal beauty as this.

These were gardens of glowing light, of luminous color! Trees and shrubs bore masses of blossoms that glowed burning red, cool green, turquoise blue, and every shade between. The soft breeze that brought heavy perfume from them shook them gaily like a forest of shining flame-flowers, transcendently lovely.

Later, Gordon was to learn that these luminous flowers were cultivated on several highly radioactive worlds of the star Achernar, and were brought here and planted in beds of similarly radioactive soil. But now, suddenly coming on them, they were stunning.

Behind him, the massive terraces of the gigantic oblong palace shouldered the stars. Glowing lights flung boldly in step on climbing step against the sky! And the three clustered moons above poured down their mingled radiance to add a final unreal touch.

'Beautiful, beyond words,' Gordon murmured, enthralled by the scene.

Lianna nodded. 'Of all your world of Throon, I love these gardens the best. But there are wild, unpeopled worlds far in our Fomalhaut Kingdom that are even more lovely.'

Her eyes kindled and for the first time he saw emotion conquer the regal composure of her lovely little face.

'Lonely, unpeopled worlds that are like planets of living color, drenched by the wonderful auroras of strange suns! I shall take you to see them when we visit Fomalhaut, Zarth.'

She was looking up at him, her ash-gold hair shining like a crown in the soft light.

She expected him to make love to her, Gordon thought. He was – or at least, she thought he was – her fiance, the man she had chosen to marry. He'd have to keep up his imposture, even now.

Gordon put his arm around her and bent to her lips. Lianna's slim body was pliant and warm inside the shimmering white gown, and her half-parted lips were dizzyingly sweet.

'I'm a cursed liar!' Gordon thought, dismayed. 'I'm kissing her because I *want* to, not to keep up my role!'

He abruptly stepped back. Lianna looked up at him with sheer amazement on her face.

'Zarth, what made you do that?'

Gordon tried to laugh, though that thrillingly sweet contact still seemed trembling through his nerves.

'Is it so remarkable for me to kiss you?' he countered.

'Of course it is – you never did before!' Lianna exclaimed. 'You know as well as I that our marriage is purely a political pretense!'

Truth crashed into Gordon's mind like a blast of icy cold, sweeping the fumes of *saqua* from his brain.

He had made an abysmal slip in his imposture! He should have guessed that Lianna didn't *want* to marry Zarth Arn any more than he wanted to marry her – that it was purely a political marriage and they but two pawns in the great game of galactic diplomacy.

He had to cover up this blunder as best he could, and quickly! The girl was looking up at him with that expression of utter mystification still on her face.

'I can't understand you doing this when you and I made agreement to be mere friends.'

Gordon desperately voiced the only explanation possible, one perilously close to the truth.

'Lianna, you're so beautiful I couldn't help it. Is it so strange I should fall in love with you, despite our agreement?'

Lianna's face hardened and her voice had scorn in it. 'You in love with *me?* You forget that I know all about Murn.'

'Murn?' The name rang vaguely familiar in Gordon's ears. Jhal Arn had mentioned 'Murn.'

Once more Gordon felt himself baffled by his ignorance of vital facts. He was cold sober now, and badly worried.

'I – I guess maybe I just had too much *saqua* at the Feast, after all,' he muttered.

Lianna's amazement and anger had faded, and she seemed to be studying him with a curiously intent interest.

He felt relief when they were interrupted by a gay throng streaming out into the gardens. In the hours that followed, the presence of others made Gordon's role a little easier to play.

He was conscious of Lianna's gray eyes often resting on him, with that wondering look. When the gathering broke up and he accompanied her to the door of her apartments, Gordon was uneasily aware of her curious, speculative gaze as he bade her good night.

He mopped his brow as he went on the gliding motowalk to his own chambers. What a night! He had had about as much as one man could bear!

Gordon found his rooms softly lit, but the blue servant was not in evidence. He tiredly opened the door of his bedroom. There was a quick rush of little bare feet. He froze at sight of the girl running toward him, one he had never seen before.

She seemed of almost childish youthfulness, with her dark hair falling to her bare shoulders and her soft, beautiful little face and dark-blue eyes shining with gladness. A child? It was no child's rounded figure that gleamed whitely through the filmy robe she wore!

Gordon stood, stupefied by this final staggering surprise in an evening of surprises, as the girl ran and threw soft bare arms around his neck.

'Zarth Arn!' she cried. 'At last you've come! I've been waiting so long!'

7

Star-Princess

John Gordon for the second time that night held in his arms a girl who thought he was the real Zarth Arn. But the dark-haired, lovely young girl who had thrown her arms around him was far different from the proud Princess Lianna.

Warm lips pressed his own in eager passionate kisses, as he stood bewildered. The dark hair that brushed his face was soft and perfumed. For a moment, impulse made Gordon draw her lithe figure closer.

Then he pushed her back a little. The beautiful little face that looked up at him was soft and appealing.

'You never told me that you had come back to Throon!' she accused. 'I didn't know until I saw you at the Feast!'

Gordon stumbled for an answer. 'I didn't have time. I—'

This final surprise of the day had staggered him badly. Who was this lovely young girl? One with whom the real Zarth Arn had been conducting an intrigue?

She was smiling up at him fondly, her little hands still resting on his shoulders.

'It's all right, Zarth. I came up right after the Feast and I've been waiting for you.'

She snuggled closer. 'How long will you be staying on Throon? At least, we'll have these few nights together.'

Gordon was appalled. He had thought his fantastic imposture difficult before. But *this*—!

A name suddenly bobbed into his thoughts, a name that both Jhal Arn and Lianna had mentioned as though he knew it well. The name of 'Murn.' Was it the name of this girl?

He thought it might be. To find out, he spoke to her diffidently.

'Murn—'

The girl raised her dark head from his shoulder to look at him inquiringly.

'Yes, Zarth?'

So this was Murn? It was this girl of whom Lianna had mockingly reminded him. So that Lianna knew of his intrigue?

Well, the name was something, anyway. Gordon was trying to grope his way through the complexities of the situation. He sat down, and Murn promptly nestled in his lap.

'Murn, listen – you shouldn't be here,' he began huskily. 'Suppose you were seen coming to my apartment?'

Murn looked at him with astonishment in her dark blue eyes. 'What difference does that make, when I'm your wife?'

His wife? Gordon, for the twentieth time that day, was smitten breathless by the sudden, complete destruction of his preconceived ideas.

How in Heaven's name could he keep up the part of Zarth Arn when he didn't know the most elementary facts about the man? Why hadn't Zarth Arn or Vel Quen told him these things?

Then Gordon remembered. They hadn't told him because it wasn't supposed to be necessary. It had never been dreamed that Gordon, in Zarth Arn's body, would leave Earth and come to Throon. That raid of Shorr Kan's emissaries had upset all the plan, and had introduced these appalling complications.

Murn, her dark head snuggled under his chin, was continuing in a plaintive voice.

'Even though I'm only your morganatic wife, surely there's nothing wrong about my being here?'

So that was it! A morganatic, an unofficial, wife! That custom of old had survived to the days of these star-kings!

For a moment, John Gordon felt a hot anger against the man whose body he inhabited. Zarth Arn, secretly married to this child whom he could not acknowledge publicly and at the same time preparing for a state marriage with Lianna – it was a nasty business!

Or was it? Gordon's anger faded. The marriage with Lianna was purely a political device to assure the loyalty of the Fomalhaut Kingdom. Zarth had understood that, and so did Lianna. She knew all about Murn, and apparently had not resented. Under those circumstances, was Zarth Arn not justified in secretly finding happiness with this girl he loved?

Gordon suddenly woke again to the fact that Murn did not doubt for a moment that he was her loved husband – and that she had every idea of spending the night here with him!

He lifted her from his lap and rose to his feet, looking down at her uncertainly.

'Murn, listen, you must not spend tonight here,' he told her. 'You will have to avoid my apartment for these next few weeks.'

Murn's lovely face became pale and stricken. 'Zarth, what are you saying?'

Gordon racked his brain for an excuse. 'Now don't cry, please. It isn't that I don't love you any more.'

Murn's dark blue eyes had filled with tears. 'It's Lianna! You've fallen in love with her. I saw how you paid attention to her at the Feast!'

The pain in her white face made it seem more child-like than ever. Gordon cursed the necessities of the situation. He was deeply hurting this girl.

He took her face between his hands. 'Murn, you must believe me when I tell you this. Zarth Arn loves you as much as ever – his feelings have not changed.'

Murn's eyes searched his face, and the intense earnestness in it and in his voice seemed to convince her. The pain left her face.

'But if that's so, Zarth, then why—'

Gordon had thought of an excuse, by now. 'It's because of the marriage with Lianna, but *not* because I love the princess,' he said.

'You know, Murn, that the marriage is designed to assure the support of the Fomalhaut Kingdom in the coming struggle with the Cloud.'

Murn nodded her dark head, her eyes still perplexed. 'Yes, you explained that to me before. But I still don't see why it should come between us. You said it wouldn't, that you and Lianna had agreed to regard it as a mere form.'

'Yes, but right now we must be careful,' Gordon said quickly. 'There are spies of Shorr Kan here at Throon. If they discovered I have a secret morganatic wife, they could publish the fact and wreck the marriage.'

Murn's soft face became understanding. 'Now I see. But Zarth, aren't we going to see each other at all?'

'Only in public, for a few weeks,' Gordon told her. 'Soon I shall leave Throon again for a little while. And I promise you that when I come back it will all be the same between us as before.'

And that was truth, Gordon fervently hoped! For if he could get to Earth and effect the re-exchange of bodies, it would be the *real* Zarth Arn who would come back to Throon.

Murn seemed relieved in mind but still a little rueful, as she threw on a black silk cloak and prepared to leave.

She raised herself on tiptoe to press warm lips lovingly to his. 'Good night, Zarth.'

He returned the kiss, not with passion but with a queer tenderness. He could understand how Zarth Arn had fallen in love with this exquisite, child-like girl.

Murn's eyes became a little wider, faintly puzzled, as she looked up at him after that kiss.

'You are somehow different, Zarth,' she murmured. 'I don't know how—'

The subtle instinct of a woman in love had given her vague warning of the incredible change in him, Gordon knew. He drew a long breath of relief when she had gone.

Gordon stretched himself on the bed in the little sleeping-room, but found his muscles still tense as steel cords. Not until he had lain many minutes staring at the glowing moonlight that streamed into the dark room, did his nerves relax a little.

One paramount necessity cried aloud in Gordon's mind. He had to get out of this crazy imposture – at the earliest possible moment! He couldn't much longer carry on his weird impersonation of one of the focal figures in the approaching crisis of the great star-kingdoms. Yet how? How was he to get back to Earth to re-exchange bodies with Zarth Arn?

Gordon awoke next morning to glimmering white dawn and found the blue Vegan servant standing beside his bed.

'The princess Lianna asks you to breakfast with her, highness,' the servant informed.

Gordon felt quick surprise and worry. Why had Lianna sent this invitation? Could she suspect something? No, impossible. And yet—

He bathed in a little glass room where, he found by pushing buttons at hazard, he could cause soapy, salty or perfumed waters of any temperatures to swirl up neck-high around him.

The Vegan had a silken white suit and cloak ready for him. He dressed quickly, and then went through the palace to Lianna's apartments.

These were suites of fairy-like pastel-walled rooms beyond which one of the broad, flower-hung terraces looked out over Throon. Boyish in blue slacks and jacket, Lianna greeted him on the terrace.

'I have had breakfast laid here,' she told him. 'You are just in time to hear the sunrise music.'

Gordon was astonished to detect a faint shyness in Lianna's gaze as she served him iced, red-pulped fruits and winy purple beverage. She did not now seem the regally proud princess of the night before.

And what was the sunrise music? He supposed that was another of the things he should know but didn't.

'Listen, it is beginning now!' Lianna said suddenly.

High around the city Throon loomed the crystal peaks of the Glass Mountains, lofty in the sunrise. Down from those glorious distant peaks now shivered pure, thrillingly sweet notes of sound.

Storm of music broke louder and louder from the glittering peaks! Wild, angelic arpeggios of crystalline notes rang out like all the bells of heaven. Tempests of tiny tinklings like pizzicati of fairy strings was background to the ringing chords.

Gordon realized now that he was hearing the sounds given forth by the sudden expansion of the glassy peaks as Canopus' rays warmed them. He heard the crystal music reach its ringing crescendo as the big white sun rose higher. Then it died away in a long, quivering note.

Gordon exhaled a long breath. 'That was the most wonderful thing I've ever heard.'

Lianna looked at him, surprised. 'But you've heard it many times before.'

He realized he had made another slip. They had walked to the rail of the terrace, and Lianna was looking up at him intently.

She suddenly asked a question that startled him. 'Why did you send Murn away last night?'

'How did you know about that?' he exclaimed.

Lianna laughed softly. 'You should know there are no secrets in this palace. I've no doubt it is buzzing right now with the news that we breakfasted together.'

Was that so? Gordon thought in dismay. In that case, he might have some explaining to do to Murn when next they met.

'Did you and she quarrel?' Lianna persisted. Then she flushed slightly and added, 'Of course, it's really none of my affair.'

'Lianna, it is your affair,' Gordon said impulsively. 'I only wish—'

He stopped. He could not go on, to say that he only wished he could tell her the truth.

He did wish that with all his heart and soul, at this moment. Murn was adorable, but it was Lianna whom he would never forget.

Lianna looked up at him with puzzled gray eyes. 'I don't understand you as well as I thought I did, Zarth.'

She was silent for a moment, and then suddenly spoke a little breathlessly.

'Zarth, I can't fence with people. I have to speak straight out. Tell me – did you really mean it when you kissed me last night?'

Gordon's heart jumped, and the answer sprang from his lips. 'Lianna, I did!'

Her gray eyes looked up at him gravely, wondering. 'It seemed strange yet I felt you did. Yet I still can hardly believe—'

She suddenly, with the imperiousness that betrayed regal training, put her hands on his shoulders. It was open invitation to kiss her again.

Not if the whole palace had crumbled about them could Gordon have resisted doing so. And again, the feel of her slim, electrically alive figure in his arms, the touch of sweet, breathless lips, shook him.

'Zarth, you've changed!' Lianna whispered, wonderingly, unconsciously repeating Murn. 'I almost believe that you love me—'

'Lianna, I do!' burst from Gordon. 'I have, from the first moment I saw you!'

Her eyes softened, clung brilliantly to his. 'Then you want our marriage to be a real one? You would divorce Murn?'

Gordon came to himself with a crashing shock. Good God, what was he doing?

He couldn't compromise the real Zarth, who loved Murn with all his heart.

8

The Spy from the Cloud

Gordon was temporarily delivered from his impasse of bewilderment by a providential interruption. It came from a chamberlain who hesitantly emerged onto the terrace.

'Highness, your father requests you and the Princess Lianna to come to the tower-suite,' he told Gordon, bowing.

Gordon seized upon the chance to evade further discussion. He said awkwardly, 'We had better go at once, Lianna. It may be important.'

Lianna remained looking at him with steady gaze, as though expecting him to say more. But he didn't.

He *couldn't!* He couldn't tell her that he loved her, only to have the real Zarth Arn come back and deny it!

She was silent as they followed the chamberlain by gliding ramps up to the highest tower of the palace. Here were rooms whose glass walls looked out over all the shimmering towers of Throon and the stupendous encircling panorama of glassy peaks and sea.

Arn Abbas was restlessly pacing the room, a giant, dominating figure. The thin-faced Chief Councillor, Orth Bodmer, was speaking to him, and Jhal Arn was also present.

'Zarth, this matter concerns you and Lianna both,' Arn Abbas greeted them.

He explained curtly. 'The crisis between us and the League is deepening. Shorr Kan has called all League star-ships home to the Cloud. And now I'm afraid the Hercules Barons are wavering toward him.'

Gordon quickly recalled the lukewarm attitude of Zu Rizal and the other Hercules Baron the night before.

Arn Abbas' massive face was dark. 'I sounded Zu Rizal last night after the Feast. He said the Barons couldn't commit themselves to full alliance with the Empire. They're worried by persistent rumors to the effect that Shorr Kan has some powerful new weapon.

'I believe, though, that Zu Rizal doesn't represent the feelings of all the Barons. They may be doubtful but they don't want to see the Cloud conquer. I think they can be brought into full alliance with the Empire. And I'm going to send you to accomplish that, Zarth.'

'Send *me*?' Gordon exclaimed, startled. 'But I couldn't carry out a mission like that!'

'Who could carry it out better, highness?' Orth Bodmer said earnestly to him. 'As the emperor's own son, your prestige would make you a potent ambassador.'

'We're not going to argue about it – you're going whether you like it or not!' snapped Arn Abbas.

Gordon was swept off his feet. He to act as ambassador to the great star-lords of Hercules Cluster? How could he?

Then he saw a chance in this. Once in space on that mission, he might manage to touch at Earth and would then be able to re-exchange bodies with the real Zarth Arn! If he could do that –

'This means,' Arn Abbas was saying, 'that your marriage to Lianna must take place sooner than we planned. You must leave for Hercules in a week. I shall announce that your marriage to Lianna will be solemnized five days from now.'

Gordon felt as though he had suddenly stepped through a trapdoor into an abyss.

He had assumed that this marriage lay so far in the future he didn't need to worry about it! Now his assumption was wrecked!

He desperately voiced protest. 'But is it necessary for us to hold the marriage before I go to Hercules as an ambassador?'

'Of course it is!' declared Arn Abbas. 'It's vital to hold the western star-kingdoms to us. And as husband of the princess of Fomalhaut Kingdom, you'll carry more weight with the Barons.'

Lianna looked at Gordon with that curiously steady gaze and said, 'Perhaps Prince Zarth has some objection?'

'Objection? What the devil objection could he have?' demanded Arn Abbas.

Gordon realized that open resistance would do him no good. He had to stall for time, as he had been doing since he was first flung into this involuntary impersonation.

He'd surely find a way somehow to dodge this nightmare complication. But he'd have to have time to think.

He said lamely, 'Of course it's all right with me if Lianna approves.'

'Then it's settled,' said Arn Abbas. 'It's short notice but the star-kings can get here in time for the ceremony. Bodmer and I will frame the announcement now.'

That was a dismissal, and they left the room. Gordon was glad that Jhal Arn came with them, for the last thing he wanted at this moment was to face Lianna's clear, questioning eyes.

The next few days seemed utterly unreal to Gordon. All the palace, all the city Throon, hummed with activity of preparations. Hosts of servants were busy, and each day swift star-ships arrived with guests from the more distant parts of the Empire and the allied kingdoms.

Gordon was at least relieved that he hardly saw Lianna in this hectic time except at the magnificent feasts that celebrated the coming event. Nor had he seen Murn, except at a distance. But time was running out and he had not found any way out of this fantastic impasse.

He couldn't tell them the truth about himself. That would break his solemn promise to Zarth Arn. But then what was he to do? He racked his brain, but on the eve of the appointed day he still had found no solution.

That night in the Hall of Stars was held the great reception for the royal and noble guests who had come from far across the galaxy for the wedding. The scene was one of staggering splendor.

Gordon and Lianna stood on the raised reception-dais, with Arn Abbas' giant figure on one side of them and Jhal Arn and his beautiful wife Zora on the other. Behind them were Commander Corbulo and Orth Bodmer and the other highest officials of the Empire.

The brilliant throng whom chamberlains announced as they streamed toward the dais, the majestic magnificence of the Hall of Stars, the televisor screens through which he knew half the galaxy was watching – all this numbed John Gordon.

He felt more and more like a man in a strange and impossible dream. Surely he would wake up at any moment and find himself back in his own 20th Century world?

'The King of the Cygnus Suns!' rang the chamberlain's measured announcements. 'The King of Lyra!'

They streamed before Gordon in a blurred succession of faces and voices. He recognized but few of them – the cold-eyed Zu Rizal of the Hercules Barons, young Sath Shamar of Polaris, one or two others.

'The King-Regent of Cassiopeia! The Counts of the Marches of Outer Space!'

Lesser luminaries and officials of the Empire continued the procession to the dais. Among these last came a bronzed naval captain who offered Gordon a thought-spool as he bowed.

'A small petition from my squadron to your highness on this happy occasion,' the officer murmured. 'We hope that you will listen to it.'

Gordon nodded. 'I will, captain—'

He was suddenly interrupted by Commander Corbulo. The grizzled naval chief had been staring at the bronzed officer's insignia and he suddenly pushed forward.

'No officer of that squadron should be nearer here than Vega right now!' snapped Corbulo. 'What is your name and division-number?'

The bronzed captain looked suddenly gray and haggard. He recoiled, his hand darting into his jacket.

'That man's a spy, perhaps an assassin!' yelled Corbulo. 'Blast him!'

The detected spy already had a short, stubby atom-pistol flashing in his hand.

Gordon swept Lianna swiftly behind him. He whirled back then toward the other.

But, at Corbulo's shouted command, from secret apertures high in the walls of the Hall of Stars had flicked down swift atom-pellets that tore into the spy's body and instantly exploded. The man fell to the floor, a torn, blackened corpse.

Screams rent the air, as the crowd recoiled in sudden panic. Gordon was as stunned as everyone else in the Hall by what had happened.

But Arn Abbas' rumbling roar rose quickly to dominate the scene. 'There is nothing to fear! The man is dead, thanks to Corbulo's vigilance and our guards inside the walls!'

The big ruler shot orders. 'Take the body into another room. Zarth, you and Jhal come along. Corbulo, have that thought-spool ray-searched, it may be dangerous. Lianna, will you reassure our guests?'

Gordon went with the giant emperor into another, smaller room where the blasted body of the spy was quickly carried.

Jhal Arn bent over the body, ripped away the scorched jacket. The mangled torso was not bronze in color like the face. It was a curiously pallid white.

'A Cloud-man! A League spy, as I thought!' snapped Arn Abbas. 'One of Shorr Kan's agents in clever disguise!'

Jhal Arn looked puzzled. 'Why did he come here? He wasn't primarily trying to assassinate any of us – he didn't draw his weapon until he was detected.'

'The thought-spool he was trying to give Zarth may tell us something,' muttered the ruler. 'Here's Corbulo.'

Commander Corbulo had the thought-spool in his hand. 'It's been thoroughly ray-examined and is a simple thought-spool and nothing more,' he reported.

'It's cursed strange!' rumbled Arn Abbas, his face dark. 'Here, put the spool in this reader and we'll listen to it.'

The thought-spool was inserted in the reading-mechanism on the desk. Arn Abbas flicked the switch.

The spool started unwinding. Gordon felt the impact of its recorded, amplified thought-pulsations beating into his mind as into the minds of the others.

A clear, resonant voice seemed speaking in his mind as he listened.

'Shorr Kan to the Prince Zarth Arn. It is unfortunate that the arrangements we agreed on for bringing you to the Cloud were thwarted by the chance interference of an Empire patrol. I regret this as much as you do. But rest assured that I will make new arrangements at once for getting you here in safety and secrecy.

'The terms upon which we agreed still stand. As soon as you join forces with me and impart to us the secret of the Disruptor, we of the Cloud will be able to attack the Empire without fear of defeat and you will be publicly recognized as my co-equal in ruling the entire galaxy. Make no move that might arouse suspicion, but wait until my trusted agents are able to bring you safely to me.'

9

In the Palace Prison

To Gordon, at first, that thought-message did not make sense. A message from Shorr Kan to him, to Zarth Arn?

Then as the significance of it sank in, he felt a shock of bewilderment and dismay. And his dismay deepened as he encountered the raging eyes of Arn Abbas.

'By Heaven, my own son a traitor to the Empire!' cried the ruler. 'My own son intriguing secretly to betray us to the Cloud!'

Gordon found his voice. 'This message is a lie! I never made any arrangements with Shorr Kan, nor had any discussions with him!'

'Then why would he send you such a secret message as this!' roared the emperor.

Gordon caught desperately at the only explanation that suggested itself to him.

'Shorr Kan must have sent this message hoping it would be discovered and make trouble! There can be no other reason.'

Jhal Arn, whose handsome face was deeply troubled, spoke quickly.

'Father, that sounds possible enough. It's impossible to believe that Zarth could be a traitor.'

'Bah, it's too thin!' raged Arn Abbas. 'Shorr Kan is too clever to devise such a harebrained plan that would gain him so little. Why, his spy was only detected at all by the mere chance of Corbulo noticing his naval insignia.'

His massive face darkened. 'Zarth, if you *have* been secretly plotting with the Cloud, the fact that you're my son won't save you!'

'I swear I haven't!' Gordon cried. 'I didn't arrange with those League raiders to come to Earth for me. And why in the world should I betray the Empire?'

'You're my second son,' Arn Abbas reminded grimly. 'You may have secretly envied Jhal the succession, all the time you pretended to be absorbed in your scientific studies. Such things have happened!'

If his position had seemed nightmare to John Gordon before, it seemed doubly nightmare now.

'This thing is going to be sifted to the bottom!' roared Am Abbas. 'In the meantime, you'll remain locked up in the palace prison!'

Jhal Arn protested. 'You can't send Zarth down there!'

Commander Corbulo supported the protest. 'At least for appearance's sake, confine Prince Zarth to his own quarters.'

Arn Abbas glared at them. 'Have you two lost your wits? Don't you realize that if Zarth *is* a traitor, he represents mortal danger to the Empire?

'He knows the secret of the Disruptor, that only Jhal and I beside him know! Let Shorr Kan get that secret, and the Cloud will strike like lightning! Do you want to take a chance of that?'

'But the wedding tomorrow, the guests –' Jhal began.

'Announce that Prince Zarth was suddenly taken ill,' snapped the ruler. 'Corbulo, you take him down to the prison. And you're responsible for him with your life!'

Gordon's thoughts were whirling wildly. Suppose he told them the truth, the *real* truth? Suppose he told them that he was only Zarth Arn in physical body and was really John Gordon of the 20th Century? Surely Zarth Arn couldn't blame him for breaking his pledge of secrecy *now?*

But would they believe if he told? He knew that they wouldn't. No one would believe that incredible story. Zarth Arn had kept his method of mind-exchange secret, and no one even dreamed of its possibility. They'd think he was merely trying a desperate, wild lie to save himself.

Gordon's shoulders sagged. He made no further protest but dully went with Commander Corbulo out of the room.

On the corridor motowalk that bore them downward to the lower levels of the palace, Corbulo spoke to him bluntly.

'Zarth, I don't believe a word of all this talk of treachery on your part. I have to lock you up, but you can depend on me to do everything I can to clear you.'

The unexpected support from the veteran officer pulled Gordon a little out of his stunned despair.

'Corbulo, I swear the whole thing is some kind of frame-up! Surely my father can't believe I'd really betray the Empire?'

'You know as well as I what a violent temper Arn Abbas has,' said the Commander. 'But as soon as he cools off, I'll make him listen to reason.'

Deep down beneath the great palace they came to a massive metal door. Corbulo flashed a tiny beam from a heavy ring on his finger, into a needle-hole in the door. It slid aside and revealed a square, bare little metal room.

'This is a cell of your father's secret prison, Zarth. I never thought I'd be locking you in here. But don't worry – we'll do our best to change Arn Abbas' mind.'

Gordon gripped his hand gratefully, and entered the room. The massive door slid shut.

The room had only a cot with a thin pad for furniture. There were two taps in the wall, one for water and the other for nutritional fluid. Walls, floor and ceiling were of solid metal.

Gordon sat down heavily. At first, he felt a little cheered by Corbulo's assurance of support. But then his hope faded. Even if Corbulo and Jhal believed in him, how could they prove his innocence?

And, the thought forced into his mind, what if he really *was* guilty of treachery? What if Zarth Arn, the real Zarth Arn, had in the past been intriguing with Shorr Kan?

Gordon shook his head. 'No, I can't believe that! Zarth Arn was a scientific enthusiast, not a schemer. And if he'd been plotting with the Cloud, he'd not have exchanged minds with me.'

But if Zarth Arn had been innocent of intrigue, why had Shorr Kan sent him that message referring to their past discussions?

Gordon gave it up. 'I'm just out of my depth. I should have known that my ignorance would get me into some disaster if I tried to play Zarth's part!'

He thought miserably of Lianna. They'd have to tell her what had happened, even if they kept it concealed from everyone else.

Would she too think him a traitor? That possibility stung Gordon to despair.

He was for a time in a fever of self-torment, but finally a despairing apathy succeeded it. After hours, he slept.

Gordon estimated it was evening of the next day when he awoke. The door opening had aroused him. He stood up, and then stared incredulously at the two figures entering.

One was Corbulo's stocky form. But the other, the slimmer figure in dark jacket and slacks –

'Lianna!' Gordon exclaimed. 'What are you doing down here?'

She came toward him, her face pale but her gray eyes alight as she put her small hands on his shoulders. Her words came in a rush.

'Zarth, they told me all about your father's accusation. Arn Abbas must be mad!'

His eyes hungrily searched her face. 'You don't believe I'm a traitor, Lianna?'

'I *know* you are not!' she exclaimed. 'I told Arn Abbas so, but he was too angry to listen to me.'

Gordon felt a wave of sharp emotion. 'Lianna, I think it was what you might believe that tortured me most!'

Corbulo came forward, his grizzled face grave. 'You must talk quickly, princess! We must be out of here with Zarth Arn in twenty minutes, to keep my schedule.'

'Out of here with *me?*' Gordon repeated. 'You mean you're going to let me leave here?'

Corbulo nodded curtly. 'Yes, Zarth, I made up my mind and told the princess this evening. I'm going to help you escape from Throon.'

Gordon warmed to this hard-faced Commander. 'Corbulo, I appreciate your faith in me. But it would look like running away.'

'Zarth, you have to go!' Corbulo told him earnestly. 'I thought I could bring your father around. But unfortunately, in your apartments were discovered other incriminating messages to you from Shorr Kan!'

Gordon was stupefied. 'Then they're fakes, planted there on purpose to incriminate me!'

'I believe that, but they've deepened your father's raging belief in your guilt,' Corbulo declared. 'I fear that in his present anger, he may order you executed as a traitor!'

The Commander added, 'I'm not going to let him do that and then regret it later when you're proved innocent. So you must get away from Throon until I can prove your innocence!'

Lianna added eagerly, 'We have it all planned, Zarth. Corbulo has a light naval cruiser with trusted officers waiting at the spaceport. That ship will take us up to my Fomalhaut Kingdom. We'll be safe there until Corbulo and your brother can prove you're not guilty.'

Gordon was more deeply astonished. 'You say – *we?* Lianna, you'd go with me, a fugitive? Why?'

For answer, firm, warm arms went around his neck and soft lips pressed his in quivering, sweet contact.

Her voice was a husky whisper. 'That is why, Zarth.'

Gordon's mind whirled. 'You mean that you love me? Lianna, is it true?'

'I have, since the night of the Feast of Moons when you kissed me,' she whispered. 'Until then, I had liked you but that was all. But since then, you've been somehow different.'

Gordon's arms tightened around her 'Then it's the different Zarth Arn, the new Zarth Arn, you love?'

She looked up at him steadily. 'I have just told you so.'

There deep in the secret prison beneath the great palace of Throon, Gordon felt a wild, soaring joy that blotted from his mind all consciousness of the deadly web of peril and intrigue in which he was caught.

It was he himself, even though in a stranger's physical body, who had won Lianna's love! Though she might never know it, it was not Zarth Arn she loved but John Gordon!

10

Flight into the Void

The secret of his identity trembled on Gordon's lips. He wanted with all his soul to tell Lianna that he was Zarth Arn only in physical body, that he was really John Gordon of the past.

He couldn't do it, he had to keep his pledge to Zarth Arn. And after all, what good would it do to tell her when he had to leave her eventually and go back to his own time?

Could any self-devised torment be more damnable? To be forced to separate himself by half a universe and two thousand centuries of time from the only girl he had ever really loved?

Gordon spoke huskily. 'Lianna, you must not go with me. It's too dangerous.'

She looked up quickly with brilliant eyes. 'Does a daughter of star-kings fear danger? No, Zarth, we go together!'

She added, 'Don't you see, your father won't be able to send after you by force when you're with me in my little Fomalhaut Kingdom. The Empire needs allies too much to estrange my people thus.'

Gordon's mind raced. Here might be his chance to get to Earth! Once away from Throon, he might by some pretext get Corbulo's men to take them first to Earth and the laboratory there.

There, he could manage to re-effect the mind-exchange with the real Zarth Arn without letting Lianna know what he was doing. And the real Zarth, on returning, could surely prove his innocence.

Corbulo interrupted by coming up to them. His hard face was deeply worried.

'We cannot wait longer here! The corridors will be clear now, and it is our only chance to go.'

Disregarding Gordon's protests against her accompanying him, Lianna seized his wrist and tugged him forward.

Corbulo had opened the massive sliding door. The corridors outside were softly lighted, silent, deserted.

'We go to a little-used branch of the tubeway,' Corbulo told them hastily. 'One of my most trusted officers is waiting there.'

They hurried along the corridors, deep beneath the mighty palace of Throon. Not a sound came from the mammoth structure over their heads. These secret passages were soundproofed.

Nor did they meet anyone. But as they emerged into a wider corridor, Corbulo led the way with caution. Finally they stepped into a small room that was a vestibule to one of the tubeways. A car was waiting in the tube, and a man in naval uniform waited beside it.

'This is Thern Eldred, captain of the cruiser that will take you to Fomalhaut Kingdom,' Corbulo said quickly. 'You can trust him absolutely.'

Thern Eldred was a tall Sirian, the faintly greenish hue of his face gave evidence. He looked a hard-bitten, rangy veteran of space, but his curt face lighted as he bowed deeply to Gordon and Lianna.

'Prince Zarth, Princess – I am honored by this trust! The Commander has explained everything to me. You can rely on me and my men to get you to any part of the galaxy!'

Gordon hesitated, troubled. 'It still seems like running away.'

Corbulo swore a spaceman's oath. 'Zarth, it's your only chance! With you gone, I'll have time to dig out evidence of your innocence and bring your father around. Stay here, and he's likely to have you shot as a traitor.'

Gordon might have stayed despite that danger had it not been for the potent factor which was wholly unknown to these others – the fact that this was his only chance to get to Earth and make contact with the real Zarth Arn.

He gripped Corbulo's hand. And Lianna softly told the bluff Commander, 'You're risking much for us. I shall never forget.'

They stepped into the car. Thern Eldred hastily followed them in and touched a lever. The car started racing headlong through the darkness.

Thern Eldred glanced tensely at his watch. 'Everything has been scheduled to the minute, highness,' he told Gordon. 'My cruiser, the *Markab*, is waiting in a secluded dock at the spaceport. Ostensibly we take off to join the Sagittarius patrol.'

'You're risking your neck for us too, captain,' Gordon said earnestly.

The Sirian smiled. 'Commander Corbulo has been like a father to me. I could not refuse the trust when he asked me and my men.'

The car slowed and halted beside another little vestibule in which two naval officers armed with atom-pistols were waiting.

They saluted sharply as Gordon and Lianna stepped out. Thern Eldred quickly followed and led the way up a gliding ramp.

'Now muffle your cloaks about your faces until we get aboard the *Markab*,' he told them. 'After that, you need fear nothing.'

They emerged onto a corner of the spaceport. It was night, two golden moons strung across the blazing starry sky, casting down a warm light in which the massive ships, cranes and machines glinted dully.

Towering from the docks, dwarfing all else, loomed the black bulks of the mighty first-line battleships. As they followed Thern Eldred along the side of one, Gordon glimpsed the portentous muzzles of its heavy atom-gun batteries silhouetted against the stars.

The Sirian made a signal and held them suddenly back, as a troop of noisy sailors swaggered past. Standing there in the dark, Gordon felt the pressure of Lianna's fingers on his hand. Her face, in the dim light, smiled at him undauntedly.

Then Thern Eldred motioned them on. 'We must hurry!' he sweated. 'We're behind schedule—'

The black, fishlike mass of the *Markab* rose before them in the golden moonlight. Lights glittered from small portholes, and there was a steady throbbing of power from the stern of the light cruiser.

They followed the Sirian and his two officers up a narrow gangway toward a waiting open door in the side of the ship. But suddenly, the silence was violently broken.

Annunciators about the spaceport screamed a loud siren alarm. Then a man's hoarse, excited voice shouted from the speakers.

'General alarm to all naval personnel!' yelled that wild voice. 'Arn Abbas has just been assassinated!'

Gordon froze, wildly clutching Lianna's hand as they stopped there on the gangway.

The voice was shouting on. 'Apprehend Prince Zarth Arn wherever he is encountered! He is to be arrested immediately!'

'Good God!' cried Gordon. 'Arn Abbas murdered – and they think I escaped and did it!'

The whole great spaceport was waking to the alarm, the voice shouting its wild message over and over from a hundred annunciators. Bells were ringing, men yelling and running.

Far southward, over the distant towers of the city Throon, gleaming fliers were rushing up in the night sky and racing wildly across the heavens in half a dozen different directions.

Thern Eldred tried to urge the frozen Gordon and Lianna up the gangway. 'You must hurry, highness!' cried the Sirian. 'Your only chance is to get away at once!'

'Run away and let them think I murdered Arn Abbas?' cried Gordon. 'No! We're going back to the palace at once!'

Lianna, her face pale, swiftly supported him. 'You must return. Arn Abbas' murder will shake the whole Empire!'

Gordon had turned with her to start back down the gangway. But Thern Eldred, his green face wearing a hard, taut expression, suddenly whipped out and extended a little glass weapon.

It was a short glass rod on whose end was mounted a glass crescent that had two metal tips. He darted it toward Gordon's face.

'Zarth, it's a paralyzer! Look out!' cried Lianna, who recognized the menace of the weapon where Gordon did not.*

The tips of the glass crescent touched Gordon's chin. Lightning seemed to crash through his brain with a paralyzing shock.

He felt himself falling, every muscle frozen, consciousness leaving him. He had a dim sensation of Lianna's voice, of her staggering against him.

There was only darkness in Gordon's mind then. In that darkness he seemed to float for ages before finally light began to dawn.

He became aware that his body was tingling painfully with returning life. He was lying on a hard, flat surface. There was a steady, loud droning sound in his ears.

Gordon painfully opened his eyes. He lay on a bunk in a little metal cabin, a tiny lighted room with little furniture.

Lianna, her face colorless and her eyes closed, lay in another bunk. There was a little porthole window from which he saw a sky of blazing stars. Then Gordon recognized the droning sound as the throb of a star-ship's powerful atomic turbines and drive-generators.

'Good God, we're in space!' he thought. 'Thern Eldred stunned us and brought us—'

They were in the *Markab*, and from the high drone of its drive the light cruiser was hurtling through the galactic void at its utmost speed.

Lianna was stirring. Gordon stumbled to his feet and went to her side. He chafed her wrists and face till her eyes opened.

The girl instantly became aware of their situation, with her first glance. Remembrance came back to her.

'Your father murdered!' she cried to Gordon. 'And they think you did it, back at Throon!'

Gordon nodded sickly. 'We've got to go back. We've got to make Thern Eldred take us back.'

Gordon stumbled to the door of the cabin. It would not slide open when he tried it. They were locked in.

Lianna's voice turned him around. The girl was at the porthole, looking out. She turned a very pale face.

'Zarth, come here!'

He went to her side. Their cabin was near the bows of the cruiser, and the curve of the wall allowed them to look almost straight forward into the vault of stars into which the *Markab* was racing.

'They're not taking us toward Fomalhaut Kingdom!' Lianna exclaimed. 'Thern Eldred has betrayed us!'

* A paralyzer was a weapon designed to stun an opponent when at close quarters. It did so by releasing a brief high-voltage electroshock that travelled through the nerves to the brain.

Gordon stared into the blazing jungle of stars that spread across the sky ahead.

'What's the meaning of this? Where is Thern Eldred taking us?' Gordon asked.

'Look to the west of Orion Nebula, in the distance ahead of us!' Lianna exclaimed.

Gordon looked as she pointed through the round window.* He saw, far away in the starry wilderness ahead of their racing ship, a black little blot in the heavens. A dark, brooding blotch that seemed to have devoured a section of the starry firmament.

He knew instantly what it was. The Cloud! The distant, mysterious realm of semi-darkness within which lay the stars and planets of that League of the Dark Worlds of which Shorr Kan was master, and that was hatching war and conquest for the rest of the galaxy.

'They're taking us to the Cloud!' Lianna cried. 'Zarth, this is Shorr Kan's plot!'

* The 'windows' of a star-ship were not simple windows, but vision-screens operating by sub-spectrum rays far faster than light. So that even when a ship was moving faster than the rays of light, these windows gave a true picture of surrounding space.

11

Galactic Plot

The truth flashed over Gordon's mind. All that had happened to him since he had taken up the impersonation of Zarth Arn had been instigated by the cunning scheming of that master plotter who ruled the Cloud.

Shorr Kan's plots had reached out to involve him in gathering conflict between the giant galactic confederations, through many secret agents. And one of those agents of the powerful master of the Dark Worlds must be Thern Eldred!

'By Heaven, I see it now!' Gordon exclaimed, to the stunned girl. 'Thern Eldred is working for the Cloud, and has betrayed Commander Corbulo!'

'But why should they do this, Zarth? Why implicate you in the murder of your own father?'

'To compromise me hopelessly so that I can't return to Throon!' gritted Gordon.

Lianna had paled slightly. She looked up at him steadily, though.

'What is going to happen to us in the Cloud, Zarth?' she asked.

Gordon felt an agony of apprehension for her. It was his fault that she was in this deadly danger. She had been trying to help him, and had incurred this peril.

'Lianna, I knew you shouldn't have come with me! If anything happens to you—'

He stopped and swung around, as the door slid open. Thern Eldred stood there.

At sight of the tall Sirian standing and regarding them with a cynical smile on his pale green face, Gordon started forward in an access of hot rage.

Thern Eldred quickly drew one of the little glass weapons from his jacket.

'Please note this paralyzer in my hand,' he advised dryly. 'Unless you want to spend more time unconscious, you'll restrain yourself.'

'You traitor!' raged Gordon. 'You've betrayed your uniform, your Empire!'

Thern Eldred nodded calmly. 'I've been one of Shorr Kan's most trusted agents for years. I expect to receive his warmest commendations when we reach Thallarna.'

'Thallarna? The mysterious capital of the League?' said Lianna. 'Then we are going to the Cloud?'

The Sirian nodded again. 'We'll reach it in four days. Luckily, knowing the patrol-schedules of the Empire fleet as I do, I am able to follow a course that will prevent unpleasant encounters.'

'Then Arn Abbas was murdered by you League spies!' Gordon accused harshly. 'You *knew* it was going to happen! That's why you were in such a hurry to get us away!'

The Sirian smiled coolly. 'Of course. I was working on a schedule of split-seconds. It had to look as though you had murdered your father and then fled. We just pulled it off.'

Gordon raged. 'By heaven, you're not to the Cloud yet! Corbulo knows I didn't commit that murder! He'll put two and two together and be out to track you down!'

Thern Eldred stared at him, then threw back his head in a roar of laughter. He laughed until he had to wipe his eyes.

'Your pardon, Prince Zarth, but that's the funniest thing you've said yet!' he chuckled. 'Corbulo after me? Why, haven't you guessed yet that Corbulo himself planned this whole thing?'

'You're mad!' Gordon exclaimed. 'Corbulo is the most trusted official in the Empire!'

Thern Eldred nodded. 'Yes, but *only* an official, only Commander of the fleet. And he has ambitions beyond that post, has had them a long time. For the last few years, he and a score of others of us officers have been working secretly for Shorr Kan.'

The Sirian's eyes gleamed. 'Shorr Kan has promised that when the Empire is shattered, we shall each of us have a star-kingdom of our own to rule. And Corbulo is to have the biggest.'

Gordon's angry incredulity somehow faded a little, before the ring of truth in the Sirian's voice.

Horrified, Gordon realized that it might be true! Chan Corbulo, Commander of the Empire's great navy, might be a secret traitor for all he knew.

Evidence pointing that way rose swiftly in Gordon's mind. Why else had Corbulo broken his duty and helped him to escape? Why, at the very moment when Arn Abbas' assassination was imminent?

Thern Eldred read something of what passed in Gordon's mind, from his face. And the Sirian laughed again.

'You begin to realize now what a dupe you've been. Why, it was Corbulo himself who shot down Arn Abbas last night! And Corbulo will swear that he saw it done by *you*, Zarth Arn!'

Lianna was pale, incredulous. 'But why? Why implicate Zarth?'

'Because,' smiled the Sirian, 'it's the most effective way to split the Empire and leave it wide open to the Cloud's attack. And there's another reason that Shorr Kan will explain to you.'

The malice and triumph in Thern Eldred's eyes detonated the rage that gathered in John Gordon's mind.

He plunged forward, heedless of Thern Eldred's warning shout. He managed by a swift contortion of his body to avoid the glass paralyzer that the other jabbed at him. His fist smashed into the Sirian's face.

Thern Eldred, as he sprawled backward, had Gordon atop him like a leaping panther. But the Sirian had managed to cling to his weapon. And before Gordon could carry out his intention of wrestling it away, Thern Eldred desperately jabbed up with it again.

The crescent at the end of the glass rod touched Gordon's neck. A freezing shock smote like lightning through his body. He felt his senses darken swiftly.

When Gordon for a second time came back to consciousness, he was again lying in one of the bunks. This time, the freezing ache in his body was more painful. And this time, Lianna was sitting beside him and looking down at him with anxious gray eyes.

Her eyes lighted as he opened his own. 'Zarth, you've been unconscious more than a day! I was beginning to worry.'

'I'm – all right,' he muttered. He tried to sit up, but her little hands quickly forced him back down onto the pad.

'Don't, Zarth – you must rest until your nerves recover from the electroshock.'

He glanced at the porthole window. The vista of blazing stars outside seemed unchanged. He could glimpse the black blot of the Cloud, looking only a little larger in the distant forest of suns.

Lianna followed his glance. 'We are travelling at tremendous speed but it will still require a few days before we reach the Cloud. In that time, we may encounter an Empire patrol.'

Gordon groaned. 'Lianna, there's no hope for that. This is itself an Empire cruiser and could pass any patrol. And if Corbulo is really leader of this treachery, he'd have his patrols arranged so that this ship could pass unseen.'

'I've thought and thought about it and I still can hardly believe it,' Lianna said. 'Corbulo a traitor! It seems fantastic! And yet—'

Gordon himself no longer doubted. The evidence was too overwhelming.

'Men will betray any trust when ambition drives them, and Corbulo is ambitious,' he muttered. Then, as deeper realization came to him, 'Good God, this means that if the League does attack the Empire, the Commander of the Empire forces will sabotage their defense!'

He rose painfully from the bunk despite Lianna's protestations.

'If we could only get word back to Throon somehow! That would at least put Jhal Arn on his guard!'

Lianna shook her ash-golden head a little sadly. 'I fear there's no chance of that, once we're prisoners in the Cloud. Shorr Kan is not likely to let us go.'

It all spun in John Gordon's mind in a bewildering chaos of known and unknown factors, in the hours that followed.

A few things, though, stood out clearly. They all, everyone in this universe, thought that he was Zarth Arn. And thus it was believed that he knew the secret of the Disruptor, that mysterious scientific weapon known only to Arn Abbas and his two sons.

That was why Corbulo had risked the plot that was sending him and Lianna now as prisoners to the Cloud! Once Shorr Kan had that secret, mysterious weapon, he would have nothing to fear from the Empire whose fleet was commanded by his own man. He would attack them at once!

The *Markab* droned on and on. When the ship bells signalled evening of the arbitrary 'day,' the aspect of the starry firmament had changed. Orion Nebula flamed, now in all its titan glory far in the east.

Straight ahead, far in the distance against the remotest suns of the galaxy, brooded the black blot of the Cloud. It was visibly larger than before, and its gigantic dimensions were now becoming more clearly apparent.

Neither Thern Eldred nor any of his officers or men entered the cabin. There was no opportunity for a second attack. And after searching vainly through the room, Gordon conceded defeatedly that there was nothing in it that might facilitate escape.

Sick anxiety for Lianna's safety deepened in him. He reproached himself again for letting her accompany him on this flight.

But she did not seem afraid as she looked up at him. 'Zarth, at least we're together for a little while. It may be all of happiness we'll get.'

Gordon found his arms instinctively starting to go around her, his hand touching her shining hair. But he forced himself to step back.

'Lianna, you'd better get some sleep,' he said uncomfortably.

Lianna, looked at him with a wondering little smile. 'Why, Zarth, what's the matter?'

Gordon had never in his life wanted anything so much as to reach forth to her. But to do so would be the blackest treachery.

Treachery to Zarth Arn, who had trusted his body, his life, to Gordon's pledge! Yes, and treachery to Lianna herself.

For if he were able to reach the Earth laboratory, it would be the real Zarth Arn who would come back to her – Zarth Arn, who loved Murn and not Lianna.

'That won't ever happen!' whispered a subtle, tempting voice in Gordon's mind. 'You and she will never escape from the Cloud. Take what happiness you can, while you can!'

Gordon desperately fought down that insinuating voice. He spoke huskily to the puzzled girl.

'Lianna, you and I will have to forget all talk of love.'

She seemed stricken by amazement, unbelief. 'But Zarth, at Throon that morning you told me you loved me!'

Gordon nodded miserably. 'I know. I wish to God I hadn't. It was wrong.'

Little clouds began to gather in Lianna's gray eyes. She was white to the lips. 'You mean that you are still in love with Murn, after all?'

Gordon forced the answer to that out of strained, desperate resolve. He spoke what he knew was the exact truth.

'Zarth Arn does still love Murn. You have to know that, Lianna.'

The incredulity in Lianna's white face gave way to a hurt that went deep in her gray eyes.

Gordon had expected stormy resentment, wrath, bitter reproach. He had steeled himself against them. But he had not expected this deep, voiceless hurt, and it was too much for him.

'To the devil with my promise!' he told himself fiercely. 'Zarth Arn wouldn't hold me to it if he knew that situation – he couldn't!'

And Gordon stepped forward and grasped the girl's hand. 'Lianna, I'm going to tell you the whole truth! Zarth Arn doesn't love you – but *I* do!'

He rushed on. 'I'm not Zarth Arn. I'm an entirely different man, in Zarth Arn's body. I know it sounds incredible, but—'

His voice trailed off. For he read in Lianna's face her quick disbelief and scorn.

'Let us at least have no more lies, Zarth!' she flared.

'I tell you, it's true!' he persisted. 'This is Zarth Arn's physical body, yes. But I am a different man!'

He knew from the expression on her face that his attempt had failed. He knew that she did not believe and never would believe.

How could he expect her to believe it? If positions had been reversed, would he have credited such a wild assertion? He knew he wouldn't.

No one in this universe would credit it, now Vel Quen was dead. For only Vel Quen had known about Zarth Arn's fantastic experiments.

Lianna was looking at him, her eyes now calm and level and without a trace of emotion in her face.

'There is no need for you to explain your actions by wild stories of dual personality, Zarth. I understand clearly enough. You were simply doing what you conceived to be your duty to the Empire. You feared lest I might refuse the marriage at the last moment, so you pretended love for me to make sure of me and of Fomalhaut's support.'

'Lianna, I swear it isn't so!' Gordon groaned. 'But if you won't trust me to speak truth—'

She ignored his interruption. 'You need not have done it, Zarth. I had no thought of refusing the marriage, since I knew how much depended on my kingdom supporting the Empire.

'But there's no further need for stratagems. I will keep my promise and so will my kingdom. I will marry you, but our marriage will be only a political formality as we first agreed.'

John Gordon started to protest, then stopped. After all, the course she proposed was the only one he could take.

If the real Zarth Arn returned, his marriage with Lianna could not be anything more than political pretense.

'All right, Lianna,' Gordon said heavily. 'I repeat that I never lied to you. But it all doesn't make much difference now, anyway.'

He gestured, as he spoke, toward the porthole. Out there in the star-blazing void ahead of the rushing cruiser, the monster blot of the Cloud was looming ever bigger and closer.

Lianna nodded quietly. 'We do not have much chance of escaping Shorr Kan's clutches. But if a chance does present itself, you will find me your ally. Our personal emotions mean little compared to the urgent necessity of getting back with a warning to the Empire.'

Gordon saw less and less chance of that, in the hours that followed. For now the *Markab*, its velocity at great heights, was rushing ever nearer the Cloud.

That 'night' when the ship lights dimmed, he lay in his bunk thinking bitterly that of all men in history he had had the most ironic joke played upon him.

The girl across the cabin loved him, and he loved her. And yet soon a gulf of space and time incredible might forever separate them, and she would always believe him faithless.

12

In the Cosmic Cloud

Next 'morning' they woke to find that the cloud was colossal now ahead. Its vast blotch loomed across half the firmament, a roiling gloom that reached out angry, ragged arms of shadow like an octopus whose dark tentacles clutched at the whole galaxy.

And the *Markab* now was being companioned through space by four massive black battleships with the black disk of the League of Dark Worlds marked on their bows. They were so close, and maintained so exactly the same speed, they could be clearly seen.

'We might have known that Shorr Kan would send an escort,' Lianna murmured. She glanced at Gordon. 'He thinks that he has the secret of the Disruptor almost in his hands, in your person.'

'Lianna, set your mind at rest on one thing,' Gordon told her. 'He'll never get that secret from me.'

'I know you are not traitor to the Empire,' she said somberly. 'But the League scientists are said to be masters of strange tortures. They may force it from you.'

Gordon laughed shortly. 'They won't. Shorr Kan is going to find that he had made one bad miscalculation.'

Nearer and nearer the five ships flew toward the Cloud. All the universe ahead was now a black, swirling gloom.

Then, keeping to their tight formation, the squadron plunged into the Cloud.

Darkness swept around the ship. Not a total darkness but a gloomy, shadowy haze that seemed smothering after the blazing glory of open space.

Gordon perceived that the cosmic dust that composed the Cloud was not as dense as he had thought. Its huge extent made it appear an impenetrable darkness from outside. But once inside it, they seemed racing through a vast, unbroken haze.

There were stars in here, suns that were visible only a few parsecs away. They shone wanly through the haze, like smothered bale-fires, uncanny witch-stars.

The *Markab* and its escort passed comparatively close to some of these star-systems. Gordon glimpsed planets circling in the feeble glow of the smothered suns, worlds shadowed by perpetual twilight.

Homing on secret radar beams, the ships plunged on and on through the Cloud. Yet it was not until next day that deceleration began.

'We must be pretty nearly there,' Gordon said grimly to the girl.

Lianna nodded, and pointed ahead through the window. Far ahead in the shadowy haze burned a dull red, smoldering sun.

'Thallarna,' she murmured. 'The capital of the League of Dark Worlds, and the citadel of Shorr Kan.'

Gordon's nerves stretched taut as the following hours of rapid deceleration brought them closer to their destination.

Meteor-hail rattled off the ships. They twisted and changed course frequently. The shrilling of meteor-alarms could be heard each few minutes, as jagged boulders rushed upon them and then vanished in the automatic trip-blast of atomic energy from the ship.

Angry green luminescence that had once been called nebulium edged these stormy, denser regions. But each time they emerged into thinner haze, the sullen red sun of Thallarna glowed bigger ahead.

'The star-system of Thallarna was not idly chosen for their capital,' Lianna said. 'Invaders would have a perilous time threading through these stormy mazes to it.'

Gordon felt the sinister aspect of the red sun as the ships swung toward it. Old, smoldering, sullen crimson, it glowed here in the heart of the vast and gloomy Cloud like an evil, watching eye.

And the single planet that circled it, the planet Thallarna itself, was equally somber. Strange white plains and white forests of fungoid appearance covered much of it. An inky ocean dashed its ebon waves, eerily reflecting the bloody light of the red sun.

The warships sank through the atmosphere toward a titan city. It was black and massive, its gigantic, blocklike buildings gathered in harshly geometrical symmetry.

Lianna exclaimed and pointed to the huge rows of docks outside the city. Gordon's incredulous eyes beheld a vast beehive of activity, thousands of grim warships docked in long rows, a great activity of cranes and conveyors and men.

'Shorr Kan's fleet makes ready, indeed!' she said. 'And this is only one of their naval bases here. The League is far stronger than we dreamed!'

Gordon fought a chilling apprehension. 'But Jhal Arn will be calling together all the Empire's forces, too. And he has the Disruptor. If Corbulo can only be prevented from further treachery!'

The ships separated, the four escort battleships remaining above while the *Markab* sank toward a colossal, cubical black pile.

The cruiser landed in a big court. They glimpsed soldiers running toward it – Cloud-men, pallid-faced men in dark uniforms.

It was some minutes before the door of their own cabin opened. Thern Eldred stood in it with two alert League officers.

'We have arrived and I learn that Shorr Kan wishes to see you at once,' the

Sirian traitor told Gordon. 'I beg you to make no resistance, which would be wholly futile and foolish.'

Gordon had had two experiences with the glass paralyzers to convince him of that. He stood, with Lianna's hand on his, and nodded curtly.

'All right. The sooner we get this over with, the better.'

They walked out of the ship, their gravitation-equalizers* preventing them from feeling any difference in gravity. The air was freezing and the depressing quality was increased by the murky gloom that was thickening as the red sun set.

Cold, gloomy, shadowed forever by the haze, this world at the heart of the Cloud struck Gordon as a fitting place for the hatching of a plot to rend the galaxy.

'This is Durk Undis, a high officer of the League,' the Sirian was saying, 'The Prince Zarth Arn and the Princess Lianna, Durk.'

Durk Undis, the League officer, was a young man. But though he was not unhandsome, his pallid face and deep eyes had a look of fanaticism in them.

He bowed to Gordon and the girl, and gestured toward a doorway.

'Our Commander is waiting,' he said clippedly.

Gordon saw the gleam of triumph in his eye, and in the faces of the other rigid Cloud-men they passed.

He knew they must be exultant at this capture of one of the Empire's royal family and the striking down of mighty Arn Abbas.

'This ramp, please,' Durk Undis said, as they entered the building. He could not help adding proudly to Gordon, 'You are doubtless surprised at our capital? We have no useless luxuries here.'

Spartan simplicity, an austere bareness, reigned in the gloomy halls of the great building. Here there was none indeed of the luxury and splendor of the great palace at Throon. Uniforms were everywhere. This was the center of a military empire.

They came to a massive door guarded by a file of stalwart, uniformed Cloud-men armed with atom-guns. These stepped aside, and the door opened.

Durk Undis and the Sirian walked on either side of Gordon and Lianna into a forbidding room.

It was even more austere than the rest of the place. A single desk with its row of visors and screens, a hard, uncushioned chair, a window looking out on the black massiveness of Thallarna – these were all.

The man behind the desk rose. He was tall, broad-shouldered, about forty years of age. His black hair was close-clipped, his strong, pallid face sternly set, and his black eyes harsh and keen.

* The gravitation-equalizers were marvelously compact projectors worn in a tiny belt-case by everyone, in this star-travelling age. They automatically gave the body a positive or negative magnetic-gravitational charge that made weight the same no matter how large or small a world was visited.

'Shorr Kan, Commander of the League of the Dark Worlds!' intoned Durk Undis, with fanatic intensity. And then, 'These are the prisoners, sir!'

Shorr Kan's stern gaze fastened on Gordon's face, and then briefly on Lianna's.

He spoke in clipped tones to the Sirian. 'You have done well, Thern Eldred. You and Chan Corbulo have proved your devotion to the great cause of the League, and you will not find it ungrateful.'

He went on, 'You had better take your cruiser back at once to the Empire and rejoin your fleet lest suspicion fall on you.'

Thern Eldred nodded quickly. 'That will be wisest, sir. I shall be ready to execute any orders you send through Corbulo.'

Shorr Kan added, 'You can go too, Durk. I shall question our two unwilling guests now.'

Durk Undis looked worried. 'Leave them here with you alone, sir? It is true they have no weapons, but—'

Shorr Kan turned a stern face on the young fanatic. 'Do you think I stand in any danger from this flabby Empire princeling? And even if there were danger, do you think I would shrink from it if it was required by our cause?'

His voice deepened. 'Will not millions of men soon hazard their lives for that cause, and gladly? Should one of us shrink from any peril when upon our unswerving devotion depends the success of all we have planned?

'And we *will* succeed!' rang his voice. 'We shall take by force our rightful heritage in the galaxy, from the greedy Empire that thought to condemn us to perpetual banishment in these dark worlds! In that great common enterprise, do you believe I think of risks?'

Durk Undis bowed, almost worshipfully, and the Sirian imitated the action. They withdrew from the room.

Gordon had felt an astonishment at Shorr Kan's thundering rhetoric. But now he was further astonished.

For as the door closed, Shorr Kan's stern face and towering figure relaxed. The League commander lounged back in his chair and looked up at Gordon and Lianna with a grin on his dark face.

'How did you like my little speech, Zarth Arn?' he asked. 'I know it must sound pretty silly, but they love that kind of nonsense.'

Gordon could only stare, so amazed was he by the sudden and utter transformation in the personality of Shorr Kan.

'Then you don't believe in any of that stuff yourself?' he demanded.

Shorr Kan laughed. 'Do I look like a complete fool? Only crazy fanatics would swallow it. But fanatics are the mainspring of any enterprise like this, and I have to be the biggest fanatic of all when I'm talking to them.'

He motioned to chairs. 'Sit down. I'd offer you a drink but I don't dare to keep the stuff around here. It might be found and that would destroy the wonderful legend of Shorr Kan's austere life, his devotion to duty, his ceaseless toil for the people of the League.'

He looked at them with calmly cynical, keen black eyes for a moment.

'I know a good bit about you, Zarth Arn. I've made it my business to find out. And I know that while you're a scientific enthusiast rather than a practical man, you're a highly intelligent person. I'm also aware that your fiancee, the Princess Lianna, is not a fool.

'Very well, that makes things a lot easier. I can talk to intelligent people. It's these idiots who let their emotions rule them who have to be handled with high-sounding nonsense about destiny, and duty, and their sacred mission.'

Gordon, his first shock of surprise over, began to understand this ruler whose name shadowed the whole galaxy.

Utterly intelligent, and yet at the same time utterly cynical, ruthless, keen and cold as a sword-blade, was Shorr Kan.

Gordon felt a strange sense of inferiority in strength and shrewdness to this arch-plotter. And that very feeling made his hatred more bitter.

'You expect me to discuss things calmly with you, after having me brought here by force and branded to the galaxy as a parricide?'

Shorr Kan shrugged. 'I admit that that's unpleasant for you. But I had to have you here. You'd have been here days ago, if the men I sent to seize you at your Earth laboratory hadn't failed.'

He shook his dark head ruefully. 'It just shows how chance can upset the cleverest plans. They should have had no trouble bringing you from Earth. Corbulo had given us a complete schedule of the Empire patrols in that sector, so they could be avoided. And then that cursed Antarian captain had to make an unscheduled visit to Sol!'

The cloud-leader concluded. 'So I had to get you here some other way, Prince Zarth. And the best way was to send you an incriminating thought-message that would get you into trouble. Corbulo, of course, had orders to "discover" my messenger, and then later to assist your flight from Throon so his killing of Arn Abbas would be blamed on you!'

Gordon seized on one point in that explanation. 'Then it's true that Chan Corbulo is working for you?'

Shorr Kan grinned. 'I'll wager that was a bad shock to you, wasn't it? Corbulo is pretty cunning. He's mad for power, for a star-kingdom of his own to rule. But he's always concealed that under the bluff, honest spaceman pose that made the whole Empire admire him.'

He added, 'It may assuage your disillusion to learn that only Corbulo and a score of other officials and officers in the Empire are traitors. But they're enough to wreck the Empire fleet's chances when it comes to the showdown.'

Gordon leaned forward tensely. 'And just when is that showdown going to come?'

13

Master of the Cloud

Shorr Kan lounged back in his chair before he answered. 'Zarth Arn, that depends to some extent on whether or not you're willing to cooperate with me.'

Lianna spoke scornfully. 'By "cooperate" you mean, betray the Empire.'

The League commander was not ruffled. 'That's one way of putting it. I'd prefer to define it as simply to become realistic.'

He leaned forward and his strong, mobile face was in deep earnest as he continued.

'I'll put my cards on the table, Zarth. The League of Dark Worlds has secretly built up its fleet here stronger than the Empire navy. We have every weapon of war you have, and a brand new weapon that will play the devil with your fleet when we use it.'

'What kind of a weapon? Sounds like a bluff to me,' commented Gordon.

Shorr Kan grinned. 'You can't fish information out of me. But I will tell you that it's a weapon that can strike down enemy warships from *inside* them.'

He added, 'With that new weapon, with our powerful fleet, and above all with your Commander Corbulo secretly in our pay, your Empire fleet won't have a chance when we attack! We'd have attacked before now if it hadn't been for one thing. And that's the Disruptor.

'Corbulo couldn't tell us about the Disruptor, since only the royal house of the Empire are allowed to know about it. And while the traditions of its awful power may be exaggerated, we know that they are not baseless. For your ancestor Brenn Bir did with the Disruptor somehow completely annihilate the alien Magellanians who invaded the galaxy two thousand years ago.'

Shorr Kan's face tightened. 'You know the secret of that mysterious weapon or power, Zarth. And I want it from you!'

John Gordon had expected no less. But he continued to fence. 'I suppose,' he said ironically, 'that you're going to offer me a star-kingdom if I give you the secret of the Disruptor?'

'More than that,' Shorr Kan said levelly. 'I'm offering you the sovereignty of the whole galaxy!'

Gordon was astonished by the audacity of this man. There was something breathtaking about him.

'We agreed to talk intelligently,' Gordon snapped. 'Do you suppose me stupid enough to believe that after you conquered the Empire and power over the whole galaxy, you'd give it to me?'

Shorr Kan smiled. 'I said nothing about giving you the *power*. I spoke of giving you rule. They are different things.'

He explained rapidly. 'Once the Disruptor secret is mine, I can shatter the Empire and dominate the galaxy. But half the galaxy would still hate me as a usurper, an alien. There would be endless revolts and unrest.

'So, once I've got my hand on everything, I'd put forward Zarth Arn, legitimate son of the late Arn Abbas, as new sovereign of the galaxy! I, Shorr Kan, would merely be your trusted advisor. It would be a peaceful federation of the whole galaxy, I'd announce.'

He grinned again. 'See how much simpler it would make things for me? A legitimate emperor, no revolts, no unrest. You and Lianna would be the rulers, and enjoy every luxury and respect. I don't care for the pomp and outward show of power, and would be quite content to wield the real power from behind the throne.'

'And if I decided to use my position as nominal ruler to turn the tables on you?' Gordon asked curiously.

Shorr Kan laughed. 'You wouldn't, Zarth. The core of the armed forces would be loyal Cloud-men I could trust.'

He stood up 'What do you say? Remember that right now you're a fugitive from the Empire, sought for the murder of your own father. All that can be cleared up, the charge can be disproved, and you can live the greatest sovereign in history. Isn't it intelligent to do so?'

Gordon shrugged. 'Your proposal is certainly clever. But I'm afraid you've wasted your time. The stumbling-block is that under no circumstances will you get the Disruptor secret from me.'

He expected a burst of rage from the League ruler. But Shorr Kan merely looked disappointed.

'I was hoping you'd be clearheaded enough to discount all this nonsense about patriotism and loyalties, and use a little sense.'

Lianna flashed, 'Of course you cannot understand loyalty and honor, when you have none yourself!'

Shorr Kan looked at her frowningly, though still apparently without anger.

'No, I don't have any,' he agreed. 'What, after all, are loyalty, honor, patriotism, all those admirable qualities? Just ideas that people happen to think are praiseworthy, and therefore will die for. I'm a realist. I refuse to injure myself for any mere idea.'

He turned again to Gordon. 'Let's not talk any more about it right now. You're tired, your nerves are taut, you're in no shape to make a decision. Get a good night's rest, and think it over tomorrow – and use your brains, not your emotions. You'll surely see that I'm right.'

He added, more slowly, 'I could tell you that if you persist in refusing to cooperate, there's a highly unpleasant alternative. But I don't want to threaten you, Zarth! I want you to come in with me, not from any love of me or the League, but simply because you're smart enough to recognize your own interests.'

Gordon for the first time glimpsed the steel within the velvet glove, as he saw the glint in Shorr Kan's black eyes.

The League commander had pressed a signal-button as he spoke. The door opened and Durk Undis entered.

'Give Prince Zarth and his fiancee the best possible quarters,' Shorr Kan told the younger Cloud-man. 'They must be strictly guarded, but let the guard be unobtrusive. Any disrespect to them will be severely punished.'

Durk Undis bowed and stood waiting. Gordon took Lianna's arm and silently left the room.

All the way through the corridors and ramps of the gloomy building, Gordon felt that unsettling sense of having met a man who was far stronger than he in shrewdness and cunning, and who might be able to handle him like putty.

This huge citadel of the League of Dark Worlds was a dreary place, by night. The lights that glowed at intervals along its corridors could not dispel the insidious haze that wrapped this world.

The apartment to which they were conducted was far from luxurious. The square, white-walled rooms were strictly utilitarian in design and furniture, with transparent sections of wall looking out over the somber city Thallarna.

Durk Undis bowed stiffly to them. 'You will find nutrition-dispensers and all else needful. Let me warn you not to try venturing out of these rooms. Every exit is strictly guarded.'

When the League officer had gone, John Gordon turned and looked at Lianna, who stood by the window.

Something in the brave erectness of her little figure choked him with tenderness. He went to her side.

'Lianna, if I could assure *your* safety by giving up the secret of the Disruptor, I would,' he said huskily.

She turned quickly. 'You must not give it up! Without it, Shorr Kan still hesitates to move. And while he hesitates, there is a chance that Corbulo's treachery may be discovered.'

'There's little chance of our exposing him, I'm afraid,' Gordon said. 'There's no possibility of escape from here.'

Lianna's slim shoulders sagged a little. 'No, I realize that,' she murmured. 'Even if by some miracle we could escape this building and seize a ship, we could never find our way out through the mazes of the Cloud.'

The Cloud! It was the sky here, dark, heavy and menacing, showing no star as its ebon folds enwrapped this grim city.

That dark sky gave Gordon a feeling of claustrophobia, a sense of all the trillions of miles of shadowy gloom that encompassed him and shut him from the star-bright spaces of the galaxy outside.

Thallarna was not sleeping. Out there in the severely straight streets streamed many heavy vehicles. Fliers came and went in swarms. Thunderous reverberations droned dimly to them from the distant docks where squadrons of heavy warships were constantly coming and going.

Gordon took the couch in the living-room of their austere apartment, without expectation of being able to sleep. But his tired body relaxed in almost drugged slumber in a short time.

Dawn awoke him – a sickly, shadowy dawn that only slowly revealed the outlines of the room. He found Lianna sitting on the edge of his couch, looking down at him with curious intentness.

She flushed slightly. 'I wondered if you were awake. I have our breakfast ready. It is not bad, the nutritional fluid. Though it's likely to become monotonous.'

'I doubt if we will be here long enough to grow tired of it,' Gordon said grimly.

She looked at him. 'You think that Shorr Kan will insist on your giving him the Disruptor secret today?'

'I'm afraid so,' he said. 'If that secret is all that is holding back his attack, he'll want it as soon as possible.'

Through the hours of the gloomy day, as the red sun swept with somber slowness across the shadowy sky, they expected Shorr Kan's summons.

But it was not until night had returned that Durk Undis and four armed soldiers entered the apartment.

The young fanatic Cloud-man again bowed stiffly. 'The commander will see you now, Prince Zarth. Alone,' he added quickly, as Lianna stepped forward with Gordon.

Lianna's eyes flashed. 'I go where Zarth goes!'

'I regret that I must carry out my orders,' said Durk Undis coldly. 'Will you come now, Prince Zarth?'

Lianna apparently realized the hopelessness of further resistance. She stood back.

Gordon hesitated, then let impulse sweep him and strode back to her. He took her face between his hands and kissed her.

'Don't worry, Lianna,' he said, and turned away.

His heart beat painfully as he followed Durk Undis through the corridors. He was certain that he had seen Lianna for the last time.

Maybe better this way! he thought. Maybe better to forget her in death than to go back to his own time and be forever haunted by memory of love irrevocably lost!

Gordon's desperate thoughts received a check when he followed his guards into a room. It was not the austere study of the previous day.

This was a laboratory. There was a table, above which hung a massive metal cone connected by cables to a complicated apparatus of banked, vacuum tubes and moving tapes. Here were two thin, nervous-looking Cloud-men – and Shorr Kan.

Shorr Kan dismissed Durk Undis and the guards, and quickly greeted Gordon.

'You've slept, rested? That's good. Now tell me what you've decided.'

Gordon shrugged. 'There was no decision to make. I can't give you the secret of the Disruptor.'

Shorr Kan's strong face changed slightly in expression, and he spoke after a pause.

'I see. I might have expected it. Old mental habits, old traditions – even intelligence can't conquer them, sometimes.'

His eyes narrowed slightly. 'Now listen, Zarth. I told you yesterday that there was an unpleasant alternative if you refused. I didn't go into details because I wanted to gain your willing cooperation.

'But now you force me to be explicit. So let me assure you first of one thing. I am going to have the Disruptor secret from you, whether you give it willingly or not.'

'Torture, then?' sneered Gordon. 'That is what I expected.'

Shorr Kan made a disgusted gesture. 'Faugh, I don't use torture. It's clumsy and undependable, and alienates even your own followers. No, I have quite another method in mind.'

He gestured to the older of the two nervous-looking men nearby. 'Land Allar, there, is one of our finest psychoscientists. Some years ago he devised a certain apparatus which I've been forced to utilize several times.

'It's a brain-scanner. It literally reads the brain, by scanning the neurones, plotting the synaptic connections, and translating that physical set-up into the knowledge, memories and information possessed by that particular brain. With it, before this night is over, I can have the Disruptor secret right out of your brain.'

'That,' said John Gordon steadily, 'is a rather unclever bluff.'

Shorr Kan shook his dark head. 'I assure you it is not. I can prove it to you if you want me to. Otherwise, you must take my word that the scanner *will* take everything from your brain.'

He went on, 'The trouble is that the impact of the scanning ray on the brain for hour after hour in time breaks down the synaptic connections it scans. The subject emerges from the process a mindless idiot. That is what will happen to you if we use it on you.'

The hair bristled on Gordon's neck. He had not a doubt now that Shorr Kan was speaking the truth. If nothing else, the pale, sick faces of the two scientists proved his assertion.

Weird, fantastic, nightmarishly horrible – yet wholly possible to this latterday science! An instrument that mechanically read the mind, and in reading wrecked it!

'I don't want to use it on you, I repeat,' Shorr Kan was saying earnestly. 'For as I told you, you'd be extremely valuable to me as a puppet emperor after the galaxy is conquered. But if you persist in refusing to tell that secret, I simply have no choice.'

John Gordon felt an insane desire to laugh. This was all too ironic.

'You've got everything so nicely calculated,' he told Shorr Kan. 'But again, you find yourself defeated by pure chance.'

'Just what do you mean?' asked the League ruler, with dangerous softness.

'I mean that I can't tell you the secret of the Disruptor because I don't know it!'

Shorr Kan looked impatient. 'That is a rather childish evasion. Everyone knows that as son of the emperor you would be told all about the Disruptor.'

Gordon nodded. 'Quite true. But I happen not to be the emperor's son. I'm a different man entirely.'

Shorr Kan shrugged. 'We are gaining nothing by all this. Go ahead.'

The last words were addressed to the two scientists. At that moment Gordon savagely leaped for Shorr Kan's throat!

He never reached it. One of the scientists had a glass paralyzer ready, and swiftly jabbed it at the back of his neck.

Gordon sank, shocked and stunned. Only dimly, he felt them lifting him onto the metal table. Through his dimming vision, Shorr Kan's hard face and cool black eyes looked down.

'Your last chance, Zarth! Make but a signal and you can still avoid this fate.'

Gordon felt the hopelessness of it all, even as his raging anger made him glare up at the League commander.

The paralyzer touched him again. This shock was like a physical blow. He just sensed the two scientists busy with the massive metal cone above his head, and then darkness claimed him.

14

Dark-World Menace

Gordon came slowly to awareness of a throbbing headache. All the devil's triphammers seemed to be pounding inside his skull, and he felt a sickening nausea.

A cool glass was held to his lips, and a voice spoke insistently in his ear.

'Drink this!'

Gordon managed to gulp down a pungent liquid. Presently his nausea lessened and his head began to ache less violently.

He lay for a little time before he finally ventured to open his eyes. He still lay on the table, but the mental cone and the complicated apparatus were not now in sight.

Over him was bending the anxious face of one of the two Cloud scientists. Then the strong features and brilliant black eyes of Shorr Kan came down in his field of vision.

'Can you sit up?' asked the scientist. 'It will help you recover faster.'

The man's arm around his shoulders enabled Gordon weakly to slide off the table and into a chair.

Shorr Kan came and stood in front of him, looking down at him with a queer wonder and interest in his expression.

He asked, 'How do you feel now, John Gordon?'

Gordon started. He stared back up at the League commander.

'Then you know?' he husked.

'Why else do you think we halted the brain-scanning?' Shorr Kan retorted. 'If it weren't for that, you'd be a complete mental wreck by now.'

He shook his head wonderingly. 'By Heaven, it was incredible! But the brain-scanner can't lie. And when the first minutes of its reading drew out the fact that you were John Gordon's mind in Zarth Arn's body, and that you did *not* know the Disruptor secret, I stopped the scanning.'

Shorr Kan added ruefully. 'And I thought I had that secret finally in my grasp! The pains I've taken to fish Zarth Arn into my net, and all for nothing! But who'd dream of a thing like this, who'd guess that a man of the ancient past was inside Zarth's body?'

Shorr Kan knew! John Gordon tried to rally his dazed faculties to deal with this startling new factor in the situation.

For the first time, someone in this future universe was cognizant of the weird imposture he had carried out! Just what would that mean to him?

Shorr Kan was striding to and fro. 'John Gordon of ancient Earth, of an age two hundred thousand years in the past, here inside the brain and body of the second prince of the Empire! It still doesn't make sense!'

Gordon answered weakly. 'Didn't your scanner tell you how it happened?'

The League commander nodded. 'Yes, the outlines of the story were clear after a few minutes' scanning, for the whole fact of your imposture was uppermost in your mind.'

He uttered a soft curse. 'That young fool Zarth Arn! Trading bodies with another man across time! Letting his crazy scientific curiosity about the past take him ages away, at the very moment his Empire is in danger.'

He fastened his gaze again on Gordon. 'Why in the devil's name didn't you tell me?'

'I tried to tell you, and got nowhere with it,' Gordon reminded him.

Shorr Kan nodded. 'That's right, you did. And I didn't believe. Who the devil *would* believe a thing like this, without the brain-scanner's proof of it?'

He paced to and fro, biting his lip. 'Gordon, you've upset all my careful plans. I was sure that with you I had the Disruptor secret.'

John Gordon's mind was working swiftly now as his strength slowly returned. The discovery of his true identity changed his whole situation.

It might give him a remote chance of escape! A chance to get away with Lianna and warn the Empire of Corbulo's treachery and the imminent danger! Gordon thought he dimly saw a way.

He spoke a little sullenly to Shorr Kan. 'You're the first one to discover the truth about me. I deceived all the others – Arn Abbas, Jhal Arn, Princess Lianna. They didn't dream the truth.'

Shorr Kan's eyes narrowed a little. 'Gordon, that sounds as though you *liked* being prince of the Empire?'

Gordon laughed mirthlessly. 'Who wouldn't? Back in my own time I was a nobody, a poor ex-soldier. Then, after Zarth Arn proposed that strange exchange of bodies across time, I found myself one of the royal family of the greatest star-kingdom in the universe! Who wouldn't like that change?'

'But you had promised to go back to Earth and re-exchange bodies with Zarth Arn, according to what the scanner revealed,' pointed out Shorr Kan. 'You'd have had to give up all your temporary splendor.'

Gordon looked up at him, with what he hoped was a cynical expression.

'What the devil?' he said contemptuously to Shorr Kan. 'Do you really think I'd have kept that promise?'

The League commander stared at him intently. 'You mean that you were planning to deceive the real Zarth Arn, and keep his body and identity?'

'I hope you're not going to get righteous with me!' flared Gordon. 'It's what you would have done yourself in my place, and you know it!

'Here I was, set for life as one of the great men of this universe, about to marry the most beautiful girl I've ever seen. No one could possibly ever doubt my identity. All I had to do was simply forget my promise to Zarth Arn. What would *you* have done?'

Shorr Kan burst into laughter. 'John Gordon, you're an adventurer after my own heart! By Heaven, I see that they bred bold men back in those ancient times on Earth!'

He clapped Gordon on the shoulder, his good spirits seeming partly restored.

'Don't get downhearted because I know the truth about you, Gordon. No one else knows it, except these scientists who'll never speak. You might still be able to live out your life as Prince Zarth Arn.'

Gordon pretended to catch eagerly at the bait. 'You mean – you wouldn't give me away?'

'That's what I mean. You and I ought to be able to help each other,' Shorr Kan nodded.

Gordon sensed that the high-powered brain behind those keen black eyes was working rapidly.

He realized that trying to fool this utterly intelligent and ruthless plotter was the hardest task he had ever essayed. But unless he succeeded, Lianna's life and the Empire's safety were forfeit.

Shorr Kan helped him to his feet. 'You come with me and we'll talk it over. Feel like walking yet?'

When they emerged from the laboratory, Durk Undis stared at Gordon as though he saw a man risen from the dead.

The fanatic young Cloud-man had not expected him to emerge from that room living and sane, Gordon knew.

Shorr Kan grinned. 'It's all right, Durk. Prince Zarth is cooperating with me. We shall go to my apartments.'

'Then you already have the Disruptor secret, sir?' burst out the young fanatic eagerly.

Shorr Kan's quick frown checked him. 'Are you questioning me?' snapped the commander.

As they walked on, John Gordon's mind was busy with this byplay. It encouraged him in the belief that his dim scheme might be made to work.

But he would have to go carefully, carefully! Shorr Kan was the last man in the universe to be easily deceived. Gordon sweated with realization that he walked a sword-edge over an abyss.

Shorr Kan's apartments were as austere as the bare office in which Gordon had first seen him. There were a few hard chairs, bare floors, and in another room an uncomfortable-looking cot.

Durk Undis had remained outside the door. As Gordon looked around, Shorr Kan's smile returned.

'Miserable hole for the master of the Cloud to live in, isn't it?' he said. 'But it all helps to impress my devoted followers. You see, I've worked them up to attack the Empire by stressing the poverty of our worlds, the hardness of our lives. I daren't live soft myself.'

He motioned Gordon to a chair, and then sat down and looked at him intently.

'It's still cursed hard to believe,' he declared. 'Talking here to a man of the remotest past! What was it like, that age of yours when men hadn't even left the little Earth?'

Gordon shrugged. 'It wasn't so much different, at bottom. There was war and conflict, over and over. Men don't change much.'

The League commander nodded emphatically. 'The mob remains always stupid. A few million men fighting on your old planet, or ten thousand star-worlds ranged against each other in this universe – it's the same thing at bottom.'

He continued swiftly. 'Gordon, I like you. You're intelligent, daring and courageous. Since you *are* intelligent, you understand that I wouldn't let a mere passing liking influence me, powerfully. I think we can help each other.'

He leaned forward. 'You're not Zarth Arn. But no one in the universe knows that, but me. So, to the galaxy, you are Zarth Arn. And as such, I can use you as I hoped to use the real Zarth, to act as puppet ruler after the Cloud has conquered the galaxy.'

John Gordon had hoped for this. But he pretended startled astonishment.

'You mean, you'd make me the nominal ruler of the galaxy?'

'Why not?' retorted the other. 'As Zarth Arn, one of the Empire's royal blood, you'd still serve to quiet rebellion after the Empire is conquered. Of course, I'd wield the real power, as I said.'

He added frankly, 'From one viewpoint you're better for my purpose than the real Zarth Arn. He might have had scruples, might have given me trouble. But you have no loyalties in this universe, and I can depend on you to stick with me from pure self-interest.'

Gordon felt a brief flash of triumph. That was exactly what he had wanted Shorr Kan to think – that he, John Gordon, was merely an ambitious, unscrupulous adventurer from the past.

'You'd have everything you could desire!' Shorr Kan was continuing. 'Outwardly, you'd be the ruler of the whole galaxy. The Princess Lianna for your wife, power and wealth and luxury beyond your dreams!'

Gordon pretended a stunned, rapt wonder at the prospect. 'I, the emperor of the galaxy? I, John Gordon?'

And then suddenly, without warning, the plan he was precariously trying to carry through slipped away from Gordon's mind and the voice of the tempter whispered in his ear.

He could do this thing, if he wanted to! He could be at least nominally the supreme sovereign of the entire galaxy with all its thousand on thousands of mighty suns and circling worlds! He, John Gordon of New York, could rule a universe with Lianna at his side!

All he had to do was to join with Shorr Kan and attach his loyalty to the Cloud. And why shouldn't he do that? What tie bound him to the Empire? Why shouldn't he strike out for himself, for such power and splendor as no man in all human history had ever dreamed of attaining?

15

Mystery of the Galaxy

John Gordon fought a temptation whose unexpectedness added to its strength. He was appalled to realize that he wanted with nearly all his soul to seize this unprecedented opportunity.

It wasn't the pomp and power of galactic rule that tempted him. He had never been ambitious for power, and anyway it would be Shorr Kan who had the real power. It was the thought of Lianna that swayed him. He'd be with her always then, living by her side –

Living a lie! Pretending to be another man, haunted for the rest of his life by memory of how he had betrayed Zarth Arn's trust and wrecked the Empire! He couldn't do it! A man had his code to live by, and Gordon knew he could never break his pledge.

Shorr Kan was watching him keenly. 'You seem stunned by the prospect, Gordon. It's a tremendous opportunity for you, all right.'

Gordon rallied his wits. 'I was thinking that there are lots of difficulties. There's the Disruptor secret, for instance.'

Shorr Kan nodded thoughtfully. 'That's our biggest difficulty. And I was so sure that once I had Zarth Arn, I'd have it!'

He shrugged. 'But that can't be helped. We shall have to make our attack on the Empire without it, and rely on Corbulo to see that Jhal Arn never gets a chance to use the Disruptor.'

'You mean – assassinate Jhal Arn as he did Arn Abbas?' questioned Gordon.

The Cloud-man nodded. 'Corbulo was to do that anyway on the eve of our attack. He'll be appointed one of the regents for Jhal's child. Then it'll be even easier for him to sabotage the Empire's defense.'

Gordon realized that Shorr Kan's failure to gain the Disruptor secret was not going to stave off the League's impending attack!

'Those are *your* problems,' Gordon said bluntly. 'It's my own prospects I was thinking of. You're to make me puppet emperor when the galaxy is conquered. But if we don't have that Disruptor secret, maybe your own League forces won't accept me.'

Shorr Kan frowned. 'Why should they refuse to accept you on that account?'

'They, like everyone else, think I'm Zarth Arn and believe I know the

Disruptor secret,' Gordon pointed out. 'They'll ask, "If Zarth Arn is now on our side, why doesn't he give us that secret?"'

The Cloud-man swore. 'I hadn't thought of that difficulty. Curse the Disruptor, anyway! Its existence hampers us at every turn!'

'What *is* the Disruptor, really?' Gordon asked. 'I've had to pretend I know all about it, but I haven't any idea what it is.'

'No one has!' Shorr Kan replied. 'Yet it's been a terrible tradition in the galaxy for the last two thousand years.

'Two thousand years ago the alien, unhuman Magellanians invaded the galaxy. They seized several star-systems and prepared to expand their conquests. But Brenn Bir, one of the great scientist-kings of the Empire, struck out against them with some fearful power or weapon. Tradition says he destroyed not only the Magellanians but also the star-systems they infested, and nearly destroyed the galaxy itself!

'Just what Brenn Bir used, no one now knows. It's been called the Disruptor, but that tells nothing. The secret of it, known only to the Empire's royal house, has never been used since. But memory of it haunts the galaxy, and has maintained the Empire's prestige ever since.'

'No wonder you've tried to get hold of it before attacking the Empire,' said Gordon. 'But there's still a way we can get that secret!'

Shorr Kan stared. 'How? Jhal Arn is the only remaining one who knows about it, and we've no chance of capturing him.'

'There's one other man who knows the secret,' Gordon reminded swiftly. 'The real Zarth Arn!'

'But the real Zarth's mind is back in that remote past age in your body –' Shorr Kan began. Then he stopped, eyeing Gordon narrowly. 'You've something in mind. What?'

Gordon was tense as he unfolded the scheme on which his dim, precarious plan of escape depended.

'Suppose we can make the real Zarth tell us that secret, across time?' he proposed boldly. 'There in Zarth's laboratory on Earth are the psycho-mechanisms by which I could speak to him across time. I learned the method from Vel Quen, and I could reach him.

'Suppose I tell him – Shorr Kan's men hold me prisoner and won't release me unless I tell the Disruptor secret, which I don't know. I won't be permitted to re-exchange minds with you until they have the secret.'

'Suppose I tell the real Zarth *that?* What do you think he'll do? He doesn't want to be marooned back there in my own world and age, in my own body, for the rest of his life. This is his universe, he's got a morganatic wife here he dearly loves, he'd sacrifice anything to get back here. He'll tell us that secret, across time!'

Shorr Kan looked at him in wondering admiration. 'By Heaven, Gordon, I believe it would work! We *could* just get the Disruptor secret that way!'

He stopped and asked suddenly, 'Then when you had forced that secret out of Zarth, you'd re-exchange minds with him?'

Gordon laughed. 'Do I look like a complete fool? Of course I won't. I'll simply break the contract then and let Zarth Arn live the rest of his life back in my own time and body while I keep on playing *his* part.'

Shorr Kan threw back his head in a burst of laughter. 'Gordon, I repeat, you're a man after my own heart!'

He began to pace to and fro as seemed his habit when thinking rapidly.

'The main difficulty will be to get you to Earth to make that contact with the real Zarth,' he declared. 'Empire patrols are thick all along the frontier, and the main Empire fleet is maneuvering near the Pleiades. And Corbulo can't order that whole region cleared, without arousing suspicion.'

Shorr Kan paused, then continued. 'The only kind of League ship that has any chance of reaching Earth through all that is a phantom-cruiser. Phantoms are able to slip through tight places, where even a battle-squadron couldn't fight a way.'

Gordon, who had only the mistiest notion of what kind of a warship was mentioned, looked puzzled. 'A phantom? What's that?'

'I forgot for a moment that you're really a stranger in this age,' Shorr Kan said. 'A phantom-cruiser is a small cruiser with armament of a few very heavy atom-guns. It can become totally invisible in space.'

He explained, 'It does that by projecting a sphere of force around itself that refracts perfectly all light and radar rays. So no ship can detect it. But to hold that concealing sphere of force requires terrific power, so a phantom is only good for twenty or thirty hours travel "dark".'

John Gordon nodded understandingly. 'I get it. And it looks like the best chance to reach Earth, all right.'

'Durk Undis will go with you with a full crew of trusted men,' Shorr Kan continued.

That was bad news to Gordon. That fanatic young Cloud-man hated him, he knew.

'But if Durk Undis learns that I'm not really Zarth Arn –' he began to object.

'He won't,' Shorr Kan interrupted. 'He'll simply know that he's to take you to your laboratory on earth for a brief time, and that he's to bring you back safely.'

Gordon eyed the Cloud-man. 'It sounds as though he's to be a guard. You don't entirely trust me?'

'What the devil made you think I did?' Shorr Kan retorted cheerfully.

'I trust no man entirely. I do trust to men following their self-interest, and that's why I feel I can rely on you. But just to make sure – Durk Undis and a crew of picked men go with you.'

Again, Gordon chilled to a realization that he was playing his desperate game against a man so shrewd and skilled in intrigue that it seemed almost hopeless he could succeed.

He nodded coolly, however. 'That's fair enough. But I might also say that I don't entirely trust *you*, Shorr Kan. And for that reason, I don't go on this mission unless Lianna goes with me.'

Shorr Kan looked genuinely surprised for a moment. 'The Fomalhaut girl? Your fiancee?'

Then an ironic smile flickered in his eyes. 'So that's your weak point, Gordon – that girl?'

'I love her and I'm not going to leave her here for you to tamper with,' Gordon asserted sullenly.

Shorr Kan snorted. 'If you knew me better, you'd know that one woman means no more to me than another. Do you think I'd risk my plans for a pretty face? But if you're jealous, you can take her with you.'

He added, 'How are you going to explain it all to her, though? You can't very well tell her the truth about our deal.'

Gordon had thought of that already. He said slowly, 'I'll make up a story that you're going to let us go if I bring you certain valuable scientific secrets from my Earth laboratory.'

Shorr Kan nodded understandingly. 'That will be your best course.'

He added rapidly, 'I'll give orders at once to have our best phantom-cruiser prepared. You ought to be able to start tomorrow night.'

Gordon stood up. 'I'll be glad to get some rest. I feel as though I'd been through a grinder.'

Shorr Kan laughed. 'Man, that's nothing to what the brain-scanner would have made of you if it had run longer than a few minutes. What a twist of fate! Instead of a mindless idiot, you're to be nominal emperor of the galaxy!'

He added, his face setting for just a moment to a steely hardness, 'But never forget that your power is only nominal and that it is *I* who will give the orders,'

Gordon met his searching gaze steadily, 'I might forget it if I thought I'd gain by that. But I'm pretty sure I wouldn't. I'm pretty sure that once I'm ruler, I'll fall if you fall. So you will be able to rely on me – or on my self-interest.'

The Cloud-man chuckled. 'You're right. Didn't I say I always like to deal with intelligent people? We'll get along.'

He pressed a button. When Durk Undis quickly entered the room, he told him:

'Escort Prince Zarth back to his quarters and then return here for orders.'

All the way back through the corridors, Gordon's thoughts were feverish. Relaxation from the intolerable strain of playing his part left him trembling.

So far, his precarious scheme for escape was succeeding. He had gambled on Shorr Kan's ruthless, cynical personality reacting in a certain way, and had won.

But he well knew that this success was only the beginning. Ahead loomed far greater difficulties which he had not yet found the least way of solving.

He'd have to go ahead, even though his scheme was suicidal in riskiness! There was no other way.

When he entered the somber apartment, Lianna sprang from a chair and ran toward him. She grasped his arm.

'Zarth, you're all right?' she cried, her gray eyes shining. 'I was afraid—'

She loved him, still. Gordon knew it from her face, and again he felt that wild, hopeless rapture.

He had to fight his impulse to take her into his arms. Something of what he felt must have showed in his face, for Lianna flushed and stepped back a little.

'Lianna, I'm all right though a little shaky,' Gordon told her, sinking into a chair. 'I had a taste of Cloud science and it wasn't pleasant.'

'They tortured you? They made you tell the Disruptor secret?'

He shook his head. 'I didn't tell that secret. And I'm not going to. I convinced Shorr Kan he couldn't get it from me.'

Gordon went on, telling her as much of the truth as he could. 'I made that devil believe that I would have to go to my Earth laboratory to get that secret for him. And he's sending us to get it. We'll leave in a phantom-cruiser tomorrow night.'

Lianna's eyes flashed. 'You're going to outwit him? You have some plan?'

'I wish I did,' groaned Gordon. 'This is as far as my plan goes. It will get us out of the Cloud, that's all. Then it's up to me. Somehow, I'll have to find a way for us to escape that ship and get a warning of Corbulo's treachery to Jhal Arn.'

He added wearily, 'The only way I can think of is somehow to sabotage the phantom-cruiser so it'll be captured by Empire warships. But how to do that, I don't know. That young fanatic Durk Undis is going with a picked crew to guard us, and it won't be easy.'

Faith and courage shone in Lianna's eyes. 'You'll find a way somehow, Zarth. I know you will.'

Her faith could not overcome the chill realization in Gordon's mind that his hare-brained scheme was almost impossible.

He might be dooming both Lianna and himself by trying it. But they were doomed anyway unless he betrayed the real Zarth Arn and the Empire, and the momentary temptation to do that had left Gordon forever.

He slept heavily, well into the next day. It was dusk when Shorr Kan and Durk Undis finally came.

'Durk Undis has all his orders, and the phantom is ready,' Shorr Kan told Gordon. 'You should get to Earth in five days, and be back here in eleven.'

His face lit. 'Then I'll announce to the galaxy that we have the Disruptor secret and that Zarth Arn has joined us, and will give Corbulo the secret signal and launch the League's attack!'

Two hours later, from the huge Thallarna spaceport, the slim, shining phantom-cruiser on which Gordon and Lianna had embarked rose from its dock and plunged headlong out through the Cloud.

16

Sabotage in Space

When Gordon and Lianna had entered the *Dendra*, the phantom-cruiser that was to bear them on the mission, they were led to the mid-deck corridor by Durk Undis.

The fanatic young Cloud-man bowed stiffly to them and gestured toward the door of a small suite of two tiny cabins.

'These cabins will be your quarters. You will remain in them until we reach Earth.'

'We will *not* remain in them!' Gordon flared. 'The princess Lianna is already suffering from the confinement of the voyage here. We'll not stay cooped up in those tiny rooms for days more.'

Durk Undis' lean face hardened. 'The commander gave orders that you were to be strictly guarded.'

'Did Shorr Kan say we were to be prisoned in two tiny rooms every minute?' Gordon demanded. He saw the slight uncertainty in Durk Undis' face, and pressed his attack. 'Unless we have a chance to get a little exercise, we'll refuse to carry out this whole plan.'

The fanatic Cloud-man hesitated. Gordon had guessed rightly that Durk Undis did not want to go back to his superior and report the mission aborted by such a slight difficulty.

Finally, Durk Undis said grudgingly, 'Very well, you will be permitted to walk in this corridor twice each day. But you will not be allowed in it any other time, or when we're running "dark." '

The concession was not as much as Gordon had wanted but he guessed that it was the most he could obtain. So, with anger still assumed, he followed Lianna into the cabin-suite and heard the lock click after them.

As the *Dendra* rose from Thallarna and started arrowing out at high speed through the gloomy hazes of the Cloud, Lianna looked inquiringly at Gordon.

'The confinement does not really bother me, Zarth. You have some plan?'

'No more than the plan I already mentioned, of somehow drawing the attention of an Empire patrol to this ship so that it'll be discovered and captured,' he admitted.

He added determinedly, 'I don't know yet how it can be done but there must be a way.'

Lianna looked doubtful. 'This phantom undoubtedly has super-sensitive radar equipment, and will be able to spot ordinary patrols long before they spot us. It will dark-out till we're past them.'

The steady drone of big drive-generators building up velocity became an unwavering background, in the following hours.

The *Dendra* plunged through hails of tiny meteor-particles, through dust-currents that made it pitch and toss roughly. It often changed direction as it threaded its way out through the Cloud.

It was the middle of the following day before they emerged from the gloomy haze into the vast, clear vault of star-gemmed space. At once, the phantom-cruiser picked up still greater speed.

Gordon and Lianna looked from the window at the brilliant galactic spectacle ahead. To their astonishment, the distant spark of Canopus lay out of sight far on their left. Ahead of the *Dendra* glittered a vault of strange stars in which Orion Nebula glowed in flaming glory.

'We're not heading straight back into the Empire,' Lianna said. 'They're going to avoid the most guarded Empire frontier by swinging up west of Orion Nebula and on past the Marches of Outer Space to curve in toward Sol.'

'Going the long way around to sneak into the Empire by the back way!' Gordon muttered. 'It's probably the way that Cloud ship came that tried to kidnap me from Earth.'

His faint hopes sank. 'There's less chance of an Empire patrol catching us, if we're going through a little-travelled region.'

Lianna nodded. 'We are not likely to meet more than a few patrol cruisers, and Durk Undis can slip past them under dark-out.'

Discouragedly, Gordon stared out at the brilliant scene. His gaze shifted to the direction in which he knew Canopus must lie.

Lianna caught the direction of his gaze and looked up at him questioningly. 'You are thinking of Murn?'

It startled Gordon. He had almost forgotten the dark, lovely girl whom the real Zarth Arn loved.

'Murn? No! I was thinking of that black traitor Corbulo, spinning his plots back there on Throon and just waiting his chance to murder Jhal Arn and wreck the Empire's defenses.'

'That is the greatest danger,' Lianna agreed soberly. 'If they could only be warned of Corbulo's treachery, the League's plan of attack could still be foiled.'

'And we're the only ones who can warn them,' Gordon muttered.

Yet on the third day after this, he had to confess to himself that it seemed more than ever an impossibility.

The *Dendra* was by now well inside the boundaries of the Empire, beating northward on a course that would take it just west of the gigantic, glowing Orion Nebula.

Once beyond the great Nebula, they would fly northwestward along the little-travelled edges of the Marches of Outer Space. Few Empire warships would be in the region bordering that wild frontier of unexplored star-systems. And Sol and its planet Earth would be nearby, then.

Twice during these three days, an alarm bell had rung through the *Dendra* as its radar operators detected Empire warships nearby. Each time, in their cabins, Gordon and Lianna had seen the whole vault of space outside the window suddenly blacked out.

Gordon had exclaimed in astonishment when it first happened. 'What's wrong? All space has gone dark!'

Lianna looked at him in surprise. 'They've turned on the dark-out of our ship. You surely remember that when a phantom-cruiser runs dark, those inside it can see nothing of outside space?'

'Oh, of course,' Gordon said hastily. 'It's been so long since I've been in one of these craft that I'd forgotten.'

He understood now what was happening. The new, loud whine that permeated the cruiser was the sound of the dark-out generators that were flinging an aura of potent force around the ship.

That aura slightly refracted every ray of light or radar beam that struck it, so that the phantom-cruiser could neither be seen or ranged by radar. Of necessity, that deflection of all outside light left the cruiser moving in utter darkness.

Gordon heard the dark-out generators down in the lower deck whining for nearly an hour. They apparently required almost all the power of the ship, the drive-machinery merely purring and the ship moving almost on inertia.

The thing happened again the following morning, when the *Dendra* was drawing up closer to the west borders of Orion Nebula. That glowing mass now stretched billions of miles across the firmament beside them.

Gordon saw many hot stars inside the Nebula. He recalled that it was their electron-barrage that excited the hazy dust of the Nebula to its brilliant glow.

That 'evening,' he and Lianna were walking in the long corridor under the close scrutiny of an armed Cloud-man when the alarm bell again rang sharp warning through the ship.

The Cloud-man instantly stepped forward. 'Dark-out! Return to your cabins immediately!'

Gordon had hoped for a chance like this and resolved to seize it. They might never have another.

As the familiar whine of the dark-out came on, as he and Lianna moved toward their cabins, he leaned to whisper to her.

'Act faint and collapse just as we enter the cabin!'

Lianna gave not a sign of hearing him, except that her fingers quickly pressed his hand.

The Cloud-officer was a half-dozen paces behind them, his hand resting on the butt of his atom-pistol.

Lianna, at the door of the cabin, tottered weakly and pressed her heart.

'Zarth, I feel ill!' she whispered huskily, then began to sag to the floor.

Gordon caught her, held her. 'She's fainted! I knew this confinement would be too much for her!'

He turned angrily toward the startled Cloud-man. 'Help me get her into the cabin!' Gordon snapped.

The officer was anxious to get them out of the corridor. His orders had been that they were immediately to be reconfined whenever a dark-out began.

Zeal to obey his orders betrayed him. The Cloud-man stepped forward and stooped to help pick up Lianna and carry her inside.

As he did so, Gordon acted! He callously let Lianna fall to the floor, and snatched at the butt of the Cloud-man's atom-gun.

So swift was his movement that he had the gun out of its holster before the other realized it. The Cloud-man began to straighten and his mouth opened to yell an alarm.

Gordon smashed the barrel of the heavy atom-pistol against the man's temple below his helmet. The officer's face relaxed blankly, and he slumped like a bag of rags.

'Quick, Lianna!' sweated Gordon. 'Into the cabin with him!'

Lianna was already on her feet. In an instant, they had dragged the limp form into the little room and shut the door.

Gordon stooped over the man. The skull was shattered.

'Dead,' he said swiftly. 'Lianna, this is my chance!'

He was beginning to strip off the dead man's jacket. She flew to his side. 'Zarth, what are you going to do?'

'There must be at least one Empire patrol cruiser nearby,' Gordon rasped. 'If I can sabotage the *Dendra's* dark-out equipment, the patrol will spot us and capture the ship.'

'More likely they'll blow it to fragments!' Lianna warned.

His eyes held hers. 'I know that, too. But I'm willing to take the chance if you are.'

Her gray eyes flashed. 'I'm willing, Zarth. The future of the whole galaxy hangs in the balance.'

'You stay here,' he ordered. 'I'll put on this fellow's uniform and helmet and it may give me a little better chance.'

In a few minutes, Gordon had struggled into the dead man's black uniform. He jammed on the helmet, then holstered the atom-gun and slid out into the corridor.

The dark-out was still on, the *Dendra* cautiously groping its way through self-induced blackness. Gordon started aft.

He had already, during these past days, located the sound of the dark-out generators as coming from aft on the lower deck. He hastened in the direction of that loud whine.

There was no one in the corridor. During dark-out, every man and officer was at action stations.

Gordon reached the end of the corridor. He hurried down a narrow companionway to the lower deck. Here doors were open, and he glanced into the big drive-generator rooms. Officers stood at flight-panels, men watched the gauges of the big, purring energy-drive.

An officer glanced up surprisedly as Gordon quickly passed the door. But his helmet and uniform seemed to reassure the Cloud-man.

'Of course!' Gordon thought. 'The guard I killed would be just returning to his station from locking us up!'

He was now closer to the loud whine of the dark-out generators. They were just forward of the main drive-machinery rooms, and the door of the dark-out room was also open.

Gordon drew his atom-pistol and stepped into the doorway. He looked into a big room whose generators were emitting that loud whine. One whole side of it was a bank of giant vacuum tubes that pulsed with white radiance.

There were two officers and four men in the room. An officer at the switch-panel beyond the tubes turned to speak to a man, and glimpsed Gordon's taut face in the doorway.

'Zarth Arn!' yelled the officer, grabbing for his gun. 'Look out!'

Gordon triggered his pistol. It was the first time he had used one of these weapons and his ignorance betrayed him.

He was aiming at the vacuum tubes across the room but the gun kicked high in his hand. The exploding pellet blasted the ceiling. He flung himself down in a crouch as a pellet from the officer's pistol flicked across the room. It struck the doorframe above his head, flaring instantly.

'General alarm!' the officer was yelling. 'Get—'

Gordon triggered again at that moment. This time he held his weapon down. The atomic pellets from his pistol exploded amid the bank of giant tubes.

Electric fire mushroomed out into the dark-out room! Two men and an officer screamed as raging violet flames enveloped them.

The officer with the gun swung around, appalled. Gordon swiftly shot him. He shot then at the nearest big generator.

His pellet only fused its metal shield. But the giant vacuum tubes were still popping, the whole room an inferno. The two men left there staggered in the violet fires, screaming and falling.

Gordon had recoiled into the corridor. He yelled exultantly as he saw the blackness outside the window suddenly replaced by a vault of brilliant stars.

'Our dark-out has failed!' yelled a voice on one of the upper decks.

Bells shrilled madly. Gordon heard a rush of feet as Cloud-men started pouring down from an upper deck toward the dark-out room.

17

Wrecked in the Nebula

Gordon glimpsed a dozen League soldiers bursting into the farther end of this lower-deck corridor. He knew that his game was up, but he turned his atom-pistol savagely loose upon them.

The pellets flew down the passage and exploded. The little flares of force blasted down half the Cloud-men there. But the others raced forward with wolfish shouts. And his pistol went dead in his hand, its loads exhausted.

Then it happened! The whole fabric of the *Dendra* rocked violently and there was a crash of riving plates and girders. All space outside the ship seemed illuminated by a brilliant flare.

'That Empire cruiser has spotted us and is shelling us!' yelled a wild voice. 'We're hit!'

Continued rending crash of parting struts and plates was accompanied by the shrill singing of escaping air. Then came the quick *slam-slam* of automatic bulkheads closing.

The corridor in which Gordon stood was suddenly divided by the automatic doors closing! He was cut off from the men at its end.

'Battle-stations! Space-suits on!' rang Durk Undis' sharp voice from the annunciators throughout the ship. 'We're crippled and have to fight it out with that Empire cruiser!'

Bells were ringing, alarms buzzing. Then came the swift shudder of recoil from big atom-guns broadsiding. Far away in space, out there in the vast blackness, Gordon glimpsed points of light suddenly flaring and vanishing.

A duel in space, this! His sudden sabotage of the dark-out concealment had exposed the *Dendra* to the Empire cruiser which it had been trying to evade. That cruiser had instantly opened fire.

'Lianna!' Gordon thought wildly. 'If she's been hurt—'

He turned and scrambled up the companionway to the middeck.

Lianna came running to meet him in the corridor there. Her face was pale but unafraid.

'There are space-suits in the locker here!' she exclaimed. 'Quick, Zarth! The ship may be hit again any moment!'

The girl had kept her head enough to find one of the lockers of space-suits placed at strategic locations throughout the ship.

In their cabin, she and Gordon hastily struggled into the suits. They were of stiffened metallic fabric, with spherical glassite helmets whose oxygenators started automatically when they were closed.

Lianna spoke, and he heard her voice normally by means of the short-range audio apparatus built into each suit.

She cried to him, 'That Empire cruiser is going to shell this ship to fragments now that it can't go dark!'

Gordon was dazed by the strangeness of the scene from the windows. The *Dendra*, maneuvering at high speed to baffle the radar of the other ship, was loosing its heavy atom-shells continuously.*

Far in space, tiny pinpoints of light flared and vanished swiftly. So tremendous was the distance at which this duel was being conducted, that the gigantic flares of the exploding atom-shells were thus reduced in size.

Space again burst into blinding light about them as the Empire cruiser's shells ranged close. The *Dendra* rocked on its beam-ends from the soundless explosions of force.

Gordon and Lianna were hurled to the floor by the violent shocks. He was aware that the drone of the drive-generators had fallen to a ragged whine. More automatic bulkheads were slamming shut.

'Drive-rooms half wrecked!' came a shout through his space-suit audiophone. 'Only two generators going!'

'Keep them running!' rang Durk Undis' fierce order. 'We'll disable that Empire ship with our new weapon, in a few moments!'

Their new weapon? Gordon swiftly recalled how Shorr Kan had affirmed that the League had a potent new weapon of offense that could strike down any ship.

'Lianna, they've got their hands too full to bother with us right now!' Gordon exclaimed. 'This is our chance to get away! If we can get off in one of the spaceboats, we can reach that Empire ship!'

Lianna did not hesitate. 'I am willing to try it, Zarth!'

'Then come on!' he exclaimed.

The *Dendra* was still rocking wildly, and he steadied Lianna as he led the way hastily down the corridor.

The space-suited gunners in the gun-galleries they passed were too engrossed in the desperate battle to glimpse them.

They reached the hatch in whose wall was a closed valve leading to one of the space life-boats attached to the hull. Gordon fumbled frantically for a moment with the valve.

'Lianna, I don't know how to open this! Can you do it?'

She swiftly grasped the catches, pulled at them. But there was no response.

* The shells of the big atom-guns used in space battle were self-propelled by jetting the sub-spectrum pressure rays that hurled them many times faster than light.

'Zarth, the automatic trips have locked! That means that the space-boat is wrecked and unusable!'

Gordon refused to let despair conquer him: 'There are other space-boats! On the other side—'

The *Dendra* was still rocking wildly, its parting girders cracking and screeching. Shells were still exploding blindingly outside.

But at that moment they heard a fiercely exultant cry from Durk Undis.

'Our weapon has disabled them! Now give them full broadsides!'

Almost instantly came a thin cheer. 'We got them!'

Through the porthole beside the hatch, Gordon glimpsed far out there in the void a sudden flare like that of a new nova. It was no pinpoint of light this time, but a blazing star that swiftly flared and vanished.

'They've destroyed the Empire cruiser somehow!' cried Lianna.

Gordon's heart sank. 'But we can still get away if we can get to one of the other space-boats!'

They turned to retrace their way. As they did so, two dishevelled Cloud officers burst into the cross-corridor.

'Get them!' yelled one. They started to draw their atom-pistols from the holsters of their space-suits.

Gordon charged desperately, the heel of the staggering ship hurling him into the two men. He rolled with them on the corridor floor, fiercely trying to wrest a weapon from one.

Then more voices rang loud about him. He felt himself seized by many hands that tore him loose from his antagonists. Hauled to his feet, panting and breathless, Gordon found a half-dozen Cloud-men holding Lianna and himself.

Durk Undis' fierce, flushed face was recognizable inside the glassite helmet of the foremost man.

'You traitor!' he hissed at Gordon. 'I *told* Shorr Kan no spawn of the Empire could be depended on!'

'Kill them both now!' urged one of the raging Cloud-men. 'It was Zarth Arn who sabotaged the dark-out and got us into this fix!'

'No, they don't die yet!' snapped Durk Undis. 'Shorr Kan will deal with them when we get back to the Cloud.'

'*If* we get back to the Cloud,' corrected the other officer bitterly. 'The *Dendra* is crippled, its last two generators will barely run, the space-boats are wrecked. We couldn't make it halfway back.'

Durk Undis stiffened. 'Then we'll have to hide out until Shorr Kan can send a relief ship for us. We'll call him by secret wave and report what has happened.'

'Hide out where?' cried another Cloud-officer. 'This is Empire space! That patrol-cruiser undoubtedly got off a flash report before we finished it.

This whole sector will be searched by Empire squadrons within twenty-four hours!'

Durk Undis bared his teeth. 'I know. We'll have to get out of here. And there's only one place to go.'

He pointed through a porthole to a brilliant coppery star that shone hotly just a little inside the glowing haze of huge Orion Nebula.

'That copper sun has a planet marked uninhabited on the charts. We can wait there for help. The cursed Empire cruisers won't look long for us if we jettison wreckage to make it appear we were destroyed.'

'But the charts showed that that sun and its planet are the center of a dust-whorl! We can't go there!' objected another Cloud-man.

'The whorl will drift us in, and a high-powered relief ship will be able to come in and get back out,' Durk Undis insisted. 'Head for it with all the speed you can get out of the generators. Don't draw power yet to message Thallarna. We can do that after we're safe on that world.'

He added, pointing to Gordon and Lianna, 'And tie these two up and keep a man with drawn gun over them every minute, Linn Kyle!'

Gordon and Lianna were hauled into one of the metal cabins whose walls were badly bulged by the damage of battle. They were dumped into two recoil-chairs mounted on rotating pedestals.

Plastic fetters were snapped to hold their arms and legs to the frame of the chairs. The officer Linn Kyle then left them, with a big Cloud-soldier with drawn atom-pistol remaining guard over them.

Gordon managed to rotate his chair by jerks of his body until he faced Lianna.

'Lianna, I thought we had a chance but I've just made things worse,' he said huskily.

Her face was unafraid as she smiled at him through her glassite helmet.

'You had to try it, Zarth. And at least you've thwarted Shorr Kan's scheme.'

Gordon knew better. He realized sinkingly that his attempt to get the *Dendra* captured by Empire forces had been a complete failure.

Whatever was the new, potent weapon the Cloud-men had used, it had been too much for the Empire cruiser. He had succeeded only in proving to the Cloud-men and Shorr Kan that he was their enemy.

He'd never have a chance now to warn Throon of Corbulo's treachery and the impending attack! He and Lianna would be dragged back to the Cloud and to Shorr Kan's retribution.

'By God, not that!' Gordon swore to himself. 'I'll make them kill us before I let Lianna be taken back there!'

The *Dendra* throbbed on for hours, limping on its last two generators. Then it cut off power and drifted. Soon the ship was entering the strange glow of the gigantic nebula.

At intervals came ominous cracklings and creakings from many parts of the ship. When a guard came to relieve their watch-dog, Gordon learned from the brief talk of the two Cloud-men that only eighteen men remained alive of the officers and crew.

The staggering ship began some hours later to buck and lurch in the grip of strong currents. Gordon realized they must be entering the great dust-whorl in the nebula to which Linn Kyle had referred.

More and more violent grew the bucking until the *Dendra* seemed shaking itself apart. Then came a loud crash, and a singing sound that lasted for minutes.

'The air has all leaked out from the ship now,' Lianna murmured. 'Without our space-suits, we'd all be dead.'

Death seemed close to John Gordon, in any case. The crippled ship was now in the full grip of the mighty nebula dust-current that was bearing it on toward a crash on the star-world ahead.

Hours passed. The *Dendra* was now using the scant power of its two remaining generators again, to keep from being drawn into the coppery sun they were nearing.

Gordon and Lianna could get only occasional glimpses of their destination, through the porthole. They glimpsed a planet revolving around that copper-colored star – a yellow, tawny world.

Durk Undis' voice rang in a final order. 'Strap in for crash-landing!'

The guard who watched Gordon and Lianna strapped himself into a recoil-chair beside them. Air began to scream through the wreck.

Gordon had a flashing glimpse of weird ocher forests rushing upward. The generators roared loud in a brief deceleration effort. Then came a crash that hurled Gordon into momentary darkness.

18

Monster Men

Gordon came to himself, dazed and shaken, to find that it was Lianna's anxious voice that had aroused him.

The girl was leaning toward him from the chair in which she was bound. Her face was worried.

'Zarth, I thought for a moment you were really hurt! Your recoil-chair almost broke loose completely.'

'I'm all right,' Gordon managed to answer. His eyes swung to take in the scene. 'We've landed, all right!'

The *Dendra* was no longer a ship. It was now a twisted, wrecked mass of metal whose voyaging was forever ended.

Walls had bulged like paper, metal girders and struts had been shorn away like cardboard, by the impact of the crash. Hot coppery sunlight streamed through a gaping rent in the cabin wall. Through that opening, Gordon could glimpse the scene outside.

The wreck lay amid towering ocher jungles of strange trees whose broad leaves grew directly from their smooth yellow trunks. Trees and brush and strange shrubs of yellow-and-black flowers had been crushed by the fall of the wreck. Golden spore-dust drifted in the metallic sunlight, and strange webbed-winged birds or creatures flew through the ocher wilderness.

To Gordon's ears came the ragged hum of atomic turbines and generators, close to them in the wreck.

'Durk Undis' men have been working to start the two generators,' Lianna said. 'They were not badly damaged, it seems.'

'Then they're going to send a call back to the Cloud,' Gordon muttered. 'And Shorr Kan will send another ship here!'

The officer Linn Kyle came into their cabin, no longer wearing a space-suit.

'You can take the suits off the prisoners,' Linn Kyle told their guard. 'Keep them fettered in the chairs, though.'

Gordon was relieved to get rid of the heavy suit and helmet. He found the air breathable but laden with strange, spicy scents.

Just across the corridor from their prison was the stereo room. They heard a transmitter there soon begin its high-pitched whine. Then the taut voice of Durk Undis reached them.

'Calling headquarters at Thallarna! *Dendra* calling!'

Lianna asked, 'Won't their call arouse attention? If it's heard by Empire warships, it will.'

Gordon had no hope of that. 'No, Durk Undis mentioned a secret wave they would use. No doubt that means they can call Thallarna without being overheard.'

For minutes, the calls continued. Then they heard Durk Undis order the transmitter turned off.

'We'll try again,' they heard him say. 'We've got to keep trying until we reach headquarters.'

Gordon hitched his recoil-chair around by imperceptible jerks of his body. He could now look across the shattered corridor into the Stereo room, whose door sagged from its frame.

In there, two hours later, he saw Durk Undis and his operator again try to reach Thallarna with a call. As the generators astern began humming, the operator closed the switches of his transmitter and then carefully centered a series of vernier dials on his panel.

'Be careful to keep exactly on the wave,' Durk Undis cautioned. 'If the cursed Empire ships get even a whisper of our call, they'll run a direction-fix on it and be here to hunt us.'

Then, again, began the series of calls. And this time, Durk Undis succeeded in obtaining a response.

'*Dendra* calling, Captain Durk Undis speaking!' he exclaimed eagerly into the transmitter. 'I can't go stereo, for lack of power. But here's my identification.'

He uttered a series of numbers, evidently a prearranged identification code. Then he rapidly gave the space coordinates of the planet inside the nebula where the wreck lay, and reported the battle and its sequel.

Shorr Kan's ringing voice came from the receiver of the apparatus.

'So Zarth Arn tried to sabotage the mission? I didn't think he was such a fool! I'll send another phantom-cruiser for you at once. Maintain silence until it arrives, for the Empire fleet mustn't suspect you're in their realm.'

'I assume that we will not now be continuing the mission to Earth?' said Durk Undis.

'Of course not!' snapped Shorr Kan. 'You'll bring Zarth Arn and the girl back to the Cloud. Above all, he mustn't get away to carry any news to Throon!'

Gordon's heart chilled as he heard. Lianna looked mutely at him.

Durk Undis and the other Cloud-men were jubilant. Gordon heard the fanatic young captain give his orders.

'We'll maintain sentries around the wreck. We don't know what kind of creatures are in these jungles. Linn Kyle, you command the first watch.'

Night swept upon the ocher jungles as the coppery sun sank. The dank breath of the forest became stronger.

The night was like one of wondrously glowing moonlight, for the flaring nebula sky dripped strange radiance upon the brooding jungles and the wreck.

Out of the nebula-illuminated jungle there came a little later the echo of a distant cry. It was a throaty, bestial call, but with a creepy human quality in its tones.

Gordon heard Durk Undis' sharp voice. 'That must be a beast of some size! Keep your eyes open.'

Lianna shivered slightly. 'They tell strange tales of some of these lost worlds in the nebula. Few ships ever dare to enter these dust-whorls.'

'Ships are going to enter this one, if I can bring it about,' muttered Gordon. 'We're not going back to the Cloud!'

He had discovered something that gave him a faint hope. The recoil-chair in which he was fettered had suffered like the rest of the wreck from the shock of the crash-landing. The metal frame of the chair was slightly cracked along the arm to which his wrist was fettered.

The crack was a slight one, not affecting the strength of the chair. But it presented a slightly raised and ragged edge. Against this roughened edge, Gordon began secretly rubbing the plastic fetter on his wrist.

Gordon realized the improbability of this small abrasion severing the plastic. But it was at least a possibility, and he kept it up by imperceptible movements until his muscles ached.

Toward morning, they were awakened from doze by a repetition of the weird, throaty call in the distant forests. The next day, and the next, passed as the Cloud-men waited. But on the third night, horror burst upon them.

Soon after nightfall that night, a yell from one of the Cloud-men sentries was followed by the crash of an atom-pistol.

'What is it?' cried Durk Undis.

'Creatures that looked like men – but they melted, when I fired at them!' cried another voice. 'They disappeared like magic!'

'There's another! And more of them!' cried a third Cloud-man. 'See!'

Guns went off, the explosion of their atomic pellets rocking the night. Durk Undis yelled orders.

Lianna had swung her chair around on its pedestal, toward the porthole. She cried out.

'Zarth! Look!'

Gordon managed to hitch his chair around also. He stared at the unbelievable sight outside the porthole.

Out there, manlike creatures in scores were pouring out of the jungle toward the wreck. They looked like tall, rubbery human men. Their eyes were blazing as they charged.

Durk Undis and his men were using their atom-pistols. The blinding flare of the atomic pellets darkened the soft nebula-glow.

But wherever those pellets blasted the strange invaders, the rubbery men simply melted. Their bodies melted down into viscous jelly that flowed back over the ground in slow retreat.

'They're coming from the other side too!' yelled the warning of Linn Kyle.

Durk Undis' voice rang imperatively. 'Pistols won't hold them off long! Linn, take two men and start the ship's generators. Hook a jet-cable to them and we can spray these creatures with pressure-rays!'

Lianna's eyes were distended by horror, as they witnessed the rubbery horde seize two of the Cloud-men and bear them back into the jungles.

'Zarth, they are monsters! Not men, yet not beasts—'

Gordon saw that the fight was going badly. The rubbery horde had pressed Dick Undis' men back close against the wreck.

It seemed that the weird attackers could not be harmed. For those who were hit simply melted to jelly and flowed away.

The generators in the wreck began humming loudly. Then Linn Kyle and his two men emerged dragging a heavy cable. At the end of this they had hastily attached one of the pressureray jet projectors that ordinarily propelled the ship.

'Use it, quickly!' shouted Durk Undis. 'The brutes are too much for us!'

'Stand clear!' yelled Linn Kyle.

He switched on the heavy ray-projector he held. Blinding beams of force leaped from it and cut through the rubbery horde. The ground instantly became a horrible stream of creeping, flowing jelly.

The monstrous attackers sullenly retreated. And the viscous slime upon the ground retreated also toward the shelter of the jungle.

There came then a raging chorus of unhuman, throaty shouts from out in the ocher forest.

'Quick, rig other jet-projectors!' Durk Undis ordered. 'It's all that will keep them off. We need one on each side of the wreck.'

'What in the name of all devils *are* the things?' cried Linn Kyle, his voice shrill with horror.

'There's no time for speculating on that!' rapped the other. 'Get those projectors ready.'

Gordon and Lianna witnessed another attack, a half-hour later. But this time, four jets of pressure-rays met the rubbery horde. Then the attacks desisted.

'They've gone!' sweated a Cloud-man. 'But they carried off two of us!'

As the generators were turned off, Gordon heard a new sound from the distance.

'Lianna, hear that?'

It was a pulsing, throbbing sound like the deep beat of distant drums. It came from far westward in the nebula-lit jungle.

Then, breaking into the throbbing drumbeat, there came a faint, agonized series of human screams. There swelled up a triumphant chorus of throaty shouts, then silence.

'The two Cloud-men who were captured,' Gordon said sickly. 'God knows what happened to them out there.'

Lianna was pale. 'Zarth, this is a world of horror. No wonder the Empire has left it uncolonized.'

The menace to themselves seemed doubled, to Gordon. Almost, to assure Lianna's safety from the nightmare terrors of this planet, he would have gone willingly back to the Cloud.

But his determination returned. They'd get away, but not to go back to the hands of Shorr Kan if he could help it!

He forced himself to continue the slow, squirming movements that rubbed his plastic fetter against the rough crack in the chair-frame. Finally in weariness he slept, to awaken hours after dawn.

In the coppery sunlight, the ocher jungles were deceptively peaceful looking. But captives and captors alike knew now what weird horror brooded out in those golden glades.

Gordon, through the long day, continued to squirm and hitch to increase the abrasion on the fetter. He desisted only when the eyes of their guard were upon him.

Lianna whispered hopefully, 'Do you think you can get free?'

'By tonight I should be able to wear it through,' he murmured.

'But then? What good will it do? We can't flee out there into the jungle!'

'No, but we can call help,' Gordon muttered. 'I've thought of a way.'

Night came, and Durk Undis gave his men sharp orders. 'Two men on each of those jet-projectors, ready to repel the creatures if they come! We'll keep the generators running continuously.'

That was welcome news, to Gordon. It made more possible the precarious scheme he had evolved.

He felt that by now the tough plastic must be abraded halfway through. But it still felt too strong to break.

The generators had begun humming. And the worried Cloud-men had not long to wait for the attack they dreaded. Once more from the nebula-illumined jungles came the weird, throaty shouts.

'Be ready the minute they appear!' called Durk Undis.

With a chorus of throaty cries, the rubbery horde rolled in a fierce wave out of the jungle. Instantly the jet projectors released beams of the powerful pressure-rays upon them.

'It's holding them back! Keep it up!' Durk Undis cried.

'But they don't *die!*' cried another man. 'They melt down and flow away!'

Gordon realized this was his opportunity. The Cloud-men were all engaged out there in defending the wreck, and the generators were running.

He expanded his muscles in an effort to break his fetter. But he had misjudged its strength. The tough plastic held.

Again he tried, straining wildly. This time the fetter snapped. Hastily, he unfastened the other fetters.

He got to his feet and quickly freed Lianna. Then he hurried across the corridor toward the Stereo room just opposite.

'Watch and warn me if any of the Cloud-men come back in here!' he told the girl. 'I'm going to try to start the transmitter.'

'But do you know enough about it to send out a call?' asked Lianna.

'No, but if I can start it up, *any* untuned wave will direct instant attention to this planet,' Gordon explained swiftly.

He fumbled in the dimness of the room for the switches he had observed the operator use to start the transmitter.

Gordon closed them. The transmitter remained dead. There was no whine of power, no glow of big tubes. A baffled feeling grew in him as he realized the failure of his plan.

19

World of Horror

Gordon forced himself to remain calm despite the wild din of struggle outside the wreck. He went over the switches he had seen the operator use to start the transmitter.

He had missed one! As he closed it, the motor-generators in the Stereo room broke into loud life, and the big vacuum tubes began glowing.

'The generators must be failing! Our jets are losing power!' came a cry from one of the Cloud-men outside the wreck.

'Zarth, you're drawing so much power from the two generators that it's cutting their ray-jets!' warned Lianna. 'They'll be in here to find out what's wrong!'

'I only need a moment!' Gordon sweated, bending tensely over the bank of vernier dials.

It was impossible, he knew, for him to try sending any coherent message. He knew almost nothing about this complicated apparatus of future science.

But if he could send out any kind of untuned signal, the very fact of such a signal coming from a supposedly uninhabited planet would surely arouse the suspicion of the Empire cruisers searching out there.

Gordon spun the verniers at random. The equipment sputtered, hummed and faltered, beneath his ignorant handling.

'The brutes are getting through!' Durk Undis' voice yelled. 'Linn, get in there and see what's wrong with the generators!'

The battle outside was closer, fiercer. Lianna uttered a cry of warning.

Gordon whirled around. Linn Kyle stood, wild and dishevelled, in the door of the Stereo room.

The Cloud-man uttered an oath and grabbed out his atom-pistol. 'By God, I might have known—'

Gordon dived for him, tackled him and brought him to the floor with a crash. They struggled furiously.

Through the increasing din, Gordon heard Lianna's horrorladen scream. And he glimpsed weird figures pouring into the room from astern and seizing the terrified girl.

The rubbery attackers! The spawn of this crazy nebula world had broken through Durk Undis' weakened defenses and were inside the wreck!

'Lianna!' Gordon yelled hoarsely, as he saw the girl borne swiftly from her feet by clutching hands.

The blank faces, the ghastly eyes of the rubbery aliens were close to him as he tore free from Linn Kyle and tried to rise.

He couldn't! The rubbery bodies were piling on him and on the Cloud-man. Arms that felt like tentacles grasped and lifted them. Linn Kyle's wild shot hit one and it melted to crawling jelly, but the others seized the Cloud-man.

Crash of atom-pistols thundered through the corridors of the wreck. Durk Undis' high voice rang over the wild uproar.

'Drive them out of the ship and hold the doors until we can get the ray-jets going again!'

Gordon heard Linn Kyle's yell choked off in his throat as he himself and the Cloud-man were swung swiftly up off their feet. The rubbery horde was retreating out of the shattered stern of the wreck, and were taking the two and Lianna with them.

Gordon fought to free himself of the clutching rubbery arms, and couldn't. He realized with horror that his weakening of the Cloud-men's defense to send his desperate call had exposed Lianna and himself to a more ghastly peril.

'Durk, they have us!' screeched Linn Kyle. Through the crash of guns and yells, Gordon heard the other's startled cry.

But they were out of the wreck now, and their captors were bounding with them through the towering jungle. The whole rubbery horde was retreating into the nebula-lit forest as Durk Undis and his remaining men got their ray-jets in action again.

Gordon's senses swam. These hideous captors hurtled through the jungle with him like preternaturally agile apes. Lianna and Linn Kyle were borne along as swiftly. Down from the flaming nebula sky dripped a glowing radiance that silvered the unearthly forest.

The pace of their strange captors quickened, after some minutes of travel through the jungle. Now rock slopes began to lift from the thick forest.

The weird horde swept with them into a deep stony gorge. It was a place more awesome than the jungle. For its rock cliffs gleamed with a faint light that was no reflection of the nebula sky, but was intrinsic.

'Radioactive, those cliffs,' Gordon thought numbly. 'Maybe it explains these unholy freaks—'

Speculation was swept from his mind by the hideous clamor that arose. There were hordes of the rubbery creatures here in the gorge. They greeted the captives with throaty, deafening cries.

Gordon found himself held tightly beside Lianna. The girl's face was deathly white.

'Lianna, you're not hurt?'

'Zarth, no! But what are they going to do to us?'

'My God, I don't know!' he husked. 'They had some reason for taking us alive.'

The quasi-human horde had seized on Linn Kyle! They were stripping all clothing off the Cloud-man's body.

Throaty clamor like the applause of an infernal audience rose loudly as Linn Kyle was now borne forward. Rubbery creatures squatting on the ground beat it with their limbs in a drumming rhythm.

Linn Kyle, struggling wildly, was carried quickly on down the gorge. Then as the horde parted to permit his passage, Gordon glimpsed where they were bearing the Cloud-man.

At the center of the gorge, ringed by faintly glowing radioactive rocks, lay a sunken pool twenty yards across. But it was not a pool of water, but of *life!*

A great, twitching, crawling mass of jelly-like life, heaving and sucking beneath the light of the flaring nebula-sky.

'What is it?' cried Lianna. 'It looks living!'

The final horror assaulted Gordon's reeling mind. For now he saw the things around the edges of the pool.

Little jelly-like things like miniature human bodies budded out of that mass of viscous life! Some were attached to the main mass by mere threads. One broke free in that moment and came walking uncertainly up the bank.

'God in Heaven!' he whispered. 'These creatures come from the pool of life. They're *born* from it!'

Linn Kyle's screams ripped the din of throaty shouts and drumming rhythm. The rubbery creatures who held the Cloud-man tossed his naked body into the viscous pool!

The Cloud-man screamed again, horribly. Gordon turned aside his gaze, retching.

When he looked again, Linn Kyle's body was engulfed by the viscous jelly that swirled hungrily over it. In a few moments the Cloud-man was gone, absorbed into the pool of life.

'Lianna, don't look!' Gordon cried hoarsely.

He made a mad attempt to free himself. He might as well have been a child in the grasp of those rubbery arms.

But his attempt drew attention to himself. The creatures began to tear away his clothing. He heard Lianna's smothered cry.

Crash of atom-pistols thundered through the infernal din of drumming and shouting! Pellets exploded in blinding fire amid the swarming horde. Rubbery creatures staggered, fell, melted into jelly that promptly flowed back toward the pool!

'Durk Undis!' yelled Gordon. He had glimpsed the young Cloud-captain's narrow face and blazing eyes, forcing through the horde at the head of his men.

'Get Zarth Arn and the girl, quick!' yelled Durk Undis to his men. 'Then back to the wreck!'

Gordon almost admired the ruthless young fanatic, at that moment. Durk Undis had been ordered by Shorr Kan to bring Gordon back to the Cloud, and he'd carry out that order or die trying.

The monstrous horde swirled in crazy uproar, momentarily stunned by the unexpected attack. Gordon wrenched free from the two creatures who still held him. He reached Lianna's side.

It was a crazy chaos of whirling, quasi-human figures and exploding atom-pellets, of Durk Undis' yells and the throaty uproar of the horde.

As the bewildered horde fell back for a moment, Durk Undis and his men blasted the last creatures still around Lianna and Gordon. Next moment, with Gordon and the half-senseless girl in their midst, the Cloud-men hastily retreated back out of the gorge.

'They're coming after us!' yelled one of the men beside Gordon.

Gordon perceived that the ghastly horde had recovered presence of mind. With a hideous throaty clamor, the unhuman mob crashed into the jungle in pursuit.

They made half the distance back to the wreck of the *Dendra*, before the jungle ahead of them swarmed also with the creatures.

'They're all around us – have cut us off!' Durk Undis exclaimed. 'Try to fight through!'

It was hopeless and he knew it, and Gordon knew it. A dozen atom-pistols couldn't hold off that mindless horde for long.

Gordon stood with Lianna behind him, using a clubbed branch he tore from a fallen tree as a bludgeon against the swarming, rubbery attackers. With it, he could at least kill Lianna before they dragged her back to that ghastly pool of life!

The whole nightmare fight was suddenly shadowed by a big black mass dropping down on them from the flaming nebula sky!

'It's a ship!' screamed one of the Cloud-men. 'One of *our* ships!'

A phantom-cruiser with the black, blotlike insignia of the Cloud on its bows thundered down upon them with krypton searchlights flaring to light the whole scene.

The rubbery horde retreated in sudden panic. As the cruiser crushed to a landing in the jungle close by, Cloud-soldiers with atom-guns sprang from it.

Gordon, raising Lianna's half-senseless form from the ground, found Durk Undis covering him with an atom-pistol. The newcomers were hastily approaching.

'Holl Vonn!' Durk Undis greeted the stocky, crop-haired Cloud-captain who was foremost. 'You got here just in time!'

'So it seems!' exclaimed Holl Vonn, staring horrifiedly at the viscous living jelly still creeping away from the scene of battle. 'What in God's name were those things that were attacking you?'

'They're creatures of this crazy planet,' Durk Undis panted. 'I think they were human once – human colonists who mutated under radioactive influence. They've got a strange new reproduction-cycle, being born from a pool of life and going back to it when hurt to be born again.'

He continued swiftly. 'That can be told later. The thing now is to get away from here at once. There must already be Empire squadrons searching the whole area west of the nebula.'

Holl Vonn nodded quickly. 'Shorr Kan said to bring Zarth Arn and Lianna back to the Cloud at once. We'd better run eastward through the nebula and then beat back southward along the Rim.'

Gordon had revived Lianna. She was looking wonderingly at the towering ship and the armed Cloud-men.

'Zarth, what happened? Does this mean—'

'It means that we're going back to the Cloud, to Shorr Kan,' he said hoarsely.

Durk Undis motioned curtly to the new Cloud-ship. 'Into the *Meric*, both of you.'

Holl Vonn suddenly stiffened. 'Listen – by heaven!'

His square face was suddenly livid as he pointed wildly upward.

Four massive shapes were rushing down on them from the nebula-sky! Not phantoms these, but big cruisers with heavy batteries of atom-guns along their sides with the flaring comet-emblem of the Mid-Galactic Empire on their bows.

'An Empire squadron!' yelled Holl Vonn wildly. 'We're trapped here! They've already spotted us!'

Gordon felt sudden wild hope. His desperate expedient had succeeded, had brought one of the searching Empire squadrons to this world!

20

Doom off the Pleiades

Durk Undis uttered a raging exclamation as the Empire cruisers swooped from the sky.

'To the ship! We'll cut our way back through them to space!'

'We've not a chance!' cried Holl Vonn, his face deathly as he started to run toward his ship. 'They've caught us flat!'

Durk Undis froze for a second, then whipped out his atom-pistol again. He whirled around toward Gordon and Lianna.

The young fanatic's eyes were flaming. 'Then we'll finish Zarth Arn and Lianna right here! Shorr Kan's orders – no matter what happens to us, these two must not get back to Throon!'

Gordon lunged at him as he spoke! In the few seconds since the Empire cruisers had appeared, Gordon had realized that in this desperate emergency the Cloud-man would kill himself and Lianna rather than let them escape.

He had bunched himself an instant before Durk Undis swung around with the weapon. He hit the Cloud-man like a human projectile. Durk Undis was hurled violently backward.

Holl Vonn was running into his ship, shouting orders. As Durk Undis sprawled, Gordon seized Lianna's hand and darted with her into the concealment of the nebula-lit jungle.

'If we can keep out of it for a few moments, we're saved!' he told her. 'Those Empire ships will come down here to search.'

'Holl Vonn is charging them!' cried Lianna, pointing upward.

Thunderous roar of generators screaming with power broke upon the air as the long, slim mass of Holl Vonn's phantom, the *Meric*, hurtled up into the glowing sky.

Gordon saw then that whatever else the men of the Cloud might be, they were not cowards. Knowing himself trapped, knowing instant destruction was the penalty for being caught here in Empire space after the destruction of an Empire ship, Holl Vonn came out fighting!

Atom-guns of the *Meric* volleyed exploding shells at the swooping Empire ships. The nebula sky seemed to burst into blinding brilliance with the explosions.

It was magnificent but hopeless, that charge of one phantom against four heavy cruisers. The great batteries of the cruisers seemed literally to smother the *Meric* in atom-shells.

Blossoming flowers of atomic fire unfolded and momentarily concealed the Cloud ship. Then it was revealed as a fusing, fiery wreck that hurtled headlong across the sky to crash in the distant jungle.

'Zarth, look out!' screamed Lianna at that instant, and pushed Gordon aside.

An atomic pellet flicked close past his face and exploded in a nearby thicket!

Durk Undis, his face deadly, was close by and was raising his weapon to fire again. Lianna had desperately grasped his arm.

Gordon realized then the tenacity of the young Cloud-captain, who had remained and followed to kill Lianna and himself.

'By Heaven, I'll finish it now!' Durk Undis was exclaiming, hurling Lianna violently away from him with a sweep of his arm.

Gordon, charging, reached him at that moment. The Cloud-man uttered a sound of sudden agony as Gordon fiercely twisted his arm.

The atom-pistol dropped from his fingers. Eyes blazing, he kneed Gordon in the stomach and smashed hard fists into his face.

Gordon hardly felt the blows, in his overpowering passion. He rocked forward and fell with the Cloud-man as they grappled.

Braced with his back against the trunk of a towering golden tree, Durk Undis got his hands on Gordon's throat and squeezed.

Gordon felt a roaring in his ears, and a sudden blackness swept over him. His groping hands grabbed the Cloud-man's bristling black hair. He hammered Durk Undis' head violently back against the tree.

He was so deep in that roaring blackness that it was only after many minutes that Lianna's voice penetrated his ears.

'Zarth, it's over! He's dead!'

Gordon, gulping air into starved lungs, felt his senses clearing. He found himself still gripping Durk Undis' hair.

The whole back of the Cloud-man's skull was a bloody mess where he had hammered it again and again against the tree-trunk.

He staggered up to his feet, sick, almost retching. Lianna sprang to his side as he swayed.

'Lianna, I didn't see him. If you hadn't cried out and rushed him, he'd have killed me.'

A stern new voice rang suddenly from close by. Gordon staggered around to face that direction.

Gray-uniformed Empire soldiers with raised atom-guns were forcing through the soft-lit jungle toward them. One of the Empire cruisers had landed nearby, while the others still hovered overhead.

The man who spoke was a hard-eyed, handsome young Empire captain who stared wonderingly at Gordon's dishevelled figure and Lianna.

'You two don't look like Cloud-people! But you were with them—'

He stopped suddenly and took a step forward. His eyes peered at Gordon's bruised, bloody face.

'Prince Zarth Arn!' he cried, stupefied. Then his eyes flamed hatred and passion. 'By Heaven, we've caught you! And with Cloud-men! You joined *them* when you fled from Throon!'

A quiver of passion ran through all the Empire soldiers who had gathered. Gordon saw mortal hatred in their eyes.

The young captain stiffened. 'I am Captain Dar Carrul of the Empire navy and I arrest you for the assassination of the late emperor and for treason!'

Gordon, dazed as he was, found his voice at that. 'I didn't murder Arn Abbas! And I didn't join the Cloud – I was held prisoner by these Cloud-men and only just escaped before you came!'

He pointed at the corpse of Durk Undis. '*He* tried to kill me before letting me escape! And what brought you to this planet searching? An untuned signal-wave from here, wasn't it?'

Dar Carrul looked startled. 'How did you know that? Yes, it is true that our operators detected such a signal coming from this uninhabited world, when we were searching space west of the nebula.'

'Zarth sent that signal!' Lianna told him. 'He used that method to attract Empire ships here!'

Dar Carrul looked a little bewildered. 'But everyone knows you killed your father! Commander Corbulo saw you do it! And you fled from Throon—'

'I didn't flee, I was carried off,' Gordon declared. He cried earnestly, 'All I ask is to be taken to Throon to tell my story!'

Dar Carrul seemed more and more perplexed by the unexpected turn of the situation.

'You will certainly be taken to Throon for trial,' he told Gordon. 'But it is not for a mere squadron captain to handle such a grave matter as this one. I will take you under guard to our main squadron and report for instructions.'

'Let me talk at once by stereo to my brother, to Jhal Arn!' pleaded Gordon tautly.

Dar Carrul's face tightened. 'You are a proclaimed fugitive, charged with the gravest of crimes against the Empire. I cannot allow you to send messages. You must wait until I receive instructions.'

He made a gesture, and a dozen soldiers with drawn atom-guns stepped forward around Gordon and Lianna.

'I must ask you to enter our ship at once,' the young captain said clippedly.

Ten minutes later, the cruiser took off from the nebula-world of horror.

With the other three Empire cruisers, it raced out westward through the vast glow of Orion Nebula.

In the cabin in which they two had been placed under guard, Gordon paced furiously to and fro.

'If they only let me tell Jhal Arn of the danger, of Corbulo's treachery!' he rasped. 'If that has to wait till we're taken to Throon, it might be too late!'

Lianna looked worried. 'Even when we get to Throon, it may not be easy to convince Jhal Arn of your innocence, Zarth.'

Gordon's taut anger was chilled by that. 'But they've got to believe me! They surely won't credit Corbulo's lies when I tell them the truth?'

'I hope not,' Lianna murmured. She added with a flash of pride, 'I will corroborate your story. And I am still princess of Fomalhaut Kingdom!'

Hours seemed to drag as the cruisers hurtled headlong out of Orion Nebula, and on westward through open space.

Lianna slept exhaustedly after a time. But Gordon could not sleep. His very nerve seemed taut as he sensed the approaching climax of the gigantic galactic game in which he had been but a pawn.

He *must* convince Jhal Arn of the truth of his story! And he must do so quickly, for as soon as Shorr Kan learned that he had escaped to tell the truth, the master of the Cloud would act swiftly.

Gordon's head ached. Where would it all end? Was there any real chance of his clearing up this great tangle and getting to Earth for the re-exchange of bodies with the real Zarth Arn?

Finally the cruisers decelerated. Orion Nebula was now a glow in the starry heavens far behind them. Close ahead lay the shining clusters of suns of the Pleiades. And near the Pleiades' famous beacon-group there stretched a far-flung echelon of tiny sparks.

The sparks were ships! Warships of the Mid-Galactic Empire's great navy cruising here off the Pleiades, one of the many mighty squadrons watching and warding the Empire's boundaries!

Lianna had awakened. She looked out with him as the cruiser slowly moved past gigantic battleships, columns of grim cruisers, slim phantoms and destroyers and scouts.

'This is one of the main battle-fleets of the Empire,' she murmured.

'Why are we being kept here, instead of letting us give our warning?' sweated Gordon.

Their cruiser drew up alongside a giant battleship, the hulls grating together. They heard a rattle of machinery.

Then the cabin door opened and young Dar Carrul entered. 'I have received orders to transfer you at once to our flagship, the *Ethne*.'

'But let us talk first by stereo to Throon, to the Emperor!' Gordon cried. 'Man, what we have to tell may save the whole Empire from disaster!'

Dar Carrul shook his head curtly. 'My orders are that you are to send no messages but are to be transferred immediately. I presume that the *Ethne* will take you at once to Throon.'

Gordon stood, sick with disappointment and hope delayed. Lianna plucked his arm.

'It won't take long for that battleship to reach Throon, and then you'll be able to tell,' she encouraged.

The two went with guards around them down through the cruiser to a hatchway. From it a short tubular gangway had been run to the battleship.

They went through it under guard of soldiers from the battleship. Once inside the bigger ship, the gangway was cast off and the airlock closed.

Gordon looked around the vestibule chamber at officers and guards. He saw the hatred in their faces as they looked at him. They too thought him assassin of his father, traitor to the Empire!

'I demand to see the captain of this battleship immediately,' he rasped, to the lieutenant of guards.

'He is coming now,' answered the lieutenant icily, as a tramp of feet came from a corridor.

Gordon swung toward the newcomers, with on his lips a fiery request to be permitted to call Throon. He never uttered it.

For he was looking at a stocky, uniformed figure, a man whose grizzled, square face and bleak eyes he knew only too well.

'Corbulo!' he cried.

Commander Corbulo's bleak eyes did not waver as his harsh voice lashed out at Gordon.

'Yes, traitor, it is I. So you two have been caught at last?'

'You call me traitor!' Gordon choked. 'You yourself the greatest traitor in all history—'

Chan Corbulo turned coldly toward the tall, swarthy Arcturian captain who had entered with him and was glaring at Gordon.

'Captain Marlann, there is no need to take this assassin and his accomplice to Throon for trial. I *saw* them murder Arn Abbas! As Commander of the Empire fleet, I adjudge them guilty by space-law and order them executed immediately!'

21

Mutiny in the Void

Gordon's mind rocked to disastrous realization. As he stared frozenly into Chan Corbulo's grim triumphant face, he understood what had happened.

As Commander of the Empire navy, Corbulo had received the report of the capture of Gordon and Lianna. The archtraitor had known that he must not let Gordon return to Throon with what he knew. So he had swiftly come here and ordered the two captives brought aboard his own flagship to do away with them before they could tell what they knew.

Gordon looked wildly around the circle of officers. 'You've got to believe me! I'm no traitor! It was Corbulo himself who murdered my father and who is betraying the Empire to Shorr Kan!'

He saw hard, cold unbelief and bitter hatred in the officers' faces. Then Gordon recognized one familiar face.

It was the craggy red face of Hull Burrel, the Antarian captain who had saved him from the Cloud-raiders on Earth. He remembered now that for that, Hull Burrel had been promoted aide to the Commander.

'Hull Burrel, you surely believe me!' Gordon appealed. 'You know that Shorr Kan tried to have me kidnapped before.'

The big Antarian scowled. 'I thought then he did. I didn't know then you were secretly in league with him, that all that was just pretense.'

'I tell you, it wasn't pretense!' Gordon cried. 'You've all let Corbulo pull the wool over your eyes.'

Lianna, her gray eyes blazing in her white face, added, 'Zarth speaks the truth! Corbulo is the traitor!'

Chan Corbulo made a brusque gesture. 'We've had enough of these wild lies. Captain Marlann, see that they are locked out into space at once. It's the most merciful manner of execution.'

The guards stepped forward. And then, as Gordon felt the bitterness of despair, he glimpsed the satisfied smirk in Corbulo's eyes and it stung him to a final desperate effort.

'You're letting Corbulo make fools of you all!' he raged. 'Why is he so set on executing us instantly, instead of taking us to Throon for trial! Because he wants to silence us! We know too much!'

At last, Gordon perceived that he had made a little impression on the officers. Hull Burrel and others looked a little doubtful.

The Antarian glanced questioningly at Corbulo. 'Commander, I beg you will pardon me if I'm overstepping my position. But perhaps it would be more regular to take them to Throon for trial.'

Val Marlann, the swarthy Arcturian captain of this battleship, supported Hull Burrel. 'Zarth Arn is one of the royal family, after all. And the princess Lianna is a ruler in her own right.'

Lianna said swiftly, 'This execution means that Fomalhaut Kingdom will break its alliance with the Empire, remember!'

Chan Corbulo's square face stiffened in anger. He had been confident that Gordon and Lianna were on the brink of death, and this slight hitch irritated him.

His irritation made Corbulo do the wrong thing. He tried to ride roughshod over the objections just advanced.

'There is no need to take black traitors and assassins to Throon!' he snapped. 'We will execute them at once. Obey my orders!'

Gordon seized on that opportunity to make a flaming appeal to the gathered officers.

'You see? Corbulo will never let us go to Throon to tell what we know! Has he even reported our capture to the Emperor?'

Hull Burrel, with gathering trouble on his craggy face, looked at a young Earthman officer.

'You are communication-officer, Verlin. Has any report of Zarth Arn's capture been made to the Emperor?'

Corbulo exploded in rage. 'Burrel, how dare you question my conduct? By God, I'll break you for this!'

The young Earthman, Verlin, looked uncertainly at the raging Commander. Then he hesitantly answered Hull Burrel's question.

'No report of any kind has been made to Throon. The Commander ordered me to make no mention of the capture yet.'

Gordon's voice crackled. 'Doesn't that at least make you doubt?' he cried to the frowning officers. 'Why should Corbulo keep my capture secret from my brother? It's because he knows Jhal Arn would order us brought to Throon for judgment, and he doesn't want that!'

And Gordon added passionately, 'We do not ask for any pardon, for any clemency. If I'm guilty, I deserve execution. All I ask is to be taken to Throon for trial. If Corbulo persists in refusing that, it can only be because he is the traitor I say he is!'

Faces changed expression. And Gordon knew that he had finally awakened deep doubt in their minds.

'You're throwing away the Empire fleet if you let this traitor command it!' he pressed. 'He's in league with Shorr Kan. Unless you let me go to Throon to prove that, the fleet and Empire are doomed!'

Hull Burrel looked around his fellow officers, and then at Chan Corbulo. 'Commander, we mean no disrespect. But Zarth Arn's demand for a trial is reasonable. He should be taken to Throon.'

A low chorus of supporting voices came from the other officers. Deep ingrained as was their discipline, deeper still was the doubt and the fear for the Empire that Gordon had awakened.

Corbulo's face flared dull red with fury. 'Burrel, you're under arrest! By God, you'll take the spacewalk with these two for your insubordination! Guards, seize him!'

Tall, swarthy Captain Val Marlann stepped forward and intervened.

'Wait, guards! Commander Corbulo, you are supreme officer of the Empire fleet but I am captain of the *Ethne*. And I agree with Burrel that we cannot summarily execute these prisoners.'

'Marlann, you're captain of the *Ethne* no longer!' raged Corbulo. 'I hereby remove you and take personal command of this ship.'

Val Marlann stiffened in open defiance as he rasped an answer.

'Commander, if I'm wrong I'm willing to take the consequences. But by God, something about all this does smell to Heaven! We're going to Throon and find out what it is!'

Gordon heard the mutter of agreement from the other officers. And Chan Corbulo heard it also.

The baffled rage on his grizzled face deepened, and he uttered a curse.

'Very well, then – to Throon! And when I get through with you at the courts-martial there, you'll wish you'd remembered your discipline. Insubordination in high space! Just wait!'

And Corbulo turned angrily and shouldered out of the room, going forward along a corridor.

Burrel and the other officers looked soberly at each other. Then Val Marlann spoke grimly to Gordon.

'Prince Zarth, you'll get the trial at Throon you asked for. And if you've not told the truth, it's our necks.'

'It must be the truth!' Hull Burrel declared. 'I never could understand why Zarth Arn should murder his own father! And why would Corbulo be so wild to execute them if the commander had nothing to hide?'

At that moment, from the annunciators throughout the ship, broke a loud voice.

'Commander Corbulo, to all hands! Mutiny has broken out on the *Ethne!* Captain Val Marlann and his chief officers, my aide Hull Burrel, and Prince Zarth and Princess Lianna are the ringleaders! All loyal men arm and seize the mutineers!'

Hull Burrel's blue eyes flashed an arctic light. 'He's raising the ship against us! Val, get to the annunciators and call off the men! You can convince them!'

The officers plunged for the corridors leading up into the interior of the mighty battleship.

Gordon cried, 'Lianna, wait here! There may be fighting!'

Then, as he ran with Hull Burrel and the others through the corridors, they heard a growing uproar somewhere ahead.

The great battleship was suddenly in chaos, alarm bells ringing, voices yelling from the annunciators, feet pounding through the corridors.

The spacemen who had rushed to obey the supreme commander's order were now bewildered by a clash of authority. Some, who tried to obey and arrest Val Marlann and his officers, were instantly attacked by those of their own comrades who remained loyal to the ship's captain.

In most of the ship, the crew had not had time to arm. Improvised metal clubs and fists took the place of atom-pistols. Battle joined and raged swiftly in crewrooms, in gun-galleries, in corridors.

Gordon and Hull Burrel found themselves with Val Marlann in the midst of a seething, battling mob in the main mid-deck corridor.

'I've got to get through to an annunciator switchboard!' cried Val Marlann. 'Help me crash through them!'

Gordon and the big Antarian, with Verlin, the young communication officer, joined him and plunged into the crazy fight.

They got through, but left big Hull Burrel battling a knot of spacemen back in the mob.

Val Marlann yelled into the annunciator switchboard. 'Captain Marlann to all hands! Cease fighting! The announcement of mutiny was a fake, a trick! Obey me!'

Verlin grabbed Gordon's arm as a distant whine of power reached their ears over the din.

'That's the stereo-transmitter going!' the young communication officer cried to Gordon. 'Corbulo must be calling for help from the other ships of the fleet!'

'We've got to stop that!' Gordon cried. 'Lead the way!'

They raced forward along a corridor, then cross-ship and up a companionway to the top deck.

Val Marlann's orders thundering from the annunciators seemed to be rapidly quieting the uproar in the ship. Its crew knew his voice better than any other. Long habit brought them to obey.

Verlin and Gordon plunged into a big, crowded Stereo room whose tubes and motor-generators were humming. Two bewildered-looking technicians were at the patrol panel.

Chan Corbulo, an atom-pistol gripped in his hand, stood on the transmitter-plate speaking loudly and rapidly.

'– command all nearby battleships to send boarding parties aboard the *Ethne* at once to restore order! You will arrest—'

Corbulo, from the tail of his eye, saw the two men burst into the room. He swung swiftly around and triggered his pistol.

The pellet that flew from it was aimed at Gordon. But Verlin, plunging ahead, took it full in his breast.

Gordon tripped headlong over the falling body of the young Earthman. That stumble made Corbulo's quick second shot flick just over Gordon's head.

As he fell, Gordon had hurled himself forward. He tackled Corbulo's knees and brought him crashing to the floor.

The two technicians ran forward and hauled Gordon off the Commander. But their grip on him relaxed when they glimpsed his face.

'Good God, it's Prince Zarth Arn!' one of them cried.

Instinctive respect for the ruling house of the Empire confused the two men. Gordon wrenched free from them and grabbed for the pistol in Verlin's holster.

Corbulo had regained his feet, on the other side of the room. He was again raising his weapon.

'*You'll* never go to Throon!' he roared. 'By—'

Gordon shot, from where he crouched on the floor. The atomic pellet, loosed more by guess than by aim, hit Corbulo's neck and exploded. It flung him backwards as though a giant hand had hit him.

Val Marlann and Hull Burrel came bursting into the stereoroom with other officers. The whole great ship seemed suddenly quiet.

Marlann bent over Corbulo's blasted body. 'Dead!'

Hull Burrel, panting, his face flaming, told Gordon grimly, 'We've killed our Commander. God help us if your story is not true, Prince Zarth!'

'It's true – and Corbulo was only one of a score of traitors in Shorr Kan's hire,' Gordon husked, shaken with reaction. 'I'll prove it all at Throon.'

The image of a dark, towering Centaurian battleship captain suddenly appeared on the receiver-plate of the stereo.

'Vice-Commander Ron Giron calling from the *Shaar!* What the devil is going on aboard the *Ethne?* We're coming alongside to board you as Commander Corbulo ordered.'

'No one will board this ship!' Val Marlann answered swiftly. 'We're going at once to Throon.'

'What does this mean?' roared the vice-commander. 'Let me speak to Commander Corbulo himself!'

'You can't – he's dead,' clipped Hull Burrel. 'He was betraying the fleet to the Cloud. At Throon, we'll prove that.'

'It *is* mutiny, then?' cried Ron Giron. 'You'll stand by for boarding parties and consider yourselves under arrest, or we'll open fire!'

'If you fire on the *Ethne*, you'll destroy the Empire's only chance to foil

Shorr Kan's plot!' cried Val Marlann. 'We've staked our lives on the truth of what Prince Zarth Arn has told us, and we're taking him to Throon.'

John Gordon himself stepped forward to make an appeal to the glaring vice-commander.

'Commander Giron, they're telling you the truth! Give us this chance to save the Empire from disaster!'

Giron hesitated. 'This is all insane! Corbulo dead and accused of treachery, Zarth Arn returned—'

He seemed to reach decision. 'It's beyond me but they can sift it at Throon. To make sure that you go there, four battleships will escort the *Ethne*. They'll have orders to blast you if you try to go anywhere but Throon!'

'That's all we ask!' Gordon cried. 'One more word of warning! A League attack may come at any time now. I know it is coming, and soon.'

Commander Giron's towering figure stiffened. 'The devil you say! But we've already taken all possible dispositions. I'll call the Emperor and report all this to him.'

The image disappeared. Through the portholes, they saw four big battleships move up and take positions on either side of the *Ethne*.

'We start for Throon at once,' Val Marlann said swiftly. 'I'll give the orders.'

As the officer hurried out, and annunciators and bells started buzzing through the ship, Gordon asked a question.

'Am I to consider myself still a prisoner?'

'Blazes, no!' Hull Burrel exclaimed. 'If you've told us the truth, there's no reason to keep you a prisoner. If you haven't told the truth, then we're due for court-martial and execution anyway!'

Gordon found Lianna in the corridor, hurrying in search of him. He told her rapidly what had happened.

'Corbulo dead? One great danger removed!' she exclaimed. 'But Zarth, now our lives and the Empire's fate depend on whether we can prove to your brother that our story is true!'

At that moment the mighty *Ethne* began to move ponderously through the void, as its great turbines roared loud.

In a few minutes, the big battleship and its four grim escorts were hurtling headlong across the starry spaces toward Throon.

22

Galactic Crisis

Huge, glaring white Canopus flared in the star-sown heavens in blinding splendor, as the five great battleships rushed toward it at rapidly decreasing speed.

Once again, John Gordon looked from a ship's bridge at the glorious capital sun of the Empire and its green, lovely world. But how much had happened since first he had come to Throon!

'We dock at Throon City in two hours,' Hull Burrel was saying. And he added grimly, 'There'll be a reception committee waiting for us. Your brother has been advised of our coming.'

'All I ask is a chance to prove my story to Jhal,' declared Gordon, 'I'm sure I can convince him.'

But, inwardly, he had a sickening feeling that he was *not* entirely sure. It all depended on one man, and on whether Gordon had correctly judged that man's reactions.

All the hours and days of the headlong homeward flight across the Empire, Gordon had been tortured by that haunting doubt. He had slept but little, had scarcely eaten, consumed by growing tension.

He *must* convince Jhal Arn! Once that was done, once the last traitor was rooted out, then the Empire would be ready to meet the Cloud's attack. His, John Gordon's, duty would be fulfilled and he could return to Earth for his re-exchange of bodies with the real Zarth Arn. And the real Zarth could come back to help defend the Empire.

But Gordon felt an agony of spirit every time he thought of that re-exchange of bodies. For on that day when he returned to his own time, he would be leaving Lianna forever.

Lianna came into the wide bridge as he thought of her. She stood beside him with her slim fingers clasping his hand encouragingly as they looked ahead.

'Your brother will believe you, Zarth – I know he will.'

'Not without proof,' Gordon muttered. 'And only one man can prove my story. Everything hinges on whether or not he has heard of Corbulo's death and my return, and has fled.'

That tormenting uncertainty deepened in him as the five big battleships swung down toward Throon City.

It was night in the capital. Under the light of two hurtling moons glimmered the fairylike glass mountains and the silver sea. The shimmering towers of the city rose boldly in the soft glow, a pattern of lacy light.

The ships landed ponderously in docks of the naval spaceport. Gordon and Lianna, with Hull Burrel and Captain Val Marlann, emerged from the *Ethne* to be met by a solid mass of armed guards.

Two officers walked toward them, and with them came Orth Bodmer, the Chief Councillor. Bodmer's thin face was lined with deep worry as he confronted Gordon.

'Highness, this is a sorry homecoming!' he faltered. 'God send you can prove your innocence!'

'Jhal Arn has kept our return and what happened out there off the Pleiades a secret?' Gordon asked quickly.

Orth Bodmer nodded. 'His Highness is waiting for you now. We are to go at once to the palace by tubeway. I must warn you that these guards have orders to kill instantly if any of you attempt resistance.'

They were swiftly searched for weapons, and then led toward the tubeway. Guards entered the cars with them. They had seen no one else, the whole spaceport having been cleared and barred off.

It seemed a dream to John Gordon as they whirled through the tubeway. Too much had happened to him, in too short a time. The mind couldn't stand it. But Lianna's warm clasp of his hand remained a link with reality, nerving him for this ordeal.

In the great palace of Throon, they went up through emptied corridors to the study in which Gordon had first confronted Arn Abbas.

Jhal Arn sat now behind the desk, his handsome face a worn mask. His eyes were utterly cold and expressionless as they swept over Gordon and Lianna and the two space-captains.

'Have the guards remain outside, Bodmer,' he ordered the Councillor in a toneless voice.

Orth Bodmer hesitated. 'The prisoners have no weapons. Yet perhaps—'

'Do as I order,' rasped Jhal Arn. 'I have weapons here. There's no fear of my brother being able to murder *me*.'

The nervous Chief Councillor and the guards went out and closed the door.

Gordon was feeling a hot resentment that burned away all that numb feeling of unreality.

He strode a step forward. 'Is this the kind of justice you're going to deal the Empire?' he blazed at Jhal Arn. 'The kind of justice that condemns a man before he's heard?'

'Heard? Man, you were *seen*, murdering our father!' cried Jhal Arn, rising. 'Corbulo saw you, and now you've killed Corbulo too!'

'Jhal Arn, it is not so!' cried Lianna. 'You must listen to Zarth!'

Jhal Arn turned somber eyes on her. 'Lianna, I have no blame for you. You love Zarth and let him lead you into this. But as for him, the studious, scholarly brother I once loved, the brother who was plotting all the time for power, who struck our father down—'

'Will you listen?' cried Gordon furiously. 'You stand there mouthing accusations without giving me a chance to answer them!'

'I have heard your answers already,' rasped Jhal Arn. 'Vice-Commander Giron told me when he reported your coming that you were accusing Corbulo of treachery to cover up your own black crimes.'

'I can prove that if you'll just give me a chance!' Gordon declared.

'What proof can you advance?' retorted the other. 'What proof, that will outweigh the damning evidence of your flight, of Corbulo's testimony, of Shorr Kan's secret messages to you?'

Gordon knew that he had come to the crux of the situation, the crisis upon which he would stand or fall.

He talked hoarsely, telling of Corbulo's treacherous assistance in helping Lianna and him escape, of how that escape had been timed exactly with the assassination of Arn Abbas.

'It was to make it look as though I'd committed the murder and fled!' Gordon emphasized. 'Corbulo himself struck down our father and then said he'd seen me do it, knowing I wasn't there to deny the charge!'

He narrated swiftly how the Sirian traitor captain had taken him and Lianna to the Cloud, and briefly summarized the way in which he had induced Shorr Kan, by pretending to join him, to allow him to go to Earth. He did not, could not, tell how his ruse had hinged on the fact that he was really not Zarth Arn at all. He couldn't tell that.

Gordon finished his swift story, and saw that the black cloud of bitter disbelief still rested on Jhal Arn's face.

'The story is too fantastic! And it has nothing to prove it but your word and the word of this girl who's in love with you. You said you could prove your tale!'

'I can prove it, if I'm given a chance,' Gordon said earnestly.

He continued swiftly. 'Jhal, Corbulo was not the only traitor in high position in the Empire. Shorr Kan himself told me there were a score of such traitors, though he didn't name them.

'But one traitor I know to be such is Thern Eldred, the Sirian naval captain who took us to the Cloud! He can prove it all, if I can make him talk!'

Jhal Arn frowned at Gordon for a moment. Then he touched a stud and spoke into a panel on the desk.

'Naval Headquarters? The Emperor speaking. There is a captain in our forces named Thern Eldred, a Sirian. Find out if he's on Throon. If he is, send him here immediately under guard.'

Gordon grew tense as they waited. If the Sirian were away in space, if he had somehow heard of events and had fled –

Then a sharp voice finally came from the panel. 'Thern Eldred has been found here. His cruiser has just returned from patrol. He is being sent to you now.'

A half-hour later the door opened and Thern Eldred stepped inside. The Sirian had a wondering look on his hardbitten greenish face. Then his eyes fell on Gordon and Lianna.

'Zarth Arn!' he exclaimed, startled, recoiling. His hand went to his belt, but he had been disarmed.

'Surprised to see us?' Gordon rasped. 'You thought we were still in the Cloud where you left us, didn't you?'

Thern Eldred had instantly recovered his self-possession. He looked at Gordon with assumed perplexity.

'I don't understand what you mean, about the Cloud!'

Jhal Arn spoke curtly. 'Zarth claims that you took him and Lianna by force to Thallarna. He accuses you of being a traitor to the Empire, of plotting with Shorr Kan.'

The Sirian's face stiffened in admirably assumed anger.

'It's a lie! Why, I haven't seen Prince Zarth Arn and the princess since the Feast of Moons!'

Jhal Arn looked harshly at Gordon. 'You said you could prove your claim, Zarth. So far, it's only your word against his.'

Lianna broke in passionately. 'Is my word nothing, then? Is a Princess of Fomalhaut to be believed a liar?'

Again, Jhal Arn looked at her somberly. 'Lianna, I know you would lie for Zarth Arn, if for nothing else in the universe.'

Gordon had expected the Sirian's denial. And he was counting on his estimate of this man's character, to get the truth out of him.

He stepped forward to confront the man. He kept his passionate anger restrained, and spoke deliberately.

'Thern Eldred, the game is up. Corbulo is dead, the whole plot with Shorr Kan is about to be exposed. You haven't a chance to keep your guilt hidden, and when it's exposed it'll mean execution for you.'

As the Sirian started to protest, Gordon continued swiftly, 'I know what you're thinking! You think that if you stick to your denials you can face me down, that that's your only chance now to save your skin. But it won't work, Thern Eldred!

'The reason it won't work is because your cruiser, the *Markab*, had a full crew in it when it took us to the Cloud. I know those officers and men had been bribed to support you, that they'll deny ever going to the Cloud. They'll deny it, at first. But when pressure is put on them, there's bound to be at least one weak one among them who'll confess to save himself!'

Now, for the first time, Gordon saw doubt creep into the Sirian's eyes. Yet Thern Eldred angrily shook his head.

'You're still talking nonsense, Prince Zarth! If you want to question my men in the *Markab*, go ahead. Their testimony will show that you're not telling the truth.'

Gordon pressed his attack, his voice ringing now. 'Thern Eldred, you can't bluff it out! You know one of them will talk! And when he does, it's execution for you.

'There's only one way you can save yourself. That's to turn evidence against the other officials and officers in this plot with you, the others who have been working for Shorr Kan. Give us their names, and you'll be allowed to go scot-free out of the Empire!'

Jhal Arn sternly interrupted. 'I'll sanction no such terms! If this man is a traitor, he'll suffer the penalty.'

Gordon turned passionately to him. 'Jhal, listen! He deserves death for his treachery. But which is most important – that he be punished, or that the Empire be saved from disaster?'

The argument swayed Jhal Arn. He frowned silently for a moment, and then spoke slowly.

'Very well, I'll agree to let him go free if he does make any such confession and names his confederates.'

Gordon swung back to the Sirian. 'Your last chance, Thern Eldred! You can save yourself now, or never!'

He saw the indecision in Thern Eldred's eyes. He was staking everything on the fact that this Sirian was a ruthless realist, ambitious, selfish, with no real loyalty to anyone but himself.

And Gordon's gamble won. Confronted by the imminence of discovery, presented with a loophole by which he might save his own skin, Thern Eldred's defiant denials broke down.

He spoke huskily. 'I have the Emperor's word that I am to go scot-free, remember?'

'Then you *were* in a plot?' raged Jhal Arn. 'But I'll keep my word. You'll go free if you name your confederates, as soon as we have seized them and verified what you tell.'

Thern Eldred was ghastly pale but tried to smile. 'I know when I'm in a trap, and I'm cursed if I'll get myself killed just for loyalty to Shorr Kan. He wouldn't do it for me!'

He went on, to Jhal Arn. 'Prince Zarth has told the truth. Chan Corbulo was leader of the little clique of officials who planned to betray the Empire to the Cloud. Corbulo killed Arn Abbas, and had me carry off Zarth and Lianna so they'd be blamed. Everything the prince has said is true.'

Gordon felt his eyes blur, his shoulders sag, as those words brought shaky relief from his intolerable strain of many days.

He felt Lianna's warm arms around him, heard her eager voice as big Hull Burrel and Val Marlann excitedly slapped his back.

'Zarth, I knew you'd clear yourself!'

Jhal Arn, face pale as death, came toward Gordon. His voice was hoarse when he spoke.

'Zarth, can you ever pardon me? My God, how was I to know? I'll never forgive myself!'

'Jhal, it's all right,' Gordon stumbled. 'What else were you to think when it was so cunningly planned?'

'The whole Empire shall soon know the truth,' Jhal Arn exclaimed. He swung to Thern Eldred. 'First, the names of the other traitors.'

Thern Eldred went to the desk and wrote for minutes. He silently handed the sheet to Jhal Arn, who then summoned guards forward.

'You'll be confined until this information is verified,' he told the Sirian sternly. 'Then I'll keep my promise. You shall go free – but the tale of your treachery will follow you to the remotest stars!'

Jhal Arn turned his eyes to the list of names, when the guards had taken the Sirian out. He cried out, stunned, 'Good God, look!'

Gordon saw. The first name on the list was 'Orth Bodmer, Chief Councillor of the Empire.'

'Bodmer a traitor? It's impossible!' Jhal Arn cried. 'Thern Eldred has merely accused him because of some grudge.'

Gordon frowned. 'Perhaps. But Corbulo was as trusted as Orth Bodmer, remember!'

Jhal Arn's lips tightened. He spoke sharply into a panel on the desk. 'Tell Councillor Bodmer to come in at once.'

The answer was quick. 'Councillor Bodmer left the anteroom some time ago. We do not know where he went.'

'Find him and bring him here at once!' ordered Jhal Arn.

'He fled when he saw Thern Eldred brought in here to be questioned!' cried Gordon. 'Jhal, he *knew* the Sirian would expose him!'

Jhal Arn sank into a chair. 'Bodmer a traitor! Yet it must be so. And look at these other names. Byrn Ridim, Korrel Kane, Jon Rollory – all trusted officials.'

The guard-captain reported. 'Highness, we can't find Orth Bodmer anywhere in the palace! He wasn't seen to leave, but isn't to be found!'

'Send out a general order for his arrest,' snapped Jhal Arn. He handed the list of names to the guard-captain. 'And arrest all these men instantly. But do so without arousing attention.'

He looked haggardly at Gordon and Lianna. 'All this treachery has already shaken the Empire! And the southern star-kingdoms are wavering! Their envoys have requested urgent audience with me tonight, and I fear they mean to throw off their alliance with the Empire!'

23

The Secret of the Empire

Gordon suddenly noticed that Lianna's slim figure was sagging with weariness. He uttered an exclamation of self-reproach.

'Lianna, you must be half dead after all you've been through!'

Lianna tried to smile. 'I'll admit that I won't be sorry to rest.'

'Captain Burrel will see you to your apartments, Lianna,' said Jhal Arn. 'I want Zarth to be here with me when the star-kingdom envoys come, to impress on them that our royal house is again united.'

He added to Hull Burrel and Val Marlann, 'You two and all your men are completely cleared of the mutiny charge, of course. I'm your debtor for life for helping to expose Corbulo and save my brother.'

When they had escorted Lianna out, Gordon sank tiredly into a chair. He was still feeling reaction after the long strain.

'Zarth, I'd rather let you rest too but you know how vital it is to hold the star-kingdoms when this crisis is deepening,' Jhal said. 'Curse that black devil, Shorr Kan!'

A servant brought *saqua* and the fiery liquor cleared Gordon's numbed mind and brought strength back into his weary body.

Presently a chamberlain opened the door of the room, bowing low.

'The ambassadors of the Kingdoms of Polaris, of Cygnus, of Perseus and of Cassiopeia, and of the Baronies of Hercules Cluster!'

The envoys, in full dress uniforms, stopped in amazement when they saw Gordon standing beside Jhal Arn.

'Prince Zarth!' exclaimed the chubby Hercules envoy. 'But we thought—'

'My brother has been completely cleared and the real traitors have been apprehended,' Jhal informed them. 'It will be publicly announced within the hour.'

His eyes ran over their faces. 'Gentlemen, for what purpose have you requested this audience?'

The chubby Hercules ambassador looked at the grave, aged envoy from Polaris Kingdom. 'Tu Shal, you are our spokesman.'

Tu Shal's lined old face was deeply troubled as he stepped forward and spoke.

'Highness, Shorr Kan has secretly just offered all our kingdoms treaty of friendship with the League of Dark Worlds! He declares that if we cling to our alliance with the Empire, we are doomed.'

The Hercules ambassador added, 'He has made the same offer to us Barons, warning us not to join the Empire.'

Jhal Arn looked swiftly at Gordon. 'So Shorr Kan is now sending ultimatums? That means he is almost ready to strike.'

'We none of us have any love for Shorr Kan's tyranny,' Tu Shal was saying. 'We prefer to hold to the Empire that stands for peace and union. But it is said that the Cloud has prepared such tremendous armaments and has such revolutionary new weapons that they'll carry all before them if war comes.'

Jhal Arn's eyes flashed. 'Do you dream he can conquer the Empire when we have the Disruptor to use in case of necessity?'

'That's just it, highness!' said Tu Shal. 'It's being said that the Disruptor was never used but once long ago, and that it proved so dangerous then that you would not dare to use it again!'

He added, 'I fear that our kingdoms will desert their allegiance to the Empire unless you prove that that is a lie. Unless you prove to us that you do dare to use the Disruptor!'

Jhal Arn looked steadily at the envoys as he answered. And his solemn words seemed to Gordon to bring the whisper of something alien and supernally terrible into the little room.

'Tu Shal, the Disruptor is an awful power. I will not disguise that it is dangerous to unchain that power in the galaxy. But it was done once when the Magellanians invaded, long ago.

'And it will be done again, if necessary! My father is dead, but Zarth and I can unloose that power. And we *will* unloose it and rive the galaxy before we let Shorr Kan fasten tyranny on the free worlds!'

Tu Shal seemed more deeply troubled than before. 'But highness, our kingdoms demand that we *see* the Disruptor demonstrated before they will believe!'

Jhal's face grew somber. 'I had hoped that never would the Disruptor have to be taken from its safekeeping and loosed again. But it may be that it would be best to do as you ask.'

His eyes flashed. 'Yes, it may be that when Shorr Kan learns that we can still wield that power and hears what it can do, he will think twice before precipitating galactic war!'

'Then you will demonstrate it for us?' asked the Hercules envoy, his round face awed.

'There's a region of deserted dark-stars fifty parsecs west of Argol,' Jhal Arn told them. 'Two days from now, we'll unchain the power of the Disruptor there for you to see.'

Tu Shal's troubled face cleared a little. 'If you do that, our kingdoms will utterly reject the overtures of the Cloud!'

'And I can guarantee that the Barons of the Cluster will declare for the Empire!' added the chubby envoy from Hercules.

When they had gone, Jhal Arn looked with haggard face at Gordon. 'It was the only way I could hold them, Zarth! If I'd refused, they'd have been panicked into submitting to Shorr Kan.'

Gordon asked him wonderingly, 'You're really going to unloose the Disruptor to convince them?'

The other was sweating. 'I don't want to, God knows! You know Brenn Bir's warning as well as I do! You know what nearly happened when *he* used it on the Magellanians two thousand years ago!'

He stiffened. 'But I'll run even that risk, rather than let the Cloud launch a war to enslave the galaxy!'

Gordon felt a deeper sense of wonder and perplexity, mixed with cold apprehension.

What was it, really, the age-old secret power which even Jhal Arn who was its master could not mention without fear?

Jhal Arn continued urgently. 'Zarth, we'll go down now to the Chamber of the Disruptor. It's been long since either of us was there, and we must make sure everything is ready for that demonstration.'

Gordon for the moment recoiled. He, a stranger, couldn't pry into this most guarded secret in the galaxy!

Then he suddenly realized that it made little difference if he did see the thing. He wasn't scientist enough to understand it. And in any case, he'd be going back soon to his own time, his own body.

He'd have to find a chance to slip away to Earth in the next day or so, without letting Jhal Arn know. He could order a ship to take him there.

Once again, at that thought, came the heartbreaking realization that he was on the verge of parting forever from Lianna.

'Come, Zarth!' Jhal was saying impatiently. 'I know you must be tired, but there's little time left.'

They went out through the anteroom, Jhal Arn waving back the guards who sprang to accompany them.

Gordon accompanied him down sliding ramps and through corridors and down again, until he knew they must be deeper beneath the great palace of Throon than even the prison where he had been confined.

They entered a spiral stair that dropped downward into a hall hollowed from the solid rock of the planet. From this hall, a long, rock-hewn corridor led away. It was lighted by a throbbing white radiance emitted by luminous plates in its walls.

As Gordon walked down this radiant corridor with Jhal Arn, he felt an astonishment he could hardly conceal. He had expected great masses of guards, mighty doors with massive bolts, all kinds of cunning devices to guard the most titanic power in the galaxy.

Instead, there seemed nothing whatever to guard it! Neither on the stair nor in this brilliant corridor was there anyone. And when Jhal Arn opened the door at the corridor end, it was not even locked!

Jhal Arn looked through the open door with Gordon from the threshold.

'There it is, the same as ever,' he said with a strong tinge of awe in his voice.

The room was a small, round one hollowed also from solid rock and also lighted by throbbing white radiance from wall-plates.

Gordon perceived at the center of, the room the group of objects at which Jhal Arn was gazing with such awe.

The Disruptor! The weapon so terrible that its power had only once been unloosed in two thousand years!

'But what *is* it?' Gordon wondered dazedly, as he stared.

There were twelve big conical objects of dull gray metal, each a dozen feet long. The apex of each cone was a cluster of tiny crystal spheres. Heavy, vari-colored cables led from the base of the cones.

What complexities of unimaginable science lay inside the cones, he could not even guess. Beside heavy brackets for mounting them, the only other object here was a bulky cubical cabinet on whose face were mounted a bank of luminous gauges and six rheostat switches.

'It draws such tremendous power that it will have to be mounted on a battleship, of course,' Jhal Arn was saying thoughtfully. 'What about the *Ethne* you came in? Wouldn't its turbines provide enough power?'

Gordon floundered. 'I suppose so. I'm afraid I'll have to leave all that to you.'

Jhal Arn looked astounded. 'But Zarth, you're the scientist of the family. You know more about the Disruptor than I do.'

Gordon hastily denied that. 'I'm afraid I don't know. You see, it's been so long that I've forgotten a lot about it.'

Jhal Arn looked incredulous. 'Forgotten about the Disruptor? You must be joking! That's one thing we don't forget! Why it's drilled into our minds beyond forgetfulness on the day when we're first brought down here to have the Wave tuned to our bodies!'

The Wave? What was that? Gordon felt completely at sea in his ignorance.

He advanced a hasty explanation. 'Jhal, I told you that Shorr Kan used a brain-scanning device to try to learn the Disruptor secret from me. He couldn't – but in my deliberate effort to forget it so he couldn't, I seem really to have lost a lot of the details.'

Jhal Arn seemed satisfied by the explanation. 'So that's it! Mental shock, of course. But of course you still remember the main nature of the secret. Nobody *could* forget that.'

'Of course, I haven't forgotten that,' Gordon was forced to prevaricate hastily.

Jhal drew him forward. 'Here, it will all come back to you. These brackets are for mounting the force-cones on a ship's prow. The colored cables hook to the similarly colored binding-posts on the control-panel, and the transformer leads go right back to drive-generators.'

He pointed at the gauges. 'They give the exact coordinates in space of the area to be affected. The output of the cones has to balance exactly, of course. The rheostats do that—'

As he went on, John Gordon began dimly to perceive that the cones were designed to project force into a selected area of space.

But what kind of force? What did they *do* to the area or object on which they acted, that was so awful? He dared not ask that.

Jhal Arn was concluding his explanation. '– so the target area must be at least ten parsecs from the ship you work from, or you'll get the backlash. Don't you remember it all now, Zarth?'

Gordon nodded hurriedly. 'Of course. But I'm glad just the same that it will be your job to use it.'

Jhal looked more haggard. 'God knows I don't want to! It has rested here all these centuries without being used. And the warning of Brenn Bir still is true.'

He pointed up, as he spoke, to an inscription on the opposite wall. Gordon read it now for the first time.

'To my descendants who will hold the secret of the Disruptor that I, Brenn Bir, discovered. Heed my warning! Never use the Disruptor for petty personal power! Use it only if the freedom of the galaxy is menaced!

'This power you hold could destroy the galaxy. It is a demon so titanic that once unchained, it might not be chained again. Take not that awful risk unless the life and liberty of all men are at stake!'

Jhal Arn's voice was solemn. 'Zarth, when you and I were boys and were first brought down here by our father to have the Wave tuned to us, we little dreamed that a time might come when we would think of using that which has lain here for so long.'

His voice rang deeper. 'But the life and liberty of all men *are* at stake, if Shorr Kan seeks to conquer the galaxy! If all else fails, we must take the risk!'

Gordon felt shaken by the implications of that warning. It was like a voice of the dead, speaking heavily in this silent room.

Jhal turned and led the way out of the room. He closed the door and again Gordon wondered. No lock, not bolts, no guard!

They went down the long radiant corridor and emerged from it into the softer yellow light of the well of the spiral stair.

'We'll mount the equipment on the *Ethne* tomorrow morning,' Jhal Arn was saying. 'When we show the star-kingdom envoys—'

'You will never show them anything, Jhal Arn!'

Out from beneath the spiral stair had sprung a dishevelled man who held an atom-pistol levelled on Gordon and Jhal Arn.

'Orth Bodmer!' cried Gordon. 'You were hiding in the palace all the time!'

Orth Bodmer's thin face was colorless, deadly, twitching in a pallid smile.

'Yes, Zarth,' he grated. 'I knew the game was up when I saw Thern Eldred brought in. I couldn't get out of the palace without being swiftly traced and apprehended, so I hid in the deeper corridors.'

His smile was ghastly now. 'I hid, until as I had hoped you came down here to the Chamber of the Disruptor, Jhal Arn! I've been waiting for you!'

Jhal's eyes flashed. 'Just what do you expect to gain by this?'

'It is simple,' rasped Bodmer. 'I know my life is forfeit. Well, so is your life unless you spare mine!'

He stepped closer, and Gordon read the madness of fear in his burning eyes.

'You do not break your word when it is given, highness. Promise me that I shall be pardoned, and I will not kill you now!'

Gordon saw that panic had driven this rabbity, nervous traitor to insane resolve.

'Jhal, do it!' he cried. 'He's not worth risking your life for!'

Jhal Arn's face was dull red with fury. 'I have let one traitor go free, but no more!'

Instantly, before Gordon could voice the cry of appeal on his lips, Orth Bodmer's atom-pistol crashed.

The pellet tore into Jhal Arn's shoulder and exploded there as Gordon plunged forward at the maddened traitor.

'You murdering lunatic!' cried Gordon fiercely, seizing the other's gun-wrist and grappling with him.

For a moment, the thin Councillor seemed to have superhuman strength. They swayed, stumbled, and then reeled together from the hall into the brilliant white radiance of the long corridor.

Then Orth Bodmer screamed! He screamed like a soul in torment, and Gordon felt the man's body relax horribly in his grasp.

'The Wave!' screeched Bodmer, staggering in the throbbing radiance.

Even as the man screamed, Gordon saw his whole body and face horribly blacken and wither. It was a shrivelled, lifeless body that sank to the floor.

So ghastly and mysterious was that sudden death, that for a moment Gordon was dazed. Then he suddenly understood.

The throbbing radiance in the corridor and in the Chamber of the Disruptor was the Wave that Jhal Arn had spoken of! It was not light but a terrible, destroying force – a force so tuned to individual human bodily vibrations that it blasted every human being except the chosen holders of the Disruptor secret.

No wonder that no locks or bolts or guards were needed to protect the Disruptor! No man could approach it without being destroyed, except Jhal Arn and Gordon himself. No, not John Gordon but Zarth Arn – it was Zarth Arn's physical body that the Wave was tuned to spare!

Gordon stumbled out of that terrible radiance back into the hall. He bent over the prone form of Jhal Arn.

'Jhal! For God's sake—'

Jhal Arn had a terrible, blackened wound in his shoulder and side. But he was still breathing, still alive.

Gordon sprang to the stair and shouted upward. 'Guards! The Emperor has been hurt!'

Guards, officers, officials, came pouring down quickly. Jhal Arn by then was stirring feebly. His eyes opened.

'Bodmer – guilty of this attack on me!' he muttered to them. 'Is Zarth all right?'

'I'm here. He didn't hit me, and he's dead now,' Gordon husked.

An hour later, he waited in an outer room of the royal apartments high in the palace. Lianna was there, striving to comfort Jhal Arn's weeping wife.

A physician came hurriedly from the inner room to which Jhal Arn had been taken.

'The emperor will live!' he announced. 'But he is terribly wounded, and it will take many weeks for him to recover.'

He added worriedly, 'He insists on Prince Zarth Arn coming in.'

Gordon uncertainly entered the big, luxurious bedroom. The two women followed. He stooped over the bed in which Jhal Arn lay.

Jhal Arn whispered an order. 'Bring a stereo-transmitting set. And order it switched through for a broadcast to the whole Empire.'

'Jhal, you mustn't try it!' Gordon protested. 'You can make announcements of my being cleared in another way than that.'

'It's not only that that I have to announce,' Jhal whispered. 'Zarth, don't you realize what it means for me to be stricken down at the very moment when Shorr Kan's plans are reaching their crisis?'

The stereo transmitter was hastily brought in. Its viewer-disk swung to include Jhal Arn's bed, and Gordon and Lianna and Zora.

Jhal Arn painfully raised his head on the pillow, his white face looking into the disk.

'People of the Empire!' he said hoarsely. 'The same traitorous assassins who murdered my father have tried to murder me, but have failed. I shall in time be well again.

'Chan Corbulo and Orth Bodmer – *they* were the ringleaders of the group! My brother Zarth Arn has been proved completely innocent and now resumes his royal rank.

'And since I am thus stricken down, I appoint my brother Zarth Arn as regent to rule in my place until I recover. No matter what events burst upon us, give your allegiance to Zarth Arn as leader of our Empire!'

24

Storm Over Throon

Gordon uttered an involuntary exclamation of dismayed amazement.

'Jhal, no! I can't wield the rule of the Empire, even for a short time!'

Jhal Arn had already made a feeble gesture of dismissal to the technicians. They had quickly switched off the stereo apparatus as he finished speaking, and were now withdrawing.

At Gordon's protest, Jhal Arn turned his deathly-white face and answered in an earnest whisper.

'Zarth, you must act for me. In this moment of crisis when the Cloud darkens across the galaxy, the Empire cannot be left without a leader.'

Zora, his wife, seconded the appeal to Gordon. 'You're of the royal house. You alone can command allegiance now.'

Gordon's mind whirled. What was he to do? Refuse and finally reveal to them the unguessed truth of his identity and his involuntary imposture?

He couldn't do that now! It *would* leave the Empire without a head, would leave all its people and its allies confused and bewildered, would make them imminent prey for the attack of the Cloud.

But on the other hand, how could he carry out the role when he was still so ignorant of this universe? And how then could he get away to Earth to contact the real Zarth Arn across time?

'You have been proclaimed regent to the Empire and it is impossible to retract that now,' said Jhal Arn, in a weak whisper.

Gordon's heart sank. It *was* impossible to retract that proclamation without throwing the Empire into even deeper confusion.

There was only one course open to him. He would have to occupy the regency until he could slip away to Earth as he'd planned. When they had re-exchanged bodies, the real Zarth could come back to be regent.

'I'll do my best, then,' Gordon faltered. 'But if I blunder—'

'You won't,' Jhal Arn whispered. 'I trust everything in your hands, Zarth.'

He sank back on his pillow, a spasm of pain crossing his white face. Hastily, Zora called the physicians.

The physicians waved them all from the room. 'The emperor must not exert himself further or we will not answer for the consequences.'

In the splendid outer rooms, Gordon found Lianna at his side. He looked at her shakenly.

'Lianna, how can *I* lead the Empire and hold the star kings' allegiance, as Jhal would have done?'

'Why can't you?' she flashed. 'Aren't you son of Arn Abbas, of the mightiest line of rulers in the galaxy?'

He wanted to cry to her that he was not, that he was only John Gordon of ancient Earth, utterly unfit for such vast responsibility.

He couldn't. He was still caught in the web that had bound him since first – how long ago it seemed! – he had for adventure's sake entered his pact across time with Zarth Arn. He still had to play out the role until he could regain his own identity.

Lianna imperiously waved aside the chamberlains and officials who already were swarming around him.

'Prince Zarth is exhausted! You will have to wait until morning.'

Gordon indeed felt drunk with exhaustion, his feet stumbling as he went with Lianna up through the palace to his own old apartment.

She left him there. 'Try to sleep, Zarth. You'll have the whole weight of the Empire on you tomorrow.'

Gordon had thought he could not possibly sleep, but he was no sooner in bed than drugged slumber overcame him.

He awoke the next morning to find Hull Burrel beside him. The big Antarian looked at him a little uncertainly.

'Princess Lianna suggested that I act as your aide, highness.'

Gordon felt relieved. He needed someone he could trust, and he had a strong liking for this big, bluff captain.

'Hull, that's the best idea yet. You know I've never been trained for rule. There's so much that I ought to know, and don't.'

The Antarian shook his head. 'I hate to tell you, but things are piling up fast for you to decide. The envoys of the southern star-kingdoms ask another audience. Vice-Commander Giron has called twice in the last hour from the fleet, to talk to you.'

Gordon tried to think, as he quickly dressed. 'Hull, is Giron a good officer?'

'One of the best,' the Antarian said promptly. 'A hard disciplinarian but a fine strategist.'

'Then,' Gordon said, 'we'll leave him in command of the fleet. I'll talk to him shortly.'

He had to nerve himself for the ordeal of walking down with his new aide through the palace, of replying to bows, of playing this part of regent-ruler.

He found Tu Shal and the other star-kingdom envoys awaiting him in the little study that was the nerve-center of Empire government.

'Prince Zarth, all our kingdoms regret the dastardly attack on your brother,' said the Polarian. 'But this will not prevent your demonstrating the Disruptor for us as your brother agreed?'

Gordon was appalled. In the whirl of the night's events, he had almost forgotten that promise.

He tried to evade the question. 'My brother is badly stricken, as you know. He is unable to carry out his promise.'

The Hercules envoy said quickly, 'But *you* know how to wield the Disruptor, Prince Zarth. You could carry out the demonstration.'

That was the devil of it, Gordon thought dismayedly. He didn't know the details of the Disruptor! He had learned something from Jhal Arn of how the apparatus was operated, but he still hadn't any idea of just what that mysterious, terrible force could do.

'I have heavy duties as regent of the Empire while my brother is helpless, and I may have to postpone that demonstration for a little while,' he told them.

Tu Shal's face grew grave. 'Highness, you must not! I tell you that failure to give us this reassurance would strengthen the arguments of those who claim the Disruptor is too dangerous to use. It would turn the wavering parties in our kingdoms toward deserting the Empire!'

Gordon felt trapped. He couldn't let the Empire's vital allies desert. Yet how could he wield the Disruptor?

He might be able to learn more from Jhal Arn about it, he thought desperately. Enough so that he could try to wield the Disruptor in at least this demonstration?

He made his voice stern, determined. 'The demonstration will be made at the first possible moment. This is all I can say.'

It did not satisfy the worried envoys, he could see. They looked furtively at each other.

'I will report that to the Barons,' said the chubby envoy of Hercules Cluster. The others bowed also, and left.

Hull Burrel gave him no time to reflect on the pressure that this new complication put upon him.

'Vice-Commander Giron on the stereo now, highness. Shall I put him through?'

When, a moment later, the image of the Empire naval commander appeared on the stereo-plate, Gordon saw that the towering Centaurian veteran was deeply perturbed.

'Prince Zarth, I wish first to know if I am to remain in command of the fleet or if a new commander is being sent out?'

'You're appointed full Commander, subject only to review by my brother when he resumes his duties,' Gordon said promptly.

Giron showed no elation. 'I thank you, highness. But if I am to command the fleet, the situation has reached the point where I must have political information on which to base my strategic plans.'

'What do you mean? What is the situation to which you refer?' Gordon asked.

'Our long-range radar has detected very heavy fleet-movements inside the Cloud!' was the sharp answer. 'At least four powerful armadas have left their bases in there and are cruising just inside the northern borders of the Cloud.'

Giron added, 'This suggests strongly that the League of Dark Worlds is planning a surprise attack on us in at least two different directions. In view of that possibility, it is imperative that I make my own fleet dispositions quickly.'

He flashed on the familiar stereo-map of the galaxy's great swarm of stars, with its zones of colored light that represented the Mid-Galactic Empire and the star-kingdoms.

'I've got my main forces strung in three divisions on a line here between Rigel and Orion Nebula, each division self-sufficient in battleships, cruisers, phantoms and so on. The Fomalhaut contingent is incorporated in our first division.

'This is our prearranged defense plan, but it counts on the Hercules Barons' and the Polaris Kingdom's fleets resisting any attempt to invade through their realms. It also counts on the Lyra, Cygnus and Cassiopeia fleets joining us immediately when we flash the "ready" signal. But are they going to fulfill their engagements? I must know if the allied Kingdoms are going to stand with us, before I make my dispositions.'

Gordon realized the tremendous gravity of the problem that faced Commander Giron far away in that southern void.

'Then you have already sent the "ready" signal to the allied Kingdoms?' he asked.

'I took that responsibility two hours ago, in view of the alarming League fleet movements inside the Cloud,' was Giron's curt answer. 'So far, I have had no reply from the star-kingdoms.'

Gordon sensed the crucial nature of the moment. 'Give me twenty-four more hours, Commander,' he asked desperately. 'I'll try in that time to get positive commitments from the Barons and the Kingdoms.'

'In the meantime, our position here is vulnerable,' rasped the Commander. 'I suggest that until we are certain of the Kingdoms' allegiance, we should shift our main forces westward toward Rigel to be in position to counter any stroke through Hercules and Polaris.'

Gordon nodded quickly. 'I leave that decision entirely in your hands. I'll contact you the moment that I have positive news.'

Hull Barrel looked at him soberly, as the image of the Commander saluted and vanished.

'Prince Zarth, you'll not get the Kingdoms to stand by their alliance unless you prove to them we can wield the Disruptor!'

'I know,' Gordon muttered. He came to a decision. 'I'm going to see if my brother can talk to me.'

He realized now that as the Antarian had said, only a clear demonstration of the Disruptor would hold the wavering Kingdoms.

Could *he* dare try to wield that mysterious force? He knew something of its operations from what Jhal Arn had explained, but that something was not enough. If he could only learn more!

The physicians were worried and discouraging when he went to Jhal Arn's apartments.

'Prince Zarth, he's under drugs and is not able to talk to anyone! It would strain his strength—'

'I must see him!' Gordon insisted. 'The situation demands it.'

He finally had his way but they warned him, 'A few minutes is all we can allow, or we must reject all responsibility for whatever may happen.'

Jhal Arn opened drugged, hazed eyes when Gordon bent over him. It took him moments to realize what Gordon was saying.

'Jhal, you must try to understand and answer me!' Gordon begged. 'I've got to know more about the operation of the Disruptor! You know I told you how Shorr Kan's brain-scanner made me forget.'

Jhal Arn's voice was a drowsy murmur. 'Strange, it made you forget like that. I thought none of us would ever forget, the way every detail was drilled into us when we were boys.'

His whisper trailed weakly, sleepily. 'You'll remember it all when you have to, Zarth. The force-cones to be mounted on your ship's prow in a fifty-foot circle, the cables to the transformer follow to the binding-posts of the same color, the power-leads to the generators.'

His murmur became so faint that Gordon had to bend his head close. 'Get an exact radar fix on the center of your target area. Balance the directional thrust of the cones by the gauges. Only switch in the release when all six directional thrusts are balanced—'

His voice dribbled slowly away, weaker and weaker until it was inaudible. Gordon desperately tried to arouse him.

'Jhal, don't go out on me! I've got to know more than that!'

But Jhal Arn had subsided into a drugged slumber from which he could not be awakened.

Gordon ran it all over in his mind. He knew a little more than he had before.

The procedure of operating the Disruptor was clear. But that wasn't enough. It was like giving a savage of his own time a pistol and telling him how to pull the trigger. The savage might hold the pistol's muzzle in his own face as he pulled that trigger!

'But I've got to pretend at least that I'm going to demonstrate the thing,'

Gordon thought tensely. 'That may hold the envoys of the Kingdoms until I can learn more from Jhal Arn.'

He went down with Hull Burrel to that deep-buried level of the palace in which lay the Chamber of the Disruptor.

The Antarian could not enter that corridor of deadly force that was tuned to blast every living being but Jhal Arn and himself. Gordon went in alone, and brought back the brackets for mounting the force-cones.

Hull Burrel looked even at these simple brackets in awe, as they took them up through the palace.

By tubeway, he and Hull Burrel sped to the naval spaceport outside Throon. Val Marlann and his men were waiting by the great, grim bulk of the *Ethne*.

Gordon handed over the brackets. 'These are to be mounted on the prow of the *Ethne* so that they will form a circle exactly fifty feet in diameter. You'll also make provision for a heavy power connection to the main drive-generators.'

Val Marlann's swarthy face stiffened. 'You're going to use the Disruptor from the *Ethne*, highness?' he exclaimed excitedly.

Gordon nodded. 'Have your technicians start installing these brackets immediately.'

He used the ship's stereo to call Tu Shal, the envoy of Polaris Kingdom.

'As you can see, Tu Shal, we are preparing to make the demonstration of the Disruptor. It will take place as soon as possible,' Gordon told the ambassador, with assumed confidence.

Tu Shal's troubled face did not lighten. 'It should be quickly, highness! Every capital in the galaxy is badly disturbed by rumors of the movements of Cloud fleets!'

Gordon felt almost hopeless as he sped back to the palace. He couldn't stall like this much longer. And with Jhal Arn still comatose, he couldn't learn more about the Disruptor now.

As night fell, thunder grumbled over the great palace of Throon from an electric storm moving in from the sea. When Gordon went wearily up to his apartments, he glimpsed violet flares of lightning outside its windows, eerily illuminating the looming Glass Mountains.

Lianna was waiting for him there. She greeted him anxiously.

'Zarth, terrifying rumors of impending League attack are being whispered through the palace. It is to be war?'

'Shorr Kan may only be bluffing,' he said numbly. 'If only things hold off, until—'

He had almost said, until he could get to Earth and re-exchange bodies so the real Zarth could return to bear this fearful responsibility.

'Until Jhal recovers?' Lianna said, misunderstanding. Her face softened.

'Zarth, I know the terrible strain all this is to you. But you're proving that you're Arn Abbas' son!'

He wanted to take her into his arms, to bury his face against her cheek. Some of that must have showed in his face, for Lianna's eyes widened a little.

'Zarth!' cried an eager feminine voice.

He and Lianna both turned sharply. Gordon immediately recognized the lovely, dark-haired girl who had entered his rooms.

'Murn!' he exclaimed.

He had almost forgotten this girl who was the real Zarth Arn's secret wife, and whom the real Zarth loved.

Amazement, then incredulity, crossed her face as she looked at Lianna. 'Princess Lianna here! I did not dream—'

Lianna said quietly, 'There need be no pretense between us three. I know quite well that Zarth Arn loves you, Murn.'

Murn colored. She said uncertainly, 'I would not have come if I had known—'

'You have more right here than I have,' Lianna said calmly. 'I shall go.'

Gordon made a movement to detain her, but she was already leaving the room.

Murn came toward him and looked up at him anxiously with soft, dark eyes.

'Zarth, before you left Throon you said you would be different when you returned, that all would be with us as before.'

'Murn, you will only have to wait a little longer,' he told her. 'Then all will be as before, I promise you.'

'I still cannot understand,' she murmured troubledly. 'But I'm happy you're cleared of that awful crime, that you've returned.'

She looked at him again with that queer shyness as she left. He knew that Murn still sensed a strangeness about him.

Gordon lay in his bed, and in his mind Lianna, Murn, Jhal Arn and the Disruptor all spun chaotically before he finally slept.

He had slept but two hours when an excited voice awoke him. The storm had broken in full fury upon Throon. Blinding lightning danced continuously over the city, and thunder was bellowing deafeningly.

Hull Burrel was shaking him, and the Antarian's craggy face was dark and taut with excitement.

'The devil's to pay, highness!' he cried. 'The Cloud's fleets have come out and crossed our frontier! There's already hard cruiser-fighting beyond Rigel, ships are snuffing out by the scores, and Giron reports that two League fleets are heading toward Hercules!'

25

The Star Kings Decide

Galactic war! The war the galaxy had dreaded, the long-feared struggle to the death between the Empire and the Cloud!

And it had come at this disastrous moment when he, John Gordon of ancient Earth, bore the responsibility of leading the Empire's defense!

Gordon sprang from bed. 'League fleets heading toward Hercules? Are the Barons ready to resist?'

'They may not resist at all!' cried Hull Burrel. 'Shorr Kan is stereo-casting to them and to all the Kingdoms, warning them that resistance would be useless because the Empire is going to fail!'

'He's telling them that Jhal Arn is too near death to wield the Disruptor, and that *you* can't use it because you don't know its secret!'

As though the words were a flash illumining an abyss, Gordon suddenly realized that that was why Shorr Kan had finally struck.

Shorr Kan knew that he, John Gordon, was a masquerader inside Zarth Arn's physical body. He knew that Gordon had no knowledge of the Disruptor such as the real Zarth had.

Knowing that, the moment he had heard of Jhal Arn being stricken down, Shorr Kan had launched the League's long-planned attack. He counted on the fact that there was no one now to use the Disruptor against him. He should have realized that was what Shorr Kan would do!

Hull Burrel was shouting on, as Gordon dressed with frantic haste. 'That devil is talking by stereo to the star kings right now! You've got to hold them to the Empire!'

Officials, naval officers, excited messengers were already crowding into the room and clamoring wildly for Gordon's attention.

Hull Burrel roughly cleared them from the way as he and Gordon hastened out and raced down through the palace to the study that was the nerve-center of the Mid-Galactic Empire.

All the palace, all Throon, was waking this fateful night! Voices shouted, lights were flashing on, great warships taking off for space could be heard rushing across the storm-swept sky.

In the study, Gordon was momentarily stunned by the many telestereos that blazed with light and movement. Two of them gave view from the bridges of cruisers in the thick of the frontier fighting, shaking to thundering guns and rushing through space ablaze with atom-shells.

But then Gordon's eyes flew toward the stereo on which the dark, dominating image of Shorr Kan stood speaking. His black head bare, his eyes flashing confidently, the Cloud-man was broadcasting.

'– so I repeat, Barons and rulers of the star-kingdoms, that the Cloud's war is not directed against you! Our quarrel is only with the Empire, which has too long sought to dominate the whole galaxy under the guise of working for peaceful federation. We in the League of Dark Worlds have finally struck out against that selfish aggrandizement.

'Our League offers friendship to your Kingdoms! You need not join this struggle and be dragged down to destruction with the Empire. All we ask is that you let our fleets pass through your realms without resistance. And you shall be full, equal members in the real democratic federation of the galaxy which we shall establish when we have conquered.

'For we shall conquer! The Empire will fall. Its forces cannot stand against our mighty new fleets and weapons. Nor can their long-vaunted Disruptor save them now, for they have no one to use it. Jhal Arn, who knows it, lies stricken down – and Zarth Arn does not know how to use it!'

Shorr Kan's voice rang loud with supreme confidence as he emphasized his final declaration.

'Zarth Arn does not know that because he is not really Zarth Arn at all – he is an impostor masquerading as Zarth Arn! I have absolute proof of that! Would I have challenged the Disruptor's menace if I had not? The Empire cannot use that secret, and thus the Empire is doomed. Star kings and Barons, do not join a doomed cause and wreck your own realms!'

Shorr Kan's image faded from the stereo as he concluded that ringing declaration.

'Good God, he must have gone crazy!' gasped Hull Burrel to Gordon. 'To claim that you're not really yourself!'

'Prince Zarth!' rang an officer's excited call across the room. 'Commander Giron calling – urgent!'

Still stunned by Shorr Kan's audacious stroke to neutralize the Kingdoms, Gordon stumbled hastily to that other stereo.

In its view, Commander Ron Giron and his officers stood on a battleship's bridge, bent over their radar screens. The towering Centaurian veteran turned toward Gordon.

'Highness, what about the star-kingdoms?' he rasped. 'We've radar reports that two of the big League fleets that came out of the Cloud are now speeding west toward Hercules and Polaris. Are the Barons and the Kingdoms going to submit to them or resist? We must know that!'

'We'll know that for certain just as soon as I can contact the Kingdoms' envoys,' Gordon said desperately. 'What is your situation?'

Giron made a curt gesture. 'Only our cruiser-screens are fighting so far. Some Cloud phantoms slipped through them and are sniping at our main fleet here back of Rigel, but that's not serious yet.

'What *is* serious is that I daren't commit my main forces on this southern front if the League is going to flank me through Hercules! If the Barons and the Kingdoms are not going to join us, I'll have to fall far back westward to cover Canopus from that flank thrust.'

Gordon, staggered by the moment of awful responsibility, tried to steady his whirling thoughts.

'Avoid commitment of your main forces as long as possible, Giron,' he begged. 'I'm still hoping to hold the Kingdoms to us.'

'If they fail us now, we're in a bad fix!' Giron said grimly. 'The League has twice as many ships as we figured! They'll cut around in short order to attack Canopus.'

Gordon swung back to Hull Burrel. 'Get the ambassadors of the star kings, at once! Bring them here!'

Burrel raced out of the room. But almost at once, he returned.

'The ambassadors are already here! They just arrived!'

Tu Shal and the other envoys of the star-kingdoms crowded into the room a moment later, pale, excited and tense.

Gordon wasted no time on protocol. 'You've heard that two of Shorr Kan's fleets are heading for Hercules and Polaris?'

Tu Shal, pallid to the lips, nodded. 'The news was brought to us instantly. We have heard Shorr Kan's broadcast—'

Gordon interrupted harshly. 'I demand to know if the Barons are going to resist his invasion or allow him free passage! And I demand to know if the Kingdoms are going to honor their engagements of alliance with the Empire, or surrender to Shorr Kan's threats!'

The deathly-white Lyra ambassador answered. 'Our Kingdoms will honor their engagements if the Empire will honor its pledge! When we pledged alliance, it was because the Empire promised to use the Disruptor if necessary to protect us.'

'Have I not told you that the Disruptor will be used?' flashed Gordon.

'You promised that but you evaded demonstrating it!' cried the Polaris envoy. 'Why should you do that if you know the secret? Suppose that Shorr Kan is right and that you *are* an impostor – then we'd be throwing our realms away in a useless fight!'

Hull Burrel, carried away by anger, uttered a roar. 'Do you believe for a moment Shorr Kan's fantastic lie that Prince Zarth is an impostor?'

'Is it a lie?' demanded Tu Shal, gazing fixedly at Gordon's face. 'Shorr Kan must know *something* to assure him the Disruptor won't be used, or he'd never have risked this attack!'

'Curse it, you can see for yourself that he's Zarth Arn, can't you?' raged the Antarian captain.

'Scientific cunning can enable one man to masquerade in the disguise of another!' snapped the Hercules envoy.

Gordon, desperate in the face of this final terrible stumbling-block, seized upon an idea that crossed his mind.

'Hull, be still!' he ordered. 'Tu Shal and you others, listen to me. If I prove to you that I *am* Zarth Arn and that I can and will use the Disruptor, will your Kingdoms stand by the Empire?'

'Polaris Kingdom will!' exclaimed that envoy instantly. 'Prove that and I'll flash instant word to our capital.'

Others chimed in swiftly, with the same assurance. And the Hercules ambassador added, 'We Barons of the Cluster want to resist the Cloud, if it's not hopeless. Prove that it isn't, and we'll fight!'

'I can prove in five minutes that I am the real Zarth Arn!' rasped Gordon. 'Follow me! Hull, you come too!'

Bewilderedly, they hastened after Gordon as he went out of the room and down through the corridors and ramps of the palace.

They came thus down the spiral stair to the hall from which extended that corridor of throbbing deadly white radiance that led to the Chamber of the Disruptor.

Gordon turned to the bewildered envoys. 'You all must know what that corridor is?'

Tu Shal answered. 'All the galaxy has heard of it. It leads to the Chamber of the Disruptor.'

'Can any man go through that corridor to the Disruptor unless he is one of the royal family entrusted with it?' Gordon pressed.

The envoys began to understand now. 'No!' exclaimed the Polarian. 'Everyone knows that only the heirs of the Empire's rulers can enter the Wave that is tuned to destroy anyone except them.'

'Then watch!' Gordon cried, and stepped into the radiant corridor.

He strode down it into the Chamber of the Disruptor. He grasped one of the big gray metal forcecones. Upon the wheeled platform on which it rested, he wheeled that cone back out of the chamber and the corridor.

'Now do you believe that I'm an impostor?' he demanded.

'By Heaven, no!' cried Tu Shal. 'No one but the real Zarth Arn could have entered that corridor and lived!'

'Then you are Zarth Arn, and you *do* know how to use the Disruptor!' another cried.

Gordon saw that he had convinced them. They had thought it possible that he might be another man disguised as Zarth Arn. And they knew now that that could not be so.

What they had not even dreamed, what even Shorr Kan had not told lest it meet utter disbelief, was that he was Zarth Arn in physical body but another man in mind!

Gordon pointed to the big force-cone. 'That is part of the Disruptor apparatus. The rest of it I'll bring out, to be mounted at once on the battleship *Ethne*. And then that ship goes with me out to use the Disruptor's awful power and crush the League's attack!'

Gordon had decided, had in these minutes of strain made his fateful choice.

He *would* try to use the Disruptor! He knew its operation from Jhal Arn's explanations, even if its purpose and power were still a dread mystery to him. He would risk catastrophe to use it.

For it was his own strange imposture, involuntary though it had been, that had brought the Empire to this brink of disaster. It was his responsibility, his duty to the real Zarth Arn, to attempt this.

Tu Shal's aging face flamed. 'Prince Zarth, if you intend thus to keep the Empire's pledge, we will keep our pledge! Polaris Kingdom will fight with the Empire against the Cloud!'

'And Lyra! And we Barons!' rang the eager, excited voices. 'We'll flash word to our capitals that you're going out with the Disruptor to join the struggle!'

'Send that word at once, then!' Gordon told them. 'Have your Kingdoms place their fleets under Commander Giron's orders!'

And as the excited ambassadors hurried back up the stairs to send their messages, Gordon turned to Hull Burrel.

'Call the *Ethne*'s technicians here with a squad of guards, Hull. I'll bring out the apparatus of the Disruptor and it can be taken at once to the *Ethne*.'

Back and forth into the silent, radiant Chamber, Gordon now hastened, bringing out one by one the big, mysterious cones. He had to do this himself – no one else except Jhal Arn could enter there.

By the time he wheeled out the bulky cubical transformer, Hull Burrel was back with Captain Val Marlann and his technicians.

Working hastily, but handling the apparatus with a gingerliness that betrayed their dread, the men loaded the equipment into tubeway cars.

A half-hour later they stood in the naval spaceport beneath the shadow of the mighty *Ethne*. It and two other battleships were the only major units left here, the others already on their way to join the epochal struggle.

Under the flare of lightning and crash of thunder and rain, the technicians labored to bolt the big force-cones to the brackets already in place around the prow of the battleship. The tips of the cones pointed forward, and their cables were brought back through the hull into the Navigation room behind the bridge.

Gordon had had the cubical transformer with its control-panel set up here. He directed the hooking of the colored cables to the panel as Jhal Arn had explained. The massive power-leads were hastily run back and attached to the mighty drive-generators of the ship.

'Ready for take-off in ten minutes!' Val Marlann reported, his face gleaming with sweat.

Gordon was shaking with strain. 'One last check of the cones. There's time for it.'

He raced out into the storm, peering up at the huge, overhanging prow of the warship. The twelve cones fastened up there seemed tiny, puny.

Impossible to think that this little apparatus could produce any such vast effect as men expected! And yet –

'Take-off, two minutes!' yelled Hull Burrel from the gangway, over the din of alarm bells and shouts of hurrying men.

Gordon turned. And as he did so, through the confusion a slim figure ran toward him.

'Lianna!' he cried. 'Good God, why—'

She came into his arms. Her face was white, tear-wet, as she raised it to him.

'Zarth, I had to come before you left! If you didn't come back, I wanted you to know – I still love you! I always will, even though I know it's Murn you love!'

Gordon groaned, as he held her in his arms with his cheek against her tear-wet face.

'Lianna! Lianna! I can't promise for the future, you may find all things changed between us in the future, but I tell you now that it is you I love!'

A wave of final, bitter heartbreak seemed to surge up in him at this last moment of wild farewell.

For it was farewell forever, Gordon knew! Even if he survived the battle, it must not be he but the real Zarth Arn who would come back to Throon. And if he didn't survive –

'*Prince Zarth!*' yelled Hull Burrel's hoarse voice in his ear. 'It is time!'

Gordon, as he tore away, had a swift vision of Lianna's white face and shining eyes that he would never forget. For he knew that it was his last.

And then Hull Burrel was dragging him bodily up the gangway, doors were grinding shut, great turbines thundering, bells ringing sharp signals down the corridors.

'Take off,' warned the annunciators shrilly, and with a crash of splitting air the *Ethne* zoomed for the storm-swept heavens.

Upward it roared, and with it raced the other two battleships, bolting like metal things of thought up across the star-sown sky.

'Giron's calling!' Hull Burrel was shouting in his ear as they stumbled forward along the corridors. 'Heavy fighting now near Rigel! And the League's eastern fleets are forcing through!'

In the Navigation room where Gordon had set up the Disruptor apparatus, Commander Giron's grim image flashed from a telestereo.

Over the Commander's shoulder Gordon glimpsed a bridge-room window that looked out on a space literally alive with an inferno of bursting atom-shells, of exploding ships.

Giron's voice was cool but swift. 'We've joined fleet action with the League's two eastern forces. And we're suffering prohibitive losses. The enemy has some new weapon that seems to strike down our ships from within – we can't understand it.'

Gordon started. 'The new weapon that Shorr Kan boasted to me about! How does it operate?'

'We don't know!' was the answer. 'Ships suddenly drift out of action all around us, and don't answer our calls.'

Giron added, 'The Barons report their fleet is moving out east of the Cluster to oppose the Cloud's two fleets coming toward them. The fleets of Lyra, Polaris and the other allied Kingdoms are already coming down full speed from the northwest to join my command.'

The Commander concluded grimly, 'But this new weapon of the League, whatever it is, is decimating us! I'm withdrawing west but they're hammering us hard, and their phantoms keep getting through. I feel it my duty to warn that we can't fight long in the face of such losses.'

Gordon told him, 'We're coming out with the Disruptor and we're going to use it! But it'll take many hours for us to reach the scene.'

He tried to think, before he gave orders. He remembered what Jhal Arn had said, that the target area of the Disruptor's force must be as limited as possible.

'Giron, to utilize the Disruptor it is imperative that the League's fleets be maneuvered together. Can you somehow do that?'

Giron rasped answer. 'The only chance I have of doing that is to retreat slightly southwestward from this branch of the attack, as though I meant to go to the aid of the Barons. That might draw the Cloud's two attacking forces together.'

'Then try it!' Gordon urged. 'Fall back southwestward and give me an approximate position for rendezvous with you.'

'Just west of Deneb should be the approximate position by the time you get here,' Giron answered. 'God knows how much of our fleet will be left then if this new Cloud weapon keeps striking us down!'

Giron switched off, but in other telestereos unfolded the battle that was going on all along the line near distant Rigel.

Beside the ships that perished in the inferno of atom-shells and the stabbing attack of stealthy phantom-cruisers, the radar screen showed many Empire ships suddenly drifting out of action.

'What in the devil's name has the Cloud got that can disable our warships like that?' sweated Hull Burrel.

'Whatever it is, it's smashing in Giron's wings fast,' muttered Val Marlann tensely. 'His withdrawal may become a rout!'

Gordon turned from the dazing, bewildering stereos that showed the battle, and glanced haggardly through the bridge windows.

The *Ethne* was already hurtling at increasing velocity past the smaller Argo suns, speeding southward toward the Armageddon of the galaxy.

Gordon felt overwhelmed by dread, a panicky reaction. He had no place in this titanic conflict of future ages! He had been mad to make the impulsive decision to try to use the Disruptor!

He use the Disruptor? How could he, when he knew so little of it? How dared he unchain the ghastly power which its own discoverer had warned could rive and destroy the galaxy itself?

26

Battle Between the Stars

Throbbing, droning, quivering in every girder to the thrust of its mighty drive-jet, the *Ethne* and its two companion ships raced southward across the starry spaces of the galaxy.

For hour on hour, the three great battleships had rushed at their highest speed toward the fateful rendezvous near the distant spark of Deneb, toward which the Empire forces were retreating.

'The Barons are fighting!' Hull Burrel cried to Gordon from the telestereo into which he was peering with flaming eyes. 'God, look at the battle off the Cluster!'

'They should be drawing back by now toward the Deneb region as Giron's forces are doing!' Gordon exclaimed.

He was stunned by the telestereo scene. Transmitted from one of the Cluster ships in the thick of that great battle, it presented an almost incomprehensible vista of mad conflict.

To the eye, there was little design or purpose in the struggle. The star-decked vault of space near the gigantic ball of suns of Hercules Cluster seemed pricked with tiny flares. Tiny flares, shining forth swiftly and as swiftly vanishing! And each of those flares was the bursting of an atomic broadside far in space!

Gordon could not completely visualize that awful battle. This warfare of the far future was too strange for him to supply from experience the whole meaning of that dance of brilliant death-flares between the stars. This warfare, in which ships far, far apart groped for each other with radar beams and fired their mighty atom-guns by instant mechanical computation, seemed alien and unearthly to him.

The pattern of the battle he witnessed began slowly to emerge. The will-o'-the-wisp dance of flares was moving slowly back toward the titanic sun-swarm of the Cluster. The battle-line was crackling and sparkling north and north-west of the great sun-cluster now.

'They're pulling back, as Giron ordered!' Hull Burrel exclaimed. 'Good God, half the Barons' fleet must be destroyed by now.'

Val Marlann, captain of the *Ethne*, was like a caged tiger as he paced back and forth between the stereos.

'Look at what's happening to Giron's main fleet retreating from Rigel!' he said hoarsely. 'They're hammering it like mad now. Our losses must be tremendous!'

The stereo at which he glared showed Gordon the similar, bigger whirl of death-flares withdrawing westward from Rigel.

He thought numbly that it was as well he couldn't visualize this awful Armageddon of the galaxy as the others could. It might well shake his nerve disastrously, and he had to keep cool now.

'How long before we'll rendezvous with Giron's fleet and the Barons'?' he cried to Val Marlann.

'Twelve hours, at least,' said the other tautly. 'And God knows if there'll be any of the Barons' ships left to join up.'

'Curse Shorr Kan and his fanatics!' swore Hull, his craggy face crimson with passion. 'All these years, they've been building ships and devising new weapons for this war of conquest!'

Gordon went back across the room, to the control-board of the Disruptor apparatus. For the hundredth time since leaving Throon, he rehearsed the method of releasing the mysterious force.

'But what does that force *do* when I release it?' he wondered again, tensely. 'Does it act as a giant beam of lethal waves, or a zone of annihilation for solid matter?'

Vain speculation! It could hardly be those things. Brenn Bir would not have left solemn warning that it could destroy the galaxy, if it were!

Hours of awful strain passed as the *Ethne's* little squadron drew nearer the scene of the titan struggle. Every hour had seen the position of the Empire's forces growing worse.

Giron, retreating southwestward to join the battered Hercules fleet still fighting off the Cluster, had been joined finally by the Lyra, Polaris and Cygnus fleets near the Ursa Nebula.

The Empire commander had turned on the pursuing League armada and had fought savagely there for two hours, a staggering rearguard action that had involved both forces in the glowing Nebula.

Then Gordon heard Giron ordering the action broken off. The order, in secret scrambler-code like all naval messages, came from their own stereos.

'Captain Sandrell, Lyra Division – pull out of the Nebula! The enemy is forcing a column between you and the Cygnus Division!'

The Lyra commander's desperate answer flashed. 'Their phantoms have piled up the head of our column. But I'll—'

The message was abruptly interrupted, the stereo going dark. Gordon heard Giron vainly calling Sandrell, with no response.

'It's what happens over and over!' raged Hull Burrel. 'An Empire ship reports phantoms near, and then suddenly its report breaks off and the ship drifts silent and disabled!'

'Shorr Kan's new weapon!' gritted Val Marlann. 'If we only had an idea what it is!'

Gordon suddenly remembered what Shorr Kan had told him, when he had boasted of that weapon in Thallarna.

'– it's a weapon that can strike down enemy warships from inside them!'

Gordon repeated that to the others and cried, 'Maybe I'm crazy but it seems to me the only way they could strike down a ship from inside is by getting a force-beam of some kind in on the ship's own stereo beams! Every ship that has been stricken has been stereoing at the time!'

'Hull, it could be!' cried Val Marlann. 'If they can tap onto our stereos and use them as carrier-beams right into our own ships—'

He sprang to the stereo and hastily called Giron and told him their suspicion.

'If you use squirt transmission on our scrambler code it may baffle their new weapon!' Val Marlann concluded. 'They won't be able to get a tap on our beams in time. And keep damper-equipment in your Stereo rooms in case they do get through.'

Giron nodded understandingly. 'We'll try it. I'll order all our ships to use only momentary transmission, and assemble messages from the squirts on recorders.'

Val Marlann ordered men with 'dampers', the generators of blanketing electric fields that could smother dangerous radiation, to stand by near their own stereos.

Already, the Empire ships were obeying the order and were 'squirting' their messages in bursts of a few seconds each.

'It's helping – far fewer of our ships are being disabled now!' Giron reported. 'But we've been badly battered and the Baron's fleet is just a remnant. Shall we fall back south into the Cluster?'

'No!' Gordon cried. 'We daren't use the Disruptor inside the Cluster. You must hold them near Deneb.'

'We'll try,' Giron said grimly. 'But unless you get here in the next four hours, there'll not be many of us left to hold.'

'Four hours?' sweated Val Marlann. 'I don't know if we can! The *Ethne*'s turbines are running on overload now!'

As the *Ethne*'s small squadron rushed on southward toward the white beacon of Deneb, the great battle east of the star was reeling back toward it.

Death-dance of flaring, falling star-ships moved steadily westward through the galaxy spaces! Up from the south, the battered remnants of the Barons' valiant fleet was coming to join with the Empire and Kingdoms' fleets for the final struggle.

Armageddon of the galaxy, in truth! For now the triumphant two main forces of the Cloud were joining together in the east and rushing forward in their final overwhelming attack.

Gordon saw in the telestereo and radar screens this climactic struggle which the *Ethne* had almost reached.

'A half hour more – we might make it, we might!' muttered Val Marlann through stiff lips.

The watch officer at the main radar screen suddenly yelled. 'Phantoms on our port side!'

Things happened then with rapidity that bewildered John Gordon. Even as he glimpsed the Cloud phantom-cruisers suddenly unmasking in the radar screen, there was a titan flare in space to their left.

'One of our escort gone!' cried Hull Burrel. '*Ah!*'

The guns of the *Ethne*, triggered by mechanical computers swifter than any human mind could be, were going off thunderously.

Space around them flashed blinding bright with the explosion of heavy atom-shells which barely missed them. Two distant flares burgeoned up and died, an instant later.

'We got two of them!' Hull cried. 'The rest have darked out and they won't dare come out of dark-out again.'

Giron's voice came from the stereo, the 'squirt' transmission being pieced together by recorders to make a normal message.

'Prince Zarth, the League armada is flanking us and within the hour they'll cut us to pieces!'

Gordon cried answer. 'You've got to hold on a little longer, until—'

At that instant, in the stereo-image, Giron vanished and was replaced by pallid, black-uniformed men who raised heavy rod-shaped weapons in quick aim.

'Cloud-men! Those League phantoms have tapped our beam and are using Shorr Kan's new weapon!' screeched Burrel.

A bolt of ragged blue lightning shot from the rod-like weapon of the foremost Cloud-man in the stereo. That flash of force shot over Gordon's head and tore through the metal wall.

Invasion of the ship by stereo-images! Images that could destroy them, by that blue bolt that used the stereo-beam as carrier!

It lasted but a few seconds, then the 'squirt' switch functioned and the Cloud-men images and their weapons disappeared.

'So that's how they do it!' cried Burrel. 'No wonder they got half our ships with it before we found out about it!'

'Turn on those dampers, quick!' ordered Val Marlann. 'We're likely to get another burst from the stereo any moment!'

Gordon felt the hair on his neck bristling as the *Ethne* rushed now into the zone of battle itself. An awful moment was approaching.

Giron had the Empire and Kingdom ships massed in a short defensive line with its left flank pinned on Deneb's great, glaring white mass. The heavier columns of the League fleets were pressing it in a crackling fire of flaring ships, seeking to roll up the right flank.

Space seemed an inferno of dying ships, of flames dancing between the stars, as the *Ethne* fought forward to the front of the battle. Its own guns were thundering at the Cloud phantoms that were hanging to it steadily, repeatedly emerging from dark-out to attack.

'Giron, we're here!' Gordon called. 'Now spread your line out thinner and withdraw at full speed.'

'If we do that, the League fleets will bunch together and tear through our thinner line like paper!' protested Giron.

'That's just what I want, to bunch the League ships as much as possible!' Gordon replied. 'Quick, we'll—'

Again, the stereo-image of Giron suddenly was replaced by a Cloud-man with the rod-shaped weapon.

The weapon loosed a blue bolt – but the bolt died, smothered by the fields of the 'dampers.' Then the 'squirt' switch functioned again to cut the stereo.

'The way they've cut our communications would be enough alone to decide the battle!' groaned Hull Burrel.

In the radar screen, Gordon tensely watched the maneuver that was now rapidly taking place in space before them.

Giron's columns were falling back westward swiftly, turning to run and spreading out thinly as they did so.

'Here comes the League fleet!' cried Val Marlann.

Gordon too saw them in the screen, the massed specks that were thousands of League warships less than twelve parsecs away.

They were coming on in pursuit but they were not bunching as he had hoped. They merely held a somewhat shorter and thicker line than before.

He knew that he'd have to act, anyway. He couldn't let them get closer before unloosing the Disruptor, remembering Jhal Arn's caution.

'Hold the *Ethne* here and point it exactly at the center of the League battleline,' Gordon ordered hoarsely.

Giron's fleet was now behind them, as the *Ethne* remained facing the oncoming League armada.

Gordon was at the control-panel of the Disruptor transformer. He threw in the six switches of the bank, turning each rheostat four notches.

The gauge-needles began to creep across the dials. The generators of the mighty battleship roared louder and louder as the mysterious apparatus sucked unimaginable amperage from them.

Was that power being stored somehow in the force-cones on the prow? And what had Jhal Arn told him? Gordon tried to remember.

'– the six directional gauges must exactly balance if the thrust is not to create disaster!'

The gauges did *not* balance. He frantically touched this rheostat, then that one. The needles were creeping up toward the red critical marks, but some were too fast, too fast!

Gordon felt beads of sweat on his face, felt stiff with superhuman strain as the others watched him. He couldn't do this! He dared not loose this thing in blind ignorance!

'Their columns are coming fast – eight parsecs away now!' Val Marlann warned tightly.

Three, then four of the needles, were on the red. But the others were short. Gordon hastily notched up their rheostats.

They were all above the red mark now but did not exactly match. The *Ethne* was shaking wildly from the thunder of its straining turbines. The air seemed electric with an awful tension.

The needles matched! Each was in the red zone on the gauge, each at the same figure –

'Now!' cried Gordon hoarsely, and threw shut the main release-switch.

27

The Disruptor

Pale, ghostly beams stabbed out from the prow of the *Ethne* toward the dim region of space ahead. Those pallid rays seemed almost to creep slowly forward, fanning out as they did so.

Gordon, Hull Burrel and Val Marlann crouched at the window frozen and incapable of movement as they looked ahead. And there seemed no change.

Then the massed specks in the radar screen that marked the position of the Cloud fleet's advancing line seemed to waver slightly. A flicker seemed to run through that area.

'Nothing's happening!' Burrel groaned. 'Nothing! The thing must be—'

A point of blackness had appeared far ahead. It grew and grew, pulsing and throbbing.

And swiftly it was a great, growing blot of blackness, not the blackness of mere absence of light but such living, quivering blackness as no living man had ever seen.

On the radar screen, the area that included half the Cloud fleet's advancing battle-line had been swallowed by darkness! For there was a black blot on the screen too, a blot from which radar-rays recoiled.

'God in Heaven!' cried Val Marlann, shaking. 'The Disruptor is destroying space itself in that area!'

The awful, the unimaginable answer to the riddle of the Disruptor's dread power flashed through Gordon's quaking mind at last!

He still did not understand, he would never understand, the scientific method of it. But the effect of it burst upon him. The Disruptor was a force that annihilated, not matter, but space!

The space-time continuum of our cosmos was four-dimensional, a four-dimensioned globe floating in the extra-dimensional abyss. The thrust of the Disruptor's awful beams destroyed a growing section of that sphere by thrusting it out of the cosmos!

It flashed across Gordon's appalled mind in a second. He was suddenly afraid! He convulsively ripped open the release-switch of the thing. Then as the next second ticked, the universe seemed to go mad.

Titan hands seemed to bat the *Ethne* through space with raving power. They glimpsed stars and space gone crazy, the huge glaring white mass of

Deneb heaving wildly through the void, comets and dark-stars and meteor-drift of the void streaming insanely in the sky.

Gordon, hurled against a wall, quaked in his soul as the universe seemed to rise in mad vengeance against the puny men who had dared to lay desecrating hands on the warp and woof of eternal space.

Gordon came back to dull awareness many minutes later. The *Ethne* was whirling and tossing on furious etheric storms, but the starry vault of space seemed to have quieted from its insane convulsion.

Val Marlann, blood streaming from a great bruise on his temple, was clinging to a stanchion and shouting orders into the annunciator.

He turned a ghastly white face. 'The turbines are holding and the disturbances are quieting. That convulsion nearly threw our ships into Deneb, and quaked the stars in this whole part of the galaxy!'

'The backlash reaction!' Gordon choked. 'It was that – the surrounding space collapsing upon the hole in space the Disruptor made.'

Hull Burrel hung over the radar screen.

'Only half the Cloud ships were destroyed in the convulsion!'

Gordon shuddered. 'I can't use the Disruptor again! I won't!'

'You won't have to!' Burrel said eagerly. 'The remainder of their fleet is fleeing back in panic toward the Cloud!'

They were not to be blamed, Gordon thought sickly. To have space itself go mad and collapse around one – he would never have dared unloose that force if he had known.

'I know now why Brenn Bir warned never to use the Disruptor lightly!' he said hoarsely. 'Pray God it never will be used at all again.'

Calls came from the stereo thick and fast, stunned inquiries from Giron's ships.

'What happened?' cried the shaken Commander over and over.

Hull Burrel had not lost sight of their goal, of what they must do.

'The League fleet's in full flight toward the Cloud, or what's left of them are!' he told the Commander exultantly. 'If we follow we can smash them once and for all!'

Giron too fired at the opportunity. 'I'll order the pursuit at once.'

Back across the galactic spaces toward the shelter of the Cloud, the remnants of the League fleet were streaming. And after them, hour by hour, sped the *Ethne* and the Empire's battered fleet.

'They're finished, if we can smash Shorr Kan's rule and destroy their remaining ships!' Burrel exulted.

'You don't think Shorr Kan was with their fleet?' Gordon asked.

'He's too foxy for that – he'd be running things from Thallarna, never fear!' Val Marlann declared.

Gordon agreed, after a moment's thought. He knew Shorr Kan was no coward, but he'd have been directing his vast assault from his headquarters inside the Cloud.

The League of Dark Worlds' ships disappeared into the shelter of the Cloud long hours later. Soon afterward, the Empire fleet drew up just outside that vast, hazy gloom.

'If we go in after them, we might run into ambushes,' Giron declared. 'The place is rotten with navigational perils that we know nothing about.'

Gordon proposed, 'We'll demand their surrender, give them an ultimatum.'

'Shorr Kan will not surrender!' Hull Burrel warned.

But Gordon had them beam a stereo-cast into the Cloud toward Thallarna, and spoke by it.

'To the Government of the League of Dark Worlds! We offer you a chance to surrender. Give up and disarm under our directions and we promise that no one will suffer except those criminals who led you into this aggression.

'But refuse, and we'll turn loose the Disruptor upon the whole Cloud! We'll blot this place forever from the galaxy!'

Val Marlann looked at him, appalled. 'You'd do that? But good God—'

'I wouldn't *dare* do that!' Gordon answered. 'I'll never turn loose the Disruptor again. But they've felt its power and may be bluffed by it.'

There came no answer to their stereo-message. Again, after an hour, he repeated it.

Again, no answer. Then finally, after another wait, Giron's stern voice came.

'It seems that we'll have to go in there, Prince Zarth.'

'No, wait,' cried Hull Burrel. 'A message is coming through from Thallarna!'

In the stereo had appeared a group of wild-looking Cloud-men, some of them wounded, in a room of Shorr Kan's palace.

'We agree to your terms, Prince Zarth!' their spokesman said hoarsely. 'Our ships will be docked and disarmed immediately. You will be able to enter in a few hours.'

'It could be a trick!' Val Marlann rasped. 'It would give Shorr Kan time to lay traps for us.'

The Cloud-man in the stereo shook his head. 'Shorr Kan's disastrous tyranny is overthrown. When he refused to surrender, we rose in rebellion against him. I can prove that by letting you see him. He is dying.'

The telestereo switched its scene abruptly to another room of the palace. There before them in image sat Shorr Kan.

He sat in the chair in his austere little room from which he had directed his mighty attempt to conquer the galaxy. Armed Cloud-men were around him. His face was marble-white and there was a blasted, blackened wound in his side.

His dulling eyes looked at them out of the stereo, and then cleared for a moment as they rested on Gordon. And then Shorr Kan grinned weakly.

'You win,' he told Gordon. 'I never thought you'd dare loose the Disruptor. Fool's luck, that you didn't destroy yourself with it—'

He choked, then went on. 'Devil of a way for me to end up, isn't it? But I'm not complaining. I had one life and I used it to the limit. You're the same way at bottom, that's why I liked you.'

Shorr Kan's dark head sagged, his voice trailed to a whisper. 'Maybe I'm a throwback to your world, Gordon? Born out of my time? Maybe—'

He was dead with the words, they knew by the way his strong figure slumped forward across the desk.

'What was he talking about to you, Prince Zarth?' asked Hull Burrel puzzledly. 'I couldn't understand it.'

Gordon felt a queer, sharp emotion. Life was unpredictable. There was no reason why he should have *liked* Shorr Kan. But he knew now that he had.

Val Marlann and the other officers of the *Ethne* were exultant.

'It's victory! We've wiped out the menace of the League forever!'

The ship was in uproar. And they knew that that wild exultation of relief was spreading through their whole fleet.

Two hours later, Giron began moving his occupation forces inside the Cloud, on radar beams projected from Thallarna. Half his ships would remain on guard outside, in case of treachery.

'But there's no doubt now that they've actually surrendered,' he told Gordon. 'The advance ships I sent in there report that every League warship is already docked and being disarmed.'

He added feelingly, 'I'll leave an escort of warships for the *Ethne*. I know you'll be wanting to return to Throon now.'

Gordon told him, 'We don't need any escort. Val Marlann, you can start at once.'

The *Ethne* set out on the long journey back across the galaxy toward Canopus. But after a half-hour, Gordon gave new orders.

'Head for Sol, not Canopus. Our destination is Earth.'

Hull Burrel, amazed, protested. 'But Prince Zarth, all Throon will be waiting for you to return! The whole Empire, everyone, will be mad with joy by this time, waiting to welcome you!'

Gordon shook his head dully. 'I am not going to Throon now. Take me to Earth.'

They looked at him puzzledly, wonderingly. But Val Marlann gave the order and the ship changed its course slightly and headed for the far-distant yellow spark of Sol.

For hours, as the *Ethne* flew on toward the north, Gordon remained sitting and staring broodingly from the windows, sunk in a strange, tired daze.

He was going back at last to Earth, to his own time and his own world, to his own body. Only now at last could he keep his pledge to Zarth Arn.

He looked out at the supernally brilliant stars of the galaxy. Far, far in the west now lay Canopus' glittering beacon. He thought of Throon, of the rejoicing millions there.

'All that is over for me now,' he told himself dully. 'Over forever.'

He thought of Lianna, and that blind wave of heartbreak rose again in his mind. That, too, was over for him forever.

Hull Burrel came and told him. 'The whole Empire, the whole galaxy, is ringing with your praises, Prince Zarth! Must you go to Earth now when they are waiting for you?'

'Yes, I must,' Gordon insisted, and the big Antarian perplexedly left him.

He dozed, and woke, and dozed again. Time seemed scarcely now to have any meaning. How many days was it before the familiar yellow disk of Sol loomed bright ahead of the ship?

Down toward green old Earth slanted the *Ethne*, toward the sunlit eastern hemisphere.

'You'll land at my laboratory in the mountains – Hull knows the place,' said Gordon.

The tower there in the ageless, frosty Himalayas looked the same as when he had left it – how long ago it seemed! The *Ethne* landed softly on the little plateau.

Gordon faced his puzzled friends. 'I am going into my laboratory for a short time, and I want only Hull Burrel to go with me.'

He hesitated, then added, 'Will you shake hands? You're the best friends and comrades a man ever had.'

'Prince Zarth, that sounds like a farewell!' burst Val Marlann worriedly. 'What are you going to do in there?'

'Nothing is going to happen to me, I promise you,' Gordon said with a little smile. 'I will be coming back out to the ship in a few hours or so.'

They gripped his hand. They stood silently looking after him as he and Hull Burrel stepped out into the frosty, biting air.

In the tower, Gordon led the way up to the glass-walled laboratory where rested the strange instruments of mental science that had been devised by the real Zarth Arn and old Vel Quen.

Gordon went over in his mind what the old scientist had told him about the operation of the telepathic amplifier and the mind-transmitter. He checked the instruments as carefully as he could.

Hull Burrel watched wonderingly, worriedly. Finally, Gordon turned to him.

'Hull, I'll need your help later. I want you to do as I ask even if you don't understand. Will you?'

'You know I'll obey any order you give!' said the big Antarian. 'But I can't help feeling worried.'

'There's no cause to – in a few hours you'll be on your way to Throon again and I'll be with you,' Gordon said. 'Now wait.'

He put the headpiece of the telepathic amplifier on his head. He made sure it was tuned again to Zarth Arn's individual mental frequency as Vel Quen had instructed. Then he turned on the apparatus.

Gordon *thought*. He concentrated his mind to hurl a thought-message amplified by the apparatus, back across the abyss of dimensional time to the one mind to which it was tuned.

'Zarth Arn! Zarth Arn! Can you hear me?'

No answering thought came into his mind. Again and again he repeated the thought-call, but without response.

Wonder and worry began to grip Gordon. He tried again an hour later, but with no more success. Hull Burrel watched puzzledly.

Then, after four hours had passed, he desperately made still another attempt.

'Zarth Arn, can you hear me? It is John Gordon calling!'

And this time, faint and far across the unimaginable abyss of time, a thin thought-answer came into his mind.

'John Gordon! Good God, for days I've been waiting and wondering what was wrong! Why is it that you yourself are calling instead of Vel Quen?'

'Vel Quen is dead!' Gordon answered in swift thought. 'He was killed by League soldiers soon after I came across to this time.'

He explained hurriedly. 'There has been galactic war here between the Cloud and the Empire, Zarth. I was swept into it, couldn't get back to Earth to call you for the exchange. I had to assume your identity, to tell no one as I promised. One man did learn of my imposture but he's dead and no one else here knows.'

'Gordon!' Zarth Arn's thought was feverish with excitement. 'You've been true to your pledge, then? You could have stayed there in my body and position, but didn't!'

Gordon told him, 'Zarth, I think I can arrange the operation of the mind-transmitter to re-exchange our bodies, from what Vel Quen explained to me. Tell me if this is the way.'

He ran over the details of the mind-transmitter operation in his thoughts. Zarth Arn's thought answered quickly, corroborating most of it, correcting him at places.

'That will do it – I'm ready for the exchange,' Zarth Arn told him finally. 'But who will operate the transmitter for you if Vel Quen is dead?'

'I have a friend here, Hull Burrel,' answered Gordon. 'He does not know the nature of what we are doing, but I can instruct him how to turn on the transmitter.'

He ceased concentrating, and turned to the worried Antarian who had stood watching him.

'Hull, it is now that I need your help,' Gordon said. He showed the switches of the mind-transmitter. 'When I give the signal, you must close these switches in the following order.'

Hull Burrel listened closely, then nodded understandingly. 'I can do that. But what's it going to *do* to you?'

'I can't tell you that, Hull. But it's not going to harm me. I promise you that.'

He wrung the Antarian's hand in a hard grip. Then he readjusted the head-piece and again sent his thought across the abyss.

'Ready, Zarth? If you are, I'll give Hull the signal.'

'I'm ready,' came Zarth Arn's answer. 'And Gordon, before we say farewell – my thanks for all you have done for me, for your loyalty to your pledge!'

Gordon raised his hand in the signal. He heard Hull closing the switches. The transmitter hummed, and Gordon felt his mind hurled into bellowing blackness ...

28

Star-Rover's Return

Gordon awoke slowly. His head was aching, and he had an unnerving feeling of *strangeness*. He stirred, and then opened his eyes.

He was lying in a familiar room, a familiar bed. This was his little New York apartment, a dark room that now seemed small and crowded.

Shakily, he snapped on a lamp and stumbled out of bed. He faced the tall mirror across the room.

He was John Gordon again! John Gordon's strong, stocky figure and tanned face looked back at him instead of the aquiline features and tall form of Zarth Arn.

He stumbled to the window and looked out on the starlit buildings and blinking lights of New York. How small, cramped, ancient, the city looked now, when his mind was still full of the mighty splendors of Throon.

Tears blurred his eyes as he looked up at the starry sky. Orion Nebula was but a misty star pendant from that constellation-giant's belt. Ursa Minor reared toward the pole. Low above the roof-tops blinked the white eye of Deneb.

He could not even see Canopus, down below the horizon. But his thoughts flashed out to it, across the abysses of time and space to the fairy towers of Throon.

'Lianna! Lianna!' he whispered, tears running down his face.

Slowly, as the night hours passed, Gordon nerved himself for the ordeal that the rest of his life must be.

Irrevocable gulfs of time and space separated him forever from the one girl he had ever loved. He could not forget, he would never forget. But he must live his life as it remained to him.

He went, the next morning, to the big insurance company that employed him. He remembered, as he entered, how he had left it weeks before, afire with the thrill of possible adventure.

The manager who was Gordon's superior met him with surprise on his face.

'Gordon, you feel well enough now to come back to work? I'm glad of it!'

Gordon gathered quickly that Zarth Arn, in his body, had feigned sickness to account for his inability to do Gordon's work.

'I'm all right now,' Gordon said. 'And I'd like to get back to work.'

Work was all that kept Gordon from despair, in the next days. He plunged into it as one might into drugs or drink. It kept him, for a little of the time, from remembering.

But at night, he remembered. He lay sleepless, looking out his window at the bright stars that to his mind's eyes were always mighty suns. And always, Lianna's face drifted before his eyes.

His superior commended him warmly, after a few days. 'Gordon, I was afraid your illness might have slowed you down, but you keep on like this and you'll be an assistant manager some day.'

Gordon could have shouted with bitter laughter, the suggestion seemed so fantastic. *He* might be an assistant manager?

He, who as prince of the Empire's royal house had feasted with the star kings at Throon? He, who had captained the hosts of the Kingdoms in the last great fight off Deneb? He, who had unloosed destruction on the Cloud, and had riven space itself?

But he did not laugh. He said quietly, 'That would be a fine position for me, sir.'

And then, on a night weeks later, he heard once more a voice calling in his half-sleeping mind!

'Gordon! John Gordon!'

He knew, at once. He knew whose mind called to him. He would have known, even beyond death.

'Lianna!'

'Yes, John Gordon, it is I!'

'But how could you call – how could you even know—'

'Zarth Arn told me,' she interrupted eagerly. 'He told me the whole story, when he came back to Throon. Told me how it was you, in his body, whom I really loved!

'He wept when he told me of it, John Gordon! For he could hardly speak, when he learned all that you had done and had sacrificed for the Empire.'

'Lianna – Lianna –' His mind yearned wildly across the unthinkable depths. 'Then at least we can say goodbye.'

'No, wait!' came her silvery mental cry. 'It need not be goodbye! Zarth Arn believes that even as minds can be drawn across time, so can physical bodies, if he can perfect his apparatus.

'He is working on it now. If he succeeds, will you come to me – you yourself, John Gordon?'

Hope blazed in him, like the kindling of a new flame from ashes. His answer was a throbbing thought.

'Lianna, I'd come if it were only for an hour of life with you!'

'Then wait for our call, John Gordon! It cannot be long until Zarth Arn succeeds, and then our call will come!'

A blaring auto-horn – and Gordon awoke, the eager vibrations of that far-away thought fading from his brain.

He sat up, trembling. Had it been a dream? *Had* it?

'No!' he said hoarsely. 'It was real. I know that it was real.'

He went to the window, and looked out across the lights of New York at the great blaze of the galaxy across the sky.

Worlds of the star kings, far away across the deeps of infinity and eternity – he would go back to them! Back to them, and to that daughter of star kings whose love had called him from out of space and time.

THE WEAPON FROM BEYOND

I

The stars watched him, and it seemed to him that they whispered to him.

Die, Starwolf. Your course is run.

He lay across the pilot-chair, and the dark veils were close around his brain, and the wound in his side throbbed and burned. He was not unconscious, he knew that his little ship had come out of overdrive, and that there were things that he should do. But it was no use, no use at all.

Let it go, Starwolf. Die.

In a corner of his mind, Morgan Chane knew that it was not the stars that were talking to him. It was some part of himself that still wanted to survive and that was haunting him, prodding him, trying to get him onto his feet. But it was easier to ignore it, and lie here.

Easier, yes. And how happy his death would make his dear friends and loving comrades. Chane's fogged mind held onto that thought. And finally it brought a dull anger, and a resolve. He would not make them happy. He would live, and some day he would make those who were now hunting him very unhappy indeed.

The savage determination seemed to clear the blur of darkness a little from his brain. He opened his eyes and then, slowly and painfully, he hauled himself erect in the seat. The action pulled at his wound sickeningly, and for a few minutes he fought against nausea. Then he reached out a shaky hand toward a switch. He must first find out exactly where he was, where the last desperately hasty course he had set as he fled had brought him.

Like little red eyes, figures glowed on the board as the computer silently answered his question. He read the figures but his brain was not clear enough to translate them. Shaking his head drunkenly, he peered at the viewplate.

A mass of blazing stars walled the firmament in front of him. High-piled suns, smoky-red, pure white, pale green and gold and peacock blue, glared at him. Great canyons of darkness rifted the star-mass, rivers of cosmic dust out of which gleamed the pale witch-fires of drowned suns. He was just outside a cluster, and now Chane's blurred mind remembered that in the last desperate moment of flight, when he threw his stolen ship into overdrive before blacking out, he had jabbed the coordinates of Corvus Cluster.

Blackness, nothingness, the eternal solemn silence of the void, and the suns of the cluster pouring their mighty radiance upon the tiny needle that was his ship. His memory quickened, and he knew now why he had come here. There was a world that he knew about in this gigantic hive of stars. He could lie up there and hide, and he sorely needed such a refuge, for he had no healamp and his wound would take time to heal naturally. He thought he would be safe on that world, if he could reach it.

Unsteadily, Chane set a course, and the little ship hurtled toward the edge of the cluster at the top speed of its normal drive.

The darkness began to dim his brain again and he thought, *No, I have to stay awake, for tomorrow we raid the Hyades.*

But that could not be right, they had hit the Hyades months ago. What was the matter with his memory? Things seemed jumbled and without sense or sequence.

Sweeping out from Varna in their swift little squadron, running down the Sagittarius Passage and crosscutting Owl Nebula to come down in a surprise swoop on the fat little planet with the fat little people who squealed and panicked when he and his comrades hit their rich towns …

But that had been a long time ago. Their last raid, the one where he had got this wound, had been to Shandor Five. He remembered how on their way there they had been spotted and chased by a squadron of heavies, and had escaped them by slamming right through a star-system at full speed in normal drive. He could remember Ssander laughing and saying, 'They won't take the chances we Varnans take and that's why they never catch us.'

But Ssander is dead, and I killed him, and that is why I'm flying for my life!

It flashed across Chane's mind: he remembered the quarrel over loot on Shandor Five and how Ssander had got furious and tried to kill him and how he had killed Ssander instead. And how, wounded, he had fled from the avengers …

The dark veils had cleared away and he was here in his little ship, still fleeing, hurtling toward the cluster. He stared at it, sweat on his dark face, his black eyes wild.

He thought that he had better stop blacking out or he would not have long to live. The hunters were after him, and there was no one in the galaxy who would give aid to a wounded Starwolf.

Chane had aimed to enter the cluster at a point where one of the dark dust-rivers divided it, and he was already passing the outpost sentinel suns. Soon he could hear the tick and whisper of dust against the hull. He was keeping out of the denser drift, and the particles were not much bigger than atoms. If, at these speeds, he met particles much bigger, they would hole the ship.

Chane got into his suit and helmet. It was a prolonged effort, and the pain of it was such that he had to set his teeth to keep from groaning. It seemed to him that the wound was more agonizing than it had been, but there was no time to look at it; the heal-patch he had put over it would have to do for now.

Up the great, dark, dusty river between the cluster stars went the little ship, and often Chane's head sagged against the board. But he kept his course. The dust might prove death for him. But it could be life, for those who would come hunting could not probe far in it.

The viewplate was blurred and vague now. It looked like a window, but it was a complex mechanism functioning through probe-rays far faster than light, and his probes had little range here. Chane had to keep all his attention on the dimness ahead, and that was hard with the wound throbbing in his side and the dark fingers always reaching for his brain.

Stars loomed up in the dust, burning like muffled torches, angry red and yellow suns that the tiny ship slowly passed. A deeper spot of brooding blackness, a dead sun, lay far ahead to zenith and became a somber star-mark that he seemed to approach with unnatural slowness ...

The dim river in the stars twisted a little, and Chane changed course. The hours went on and on, and he was well inside the cluster. But it was a long way yet ...

Chane dreamed.

The good days, the morning days, that now had so suddenly ended. The going forth from Varna of the little ships that were everywhere so dreaded. The slamming out of overdrive and the swoop upon a city of a startled world, and the warning cry across the suns – *The Starwolves are out!*

And the mirthful laughter of himself and his comrades as they went in, mocking the slow sluggishness of those who resisted: Go in fast and take the plunder and beat down those who tried to stop you, fast, fast, and away to the ships again, and finally back to Varna with loot and wounds and high-hearted triumph. The good days ... could they really be ended for him?

Chane thought of that, and fed the fires of his sullen anger. They had turned against him, tried to kill him, hunted him. But no matter what they said he was one of them, as strong, as swift, as cunning as any of them, and a time would come when he would prove it. But for now he must hide, lie concealed until his wound bettered, and soon he would reach the world where he could do that.

Again there was a turning of the dark river, the dust rifting deeper into the cluster. More of the baleful witch-stars went by, and the dust whispered louder on the hull. Far ahead, a glazed, dim eye of bloody orange watched his ship approach. And presently Chane could make out the planet that moved lonesome around the lonely dying star, and he knew it for the planet of his refuge.

He almost made it.

II

His luck started running out when the blip of a ship approaching in normal drive showed up on the probe-screen. It was outside the dust, coming along the edge of the river in the stars. It would surely come close enough for its probes to spot him, even in the dust.

There were no alternatives. If the ship was one of the Varnan hunters, they would destroy him. If it was from anyplace but Varna, they would be his enemies the moment they identified his Starwolf craft. And they would identify it as such at first glance, for no world anywhere had ships like the hated Varnan ships.

He had to go deeper into hiding and there was only one place for that, and that was the denser drift. He took his little ship deeper into the dust-stream.

The whispering and ticking on the hull became louder. The larger particles outside so blurred his probe-rays that he lost track of the ship outside the dust. Similarly, they would lose track of him. Chane cut his drive and sat motionless. There was nothing to do but wait.

He did not have to wait long.

When it came, it was no more than a slight quiver that he could hardly feel. But all his instruments went out.

Chane turned. One look was enough. A bit of drift no bigger than a marble had holed the hull and had wrecked his drive-unit and converter. He was in a dead ship, and nothing he could do would make it live again. He could not even broadcast a call.

He looked at the now-blank screen, and though he could not now see the images of the stars he seemed again to hear their mocking whisper.

Let it go, Starwolf ...

Chane's shoulders sagged. Maybe it was as well this way. What future would there be for him anyway, in a galaxy where every man would be his enemy?

Sitting slumped there, in a kind of numb daze, he thought how strange it was that he should end up this way. He had always thought that it would come in a sudden blaze of battle, in some swift swooping raid across the stars. That was the end most Starwolves came to, if they went out too many times from Varna.

He had never dreamed that he would die in this slow, dull, leaden fashion, just sitting and waiting, waiting in a dead ship until his oxygen ran out.

A feeling of revulsion grew slowly in Chane's weary mind. There must be some better end for him than this, some last effort he could make, no matter how hopeless.

He tried to think it out. The only possible source of help was the ship just outside the dust-river. If he could signal them and they came to his aid, one of two things would happen: they could be the Varnans hunting him, and they would kill him; or they could be men of some other world and as soon as they saw his Starwolf ship, they would be his deadly enemies.

But what if his ship was not here? Then, they would accept him as an Earthman, for that was what he was by pure descent even though he had never seen Earth.

Chane looked back at the wrecked drive-unit and converter. They were dead, but the power-chamber that supplied energy to the converter was intact. He thought he saw a way …

It was a gamble, and he hated to bet his life on it. Yet it was better than just sitting here and dying. But he knew that he had to make his bet quickly, or he would not even have this gambling chance.

He began, slowly and clumsily, to take apart some of the instruments on the board. It was difficult work, with gloved hands, and it was even more difficult to reassemble some of the parts into the mechanism he needed. When he finished, he had a small timing-device that he hoped would work.

Chane went back to the power-chamber and began to hook his timing-device to it. He had to work fast, and his task involved bending and crouching in a very confined space, and he felt the wound in his side tearing at him like a vulture. Tears of pain blurred his vision.

Cry, he told himself. *How they'd love to know that you died crying!*

The blur went away and he forced his nerveless fingers, ignoring the pain.

When he had finished his task, he cracked the lock open and took all four of the impellers from the spacesuit rack. He went back then to the power-chamber and turned on his crude timing-device.

Then Chane went out of the ship like a scared cat, two impellers in each hand driving him out amid the stars.

He hurtled away from the little craft, with the stars doing a crazy dance around him. He had gone into a spin but there was no time to right that. There was only one thing important and that was to get as far away as possible before his timing-gadget shorted the energy chamber and destroyed the ship. Chane counted seconds in his mind as the glittering starry hosts went round and round him.

The stars paled for a moment as a white nova seemed to flare in his eyes. It went out and he was in blind darkness. But he was living. He had got far enough before the power-chamber let go and destroyed his ship.

He turned off his impellers and drifted. The men in the ship outside the dust-river should have seen that flare. They might or might not come into the dust to investigate. And if they did, they might or might not be the Varnans who wanted his life.

He swam alone in the infinite, with stars above him and below him and all around him.

He wondered if anyone had ever been so alone. His parents had been dead for years, killed by the heavy gravitation of Varna. His friends on Varna were friends no longer but hunters eager to kill him. He had always thought of himself as Varnan and now he knew that he had been wrong.

No family, no friends, no country, no world … and not even a ship. Just a suit and a few hours of oxygen and a hostile universe around him.

But he was still a Starwolf, and if he had to die he would die like one …

The grand and glittering backdrop of the cluster stars revolved slowly around him. To check his rotation might take power from the impellers that he would later need. And this way he could scan all the starfields as he turned.

But nothing moved in them, nothing at all.

Time went by. The lordly suns had been here for a long while and they were in no hurry to see the man die.

On what seemed to him his ten-millionth rotation, his eye caught something. A star winked.

He looked again, but the star was serene and steady. Were his eyes betraying him? Chane thought it likely, but he would push his bet all the way. He used his impellers to urge him in the direction of that star.

Within minutes, he knew that his eyes had not erred. For another star winked briefly as something occluded it. He strained his eyes, but it was hard to see, for the dark veils were closing around him again. The wound in his side, strained by his exertions, had opened again and he felt that his life was running out of it.

His vision cleared and he saw a black blot growing against the starfields, a blot that grew to the outline of a ship. It was not Varnan; the ships of Varna were small and needle-like. This ship had the silhouette of a Class Sixteen or Twenty and had the odd eyebrow bridge that was characteristic of the ships of old Earth. It was barely moving, coming his way.

Chane tried to formulate in his mind what story to tell to keep them from suspecting the truth about him. The darkness closed in on him but he fought it off, and flashed his impellers on and off as a signal.

He never knew how much later it was that he found the ship beside him and its airlock opening like a black mouth. He made a final effort and moved clumsily into it, and then he gave up fighting and the blackness took him.

He awoke later feeling surprisingly good. He discovered why when he found that he lay in a ship-bunk with a healamp glowing against his side. Already the wound looked dry and half-healed.

Chane looked around. The bunk-room was small. A bulb glowed in the metal ceiling, and he felt the drone and vibration of a ship in normal drive. Then he saw that a man was sitting on the edge of the opposite bunk, watching him.

The man got up and came over to him. He was older than Chane, a good bit older, and he had an oddly unfinished look about his hands and face and figure, as though he had been roughly carved out of rock by an unskilled sculptor. His short hair was graying a little and he had a long, horse-like face with eyes of no particular color.

'You cut it pretty fine,' he said.

'I did,' said Chane.

'Will you tell me what the devil a wounded Earthman is doing floating around in Corvus Cluster?' asked the other. He added, as an afterthought, 'I'm John Dilullo.'

Chane's eyes strayed to the stun-gun the Earthman wore belted around his coverall. 'You're mercenaries, aren't you?'

Dilullo nodded. 'We are. But you haven't answered my question.'

Chane's mind raced. He would have to be careful. The Mercs were known all over the galaxy as a tough lot. A very high proportion of them were Earthmen, and there was a reason for this.

Earth, long ago, had pioneered the interstellar drive that opened up the galaxy. Yet, for all that, Earth was a poor planet. It was poor because all the other planets of its system were uninhabitable, with ferociously hostile conditions and only a few scant mineral resources. Compared to the great star-systems with many rich, peopled worlds, Earth was a poverty-stricken planet.

So Earth's chief export was men. Skilled spacemen, technicians, and fighters streamed out from old Earth to many parts of the galaxy. And the mercenaries from Earth were among the toughest.

'My name's Morgan Chane,' he said. 'Meteor-prospector, operating out of Alto Two. I went too deep into the damned drift and my ship was holed. One fragment caught me in the side, and others hit my drive. I saw my power-chamber was going to blow, and I just managed to get into my suit and get out of there in time.'

He added, 'I needn't say that I'm glad you saw the flare and came along.'

Dilullo nodded. 'Well, I've only one more question for now ...' He was turning away as he spoke. Then he suddenly whirled back around, his hand grabbing out the weapon at his belt.

Chane came out of the bunk like a flying shadow. His tigerish leap took him across the wide space between them at preternatural speed, and with his left hand he wrested away the weapon while his right hand cracked Dilullo's face. Dilullo went sprawling to the deck.

Chane aimed at him. 'Is there any reason why I shouldn't use this on you?'

Dilullo fingered his bleeding lip and looked up and said, 'No particular reason, except that there's no charge in it.'

Chane smiled grimly. Then, as his fingers tightened on the butt of the weapon, his smile faded. There was no charge-magazine in it.

'That was a test,' said Dilullo, getting stiffly to his feet. 'When you were unconscious, and I fixed that healamp on you, I felt your musculature. I'd already heard that Varnan ships were raiding toward this cluster. I knew you weren't a Varnan … you could shave off the fine fur and all that but you couldn't change the shape of your head. But all the same, you had the muscles of a Starwolf.

'Then,' Dilullo said, 'I remembered rumors I'd heard from the out-worlds, about an Earthman who raided with the Varnans and was one of them. I hadn't believed them, no one believed them, for the Varnans, from a heavy planet, have such strength and speed no Earthman could keep up with them. But you could, and right now you proved it. You're a Starwolf.'

Chane said nothing. His eyes looked past the other man to the closed door.

'Do me the credit,' said Dilullo, 'of believing that I wouldn't come down here without first making sure you couldn't do what you're thinking of doing.'

Chane looked into the colorless eyes, and believed.

'All right,' he said. 'So now?'

'I'm curious,' said Dilullo, sitting down in a bunk: 'About many things. About you, in particular.' He waited.

Chane tossed him the useless weapon, and sat down. He thought for a moment, and Dilullo suggested mildly, 'Just the truth.'

'I thought I knew the truth, until now,' Chane said. 'I thought I was a Varnan. I was born on Varna … my parents were missionaries from Earth who were going to reform the wicked Varnan ways. Of course the heavy gravitation soon killed them, and it nearly killed me, but it didn't, quite, and I grew up with the Varnans and thought I was one of them.'

He could not keep the bitterness out of his voice. Dilullo, watching him narrowly, said nothing.

'Then the Varnans hit Shandor Five, and I was one of them when they did it. But there was a quarrel there about the loot, and when I struck Ssander he tried to kill me. I killed him instead, and the others turned on me. I barely got away alive.'

He added, after a moment, 'I can't go back to Varna now. "Damned Earthspawn!" Ssander called me. *Me*, as Varnan as he was in everything but blood. But I can't go back.' He sat silent, brooding.

Dilullo said, 'You've plundered and robbed and you've doubtlessly killed, along with those you ran with. But do you have any remorse about that? No.

The only thing you're sorry about is that they threw you out of the pack. By God, you're a true Starwolf!'

Chane made no answer to that. After a moment, Dilullo went on, 'We – my men and I – have come here to Corvus Cluster because we've been hired to do a job. A rather dangerous job.'

'So?'

Dilullo's eyes measured him. 'As you say, you're a Varnan in everything but blood. You know every Starwolf trick there is, and that's a lot. I could use you on this job.'

Chane smiled. 'The offer is flattering … No.'

'Better think about it,' said Dilullo. 'And think of this – my men would kill you instantly if I told them you're a Starwolf.'

Chane said, 'And you'll tell them, unless I sign up with you?'

It was Dilullo's turn to smile. 'Other people besides Varnans can be ruthless.' He added, 'Anyway, you haven't got anyplace to go, have you?'

'No,' said Chane, and his face darkened. 'No.'

After a moment he asked, 'What makes you think you could trust me?'

Dilullo stood up. 'Trust a Starwolf? Do you think I'm crazy? I trust only the fact that you know you'll die if I tell about you.'

Chane looked up at him. 'Suppose something happened to you so you couldn't tell?'

'That,' said Dilullo, 'would be unfortunate … for you. I'd see to it that, in that case, your little secret automatically became known.'

There was a silence. Then Chane asked, 'What's the job?'

'It's a risky job,' said Dilullo, 'and the more people who know about it ahead of time, the riskier it'll be. Just assume for now that you're going to gamble your neck and will very likely lose it.'

'That wouldn't grieve you too much, would it?' Chane said.

Dilullo shrugged. 'I'll tell you how it is, Chane. When a Starwolf gets killed, they declare a holiday on all decent worlds.'

Chane smiled. 'At least we understand each other.'

III

The night sky dripped silver, The world called Kharal lay in the heart of the cluster, and the system to which it belonged was close to Corvus Nebula. That great cloud was a gigantic glowing sprawl across the heavens, with the burning glory of the cluster stars around it, so that soft light and deep black shadows lay always over the planet by night.

Chane stood in the shadow of the ship and looked across the small and quiet spaceport toward the lights of the city. Those reddish lights hung in a vast pyramid against the sky. A soft wind laden with spicy scents that had an acrid background blew toward him from that direction, and it brought him the sound of a distant buzz and hum.

Hours before, Dilullo and one other Merc had been taken secretly by a Kharali car to the city under cover of darkness.

'You'll stay here,' Dilullo had told them. 'I'm taking Bollard with me, and no one else, to talk to those who want to hire us.'

Chane, remembering that, smiled. The other Mercs were in the ship, gambling. And what was there to keep him here?

He walked toward the city, under the softly glowing sky. The spaceport was dark and quiet with nothing on it but two dumpy interstellar freighters and several armed Kharali planetary cruisers. No one passed him on the road except that once there was a whizzing roar as one of the three-wheeled Kharali cars sped by. These were a city-loving people, and even those who worked the mines that were this world's wealth returned to the cities at night. The arid, flat lands stretched away, still and silver under the nebula-sky.

There was a pulse of excitement in Chane. He had visited many strange worlds, but always as one of the Starwolves, and that meant that everywhere he had been a feared and hated enemy. But now, alone as he was, who would know that he was anything but an Earthman?

Kharal was an Earth-sized planet and Chane, used to the heavy gravitation of Varna, found himself moving with a soft vagueness. But he had adjusted to that by the time he reached the city.

It was a monolithic city, carved long ago from a mountain of black rock. Thus it was a city-mountain, with high-piled galleries and windows and terraces shining ruddy light, with alien gargoyles projecting out at every level, a mammoth hive of life towering up into the soft nebula sky. Chane looked up and up, and heard the sounds from it now as a dull, throbbing roar.

He went through a great arched doorway in the base of the city-mountain. It had huge metal doors that could be closed for defense but they had not been closed for a long time and were so corroded that the reliefs upon them which pictured kings, warriors, dancers and strange beasts were vague and blurred.

Chane started up a broad stone ramp, ignoring the motoway that slid beside it. At once the bursting life and roar of the place were all around him: Men and not-men, the human Kharalis and the humanoid aborigines, voices high and light, voices guttural and throaty. They jostled under the ruddy lights, with the throng now and then giving way before a hairy humanoid who brought a lowing, hobbled and grotesque beast to market. Smells and smokes of strange foods from cookshops in the galleries, the bawl of peddlers offering their wares, and over all the haunting singsong of the Kharali multiple-flutes echoing and reechoing.

The humans of Kharal were very tall and slender people, none of them under seven feet. They looked down, with contempt in their pale blue faces, at Chane. The women turned away from him as though they had seen something defiling, and the men made remarks and laughed mockingly. A young boy, gawky in his rather soiled robe, followed close behind Chane to show that even he was inches taller than the Earthman, and the mocking titters were redoubled. Other boys took up the game, and as he went upward he acquired a jeering retinue.

Chane ignored them, climbing to still other levels, and after a little time they tired of him and went away.

He thought, *This would be a dangerous city to loot. You could easily get trapped in these galleries.*

And then he remembered that he was not a Varnan any longer, that he would not again raid with the Starwolves.

He stopped at a stall and bought a cup of stinging, almost acid, intoxicant. The Kharali who served him, when he had finished, took the cup and ostentatiously scrubbed it. There were more titters.

Chane remembered what Dilullo had told them about the Kharalis before they landed.

They were truly human, of course, like the peoples of many star-worlds. That had been a big surprise for the first explorers from Earth after they perfected the stardrive ... the fact of so many human-peopled worlds. It had turned out that Earthmen hadn't been the first, that many systems had been seeded by a star-traveling human stock so remote in the past that only vague traditions of them lingered. But this human stock had been altered in different ways by ages of evolutionary pressure, and the Kharalis were the result here.

'They consider other humans as much beneath them as their own aborigines,' Dilullo had said. 'They're utterly insular, and dislike all strangers. Be polite.'

So Chane was polite. He ignored the mocking looks and the contemptuous remarks, even though a few of the latter, uttered by Kharalis who spoke galacto, the lingua-franca of the galaxy, were perfectly understandable. He drank again, and studiously avoided looking at Kharali women, and went on climbing the ramps and stairways, stopping here and there to peer at some odd sight. When the Varnans went on a plundering raid, they had little time for sightseeing, and Chane was enjoying a new experience.

He came into a wide gallery whose one whole side was open to the nebula sky. Under the ruddy lights, there was a small crowd of Kharalis, gathered around something Chane could not see, and there was laughter from them and now and then a strange hissing sound. He worked his way, without shoving or jostling, through the ring to see what it was they watched.

Several of the humanoids were here, hairy creatures with too many arms and mild, stupid eyes. Some of them carried leather ropes curiously looped at the ends. Two of them had such ropes tied to the legs of a winged beast that was between them. It was a semi-reptilian creature half as big as a man, its body scaled and wattled, its fanged beak striking the air in brainless fury. When it made a lunge in one direction, the rope on its other leg pulled it back. When that happened, the creature's wattles turned bright red and it hissed furiously.

The tall Kharalis found it amusing. They laughed each time the wattles crimsoned, each time the wild hissing began. Chane had seen beast-baiting on many worlds, and thought it childish. He turned to make his way out of the ring.

Something whispered, and a loop wrapped itself around each of his arms. He swung around. Two Kharali men had taken trapping-ropes from the humanoids, and had used the clever cast-and-loop to fasten onto Chane. A burst of malicious laughter went up.

Chane stood still, and put a smile on his face. He looked around the circle of mirthful, mocking blue faces.

'All right,' he said in galacto. 'I understand. To you, an Earthman is a strange beast. Now let me go.'

But they were not going to let him go that easily. The rope on his left arm tugged, pulling him sharply. As he reacted to keep his balance, the rope on his right arm pulled so that he staggered.

The laughter was very loud now, drowning out the distant flutes. The wattled beast was forgotten.

'Look,' said Chane. 'You've had your little joke.'

He was keeping down his anger, he had already disobeyed orders by being here and there was no use in making it worse.

His arms suddenly flew up to horizontal, grotesquely pointing in each direction, as both Kharalis pulled simultaneously. One of the humanoids came and capered in front of Chane, pointing at him and then at the wattled beast. It was a joke that even his simple brain could understand and his merriment triggered new bursts of laughter from the blue men. They rocked with it, looking at the humanoid and then at Chane.

Chane turned his head and looked at the Kharali who held the rope on his right arm. He asked softly, 'Will you let me go now?'

The answer was a sharp and painful tug on his right arm. The Kharali looked at him with a malicious smile.

Chane moved with all the speed and strength that his Varna-grown muscles gave him on this slighter world. He leaped toward the Kharali on his right, and the surging strength of that lunge pulled the man with the left rope off his feet.

Chane dived in close to the tall, startled Kharali and thrust his arms under the man's arms, reaching upward. His hands curved out to grab the front of the Kharali's arms, near the shoulders. He put all his strength into a levering, surging embrace. There was a dull double crack, like the sound of wet sticks breaking, and Chane stepped back.

The Kharali stood, his face a mask of horror. His long, slender arms hung limp, both of them broken near the shoulders.

For a moment, the Kharalis stared silently. It was as though they could not believe it, as though a despised cur dog had suddenly become a tiger and pounced.

Chane used the moment to slide between them across the gallery to a narrow stair. Then a raging chorus went up behind him. He started running then, going up the stairs, taking three steps at a time.

He was laughing as he ran. He would not soon forget the Kharali bully, and how his face had changed from malice to open-mouthed horror.

The stair came up into a dark corridor in the rock. His eyes picked out another stairway angling off and he took it. The whole city-mountain was a labyrinth of passages.

He emerged into a broad, red-lit bazaar that seemed to run away forever and was crowded with the tall people chaffering at stalls. Behind a stall that was festooned with statuettes of blasphemously hideous little snake-armed idols, Chane spotted a narrow stair that led downward. He slid through the crowd toward it, as blue faces looked down at him in surprise.

Going up was no good; he could only get out of this place by reaching the base of the city-mountain. He had been in worse places than this, and he was not greatly worried.

The narrow stair he followed downward suddenly opened into a big room in the rock. The glowing pink lights here showed it was a little amphitheater, with robed Kharalis sitting all around its edge, looking down at a small central stage.

Three nearly-naked Kharali girls were dancing on the stage to the wailing of multiple-flutes. They danced amid glittering points of steel, six-inch pointed blades that bristled from the floor, set about fifteen inches apart. The slender blue bodies leaped and whirled, and the bare feet came down close to the cruel blades and leaped up again, and as they danced the girls threw back their long black hair and laughed.

Chane stared, fascinated. He felt an admiration that was almost love for these three girls who could laugh as they danced with danger.

Then he heard the echo of distant gongs, and a scrabble of feet coming down the stair behind them. He started to run again as his pursuers came out of the stair.

He had not thought that someone with a weapon might have joined them. Not until he heard the stun gun buzzing behind him.

IV

Dilullo sat in the big, shadowy stone hall high in the city-mountain, and felt his frustration and anger increase.

He had been sitting here for hours, and the oligarchs who ruled Kharal had not yet come. There was nobody across the table except Odenjaa, the Kharali who had contacted him at Achernar weeks ago, and who had this night brought them from the ship up into the city by secret ways.

'Soon,' said Odenjaa. 'Very soon the lords of Kharal will be here.'

'You said that two hours ago,' said Dilullo.

He was getting tired of this. The chair he sat in was damnably uncomfortable, for it had been made for taller men to sit in, and Dilullo's legs dangled like a child's.

He was pretty sure they were keeping him waiting purposely, but there was nothing he could do but compose his face and look unperturbed. Bollard, sitting nearby, looked quite unbothered, but then fat Bollard, the toughest of the Mercs, had a moon face that rarely showed anything.

The lights around the room threw a ruddy glow that hurt his eyes, but the black rock walls remained dark and brooding. Through the open window came chill night air, and with it came the whispered flutes and voices of all the levels in the vast warren beneath.

Suddenly, Dilullo felt sick of strange worlds. He had seen too many of them in a career that had gone on too long. A Merc was old at forty. What the devil was he doing out here in Corvus Cluster, anyway?

He thought sourly, 'Quit being sorry for yourself. You're here because you like to make a lot of money and this is the only way you can do it.'

Finally, the lords of Kharal came. There were six of them, tall in their rich robes, all but one of them middle-aged or elderly. They seated themselves with ceremony at the table, and only then did they look superciliously across at Dilullo and Bollard.

Dilullo had dealt with men of a good many star-worlds, though with none quite so insular as these, and he was determined not to be put into any position of inferiority in making this deal.

He said clearly and loudly in galacto, 'You sent for me.'

Then he was silent, staring at the lords of Kharal and waiting for them to answer.

Finally, the youngest Kharali, whose face had darkened with resentment, said harshly, '*I* did not send for you, Earthman.'

'Then why am I here?' demanded Dilullo. His hand waving toward Odenjaa, he said, 'This man came to me at Achernar, many weeks ago. He told me that Kharal had an enemy, the planet Vhol, the outermost world of this system. He said that your enemies of Vhol have a great new weapon which you wish destroyed. He assured me you would pay me well if I brought men and helped you.'

His deliberately patronizing statement brought scowls to the faces of all the others, except for the very oldest Kharali, whose eyes studied him coldly from a face that was a spider-web of wrinkles.

It was this oldest man who answered. 'Collectively, we did send for you, though one of us dissented. It may well be that we can use you, Earthman.'

Insult for insult, Dilullo thought. He hoped that now that they had shown proper contempt for each other, they could get down to business.

'Why are those of Vhol your enemies?' he asked.

The old man answered. 'It is simple. They covet our world's mineral wealth. They are more numerous than we, and they have a somewhat more advanced technology' – he spoke the last as though it was a dirty word – 'and so they tried to land a force and conquer us. We repelled their landing.'

Dilullo nodded. This was an old story. A star-system got space-travel, and then one of its worlds tried to take over the others and start an empire.

'But the new weapon? How did you learn of this?'

'There have been rumors,' said the old Kharali. 'Then a few months ago, a reconnoitering Vhollan cruiser was disabled by our own cruisers. There was one living officer in it, whom we captured and questioned. He told us all he knows.'

'All?'

Odenjaa, smiling, explained. 'There are certain drugs we have that can make a man unconscious, and in his unconsciousness he will answer every question, and not even remember it afterwards.'

'What did he say?'

'He said that soon Vhol would destroy us utterly, that out of Corvus Nebula they would bring a weapon which would annihilate us.'

'Out of the Nebula?' Dilullo was startled. 'But that place is a maze of drift, uncharted, dangerous ...' He broke off and then said, with a sour smile, 'I can see why you wanted to hire Mercs to do this job.'

The youngest of the lords of Kharal said something harsh and rapid in his own language, looking furiously at Dilullo.

Odenjaa translated. 'You are to know that Kharalis have died trying to enter the nebula, but that our ships lack the subtle instruments that the Vhollans and you Earthmen use.'

Dilullo thought that that was probably true. The Kharalis had not had space-travel for too long, and they were the kind of insular, tradition-ridden people who were not very good at it. They had no star-shipping at all; the ships of other stars brought them goods to exchange for the rare and valuable gems and metals of Kharal. When he came to think of it, he wouldn't want to try bucking that nebula in a planet-cruiser as they had.

He said gravely, 'If I seem to reflect on the courage of the men of Kharal, I apologize.'

The Kharali lords looked only a little less angry. 'But,' added Dilullo, 'I must know more of this. Did your captured Vhollan know anything of the nature of the weapon?'

The old Kharali spread his hands. 'No. We have questioned him many times under the drug, the last time only a few days ago, but he knows nothing more.'

'Can I talk to this Vhollan captive?' asked Dilullo.

Instantly, they became suspicious. 'Why would you want to confer with one of our enemies, if you are to work for us? No.'

For the first time, Bollard spoke, in the soft lisp that seemed so incongruous from his moon-fat face.

'It's too damn vague, John.'

'It's vague,' Dilullo admitted. 'But it might just be done.' He thought for a minute, and then he looked across the table at the Kharalis and said, 'Thirty light-stones.'

They stared at him puzzledly, and he repeated patiently, 'Thirty lightstones. That is what you will pay us if we succeed in doing this thing for you.'

They looked first incredulous, then furious. 'Thirty lightstones?' said the young Kharali lord. 'Do you think we would give little Earthmen the ransom of an emperor?'

'How much is the ransom of a world?' said Dilullo. 'Of Kharal? How many of your lightstones will your enemies take if they conquer you?'

Their faces changed, only a little. But, watching them, Bollard murmured, 'They'll pay it.'

Dilullo gave them no time to reflect on the magnitude of his demand. 'That will be the payment if we find and destroy the weapon of your enemies. But first we must learn if we can do that, and the learning will be very risky for us. Three of the lightstones will be paid to us in advance.'

They found their voices this time, snarling their anger. 'And what if you Earthmen take the three jewels and go your way, laughing at us?'

Dilullo looked at Odenjaa. 'You were the one who looked for Mercs to hire. Tell me, did you hear of Mercs ever cheating those who hired them?'

'Yes,' said Odenjaa. 'Twice it happened.'

'And what happened to the Mercs who did that?' pursued Dilullo. 'You must have heard that, too. Tell it.'

A little reluctantly, Odenjaa replied. 'It is said that other Mercs took them, as prisoners, and delivered them over to the worlds which they had swindled.'

'It is true,' said Dilullo, to those across the table. 'We are a guild, we Mercs. Nowhere in the galaxy could we operate if we did not keep faith. Three light-stones in advance.'

They still glared at him, all except the oldest man. He said coldly, 'Get the jewels for them.'

One of the men went away, and after a little time he came back and with an angry gesture sent three tiny gleaming moons rolling across the table toward the Earthmen. Tiny, thought Dilullo, but beautiful, beautiful, seeming to fill a part of the room with dancing, dazzling swirls of light. He heard Bollard suck in his breath, and it made him feel like a god to reach a hand and grasp three moons and put them in his pocket.

There was a sound at a door and Odenjaa went there, and when he came back from the door his eyes glittered at Dilullo.

'There is something that concerns you,' he said hissingly. 'One of your men has intruded, has tried to kill ...'

Two tall Kharali men came in, supporting between them a drunkenly staggering figure.

'Surprised?' said Chane, and then fell down on his face.

V

It seemed to Chane before he awoke that Dilullo's voice was speaking to him from a great distance. He knew that this could not be. He perfectly remembered how, numbed by the stun-gun's effect, he had fallen down when his captors released him.

He remembered lying flat on the floor and hearing a Kharali voice say, 'This man does not go with you. He must remain here to be punished.'

And Dilullo's voice calmly answering, 'Keep him and punish him, then,' and his captors picking him up and dragging him through many levels to a place of cells, into one of which they had thrown him.

Chane opened his eyes. Yes, he was in the rock cell, which had a barred door opening into a red-lit corridor, and in the wall opposite the door a nine-inch square loophole window looking out at the glowing night sky of Kharal.

He lay on the damp rock floor. He had sore places in his ribs, and now he remembered that they had kicked him for a while after they dragged him into this cell.

Chane felt that some of the numbness had left him, and he hauled himself to sit with his back against the wall. His head cleared. He stared around the cell, and felt a wild feeling of revulsion.

He had never been caged before. No Starwolf was ever imprisoned ... if one was caught on a raid he was ruthlessly killed at once. Of course these people didn't know he was a Starwolf in everything but appearance. That did not change his fierce claustrophobic resentment.

He was about to get up and try his strength on the thick metal door-bars when it happened again. He heard the tiny voice of Dilullo speaking to him as from a great distance.

'Chane ...?'

Chane shook his head. A stun-gun could have odd aftereffects on the nervous system.

'Chane?'

Chane stiffened. The tiny whisper was not directionless. It seemed to come from just below his own left shoulder.

He looked down at himself. There was nothing there but the button that secured the flap of the left pocket of his jacket.

He turned his head a little, and brought the pocket and its flap-button up to his ear.

'Chane!'

He heard it quite clearly now; it came out of the button.

Chane brought the button around to the front of his face and whispered into it.

'When you gave me this fine new jacket, why didn't you tell me this button was a little transceiver?'

Dilullo's voice answered dryly. 'We Mercs have our little tricks, Chane. But we don't like everyone to know them. I would have told you later, when I was sure you wouldn't desert us.'

'Thanks,' said Chane. 'And thanks for walking off and letting the Kharalis keep me.'

'Don't thank me,' said the dry voice. 'You deserved it.'

Chane grinned. 'I guess I did, at that.'

'It's too bad,' said the tiny voice of Dilullo, 'that tomorrow morning they'll take you and break both your arms, as retribution. I don't know what you'll do when they turn you out then to die slowly.'

Chane brought the button back around to his lips and whispered, 'Did you go to the trouble of calling me and letting me know about the transceiver just to express your sorrow?'

'No,' answered the voice of Dilullo. 'There's more to it than that.'

'I thought there was. What?'

'Listen carefully, Chane. The Kharalis hold a Vhollan officer prisoner, presumably in the same prison area you're in. I want that man. We're going to Vhol, and we won't be under suspicion there if we take them one of their own whom we've got free.'

Chane understood. 'But why didn't you ask the Kharalis for him?'

'They got suspicious when I even asked to talk to the man! If I'd asked them to let me take him away, they'd be convinced I was going to throw in with the Vhollans.'

'Won't they be just as suspicious if, I break this Vhollan out?' asked Chane.

Dilullo answered sharply. 'With luck, we'll be away from Kharal and their suspicions won't matter. Now don't argue, but listen. I don't want this man to know *why* you're helping him escape, so tell him you need him to guide you out, that you were brought in unconscious, and so on.'

'Neat,' said Chane. 'But you forget one thing, and that's getting out of this cell.'

'The button of your right-hand jacket pocket is a miniaturized ato-flash. Intensity six, duration forty seconds. The stud is on the back,' Dilullo said.

Chane looked down at the button. 'And how many more of these little tricks have you got?'

'We have quite a few, Chane. But you don't. I didn't trust you with more than two and didn't even tell you about those.'

'Suppose this Vhollan isn't imprisoned here, but somewhere else?' asked Chane.

Dilullo's whisper was untroubled. 'Then you'd better find him. If you come out without him, don't bother coming to the ship. We'll take off and leave you.'

'You know,' said Chane admiringly, 'there are times when I think you'd make a Starwolf.'

'One more thing, Chane. We have to come back to Kharal, if we succeed, to get our pay. So no killing. Repeat, *no killing*. Out.'

Chane got to his feet and silently flexed his arms and legs for minutes until he was sure the last numbness had left them. Then he tiptoed to the barred door, pressing his face against it.

He could see a row of similar doors opposite, and at the far end of the corridor he could just see the feet of a guard who sat sprawled in a chair there. He stepped back, and thought.

After a time he carefully unhooked both of the buttons from his jacket. The transceiver button he put into a shirt pocket. Then he took off the jacket, and got down on the floor by the barred door.

He unobtrusively wrapped the jacket around the base of one of the door-bars, leaving the bar exposed at one point. He carefully brought the tiny aperture of the button ato-flash against the bar, using his free hand to throw a fold of the jacket over the other hand and the button. Then he pressed the stud on the back of the button.

The tiny flash was veiled by the jacket, and its hiss was drowned by the cough Chane let go. He kept the flash on for twenty seconds, and then released the stud.

Little tendrils of smoke came up from scorched parts of the jacket. Chane used his hands as fans to draw the smoke into the cell, so it would go out the loophole window instead of drifting down the corridor.

He unwrapped the scorched jacket. The bar had been burned through.

Chane considered. He could burn through the bar another place and move a section, but he did not want to do that unless he had to; he might need the ato-flash again.

He put the tiny instrument in his pocket, and laid hold of the severed bar and tested it. He felt pretty sure from the feel of it that his Varnan strength was enough to bend it now. But he was also pretty sure that it would make noise.

If you stopped to think too much, you could die before you made up your mind. Chane gripped the severed bar, and let all his revulsion at being caged will his muscles into a wild surge of power.

The bar bent inward, with a metallic sound.

There was just space enough for him to squeeze out, and he went out fast, for it had to be quick or not at all.

The Kharali guard jumped up from his chair to see the Earthman bounding at him like a dark panther, with incredible speed.

Chane's hand chopped and the guard fell senseless with his hand reaching vainly toward a button on the wall. Chane eased him to the floor and then searched him, but there was no weapon on the man, and no keys. He turned, his gaze searching along the corridor. He saw nothing that looked like a spy-eye. Apparently the Kharalis, who didn't care much for gadgets, had figured the alarm-button was enough.

Apparently, also, they didn't put many people in jail, for most of the cells were empty. Chane was not surprised. From what he had seen of them, the Kharalis were the type who would get more pleasure out of executing or punishing a man in public than in jailing him.

In one cell, a humanoid lay sprawling and snoring, his hairy arms moving in his sleep. He had some swollen bruises, and from him came an overpowering stench of the acid intoxicant.

Two more cells were empty but in the next a man was sleeping. He was about Chane's size and age and he was a white man. Not swarthy white, not Earthman white, but an albino white with fine white hair. When Chane hissed and awakened him, he saw the man's eyes were not albino but a clear blue.

He jumped to his feet. He wore a short tunic quite unlike the Kharali robes, and a sort of officer's harness over it.

'Do you know the way out of this city?' Chane asked, speaking galacto.

The Vhollan's eyes widened. 'The Earthman they dragged in a while ago. How—'

'Listen,' Chane interrupted. 'I got out of the cell. I want to get out of the whole damned city. But I was unconscious when they brought me in, and don't know where I am. If I get you out of there, can you guide me? Do you know the ways?'

The Vhollan began to babble excitedly. 'Yes, yes, I know; they have taken me in and out many times, for questioning. I won't answer them, so they drug me for some reason and bring me back, but I've seen, I know ...'

'Stand back, then.' Chane bent down and used the remaining power of the ato-flash to cut through the base of a door bar. There was not quite enough power to cut through it completely.

The bar was nine-tenths severed. Chane sat down, braced his feet against the other bars, and then grabbed the nearly-severed one just above the cut. He let it go fast with a muttered curse. It was still hot.

He waited a minute, tried again, and found it had cooled enough. He braced his feet and put his back into it and pulled. The long muscles that Varna had given him slid and swelled and the nearly-severed bar broke free with a *pung*. He didn't relax, he kept pulling, and the bar bent slowly outward. The Vhollan squeezed out fast.

'You've got strength!' he exclaimed, staring.

'It only looked like it,' Chane lied. 'I'd cut through the top of the bar before I woke you.'

The Vhollan pointed toward the door at the end of the corridor opposite to the one where the guard had sat.

'The only way out,' he whispered. 'And it's always locked from the other side.'

'What's beyond it?' Chane demanded.

'Two more Kharali guards. They are armed. When the one in here wanted out, he simply called through the door to them.'

The man, Chane noted, was trying to speak quickly and to the point, but he was shaking with excitement.

Chane pondered. He could only see one way to get that door open, and so they would have to try it and see what happened.

He took the Vhollan by the arm and ran with him, silently, down the corridor to where the guard lay slumped. He had the Vhollan stand with his back against the wall, just beside the alarm button. Then Chane took the unconscious guard and leaned him up face foremost against the Vhollan.

'Hold him up,' Chane said.

It did not look too convincing, he thought. The unconscious guard was taller, and his robed figure leaned forward in a drunken, improbable way. But he did hide the Vhollan standing against the wall, and if the deception was only good for a few seconds, that should be enough.

'When I hiss, press the button and stand still,' Chane ordered, and then sped back to stand beside the door.

He hissed. A bell rang sharply on the other side of the door. The door swung open a moment later, opening into the corridor with Chane behind it.

There was a moment's pause and then two pairs of feet pounded through the door. The two Kharalis both held stun-guns and they were hurrying but not too much. They had glanced in and seen the inner guard standing with his back to them, and no prisoners out of their cells.

Chane leaped with all his speed behind them and his flat hands struck and flashed and struck again, and the two slumped down. He took the stun-gun from one of them and gave each of them a blast from it to keep them quiet for a while.

He went down the hallway and chuckled as he saw the Vhollan, trying now to get out from under the senseless body, giving the impression of wrestling with his tall Kharali burden. Chane gave that one a blast of the stun-gun, too.

He said sharply to the Vhollan, 'Out now. Take the other weapon.'

As he passed the cell where the humanoid had been sleeping, he saw that the creature had aroused and was looking out through the bars with red-rimmed, bloodshot eyes, obviously too foggy from drink to make any sense of what was going on, even if he had had the intelligence.

'Sleep, my hairy brother,' Chane said to him. 'We are neither of us fit for cities.'

They went into the room from which the two guards had come. There was no one in it and it had only one other door. That opened out onto one of the broad galleries, and no one was there, either.

The city seemed quieter, almost sleeping. Chane could hear echoes of faint fluting from somewhere beneath, and the bawl of a distant, angry voice.

'This way,' urged the Vhollan. 'The main motowalk is this way.'

'We'd never make it,' said Chane. 'There are still too many about, and they could spot us as far as they could see us by our shorter stature.'

He went across the gallery and leaned out over its low protective wall, looking out into the night.

The nebula had slid quite a way across the sky as Kharal turned toward the coming day. The silver radiance now came down slantingly, and the grotesque stone gargoyles that jutted out from the steeply-sloping face of the city-mountain threw long, distorted black shadows.

There was a gargoyle at each level, and he estimated that they were about ten levels above the ground. He decided at once.

'We'll go down the outside wall,' he said. 'It's rough and weathered, and there's the gargoyles to help us.'

The Vhollan man looked out and down. He could not get any paler than he was but he could look a little sick, and he did.

'Come along or stay, as you like,' said Chane. 'It makes no difference to me.'

And he thought, *Only the difference between life and death, that's all, if I go back without this man.*

The Vhollan gulped and nodded. They went over the low wall and started down.

It was not as easy as Chane had thought it would be. The rock was not as weathered as the slanting shadows had made it look. He clung on, his fingernails cracking, and lowered himself to the first gargoyle below him.

The Vhollan man followed, flattened with his face against the stone. He was breathing in quick gasps when he reached Chane.

They went down that way, from gargoyle to gargoyle, and each one of the stone monstrosities seemed more blasphemously obscene than the last. At the fifth one, they paused for rest. Chane, observing this one in the silvery nebula-glow, thought how ridiculous he must look, stuck up on the side of the city-mountain, sitting on the stone back of a blobby creature whose face and backside were all together.

He chuckled a little, and the Vhollan turned his white face and looked at him as if in fear.

It became much trickier near the ground, for one of the great gates was not too far away and there were a few robed figures bunched there. The two hugged the shadow like a friend, and went away, avoiding the road that led to the spaceport but going in that direction. Nobody stopped them, and the ship took them in and went away from there.

VI

The man named Yorolin kept talking and talking, filling Dilullo's little cabin with his protestations.

'There's no *reason* why you can't take me back to Vhol,' he said.

'Look,' said Dilullo. 'I've had trouble enough in this system already. We heard there was a war here and we came to sell weapons. But I land on Kharal and get run right off because one of my men is in a fight. It figures that Vhol could be just as hostile. I'm going to the third planet, Jarnath.'

'That's a semi-barbarous world,' said Yorolin. 'The humanoids there are a poor lot.'

'Well, they might be glad enough to get some modern weapons, and might have something valuable to trade for them,' said Dilullo.

Chane, sitting in a corner and listening, admired the bluff Dilullo was putting up. It was good ... good enough that Yorolin was now looking desperate.

'I belong to one of the great families of Vhol and I have influence,' he said. 'Nothing will happen to you. I guarantee it.'

Dilullo pretended doubt. 'I don't know. I'd like to do some business at Vhol, if I could. I'll think about it.' He added, 'In the meantime, you'd better get some sleep. You look as though you'd about had it.'

Yorolin nodded shakily. 'I have.'

Dilullo took him out into the narrow corridor. 'Use Doud's cabin, over there. He's standing his turn on the bridge.'

When Dilullo came back into the cabin and sat down, Chane waited for the blast. But Dilullo reached into a locker and brought out a bottle.

'Do you want a drink?'

Surprised, but not showing it, Chane nodded and accepted the drink. He didn't like it.

'Earth whisky,' said Dilullo. 'It takes getting used to.'

He sat back and looked at Chane with a bleak, steady gaze.

'What's it like on Varna?' he asked, unexpectedly.

Chane considered. 'It's a big world. But it's not a very rich world ... at least, until we got space travel.'

Dilullo nodded. 'Until the Earthmen came and taught you how to build starships, and turned you loose on the galaxy.'

Chane smiled. 'That was a long time ago but I've heard about it. The Varnans tricked the Earthmen as though they were children. They said all they wanted to do was to engage in peaceful trade with other worlds, like the Earthmen did.'

'And we've had the Starwolves ever since,' said Dilullo. 'If the independent starworlds could quit quarreling with each other just once, they could join together and go in and clean Varna out.'

Chane shook his head. 'It wouldn't be that easy. In space, no one is an even match for Varnans for no one can endure the acceleration-pressures they can.'

'But if a big enough coalition fleet moved in ...'

'It would find it tough going. There are many mighty starworlds in that arm of the galaxy. We Varnans have never raided them, instead we trade with them, our loot for their products. They benefit by us, and they'd resist any attempt by outsiders to enter their space.'

'A damned immoral arrangement, but that wouldn't bother Varnans,' grumbled Dilullo. 'I've heard they have no religion at all.'

'Religion?' Chane shook his head. 'Not a bit. That's why my parents came to Varna, but they got nowhere in their mission.'

'No religion, no ethics,' said Dilullo. 'But you've got some laws and rules. Especially when you go out on raids.'

Chane began to understand now, but he only nodded and said, 'Yes, we do.'

Dilullo refilled his own glass. 'I'll tell you something, Chane. Earth is a poor world too. So a lot of us have to go out in space to make a living. We don't raid, but we do the tough, dirty jobs of the galaxy that people don't want to do themselves.

'We're hired men. But we're independent ... we don't run in packs. Someone wants Mercs to do a job, he comes to a Merc leader with a reputation ... like me. The leader signs on the Mercs best fitted for the job, and gets a Merc ship to come in on shares. When the job's over and price of it split up, the Mercs disband. It may be a completely different bunch next time I take on an operation.

'What I'm getting at,' he continued, and now his eyes bored into Chane's face, 'is that while we're together on a job, our lives may depend on all orders being obeyed.'

Chane shrugged. 'If you'll remember, I didn't ask for any part of the job.'

'You didn't ask for it but you've got it,' Dilullo said harshly. 'You think a hell of a lot of yourself because you've been a Starwolf. I'll tell you right now that as long as you're with me you're going to be a pretty tame wolf. You'll wait when I tell you to wait, and you'll bite only when I say "Bite!" Do you understand?'

'I understand what you're saying,' answered Chane carefully. After a moment he asked. 'Do you think you can tell me what we're after on Vhol?'

'I think I can,' said Dilullo, 'for if you open your mouth about it there, you're likely to be dead. Vhol is only a waystop, Chane. What we're after is somewhere in the nebula. The Vhollans have got something in there, some kind of weapon or power that the Kharalis fear and want destroyed. That's the job we're hired for.'

He paused, then added, 'We could go straight to the nebula, and then fly around in it for years searching, without finding anything. It's better to go to Vhol and let the Vhollans *lead* us to what they've got out there. But it's going to be tricky, and if they guess what we're up to, it'll be our necks.'

Chane felt a kindling interest. He saw the face of danger and it was a face he had known all his life, since first he had been old enough to go raiding from Varna. Danger was the antagonist with whom you struggled, and if you bested him you came away with plunder and if you lost you died. But without the struggle you were simply bored, as he had been bored on this ship until now.

'How did the Kharalis find out about this Vhollan weapon?' he asked. 'Yorolin?'

Dilullo nodded. 'Yorolin told them the Vhollans had something big out there, but he didn't know what it was. But Yorolin doesn't know he told them anything … he was drugged, unconscious, when they pumped him.'

Chane nodded. 'And presently you'll let Yorolin persuade you to go to Vhol?'

'Yes,' said Dilullo. 'He won't find it too hard to get me to go there. I hope it'll be as easy for us to leave there!'

When Chane went back into the crew-room there were only four men in it, for the Mercs stood duty as crewmen in flight. They were sitting in the bunks and they had been talking, but they stopped talking when he came in.

Bollard turned his moon-fat face toward him and said, in his lisping voice, 'Well now, Chane … did you have a good time in the city?'

Chane nodded. 'I had a good time.'

'That's nice,' said Bollard. 'Don't you think that's nice, boys?'

Rutledge gave Chane a hot-eyed stare and said nothing, but Bixel, without looking up from the small instrument he was dissembling, drawled that that was real nice.

Sekkinen, a tall rawhide man with a look of gloom about him, had no time for subtleties. He said loudly to Chane, 'You were supposed to stay with the ship. You heard the order.'

'Ah, but Chane's not like us, he's something special,' said Bollard. 'He'd have to be something special, or John wouldn't take a rock-hopper prospector and make him a full-fledged Merc.'

Chane had known from the first that they resented having to accept him, but there would be more than mere resentment if they knew the truth about him.

'The only thing is,' Bollard said to him, 'that your busting in like that might just have made the Kharalis so mad that they'd have killed us. What if that had happened?'

'I'd have been sorry,' said Chane, with a sweet smile.

Bollard beamed at him. 'Sure you would. And I'll tell you what, Chane. If it ever happens again like that, to keep you from being broken-hearted about it I'll just kill you so you don't suffer all that sorrow.'

Chane said nothing. He was remembering what Dilullo had said about Mercs' lives depending on each other, and he knew that the lisped warning was in earnest.

He was thinking that these Earthmen might not be Varnans but that they could be just as dangerous in a different way, and that Mercs had not got their tough reputation for nothing. It seemed like a good time to keep his mouth shut, and get some sleep.

When he awoke the ship was in its landing-pattern around Vhol, and he joined a few of the Mercs at the forward port to look at the planet. Through drifting clouds they saw dark blue, almost tideless, oceans and the coasts of green continents.

'It looks a lot like Earth,' said Rutledge.

Chane almost asked, 'Does it?' but he managed not to ask that betraying question.

As the landing-pattern took them lower, Bixel said, 'That city's not like any on Earth. Except maybe old Venice, blown up fifty times.'

The ship was approaching a flat coast fringed by a multitude of small islands. The sea rolled between the islands in hundreds of natural waterways and on the islands were crowded the white buildings, none very lofty, of a far-stretching city. Further inland, where the land rose a little, was a medium sized spaceport and beyond it rows of tall white blocks that looked like warehouses or factories.

'A more advanced world than Kharal,' said Rutledge. 'Look, they've got at least a half-dozen starships of their own on that port, and lots of planetary types.'

When they landed and cracked the lock, Yorolin spoke first to the two white-haired young Vhollan port officials in his own language.

The Vhollan officials looked suspicious. One of them spoke in galacto to Dilullo, after Yorolin indicated him as the leader.

'You carry weapons?'

'Samples of weapons,' Dilullo corrected.

'Why do you bring them to Vhol?'

Dilullo put on a look of indignation. 'I was only doing your friend Yorolin a favor to come here at all! But maybe we can do some business here.'

The official remaining courteously unconvinced, Dilullo patiently explained.

'Look, we're Mercs and all we want to do is make a living. We heard there was some sort of war in this system so we came with some samples of late-type weapons. I wish now we'd never come! We land on Kharal and before we can even talk business to them, they run us off because one of my men got into trouble. If you people don't want to see what we've got to offer, all right, but no need to make a big thing out of it.'

Again Yorolin spoke rapidly to the official in their own tongue, and finally the official nodded.

'Very well; we allow the landing. But a guard will be placed outside your ship. None of these weapons are to be removed from it.'

Dilullo nodded. 'All right, I understand.' He turned to Yorolin. 'Now I want to get in touch with somebody in your officialdom who would be interested in buying late-type weapons. Who?'

Yorolin thought. 'Thrandirin would be the man ... I'll let him know at once.'

Dilullo said, 'I'll be right here, if he wants to get in touch with me.' He looked over the Mercs. 'While we're here, you can take turns in town liberty. Except you, Chane ... you get no liberty.'

Chane had expected that, and he saw the Mercs grinning their satisfaction. But when Yorolin understood, he made lengthy objection.

'Chane is the man who saved me,' said Yorolin. 'I want my family and friends to meet him. I insist upon it!'

Chane saw frustration and irritation appear on Dilullo's face, and he felt like grinning back but he did not.

'All right,' said Dilullo sourly. 'If you make such a point of it.'

While they waited for Vhollan guards to come, before which the port officials would not let them off the ship, Dilullo found a chance to speak privately to Chane.

'You know what we're here for. To find out what's going on in the nebula, and where. Keep your ears open but don't seem inquisitive. And, Chane ...'

'Yes?'

'I'm not convinced that Yorolin is all that grateful. It could be they'll be trying to find out some things about us from you. Watch it.'

VII

They had all been drinking and were gay, and a couple of the men were more than that. There were three girls and four men, besides Chane, and they were a merry, crowded cargo for the skimmer as it wended slowly along the crowded waterways under the glowing nebula sky.

Yorolin was singing a lilting song which the girl beside Chane, whose name was Laneeah or something that sounded like it, translated for him. It was about love and flowers and things of that sort and Chane didn't think much of it; on Varna the songs had been of raiding and fighting, of running galactic dangers and coming home with treasure. However, he liked the Vhollans, and their world being the outermost of their red-giant sun's planets, it was pleasantly tropical and not burned dry like Kharal.

The waterways were calm and the wind was only a heavy breeze laden with drifting perfume from the flowering trees that grew on either side. These islands were the pleasure part of the Vhollan city, and in fact were the only part Chane had seen except the surprisingly pretentious villa where he had met Yorolin's parents and friends, and where his party had got started.

He had remembered Dilullo's admonition to keep his ears open, but he didn't think he was going to hear anything from this crowd that would help them any.

'We don't see many Earthmen here,' said Laneeah. She spoke galacto well. 'Only a few traders now and then.'

'How do you like us?' asked Chane, feeling a wry amusement at being classed as an Earthman.

'Ugly,' she said. 'Colored hair, even black hair like yours. Faces that are red or tan, not white.' She made a small sound of disgust, but she was smiling as though she did not find him ugly at all.

It made him think suddenly of Varna and of Graal, most beautiful of the girls he had known there, and how she had contrasted her splendid fine-furred golden body with his hairlessness, and mocked him.

Then the skimmer drew in to a landing and there were many lights and jovial music and they went ashore. There was a sort of bazaar of amusements here, small peaked buildings with colored lights under the tall flowering trees, and a swarming, aimless crowd of people. The Vhollans made a handsome sight; they were proud of their white bodies and white hair and wore their knee-length tunics in brilliant colors.

In an arbor of immense flame-colored flowers they sat and had more of the fruity Vhollan wine, and Yorolin pounded his fist on the table and spoke with passion to Chane.

'Out in deep space, that's where I should be, like you. Not paddling around in a miserable planet-cruiser.'

His face was flushed with the wine and Chane felt the drink himself, and reminded himself to be careful.

'Well, why aren't you?' he asked Yorolin. 'Vhol has starships; I saw them on the spaceport.'

'Not so many,' said Yorolin. 'And it takes seniority to get a berth in one of them, but someday I'll be on one; someday …'

'Oh, stop talking about stars and come on and have some fun,' said Laneeah. 'Or Chane and I will leave you here.'

They went on, passing some places, entering others. A kaleidoscope of impressions: jugglers tossing silver bells, flowers grown from seeds in seconds and drifting down on their heads, more wine, and dancers, and still more wine.

It was in this last drinking-place, a long low room with fire-bowls in braziers for illumination and walls of flaming red, that Yorolin suddenly looked across the room and exclaimed, 'A Pyam! I haven't seen one for years! Come on, Chane; this will be something for you to tell about.'

He led Chane across the room, the others being too engaged in chatter to follow.

At a table sat a stocky Vhollan man, and on the table was a creature that was secured to the man's wrist by a thin chain. It looked like a little yellow manikin shaped like a turnip, with two small legs, its body going up to a neckless, pointed head, with two small blinking eyes and a small baby mouth.

'Can it speak galacto?' asked Yorolin, and the man with the chain nodded.

'It can. It brings me many a coin from the offworld people.'

'What the devil is it?' asked Chane.

Yorolin grinned. 'It's not related to the human, though it vaguely looks that way. It's a rare inhabitant of our forests … it's got some intelligence and one remarkable power.' He told the Vhollan, 'Have your Pyam give my friend a demonstration.'

The Vhollan spoke to the creature in his own language. The creature turned and looked at Chane, and somehow the impact of the blinking gaze was disturbing.

'Oh, yes,' it said in flat parrot-like words. 'Oh, yes, I can see memories. I can see men with golden hair and they run toward little ships on a strange world and they are laughing. Oh, yes, I can see …'

With sudden alarm, Chane realized what the strange power of the Pyam was. It could read minds and memories and babble them forth in its squeaky tones, and in a moment it would babble a secret that would be his death.

'What kind of nonsense is this?' Chane interrupted loudly. He spoke to the Vhollan man. 'Is the thing a telepath? If it is, I challenge it to read what I am thinking at this moment.'

And he turned and looked at the Pyam and as he did so he thought with fierce, raging intensity, *If you read more from my mind I will kill you, right now, right this minute.* He put all the will power he had into concentrating on that thought, into packing it with passionate conviction.

The Pyam's eyes blinked. 'Oh yes, I can see,' it squeaked. 'Oh, yes ...'

'Yes?' said Yorolin.

The blinking eyes looked into Chane's face. 'Oh yes, I can see ... nothing. Nothing. Oh, yes ...'

The Pyam's owner looked astounded. 'That's the first time it ever failed.'

'Maybe its powers don't work on Earthmen,' said Yorolin, laughing. He gave the man a coin and they turned away. 'Sorry, Chane, I thought it would be interesting for you ...'

Did you? thought Chane. *Or did you arrange for the beast to be here and lead me right to it, so it could probe my mind?*

He was taut with suspicion now. He remembered Dilullo's warning, which he had almost forgotten.

He let none of it show in his face but went back to the table with Yorolin and drank and laughed with the others. He thought, and then, after looking carelessly around the room, he came to a decision. He began to drink more heavily, and he made a show of doing so.

'Not so much,' said Laneeah, 'or you will not last the evening.'

Chane smiled at her. 'The space between the stars has no wine in it and a man can get awfully dry.'

He kept on drinking and he began to act as though he was pretty drunk. His head rang a little but he was not drunk at all, and he kept an eye on the Vhollan with the Pyam, across the room. A few people had gathered around them, and the Pyam squeaked at them, and finally they gave coins and went away.

The stocky man then picked up the Pyam, carrying it under his arm like an overgrown baby, and went out. He went out the back door, as Chane had hoped he would.

Chane gave it a few seconds and then staggered to his feet. 'I'll be back in a moment,' he said thickly, and walked a little unsteadily toward the back of the place as though heading for a place of necessity.

He heard Yorolin laugh and say, 'Our friend seems to have underestimated the wines of Vhol.'

Chane, at the back of the room, shot a glance and saw that they were not looking after him. He slipped quickly out the back door and found himself in a dark alleyway.

He saw the shadowy figure of the stocky Vhollan, going away down the alley. Chane went after him fast, going on the tips of his toes in leaping strides that made no sound. But apparently the Pyam sensed him, for it squeaked, and the man turned around sharply.

Chane's bunched fists hit him on the point of the jaw. He did not use all his strength, which he thought was foolish, but all the same he did not feel like going back to Dilullo and saying he'd killed someone.

The man fell, dragging the Pyam down with him by the chain, and the creature squeaked in horrified alarm.

Be quiet! Be very quiet, and I will not hurt you, thought Chane.

The creature became silent and cringed, as much as its absurd little legs would allow it to cringe.

Chane took the end of the chain away from the unconscious man. He dragged the Vhollan into a lightless space between two outbuildings.

The Pyam made a small whimpering sound. Chane patted its pointed head and thought, *You will not be hurt. Tell me, was your owner hired to bring you to this tavern?*

'Oh, yes,' said the Pyam. 'Gold pieces. Yes.'

Chane considered for a moment, and then asked mentally, *Can you read the thoughts of someone who is a little way off? Like across a room?*

The Pyam's squeak, despite its dogmatic affirmative opening, was doubtful. 'Oh yes. Not unless I see his face.'

Speak whispers now, thought Chane. *Whispers. No loud sound, no hurting.*

Carrying the Pyam, he slipped back to the door of the drinking-place and opened it a few inches.

The man at the table across the room, he thought, *the man I am looking at.* And he looked at Yorolin.

The Pyam began to squeak in a subdued, conspiratorial chirping.

'Oh yes ... did Chane suspect the trick? How could he ... but he looked a bit as if he did ... it didn't work anyway and I'll have to report to Thrandirin that I couldn't confirm our suspicions ... we *can't* take chances ... what's Chane doing back there ... is he being sick? Maybe I'd better go and see ...'

Chane silently slipped back into the darkness of the alley. The Pyam's little blinking eyes looked at him fearfully.

They tell me you're from the forest, thought Chane. *Would you like to return there?*

'Oh, yes. Yes!'

If I turned you loose, could you get there?

'Oh yes, oh yes, oh yes, oh yes ...'

That's enough, thought Chane. He removed the thin chain and set the Pyam down on the ground. *All right. Go, little one.*

The Pyam waddled rapidly into the shadows and went away. Chane thought that, with its telepathic sense to warn it of obstacles, it would make it.

He turned around and went back to the door. Yorolin was worried about him, and he must not keep his dear and grateful friend waiting.

VIII

The big starship came down majestically toward the spaceport, shining and magnificent in the nebula-glow, seeming to hang for a moment in the sky.

Then it settled down slowly into the area of the port that was reserved for the military ships of Vhol.

In the navigation room of the little Merc ship, Dilullo and Bixel, the radarman, stared at each other in amazement.

'That's not a warship. Perfectly ordinary cargo carrier. What's it doing in the military reservation?'

'Docking,' said Dilullo, and leaned over Bixel's shoulder to study the scanner and the radargraph.

'It came in on a fifty degree course,' said Bixel.

Dilullo nodded, his worn face harsh in the hooded glow. 'So it didn't come from the nebula ...'

'Not unless it came the long way round.'

'That's exactly what I mean. They might be going and coming by different ways, setting roundabout courses deliberately to make it difficult to get a fix on them.'

'They could be,' Bixel said, 'and that would put us in kind of a fix ... not to be funny. Couldn't we just go back to the idea that they're playing it straight? I was much happier that way.'

'So was I. Only there must be some special reason why an ordinary cargo ship plunks down in a maximum-security military area. Of course it may be something else entirely ... but if they had brought something important back from the nebula, that's what they'd do with it.' He straightened up. 'Keep tracking all arrivals and departures. Maybe some pattern will come clear.'

He got out of the cramped little room and went below to Records, an even more cramped little room, where he dug out the stock list, price list, and spec sheets for all the sample weapons he had aboard. Nobody seemed passionately interested in even talking to him about his weapons, and if they really had something tremendous out in the nebula they would hardly need them. Nevertheless, he felt that he should be ready if called upon.

A little later Rutledge summoned him, and Dilullo put the microspools in his pocket and went to the lock. Rutledge pointed. A big skimmer – the things had wheels and were ground-cars as well as watercraft – was coming fast toward them across the spaceport.

A Vhollan officer and a civilian and a bunch of armed soldiers got out of the craft and approached the Merc ship. The civilian was middle-aged, a stocky man with authority in his massive head and face. He came to Dilullo and surveyed him coldly.

'My name is Thrandirin, and I am of the Government,' he said. 'The space-port tower reported that you have been using your radar.'

Dilullo swore inwardly, but kept his face and voice untroubled. 'Of course we have. We always test radar while in dock.'

'I'm afraid,' said Thrandirin, 'that we shall have to ask you and your men to live off-ship while you're here, and visit your ship only under escort.'

'Now wait a minute,' said Dilullo angrily. 'You can't do that ... just because we tested our radar.'

'You could have been tracking our warships,' retorted Thrandirin. 'We are in a state of war with Kharal, and the movements of our ships are secret.'

'Oh, damn your war with Kharal,' said Dilullo. 'The only thing about it that interests me is money.' And that was true enough. He pulled the microspools out of his pocket and shook them in his hand. 'I'm here to sell weapons. I don't care who uses them against what, or how. The Kharalis frankly said no and kicked us out. I'd appreciate it if you Vhollans would be as honest. Do you want to buy or don't you?'

'The subject is still under discussion,' said Thrandirin.

'Which is Universal Bureaucratic for we'll get around to it sometime. How long are we expected to wait?'

The Vhollan shrugged. 'Until the decision is made. In the meantime, you will evacuate your ship within the hour. There are inns over in the port quarter.'

'Oh, no,' blazed Dilullo. 'No, I won't. I'll call my men in and take off, and the view of Vhol going away from it will be the best view we've had yet.'

A wintry quality came into Thrandirin's voice. 'I regret that we can't give you takeoff clearance at this time ... perhaps not for a few days.'

Dilullo felt the first whispering touch of a net gathering around him. 'You've no legal right to detain us if we want to leave your system, war or not.'

'It's only for your own protection,' said Thrandirin. 'We've had word that a squadron of raiding Starwolves is in the Cluster and may be near this area.'

Dilullo was genuinely startled. He had forgotten Chane's assertion that his former comrades would not easily give up the hunt for him.

On the other hand, Thrandirin was obviously using this alarm about Starwolves as an official excuse to keep him here. He doubted, looking at the Vhollan's bleak face, that the man would care if all the Mercs in creation were in danger.

He thought rapidly. There was no possibility of their defying the order, and the worst thing he could do now was to make too big a fuss. That would only confirm their suspicions.

'Oh, all right,' he said sourly. 'It's a ridiculous thing, and our ship will be left unguarded …'

'I assure you,' said Thrandirin smoothly, 'that your ship will be closely guarded at all times.'

It was a veiled warning, Dilullo thought, but he let it go. He went into the ship and called together what Mercs were there, and told them.

'Better pack a few things,' he added. 'We may be living quite a few days on Star Street.'

Star Street was not so much a place as a name. It was the name that starmen invariably gave to whatever street near a spaceport afforded fun and comfort. The Star Street of Vhol was not too much different from many others that Dilullo had walked.

It had lights and music and drink and food and women. It was a gusty, crowded place but it was not sinful, for most of these people had never heard of the Judeo-Christian ethic and did not know they were sinning at all. Dilullo did not have an easy time keeping his men with him as he looked for an inn.

A buxom woman with pale green skin and flashing eyes hailed him from the open front of her establishment, where girls of different hues and at least three different shapes preened themselves.

'The ninety-nine joys dwell here, oh Earthmen! Enter!'

Dilullo shook his head. 'Not I, mother. I crave the hundredth joy.'

'And what is the hundredth joy?'

Dilullo answered sourly. 'The joy of sitting down quietly and reading a good book.'

Rutledge broke up laughing, beside him, and the woman started to screech curses in galacto.

'Old!' she cried. 'Old withered husk of an Earthman! Totter on your way, ancient one!'

Dilullo shrugged as her maledictions followed them down the noisy street: 'I don't know but what she's right. I'm feeling fairly old, and not very bright.'

He found an inn that looked clean enough and bargained for rooms. The big common room was shadowy and empty, the inn's patrons having apparently gone forth to sample the happiness Dilullo had rejected. He sat down with the others and called for a Vhollan brandy, and then turned to Rutledge.

'You go back to the ship. The guards may not let you inside, but wait around near it and as our chaps come in from liberty, tell them where we're staying.'

Rutledge nodded and went away, Dilullo and the others drank their brandy for a little while in silence.

Then Bixel asked, 'What about it, John? Is this job blown?'

'It isn't yet,' said Dilullo.

'Maybe we shouldn't have come to Vhol.'

Dilullo felt no anger at the criticism. The Mercs were a pretty democratic lot, they would obey a leader's orders but they didn't mind telling him when they thought he was wrong. And a leader who was wrong too many times, and ended up too many missions with empty hands, would soon have a hard job getting men to follow him.

'It seemed like our best chance,' he said. 'We wouldn't get far dashing into the nebula and looking for a needle in that size of a haystack. Do you know how many parsecs across the nebula is?'

'It's a problem,' Bixel said, making the understatement of the decade, and dropped the subject.

After a while the other Mercs began to come in, most of them fairly sober. Sekkinen brought a message from Rutledge, at the spaceport.

'Rutledge said to tell you they unloaded some stuff from that cargo ship in the military port. He could see them through the fence. There were some crates, and they hustled them into the warehouse.'

'They did, did they?' Dilullo said. And added, 'That makes it even more interesting.'

He was glad when Bollard came. Despite his fat and sloppy look, Bollard was by far the ablest of his men and had been a leader himself more than once.

When Bollard had heard, he thought for a little time and then said, 'I think we've had it. I'd say, get off Vhol as soon as we can, take our three lightstones and better luck next time.'

That was a good sound point of view. With the Vhollans suspicious of them, it was going to be awfully hard to pull this one off. It made sense to do just as Bollard said.

The trouble was that Dilullo did not like getting licked. The trouble also was that Dilullo could not afford to get licked. If he fell on his face with this job it could mean the beginning of the end for him as a Merc leader. He was getting old for it. Nobody had thought much about that because of his record, but he had thought about it. Plenty. Perhaps too much. And he thought that all it would take was one big walloping failure like this to make them say he was just a bit past his work. They'd say it regretfully. They'd talk about how big he'd been in the old days. But they'd say it.

'Look,' he told Bollard. 'All is not lost. Not yet, anyway. All right, we can't use our radar to get a line on our destination. But there's another possibility. A ship came in and landed in the military port. A cargo ship, not a warship. It wouldn't land there unless it was particularly important.'

Bollard frowned. 'A supply ship for whatever they're working on in the nebula. Sure. But what does that do for us?'

'It wouldn't do anything if the ship was just loading up with supplies and going out … that is, not unless we could follow it. But it brought something with it. Rutledge saw them unload some crates and rush them into the military port warehouse.'

'Go on,' said Bollard, eyeing him with a cold and fishy eye.

'If we could get a look at what's in those crates … not just a look but an analyzer scan … something we could compare with the record-spools for point of origin … it might give us an idea of what they're doing out there, and where.'

'It might,' said Bollard. 'Or it might not. But the point is that getting in and out of that warehouse, past all their security arrangements, is going to be just about impossible.'

'Just about,' said Dilullo. 'Not absolutely. Anybody want to volunteer?'

In derisive words or by gloomy shakes of the head, they let him know what the answer was.

'Then the old Merc law applies,' said Dilullo. 'Nobody wants to volunteer for a mean job, the job goes to the last man who broke the rules.'

A beautiful smile came onto the moonlike face of Bollard. 'But of course,' he said. 'Of course. Morgan Chane.'

IX

Chane lay on his back and looked up at the nebula sky, and let his hand trail in the water as the skimmer glided silently through the channels.

'Are you going to sleep?' asked Laneeah.

'No.'

'You drank an awful lot.'

'I'm all right now,' he assured her.

He was all right, but he was still very much on guard. Yorolin had not done anything except drink some more and get highly expansive and genial, but that one glimpse the Pyam had given him into Yorolin's mind had been enough.

They had wandered along the pleasure-places and Yorolin had wanted Chane to see something he called the feeding of the Golden Ones. Chane gathered that these were some kind of sea-creatures and that feeding them was a regular event. He didn't think much of feeding fish as fun, and he had managed to separate Laneeah from the others and entice her into a skimmer ride through the islands. Yorolin had made no objection at all and Chane had found that fact suspicious.

'How long are you going to be on Vhol, Chane?'

'It's hard to say.'

'But,' said Laneeah, 'if all you're doing here is trying to sell weapons, it won't take long, will it?'

'I'll tell you what,' said Chane. 'We've got another purpose in coming to Vhol. Maybe I'd better not tell you.'

She leaned with quick interest, her clear-cut face outlined against the glowing nebula.

'What's this other thing you're doing here?' she asked. 'You can tell me.'

'All right,' he said. 'I'll tell you. We've come here for this … to grab beautiful women wherever we can find them.'

And he grabbed her and pulled her down.

Laneeah screeched. 'You're breaking my *back!*' He loosened his grip a little, laughing, and she pulled away. 'Are all Earthmen as strong as you?'

'No,' said Chane. 'You might say that I'm special.'

'Special?' she said scornfully, and slapped his face. 'You're like all Earthmen. Repulsive. Horribly repulsive.'

'You'll get used to that,' he said, not letting go of her.

The skimmer glided past the outermost islands and the open sea was like a wrinkled sheet of silver under the glowing sky. From the lights back on the pleasure island there drifted a scrap of lilting music.

There came a distant *phat!* sound from the shore and a moment later there was a muffled splash somewhere near the skimmer. It was repeated, and suddenly Laneeah jumped up in terror.

'They've started to feed the Golden Ones!' she cried out.

'So we'll miss it,' said Chane.

'You don't understand … we've drifted out onto the feeding grounds! Look …!'

Chane heard the *phat!* sound again and then saw that a big dark mass had been catapulted out from the pleasure island. The mass hit the sea not far from their skimmer, and as it floated he saw that it looked like some kind of dark, stringy fodder.

'If one did hit us, it wouldn't hurt us …' he began, but Laneeah interrupted him by screaming.

The sea was boiling furiously right next to the skimmer. The light craft rocked and tilted, and then there was a roaring, swashing sound of disturbed waters.

A colossal yellow head broke surface. It was all of ten feet across, domed and wet-glistening. It opened an enormous maw and snapped up the mass of stringy food. Then it chewed noisily, at the same time looking toward them with eyes that were huge and round and utterly stupid.

Now Chane saw that other heads were breaking surface eagerly in the whole area. Gigantic golden bodies with oddly arm-like flippers, bodies that would have made a whale look like a sprat, thrashed and broached as the creatures eagerly made for the masses of food-fiber that continued to arrive from shore.

Laneeah was still screaming. Now Chane saw that the creature nearest them, having devoured its food, was moving straight toward the skimmer. It was only too obvious that the great brainless brute took the skimmer to be an unusually large ration and was eager to devour it.

Chane picked up the emergency paddle from the bottom of the skimmer and struck with all his strength the top of the wet, domed head.

'Start the motor and steer out of here,' he shouted to Laneeah, without turning.

He raised the paddle to deal another blow. But the Golden One, instead of charging, opened its huge mouth and delivered a thunderous bawl.

Chane broke into laughter. It was obvious that nothing had ever hit the leviathan painfully in its whole life, and it was bawling like a smacked baby.

He turned his head, still laughing, and told Laneeah, 'Damn it, stop screaming and start up.'

She could not have heard him over that Brobdingnagian bellow, but the sight of Chane laughing seemed to shock her out of her hysteria. She started the little motor and the skimmer glided away.

The light craft rocked, tilted and floundered on the waves that the Golden Ones were making. Twice again one of the creatures mistook them for something edible and bore down on them and each time Chane swung the paddle. It seemed that he had guessed right and that no one or nothing had ever dared to touch these colossi, for although they could not really have felt much pain, the shock and surprise seemed to confuse them.

They reached the pleasure island and Yorolin and the others came running to them, and Laneeah, still tearful, pointed accusingly at Chane.

'He *laughed!*'

Yorolin exclaimed, 'You could have been killed! However did you drift out there?'

Chane preferred not to go into that. He said to Laneeah, 'I'm sorry. It was just that the thing's stupid surprise was so funny.'

Yorolin shook his head. 'You're not like any Earthman I ever met. There's something wild about you.'

Chane did not want Yorolin thinking along that line, and he said, 'Some more drinks seem called for.'

They had some more, and a few more than that, and by the time they dropped Chane at the spaceport, they were a noisy party and Laneeah had almost, if not quite, forgiven him.

Rutledge met Chane before he reached the ship. 'How nice of you to show up,' he said. 'I've been hanging around for hours waiting for you, though of course I haven't minded.'

'What's happened?' asked Chane.

Rutledge told him as they walked along Star Street, still ablaze with lights and raucous with rowdy sounds. Rutledge dropped off at a drinking-place to alleviate his boredom and Chane went on along to the inn.

He found Dilullo sitting alone in the common room with a half-filled glass of brandy in front of him.

He said, 'Your Starwolf friends are still after you, Chane.'

Chane listened, and then nodded. 'I'm not surprised. Ssander had two brothers in that squadron. They won't go back to Varna until they've seen my dead body.'

Dilullo looked at him thoughtfully. 'It doesn't seem to worry you much.'

Chane smiled. 'Varnans don't worry. If you meet your enemy you try to kill him and hope you succeed, but worrying before then does no good.'

'Fine,' said Dilullo. 'Well, I worry. I worry about meeting up with Varnans. I worry about these Vhollans and what they'll do next. They're definitely suspicious of us.'

Chane nodded, and told him about Yorolin and the Pyam. He added with a shrug, 'If the mission fails, it fails. Come to that, I like the Vhollans a lot better than the Kharalis.'

Dilullo eyed him. 'So do I. A lot better. But there's more to it than that.'

'What?'

'There's two things. When a Merc takes on a job, he keeps faith. The other thing is that these likable Vhollans are carrying a war of conquest to Kharal.'

'So they're going to conquer Kharal ... is that such a terrible thing?' asked Chane, smiling.

'Maybe not to a Starwolf. But an Earthman sees things differently,' said Dilullo. He drank his brandy and continued slowly. 'I'll tell you something. You Varnans look on raids and conquest as fun. Other starworlds – lots of them – see conquest as a good and right thing. But there's one world that doesn't like conquest at all, it's so peaceable. And that's Earth.'

He set his glass down. 'You know why that is, Chane? It's because Earth was a world of war and conquest for thousands of years. Our people have forgotten more about fighting than any of you will ever learn. We were soaked in conquest right up to our ears for a long, long time and that's why we don't have much use for it any more.'

Chane was silent. Dilullo said, 'Ah, what's the use of talking to you about it. You're young and you've been raised wrong. I'm not young, and I wish to heaven I was back at Brindisi.'

'That's a place on Earth?' asked Chane.

Dilullo nodded moodily. 'It's on the sea, and in the morning you can see the sun coming up out of the mists of the Adriatic. It's beautiful and it's home. The only trouble is, you can starve to death there.'

Chane said, after a moment, 'I remember the name of the place my parents came from, on Earth. It was Wales.'

'I've been there,' said Dilullo. 'Dark mountains, dark valleys. People who sing like angels and are golden-hearted friends till you get them mad, and then they're wildcats. Maybe you got something from there as well as Varna.'

After a few moments, Chane said, 'Well, so far it's a standoff. We haven't found out anything; they haven't found out anything. So what happens next?'

'Tomorrow,' said Dilullo, 'I will put on a very large and convincing show of trying to sell these people some weapons.'

'And what about me?'

'You?' said Dilullo. 'You, my friend, are going to figure out how to do the impossible, and do it quickly, cleanly, and without being seen, let alone caught.'

'Mmm,' said Chane, 'that should keep me busy for an hour or two, what do I do after that?'

'Sit and polish your ego.' He shoved the brandy bottle over. 'Settle down. I've got some talking to do. About the impossible.'

When he was finished, Chane looked at him almost with awe. 'That might even take me three hours to figure out. You have a lot of faith in me, Dilullo.'

Dilullo showed him the edges of his teeth. 'That is the only reason you're alive,' he said. 'And you'll be as sorry as the rest of us if you let me down.'

X

Next night, Chane lay in the grass well outside the military port and studied its lights. In one hand he held a six-foot roll of thin, neutral-colored cloth. His other hand held tightly to a collar that was around the neck of a snokk.

The snokk was both furious and frightened. The animals looked something like a furry wallaby, or small kangaroo. But they had a doglike disposition and ran happily in packs in some parts of the town. This one was not happy, for attached to the collar was a leather hood that completely muffled its head. It kept trying to dig its hind feet into the ground and bound away, but Chane held it.

'Soon,' he whispered soothingly. 'Very soon.'

The snokk responded with a series of growling barks that were effectively muffled by the hood.

Chane had done his homework well. Now he looked at the conical tower that rose from the central building. That was where the ring-projector was, and he had by day seen the searchlights around it, though now they were dark.

He began to crawl forward, dragging the reluctant snokk along. Chane went with every muscle tense. At any moment he would cross the edge of the ring-like aura of force projected to enclose the whole military port. When he crossed that, things would happen very quickly.

He went on, going slowly but making sure that he was set to move fast at any moment. The snokk gave him more and more trouble but he relentlessly dragged it on with him. He could see the lights and the loom of the big starships on the port, warcraft with grim, closed weapon-ports in their sides. He made out the low structure that was the warehouse.

It happened about the moment that Chane expected it to happen. A sharp alarm rang across the port, and the searchlights flashed into life. Their beams swung swiftly in his direction.

Those lights, triggered and aimed by computers linked to the ring-apparatus, could move fast. But his Varna-born reactions gave Chane a slight edge. He acted, when the alarm first sounded, with all the speed he had.

His right hand ripped the hood and collar off the head of the snokk. With the same forward motion he threw himself flat on the ground and pulled the square of neutral-colored cloth over himself and lay still.

The snokk, freed, went off across the port with great hopping leaps, sounding an outraged series of howling barks. Two searchlights instantly locked onto the animal, while the other beams wove an intricate mathematical pattern to cover the whole edge of the port.

Chane lay quite still, trying to look like a bump in the ground.

He heard a fast skimmer come out onto the port and stop some distance from him. He heard the furious barks of the snokk receding.

Someone in the skimmer swore disgustedly, and someone else laughed. Then it went away again, back the way it had come.

The searchlights, after a little more probing, went out.

Chane continued to lie still under his cloth. Three minutes later the searchlights suddenly came on again and swept the whole area once more. Then they went out again.

Chane came out from under the cloth then. He was grinning as he rolled it up.

'A Starwolf child could get in there,' he had told Dilullo when he had finished his reconnaissance. But that had just been a little bragging, and anyway, he had only come this first step: the rest of the job would not be child's work at all.

He worked his way patiently toward the warehouse, keeping to the shadows as much as possible, using his camouflage cloth whenever he stopped to listen. The warehouse, a low flat-roofed metal building, did not seem to be guarded, but if there was anything important in it, there were sure to be cunning devices to expose an intruder.

It was almost an hour before Chane stood in the dark interior of the warehouse. He had entered by the roof, first using small sensors to select an area of the roof free of alarms, then using a hooded ato-flash to cut a neat circle. If he replaced the cutout and fused it into place when he left, it might be a long time before it was noticed.

He took out his pocket-lamp and flashed its thin beam. The first thing he saw was that the crates from the cargo-ship had been unpacked.

Three objects stood upon a long trestle-table beside the crates. Chane stared at them. He walked around the table to inspect them from all sides. Then he stared at them again, shaking his head.

He had handled a lot of exotic loot in his time. He thought he could identify, or at least take a guess at, almost everything in the way of artifacts and the stuff whereof they were made.

These three objects mocked him.

They were all made of the same substance, a metal that vaguely resembled pale, hard gold, but was like nothing he had ever seen before. In form they were all different. One was a shining, fluted ribbon that reared like a snake three feet high. One was a congeries of nine small spheres, held rigidly together by short, slender rods. The third was a truncated cone, wide and thick at the base, with no openings and no decoration. They were beautiful enough to be ornaments, but somehow instinctively he knew they weren't. He could not guess at the purpose of any of them.

Still shaking his head, but reminding himself strongly that he didn't have all night, Chane took from a belt-pouch a mini-camera and a small but highly sophisticated instrument Dilullo had given him; a portable analyzer that poked and probed with fingering rays among the molecules of a substance and came up with a pretty accurate chart of its essential components. Because of its extreme miniaturization it had a limited usefulness, but within those limitations it was useful indeed. Chane applied its sensor units to the base of the spiraled golden ribbon and clicked it on, and then began snapping quick record shots with the little camera.

The truncated cone occluded a portion of the nine-sphere congeries. He reached out and moved it ... the metal was satin-smooth and chilly and surprisingly light. He leaned past it to aim the camera's tiny flash-pod at the golden spheres. And suddenly he went rigid.

There was a whisper of sound in the dark warehouse.

He swung on his heel, his hand going to the stunner inside his jacket, his little beam probing every corner. There were these enigmatic golden objects, and some piles of regulation ship-stores cases.

Nothing more. And no one.

The sound whispered a little louder. It was like someone, or something, trying to speak in a breathy murmur. Now Chane identified its source. It was coming from the cone.

He stepped back from the thing. It lay in the beam of his light, shining and still. But the breathy whisper from it grew in volume.

Now a light came up from the cone, as though emanating from the solid metal. It was not ordinary light; it was a twisting tendril of soft glowing flame. It twisted higher, endlessly pouring out of the cone, until there was a great wreath of it several feet above his head.

Then, without warning, the wreath of light exploded into a myriad of tiny stars.

The whispering voice swelled louder. The little stars above floated down in showers. They were not mere sparks or points of light: each one was different, each like a real star made inconceivably tiny.

They swirled and floated around Chane, yet he could not feel their touch. Red giants and white dwarfs, smoky orange suns and the evil-glowing quasars, and their perfection was so absolute that for a moment Chane lost perspective. They seemed to him real stars, and he was a giant standing in a cascade of swirling suns.

The murmuring voice was still louder, and now he could hear strange, irregular rhythms in it.

Someone, or something, singing?

Of a sudden, Chane realized his peril. If there was an alarm-device here triggered by sound, it could be activated by this.

He grabbed for the cone, to search for some control on it. But before his hand quite touched it, the swirling stars around him vanished and the whispering singing ceased.

He stood, a little shaken by the experience, but understanding now. This seemingly-solid cone was an instrument that reproduced audio-visual records, and was turned on or off by the mere proximity of a hand.

But who, or what, had made such a record as this?

Chane, after a moment, cautiously examined the other gold-colored objects, the fluted spiral and the congeries of spheres. But no wave of the hand produced in them any reaction.

He stood, thinking. It seemed evident that the Vhollans, who had brought these things here, had not made them. Then who had?

A people inside the nebula? One that had mastered unknown technologies? But if so ...

He heard a slight clicking sound from the door.

Instantly, Chane stiffened. There *had* been a sonic-triggered alarm in here. Guards had come, and were softly unlocking the combination of the door.

Chane thought swiftly. He ran to the golden cone. He passed his hand over it, and the whispering sound began and the tendril of light grew up from it. Chane thrust the analyzer and the camera into his pouch, already moving away.

The door clicked softly again. Chane sprang to one of the corners of the room, and crouched behind cases of stores.

In the darkness, the wreath of light above the cone exploded again into tiny stars, and the whispering swelled.

The door opened.

There were two helmeted Vhollan guards and they had lethal lasers in their hands, and they were ready to fire at once. But for just a second, their eyes were riveted by that amazing cataract of stars.

Chane's stun-gun buzzed and dropped them.

He had, he thought, only a few minutes before the guards were missed. His plans for getting out of the port required much more time than that.

A grin crossed his face and he thought, *The hell with clever plans. Do it the Starwolf way.*

The small skimmer the guards had come in stood outside the warehouse. Chane reached down and took the helmet off one of the unconscious men, and put it on his head. It would conceal the fact that his hair was not the albino white of Vhol, and it would help to hide his face. The guard's jacket concealed his non-Vhollan clothing.

He jumped into the driver's seat of the skimmer, turned it on, and went racing and screaming toward the main gateway of the military port.

The searchlights on the tower came on and locked onto him. He waved his free arm wildly as he drove up to the gateway, and shouted to the guards there. He hardly knew a word of Vhollan so he kept his shout a wordless one, relying on the screaming of the siren to make it unintelligible anyway. He pointed excitedly ahead and goosed the skimmer to its highest speed.

The guards fell away, startled and excited, and Chane drove on into the darkness, laughing. It was the old Varnan way; be as clever and tricky as you can but when cleverness won't work, smash right through before people wake up. He and Ssander had done it many times.

For a fleeting moment, he was sorry that Ssander was dead.

XI

'They didn't see me,' Chane said. 'Not to recognize me as a non-Vhollan. I can vouch for that. They didn't see me at all.'

Dilullo's face was very hard in the lamplight, the lines cut deep like knife-slashes in dark wood.

'What did you do with the skimmer?'

'Found a lonely beach, drove it out onto the water a way, and sank it.' Chane looked at Dilullo and was astonished to find himself making excuses. 'It was that damned cone, that recorder thing. I had no way of knowing what it was, and it went on all by itself when my hand got near it.' He saw Dilullo looking at him very oddly, and he hurried on. 'Don't worry about it. I came in over the roofs. Nobody saw me. Why would they suspect us? Obviously some of their own people must be overly prying or they wouldn't have all that tight security. If there are no thieves on Vhol it'll be the rarest planet in the galaxy.'

He tossed the belt pouch on Dilullo's lap. 'I got what you wanted, anyway. It's all there.' He sat down and helped himself to a drink from Dilullo's brandy bottle. The bottle, he noticed, had taken a severe beating, but Dilullo was cold and stony sober as a rock.

'Just the same,' Dilullo said, 'I think the time has come to say goodbye to Vhol.' He set the pouch aside. 'Have to wait on these till we have the ship's techlab.' He leaned forward, looking at Chane. 'What was so strange about these things?'

'The metal they were made of. The fact that they were unclassifiable as to function. Above all, the fact that they came from an area – the nebula – that doesn't have any inhabited world with a technology above Class Two level.'

Dilullo nodded. 'I wondered if you remembered that. We studied all the microfile charts on our way here from Kharal.'

'Either the microfile charts are wrong, or something else is. Because those things are not only from a very high technology, but a very alien one.'

Dilullo grunted. He got up and lifted a corner of the curtain across the window. It was already dawn. Chane turned off the lamp and a pearl-pink light flooded into the little room of the inn on Star Street.

'Could they have been weapons, Chane? Or components of weapons?'

Chane shook his head. 'The recorder thing certainly wasn't. I couldn't swear to the other two, of course, but they didn't *feel* like it.' He meant an inner feeling, the instinctive recognition by a practiced fighter for any deadly instrument.

'That's interesting,' Dilullo said. 'Did I tell you, by the way, that Thrandirin wants to inspect our wares tomorrow, with a view to buying? Go get some sleep, Chane. And when I call you, wake up fast.'

It was not Dilullo who waked him, though. It was Bollard, looking as though he had just waked up himself, or was perhaps just on the verge of going to sleep.

'If you have any possession here that you can't bear to leave behind you, bring it ... just so long as it'll fit into your pocket.' Bollard scratched his chest and yawned. 'Otherwise forget it.'

'I travel light.' Chane pulled his boots on. They were all he had taken off before he slept. 'Where's Dilullo?'

' 'Board ship, with Thrandirin and some top brass. He wants us to join him.'

Chane paused in his boot-pulling and met Bollard's gaze. The small eyes behind those fat pink lids were anything but sleepy.

'I see,' said Chane, and stamped his heel down and stood up. He grinned at Bollard. 'Let's not keep him waiting.'

'You want to go down and explain that to the guards?' He smiled back at Chane, a fat lazy man without a care in the world. 'They're posted front and back, ever since last night. Confined to quarters, Thrandirin said, for our own protection during a period of emergency. Something happened last night that upset them. He didn't say what. He only allowed Machris, the weapons expert, and one other man to go with Dilullo to the ship. So we have almost a full crew. But the guards have lasers. So it's going to be a little bit of a problem ...' Bollard seemed to ponder a moment. 'John said something about you coming in over the roofs. Could that be done by others, say, fat slobs like me?'

'I can't vouch for the construction,' Chane said, 'but if you don't fall through you shouldn't have any trouble. It'll have to be done quietly, though. These buildings aren't very high, and if they hear us we'll be in worse trouble than if we'd just butted them head on.'

'Let's try,' said Bollard, and went away, leaving Chane wishing it were night.

But it was not night. It was high noon, and the sun of Vhol shone white and bright overhead, driving a shaft of brilliance down through the trapdoor when Chane pushed it carefully open.

There was no one to be seen. Chane stepped out and waved the others after him. They came quietly up the ladder one at a time, and at intervals they went quietly across the roof, not running, in the direction Chane had pointed out.

Meanwhile, Chane and Bollard kept watch of the streets below in front of and behind the inn. Chane drew the alley because Bollard was in command and therefore got the most important post. Motionless as one of the carved stone gargoyles of Kharal, he peered down into the alley from behind a kitchen chimney. The Vhollan guards were a tough-looking lot, standing patiently in good order, not minding the sun nor the chatter of small urchins gathered to stare at them, nor the invitations of several young ladies who seemed to be telling them they could go and have a cooling drink and be back before they were missed. Chane disliked the Vhollan guards intensely. He preferred men who would loosen their tunics and sit in the shade and chaffer with the ladies.

The Mercs were not as good as Varnans, nobody was, but they were good enough, and they got off without attracting any attention from below. Bollard signaled that all was clear on his side. Chane joined him and they went on their way toward the spaceport.

The roofs of Star Street were utilitarian, ugly, and mercifully flat. The Mercs moved across them in a long irregular line, going as quickly as they could without making any running noises for people to come up and investigate. The line of buildings ended at the spaceport fence, separated from it by a perimeter road that served the warehouse area. The gate was no more than thirty yards away, and the Merc ship sat unconcernedly on its pad a quarter mile beyond.

It looked a long, long way.

Chane took a deep breath and Bollard said quietly to the Mercs, all bunched together on that ultimate roof, 'All right; once we start moving, don't stop.'

Chane opened the trapdoor and they went down through the building, not worrying now about making noise, not worrying about anything but getting where they wanted to go. There were three floors in the building. The air was stale and heavy in the corridors, sweet with too much perfume. There were a lot of doors, mostly closed. The sound of music came up from below.

They hit the ground floor running, passed through a series of ornate rooms that were chipped and worn and moth-eaten in the daylight that leaked in through the curtained windows. There were people in the rooms, of various sizes, shapes, and colors, some of them quite strange, but Chane did not have time to see exactly what they were doing. He only saw their startled eyes turned on him in the half-gloom. A towering woman in green charged at them, screeching angrily like a gigantic parrot. Then the front door slammed open with a jingling of sinful bells, and they were out in the clean hot street.

They headed for the gate. And Chane was astonished at how rapidly Bollard could make his fat legs go when he really wanted to.

There was a watchman's box beside the gate. The man inside it saw them coming. Chane could see him staring at them for what seemed like minutes as they rushed closer, and he smiled at the man, a contemptuous smile that mocked the slow reactions of the lesser breeds. He himself, or any other Starwolf, would have had the gate closed and half the onrushing Mercs shot down before the watchman's synapses finally clicked and set his hand in motion toward the switch. Actually the time lapse from initial stimulus to reaction was only a matter of seconds. But it was enough to bring Chane in stunner range. The watchman fell down. The Mercs pounded through the gate. Bollard was the last of them and Chane saw Bollard staring at him with a very peculiar expression as he passed, and only then did he realize that in the necessity of the moment he had forgotten all about being careful and had raced ahead of the others, covering the thirty yards at a speed well-nigh impossible for a normal Earthman.

He swore silently. He was going to give himself away for sure if he wasn't more careful, perhaps had already done so.

Somebody shouted, 'Here they come!'

The Vhollan guards had finally been alerted. They were coming down Star Street at the double, and in a minute, Chane knew, those needle-like laser beams would begin to flicker. He heard Bollard's almost unconcerned order to spread out. He punched the switch and jumped through as the gate began to swing. Bollard was fishing something out of his belt-pouch, a bit of plastic with a magnetic fuse-and-coupler plate. He slapped it onto the end of the gate as it swung past, just above the lock assembly. Then Chane and Bollard ran on together toward the ship.

Behind them there was a pop and an intense flash of light as the gate clanked shut. Bollard smiled. 'That fused the gate and the post together. They can cut through, of course, but it'll take 'em a couple minutes. Where did you learn to run?'

'Rock-jumping in the drift mines,' said Chane innocently. 'Does wonders for the coordination. You should try it sometime.'

Bollard grunted and saved his breath. The Merc ship still seemed a million miles away. Chane fumed at having to rein himself in to the Mercs' pace, but he did it. Finally Bollard panted, 'Why don't you go on ahead like you did before?'

'Hell,' said Chane, pretending to pant also, 'I can only do that in spurts. I blew myself.'

He panted harder, looking back over his shoulder. The guards were approaching the gate now. One of them went into the watchman's box. Chane assumed that he tried the switch, but nothing happened. The gate remained closed. Some of the guards fired through the mesh. The whip crack and flash of the lasers scarred the air behind the Mercs but the range was too long for the small power-packs in the hand weapons. Chane thanked the luck of the Starwolves that the guards had not thought they might need heavier weapons.

There was not as yet any sign of life around the Merc ship. Presumably the Vhollans within would feel perfectly safe, believing that the ship's crew was bottled up at the inn, and Chane was sure that Dilullo would see to it that the demonstration was held where the visitors wouldn't be inconvenienced by noises from outside. Still and all, there should be a guard …

There was. Two Vhollans in uniform came out of the lock to see what was going on. They saw, but they were already too late. The Mercs knocked them down neatly with their stun-guns. The skimmer in which Dilullo and the Vhollan officials had come was parked beside the boarding steps. Bollard ordered the men aboard and motioned to Chane. Together they tossed the unconscious men into the skimmer and started it, heading it back without a driver toward the fence. The guards from the inn had cut their way through the gate.

Bollard nodded. 'That all worked out real nice,' he said.

They scrambled up the steps and into the lock. The warning hooter was going, the CLEAR LOCK sign flashing red. Dilullo had not wasted any time. The inner lock door clapped shut and sealed itself almost on Chane's coattails.

Members of the crew with flight duty hurried to their stations. Chane went to the bridge room with Bollard.

There was quite a crowd in it, all Mercs but one, and all but one jubilant. The one was Thrandirin. Dilullo stood with him before the video pickup grid, so that there should not be any mistake when the message went out.

Dilullo was talking into the communicator.

'Hold your fire,' he was saying. 'We're about to take off, so clear space. And forget about your intercept procedures. Thrandirin and the two officers will be returned to you safely if you do as I say. But if anybody fires off so much as a slingshot at us, they die.'

Chane hardly heard the words. He was looking at the expression on Thrandirin's heavy, authoritative face, and it filled him with pure joy.

The drive units throbbed to life, growled, roared, screamed, and took the Merc ship skyward. And nobody fired so much as a slingshot as it went.

XII

The Merc ship hung in the edge of the nebula, lapped in radiance.

Dilullo sat in the wardroom with Bollard, studying for the hundredth time the photographs and the analyzer record on the objects in the warehouse.

'You'll wear them out with eyetracks,' Bollard said. 'They aren't going to tell you anything different from what they already have.'

'Which is nothing,' Dilullo said. 'Or worse than nothing. The photographs are clear and sharp. I see the things, therefore I know they exist. Then along comes the analyzer record and tells me they don't.'

He tossed the little plastic disc onto the table. It was blank and innocent as the day it was made, recording zero.

'Chane didn't handle it right, John. Attached the sensors wrong, or forgot to turn it on.'

'Do you believe that?'

'Knowing Chane, no. But I have to believe something, and the fault isn't in the analyzer. That's been checked.'

'And rechecked.'

'So it has to be Chane.'

Dilullo shrugged. 'That's the most logical explanation.'

'Is there another one?'

'Sure. The things are made out of some substance that the analyzer isn't programmed to identify. I.e., not on our atomic table. But we know that's ridiculous, don't we?'

'Of course we do,' said Bollard slowly.

Dilullo got up and got a bottle and sat down again. 'We're not doing anything else,' he said. 'Get Thrandirin and the two generals in here. And Chane.'

'Why him?'

'Because he saw the things. Touched them. Set one off. Heard it ... singing.'

Bollard snorted. 'Chane's fast and he's good, but I wouldn't trust him any farther than he could throw me.'

'I wouldn't either,' said Dilullo. 'So bring him.'

Bollard went out. Dilullo put his chin in his fists and stared at the disc and the photographs. Outside the hull the pale fires of the nebula glowed across infinity ... endless parsecs of infinity in three dimensions. Up in the navigation room Bixel read micro-books from the ship's library for the third time over and drank innumerable cups of coffee, keeping vigil over the radar which remained as obstinately blank as the analyzer disc.

Bollard came back with Chane and Thrandirin and the two generals, Markolin and Tatichin. The *-in* suffix was important on Vhol, it seemed, identifying a certain gens which had acquired power a long time back and hung onto it with admirable determination. They figured largely in administrative, military and space-flight areas, and they were accustomed to command. Which made them less than patient prisoners.

Thrandirin opened the game, as he always did, with the *How-long-are-you-going-to-persist-in-this-idiocy* gambit. Dilullo countered, as he always did, with the *As-long-as-it-takes-me-to-get-what-I-want* one. Then all three told him that was impossible, and demanded to be taken home.

Dilullo nodded and smiled. 'Now that we've got that out of the way, perhaps we can just sit around and have a drink or two and talk about the weather.' He passed the bottle and the glasses around the scarred table. The Vhollans accepted the liquor stiffly and sat like three statues done in marble and draped in bright tunics. Only their eyes were alive, startlingly blue and bright.

Thrandirin's eyes rested briefly on the photographs in front of Dilullo and moved away again.

'No,' said Dilullo. 'Go ahead, look at them.' He passed them down. 'Look at this, too.' He passed the disc. 'You've seen them before. There's no need to be bashful about it.'

Thrandirin shook his head. 'I say what I have said before. If I knew any more than you do about those objects I would not tell you. But I don't. I saw them in the warehouse, and that is all. I am not a scientist, I am not a technician, and I have no direct part in this operation.'

'Yet you are a government official,' said Dilullo. 'Pretty top-level, too. Top enough to dicker for weapons.'

Thrandirin made no comment.

'I find it very difficult to believe that you do not know where those things came from,' said Dilullo softly.

Thrandirin shrugged. 'I don't see why you find it difficult. You questioned us with a lie-detector of your latest type and it should have proved to you that we know nothing.'

Tatichin said brusquely, as though it were an old sore subject with him, 'Only six men know about this thing. Our ruler, his chief minister, the chief of the War Department, and the navigators who actually take the ships into the nebula. Even the captains do not know the course, and the navigators are under constant guard, virtual prisoners, both in space and on Vhol.'

'Then it must be something of tremendous importance,' Dilullo said. The three marble statues stared at him with hard blue eyes and said nothing. 'The

Kharalis questioned Yorolin under an irresistible drug. He told them that Vhol had a weapon out in the nebula, something powerful enough to wipe them off the face of their world.'

The hard blue eyes flared brighter on that, but the Vhollans did not seem too surprised.

'We assumed that they had,' said Thrandirin, 'though Yorolin could not remember anything beyond the fact that the Kharalis had drugged him. A man cannot lie under that drug, it is true. But he can tell only what is in his mind, no more, no less. Yorolin believed what he said. That does not necessarily make it so.'

Now Dilullo's eyes grew very hard and his jaw set like a steel trap. 'Your own unlying minds have told me that you too have heard this, and that you are indeed planning the conquest of Kharal. Now that being so, isn't it strange that you were interested in buying weapons from us? Ordinary puny conventional little weapons, even though rather better than the ones you have, when there's a super-weapon lying at hand here in this nebula?'

'Surely we answered that question for you,' said Thrandirin.

'Oh, yes, you said the weapons were needed to ensure the safety of the nebula. Now that doesn't make a whole lot of sense, does it?'

'I'm afraid I do not follow your line of reasoning, and I definitely do not enjoy your company.' Thrandirin rose, and the generals rose with him. 'I most bitterly regret that I did not have you imprisoned the moment you landed. I underestimated your—'

'Gall?' said Dilullo. 'Nerve? Plain stupid rashness?'

Thrandirin shrugged. 'I could not believe that you would come openly to Vhol from Kharal if you had actually taken service with the Kharalis. And of course there was Yorolin … we knew the Kharalis would never have given him up willingly, and the fact that you did help him to escape seemed to prove your story. So we hesitated. There was even some discussion' – here he looked rather coldly at Markolin – 'about hiring you for our own use against Kharal. You were very adroit, Captain Dilullo. I hope you are enjoying your triumph. But I will remind you again. Even if you should manage to find what you're seeking, they have been warned by sub-spectrum transmission from Vhol. They will be expecting you.'

'*They*? Heavy cruisers, Thrandirin? How many? One? Two? Three?'

Markolin said, 'He can't tell you, nor can I. Rest assured the force is sufficient to guard our … installation.' The hesitation before that word was so brief as to be almost unnoticeable. 'And I can assure you also that the value of our lives is not great enough to buy your safety there.'

'That is so,' said Thrandirin. 'And now we would prefer to return to our own quarters, if you please.'

'Of course,' said Dilullo. 'No, stay here, Bollard.' He spoke briefly over the ship's intercom, and in a moment another man came and took the Vhollans away. Dilullo swung around and looked at Chane and Bollard.

'They wanted to buy our weapons, and they thought of hiring us to use against Kharal.'

'I heard that,' said Bollard. 'I don't see anything too strange about it. It just means that their super-weapon isn't operational yet and won't be for some time, so they're hedging their bets.'

Dilullo nodded. 'Makes sense. What do you say, Chane?'

'I'd say Bollard was right. Only ...'

'Only what?'

'Well,' said Chane, 'that recorder thing in the warehouse. If they're constructing a weapon out here in the nebula, they sure aren't bothering to construct audio-visual recorders, and anyway it wasn't a Vhollan artifact.' Chane paused. There was something else itching at his mind, and he waited till it came clear. 'Besides, what's all this secrecy about? I can understand tight security, sure. And I can understand them being afraid that the Kharalis might hire somebody to go into the nebula, just as they did, and try to capture or destroy the weapon. But they're so afraid that they don't even trust men like Thrandirin and the generals to know where those came from or what they are.' Chane pointed to the photographs of the three golden objects. 'One of those things makes very strange music and shoots stars, but is no more than an audio-visual recorder. And what is so thunderingly secret about that? It doesn't make sense to me at all.'

Dilullo looked at Bollard, who shook his head. 'I didn't see his star-shooting recorder, so I can't say yes or no. Why not just come out and say what's on your mind, John?'

Dilullo picked up the little blank analyzer disc, the plastic zero. 'I'm beginning to think,' he said, 'that this may be more important than what Vhol does to Kharal, or vice versa. I think the Vhollans have got hold of something big, all right ... something so big that it frightens the wits out of them. Because,' he added slowly, 'I don't think they understand whatever it is, or know how to use it, any more than we do.'

There was a lengthy silence. Finally Bollard said, 'Would you care to explain that a little better, John?'

Dilullo shook his head. 'No. Because I'm only guessing, and a man's a fool to go galloping off on a wild guess. The only way we'll ever know is to find the thing and see for ourselves. And I'm beginning to think the Vhollans are right when they say we never will.'

He punched the intercom to the navigation room. 'Start a sweep pattern, Finney. Plot it to cover as much of the nebula coast as possible without leaving any gaps. That supply ship has to come from Vhol sometime, and all we need is a little bit of luck.'

The voice of Finney, the navigator, came back in tones of pure acid. 'Sure, John. Just a wee little bit of luck.'

Presently the Merc ship was on her way, an infinitesimal spider spinning a small frail web across the burning cliffs of the nebula, and everybody aboard knew what her chances were of catching the tiny fly she wanted. Particularly when the fly had ample warning.

Chane had lost all sense of the passage of time, and Dilullo was acutely aware that there had been far too much of it, when Bixel looked up from his radar screen and said, in a tone of utter disbelief:

'I've got a blip.'

Dilullo had one moment of triumphant joy. But it did not last long, for Bixel said, 'I've got another. And another. Hell, I've got a flock of them.'

Dilullo bent over the radar screen with a cold premonition clutching at his heart.

'They've changed course,' Bixel said. 'Heading straight for us now and coming fast. Awfully damned fast.'

Bollard had wedged himself into the little room and was peering over both their shoulders. 'Those aren't supply ships. Could be a squadron of Vhollan cruisers ... if they've decided they don't mind losing their friends.'

Dilullo shook his head dismally. 'Only one kind of ship is that size, moves in that kind of formation, and has that kind of speed. I guess Thrandirin wasn't lying after all, about the Starwolves.'

XIII

The first Chane knew about it was when the *Red Alert* signal came howling over the ship's intercom, followed at once by a burst of acceleration that set the ship's seams creaking and laid Chane up hard against a bulkhead. He had been stretched out in a borrowed bunk half asleep, but only half, and even that much was a major achievement. He hated waiting. He hated this business of dangling in a vacuum, waiting for another man to make the decisions. Wisdom and the instinct for survival told him he had better be patient because he had no other choice at the moment. But his physical being found it difficult to obey. It was not used to being inactive. A lifetime of training had taught it that inactivity was the next thing to being dead, a state fit only for the lesser breeds who were meant to be preyed upon. A Varnan fought hard, and when he was through fighting he enjoyed the fruits of his victory just as hard, until it was time to go fight again. Chane's metabolism revolted against waiting.

The alert and the frantic leaping of the ship were like a sudden release from prison.

He jumped up and went into the main passageway. Men were running in what appeared to be wild confusion, but Chane knew it was not, and in a matter of seconds everyone was at his station and the ship was quiet with a quivering, breathing quietness. The quiet of a very different sort of waiting.

Chane had no assigned station. He went on toward the bridge.

Dilullo's voice came rasping over the intercom, speaking to the whole ship.

'I've got a little bad news for you,' it said. 'We've got a Starwolf squadron on our tail.'

Chane froze in the passageway.

Dilullo's voice seemed to have a personal edge in it, a warning edge, as it went on, 'I repeat, we have a Starwolf squadron in pursuit.' *Talking to me*, Chane thought. *Well, and here we are. They've caught up with me, Ssander's brothers and the rest.*

Dilullo's voice continued. 'I am taking evasive action. We'll fight if we have to, but I'm going to do my damndest to run. So prepare for max stress.'

Meaning, I won't have time to warn you of abrupt changes in course or velocity. Just hang on and hope the ship holds together.

Chane stood still in the passageway, his body braced, his mind racing.

He might have been in worse spots in his career but he couldn't remember one off-hand. If the Mercs should have any reason to suspect his origin they would kill him long before Ssander's brothers could possibly reach him. And if they didn't suspect him, he would die anyway when the Starwolf squadron caught them.

Because it would catch them. Nobody got away from the Starwolves. Nobody could go fast enough, for nobody could endure physically the shattering impact of inertial stress that the Starwolves endured, maneuvering their little ships at man-killing velocities. That was what made them unbeatable in space.

The Merc ship wrenched screaming onto a tangential course. It seemed to Chane that he could feel the bulkhead bend under his hand. The blood beat up in him hard and hot. He straightened up as the ship steadied again, and went on forward to the bridge room.

It was dark there except for the hooded lights of the instrument panels. Dark enough so that the red-gold fire of the nebula seemed to fill it, pouring in through the forward viewport. Illusion, of course; the viewport was now a viewscreen and the nebula it showed was not the actuality but an FTL stimulus simulacrum. The illusion was good enough. Dilullo's head and shoulders loomed against the fire glow, and the ship plunged through rolling, whipping clouds of cold flame. The suns that set the nebula gas to burning with their light fled past like flung coals.

Dilullo looked up and saw Chane's face in the glow and said, 'What the hell are you doing here?'

'I get restless just sitting,' Chane said in a flat, quiet voice. 'I thought I might be able to help.'

The copilot, a small dark rawhide man named Gomez, said irritably, 'Get him out of here, John. I don't need any rock-hopper pilot breathing down my neck. Not now.'

Dilullo said, 'Hang on.'

Chane grabbed a support girder. Again the ship screamed and groaned. The metal bit into Chane's flesh, and again he thought he could feel it bend. The image in the viewscreen blurred to a chaotic jumble of racing sparks. Then it steadied and they were falling down a vast long chute between walls of flame, and Gomez said, 'One more time, John, and you're going to crack her bones.'

'All right,' said Dilullo. 'Here's the one more time.'

Chane heard more than the ship cry out. The men were beginning to crumple under the hammering. Gomez sagged in his chair. Blood sprang from his nose and went in dark runnels over his mouth and chin. Dilullo sighed a great sigh as the breath was squeezed from his lungs. He seemed to lean over the control panel and Chane reached forward to take the ship, drew back as Dilullo forced himself erect again, his mouth open and biting savagely on air, dragging it into him by main force and stubbornness. On the other side of the bridge room a man hung sideways against his recoil harness and did not move. Unnoticed, Chane grinned a sardonic grin, and clung to his girder, and breathed evenly against the pressure of the inertial hand that tried to crush him and could not.

Then he wondered what he was grinning about. This toughness he was so proud of was about to be his doom. The Mercs could not match it, and so the Starwolves would win.

He wondered if they knew that he was aboard the Merc ship. He didn't see how they could, for sure. But they must have tracked him to Corvus, and that would be enough. They would shake out the whole cluster until they found him or made sure he was dead.

Chane grinned again, thinking how Dilullo must be regretting his own cleverness in keeping his tame Starwolf alive. Chane felt no responsibility for the results. That had been all Dilullo's idea, and Chane could even take a certain cruel pleasure in the way he was being paid out for it.

He knew that Dilullo must be thinking the same thing. Just once Dilullo turned and met his eye, and Chane thought, *He'd give me to them now if he could, if it would save his men. But he knows it wouldn't. The Varnans couldn't let these men live, not knowing what I might have told them. Wouldn't let them live, in any case, for helping me.*

The ship lurched and staggered, slowing down. The viewscreen flickered, blanked out, became again a window onto normal space. They drifted underneath the belly of a great orange sun, veiled and misty in the cloudy fire.

After a minute Dilullo said, 'Bixel?' And again, 'Bixel!'

Bixel's voice came faintly from the navigation room. He sounded as though he was snuffing blood out of his own nose. 'I don't see anything,' he said. 'I think—' He choked and gasped and went on again, 'I think you shook 'em.'

'Just as well,' muttered Gomez, mopping himself. 'One more time and you'd have cracked *my* bones to a jelly.'

Chane said, 'They'll be along.' He saw Gomez and some of the others turn and glare at him, and he pretended weakness, sliding down along the girder to sit on the floor beside Dilullo. 'They know we can't take it like they can. They know we have to stop.'

'How did you get to be such an expert on Starwolves?' asked Gomez. Not suspiciously. Just slapping down a bigmouth. Chane slumped against his girder and shut his eyes.

'You don't have to be an expert,' he said, 'to know that.'

And how many times I've done this, he thought. *Watched a ship run and dodge and twist, half killing the men inside, and we watched and followed and waited until the strength was beaten out of them. And now I'm on the receiving end …*

Bixel said ever the intercom, 'They're here.'

The Starwolf ships dropped into normal space, showing their bright little blips like sudden sparks on the radar screen. Distant yet. Too far off to be seen. But zeroing in.

Chane's hands ached to take the controls from Dilullo, but he kept them still. It was useless anyway. The Merc ship was no stronger than the men who built it.

'Coordinates!' said Dilullo, and Bixel's tired voice answered, 'Coming.'

The computer beside the copilot's chair began to chatter. Gomez read the tapes it fed out. Chane knew what he was going to say and waited till he said it.

'They're globing us.'

Yes. Break formation and dart like flying slivers of light all around the exhausted prey. Englobe it, disable it, close and pounce.

'What the devil do they want of us?' roared Bollard's voice from the engine-room.

There was a little silence before Dilullo said, 'Maybe just to kill us. It's the nature of the beast.'

'I don't think so,' Chane said, and he thought, *I know damn well.* 'I think they'd have knocked us apart back there on first contact. I think this is a boarding action. Maybe they ... got wind of something in the nebula. Maybe they think we know.'

'Up shields,' said Dilullo.

Bollard's voice answered, 'Shields up, John. But they can batter them down. There's too many.'

'I know.' Dilullo turned to Gomez. 'Is there any gap in that globe?'

'Nothing they couldn't close long before we got there.'

Bixel's voice, high and tight, said, 'John, they're coming fast.'

Dilullo said quietly, 'Does anyone have any suggestions?'

Chane answered, 'Take them by surprise.'

'The expert again,' said Gomez. 'Go ahead, John. Take them by surprise.'

Dilullo said, 'I'm listening, Chane.'

'They think we're beat. I don't have to be an expert to know that, either. They're stronger than ordinary people, they count on that, and they count on people feeling helpless and giving up. If you suddenly bulled at them head on, I think you might break out, and you better do it fast before they blow your tail off.'

Dilullo considered, his hands poised over the controls. 'The shields won't hold for long, you know. We aren't a heavy.'

'They won't have to hold long if you go fast enough.'

'I may kill some men doing it.'

'You're the skipper,' Chane said. 'You asked, I'm only answering. But they'll die anyway if the Starwolves get hold of you. And maybe not so cleanly.'

'Yes,' said Dilullo. 'I guess you don't have to be an expert to know that, either. Full power, Bollard. And good luck all.'

He brought his hands down onto the keys.

Braced against the girder, Chane felt the acceleration slam against him, driving his spine back into the steel. The fabric of the ship moaned around him, quivered, shuddered, swayed. He thought, *She's breaking up!* and tensed himself for the whistle of air through riven plates and a sight of the nebula above his head before he died. Through the viewplate he could see the fiery veils curling past, whipped like sea-mist over their onrushing bow. Something struck them. The ship jarred and rolled. Brush lightning burned blue inside the bridge room and there was a smell of ozone. But the shield held. The ship rushed on, gaining speed. There were brutal sounds of men in agony. Chane watched Dilullo. A second blow struck. Bollard's voice, thick and choking, said, 'I don't know, John. Maybe once more.'

'Hope for twice,' said Dilullo.

Now there was something ahead of them, dark and solid in the glow. A Starwolf cruiser, diving in to block them.

'Their reactions are faster than ours,' Dilullo said in a strange half-laughing voice, and drove straight toward it.

Chane was standing now, bent forward, his belly tight and his blood pounding gloriously. He wanted to shout, *Go ahead; do it the Starwolf way! Drive, because they won't believe you have the strength or the guts to do it! Make him step aside; make him give way!*

The next two blows hit them head on. Chane could see them coming, buds of destruction loosed by the Starwolf ship to burst into full bloom against their shield. He could picture the man guiding that ship ... man, yes, human, yes, but different, shaped by the savage world of Varna to a sleek-furred magnificence of strength and speed ... the face high-boned, flat-cheeked, smiling, the long slanted eyes, cat-bright with the excitement of the chase. He would be thinking, 'They're only men, not Varnans. They'll turn back. They'll turn back.'

Somebody was shouting to Dilullo, 'Sheer off; you'll crash him!' Several people were shouting. The small cruiser seemed to leap toward them, heading straight for the eyebrow bridge and the viewport. In a couple of seconds they would have it in their laps. The cries reached a peak of hysteria and lapsed into hypnotized silence. Dilullo held course and velocity, so rigidly that Chane wondered if he was dead at his post. The Starwolf cruiser was so close now that he thought he could almost make out the shape of the pilot behind the curved port, and he tasted something in his mouth, something coppery, and knew that it was fear.

He thought he saw the face of the Starwolf pilot soften into disbelief, into belated understanding ...

In a sudden swerve that would have killed any other living thing, the cruiser went aside past their starboard bow. Chane waited for the grinding crunch of a sideswipe, but there was none.

They were out of the globe, and clear.

The viewport blanked as they passed over into jump velocity, became again a viewscreen. Dilullo leaned back in his chair and looked at Chane, his hard face looking broken in the fire glow, mottled dark in the hollows and squeezed white over the bones.

'Respite,' he said. 'They'll come again.' His voice was harsh and reedy, his lungs laboring for breath.

'But you're alive,' said Chane. 'It's only when you're dead that there isn't any chance at all.' He stared at Dilullo and shook his head. 'I've never seen anything better done.'

'And you never will,' Dilullo said, 'until I kill you.' He half fell out of the chair, looked at Gomez, shook him, then jerked a thumb at the controls. 'Take over while I check the damage.'

Chane sat down in the pilot's chair. The ship was slow and heavy under his hands, but it was good to feel any kind of a ship again. He sent it plunging deeper into the nebula, threading the denser clouds where it might be a little harder to follow.

Dilullo came back and took the controls again until Gomez could relieve him. One man was dead, and there were four sickbay cases, including General Markolin. No one but Morgan Chane was in good shape.

They dropped back into normal space in the heart of a parsec-long serpent of flame that coiled across a dozen suns.

Bixel, who had had some rest and stopped his nosebleed, sat watching his radar screen. The men slept. Even Dilullo slept, stretched out on a bench in the bridge room. Chane dozed, while time crept by with a kind of dazed sluggishness ... so much time that Chane began to hope that the hunters had given up.

But it was only a hope, and it vanished when Bixel pushed the alarm button and cried out over the intercom, 'Here they come again.'

Well, thought Chane, *it was a good try, anyway. A damned good try.*

XIV

The bright relentless little sparks flew swiftly across the radar screen. Dilullo looked at them, a cold dull sickness at the pit of his stomach. Damn them. Damn Morgan Chane and his own smartness in keeping him alive. If he hadn't kept him ...

He would be in just as much trouble, Dilullo told himself. The wolf pack was never known to let any promising prey slip through its jaws, and a Merc ship could be carrying anything ... like, say, a fortune in lightstones for the payroll.

And yet ...

He looked at Chane through the doorway, sitting quiet in the bridge room, and considered what would happen if he dropped him out of a hatchway, suited and attached to a signal flare.

He looked at the spark again, racing towards him, and he was suddenly angry. He was so angry he shook with it, and the cold sickness in him was burned away. Damn these arrogant whelps of Starwolves. He wasn't going to give up anything. Not because he knew it wouldn't stop them anyway, but because he wasn't going to be pushed and knocked around like a little boy unable to defend himself against the big boys. It was too humiliating.

He strode back to the pilot's chair and strapped in, his body protesting in every fiber as he did so. He told it to shut up.

Gomez protested, and he told him to shut up, too.

'But, John, the men can't take any more. Neither can the ship.'

'Okay,' said Dilullo. 'Then let's see to it that there's not one shred of bone or meat left for those wolves to snap their teeth on.' He shouted over the intercom to Bollard: 'Full power and never mind the shields.'

He could see the ships now. Over his shoulder he said to Chane, 'Come on up here, where you can get a good view.'

Chane stood behind him, against the girder. 'What are you going to do?'

'I'm going to make them destroy us,' Dilullo said, and pressed the keys.

The Merc ship leaped forward, toward the oncoming squadron.

Bixel's voice blasted over the intercom. 'John, I've got another one, a heavy. A heavy! Coming up on our tail!'

It was a moment before that registered. Dilullo was committed now to angry death, his whole attention fixed on the Starwolf ships. He heard Bixel all right, and he heard others shouting at him, but they were somewhere beyond a wall.

Then Morgan Chane's fingers closed on his shoulder in a grip so painful that he couldn't ignore it, and Chane was saying, 'Heavy cruiser! It must be Vhollan … the guard force Thrandirin talked about. They must have been looking out for us … picked us up when we came within range of their probes.'

Dilullo's mind broke out of frozen rage and began to work at full speed. 'Get a fix!' he snapped to Bixel. 'Estimated course and velocity.' He looked at the Starwolf ships again, this time with a kind of fiendish pleasure. 'Shields up, Bollard! Shields up! We're going to give our Starwolf friends something big to play with. Gomez … hit that aft monitor screen.'

He could see the formation of little Starwolf ships ahead of him very clearly. It was shaping into a flying U, the wings stretching out almost fondly to enfold him.

Below the viewport a screen flickered to life bringing him a picture of what was behind him. A big starcruiser loomed out of the nebula drift, closing fast. He wondered what the skipper was thinking as he saw and recognized the Starwolf squadron. He thought it must be something of a shock to him, having come after one small Merc ship only to find that the Vhollans' private preserves had been invaded by a much more numerous and deadly enemy.

It must be something of a shock to the Starwolves, too … seeing a heavy cruiser where they had expected only an exhausted prey.

The ship-to-ship band sprang to life. A man's voice shouted in sputtering galacto, 'Mercs! This is the Vhollan cruiser. Cut power immediately or we'll disable you.'

Dilullo opened his transmitter and said, 'Dilullo talking. What about the Starwolves?'

'We'll take care of them.'

'That's nice,' Dilullo said. 'Thanks. But may I remind you that I have Thrandirin and two generals aboard. I wouldn't want to take any chances with their safety.'

'Neither would I,' said the Vhollan voice grimly, 'but my orders are to stop you first and worry about your hostages second. Is that clear?'

'Perfectly,' said Dilullo, and notched his power up two steps. The ship jumped forward and he began to yaw it back and forth so that it ran toward the Starwolves the way a fox runs, never giving a clean target for a shot. It was hard on the ship, hard on the men, but not nearly so hard as the licking force-beam of the cruiser that missed them because of it.

The Starwolf formation was breaking up and scattering, so as not to provide a bunched-up target for the cruiser. It was almost in the nature of an afterthought that they fired at the Merc ship. It bucked and rolled twice as the missiles impacted on its screen, and then it was through the squadron, going away and going fast, and the monitor screen showed behind him the big

Vhollan cruiser and the Starwolf ships locked in battle, the swift wicked little ships darting and snapping at the huge heavy like dogs around a bear.

Dilullo glanced up and saw Chane's black eyes fixed upon the monitor, his expression both relieved and regretful.

Dilullo said, 'I'm sorry we can't stay around to see who wins.'

The battle faded, left behind in the glowing mists, and then even the mists were left behind as the Merc ship climbed into overdrive.

Chane said, with a ring of pride he could not quite conceal, 'They'll keep that heavy busy, all right. It has the weight, but they have the speed. They won't try to crush it ... but if nobody else interrupts, they'll just sting it to death.'

'I hope they all have fun,' said Dilullo edgily, and spoke into the intercom. 'Bixel, did you get an ECV?'

'I'm feeding it into the computer now. I'll have the backtrack in a minute.'

They waited. Dilullo saw that Chane was studying him with a new expression ... what would you call it? Respect? Admiration?

'You were really going to do it,' Chane said. 'Make them destroy us so they couldn't get anything.'

'These Starwolves,' said Dilullo, 'are too sure of themselves. Somebody, someday, is going to stand up and surprise the life out of them.'

Chane said, 'I wouldn't have believed that once, but now I'm not so sure.'

'Here it is,' said Gomez, the computer tape chattering out under his hand.

Gomez studied the tape and set up a pattern on the sky-board. 'Extrapolating from estimated course and velocity, the cruiser probably came from this area.' He punched the identifying coordinates and a microchart slid over the magnification lens and filled the area bounded by the pattern. Dilullo leaned over to study it.

The area was part of the coiled fire-snake, that part that might be likened to the head. At about the place where a parsecs-long fire-snake might have an eye, there was a star. A green star, with five planetary bodies, only one of which was large enough to be rightfully called a planet.

Dilullo became aware of somebody looking over his shoulder. It was Bollard, his round face still placid in spite of some ugly blotches that might be bruises or burst veins.

'Everything okay in engineering?' Dilullo asked.

'All okay. Though we don't deserve it.'

'Then I suppose we'd better have a look at that.'

Bollard frowned at the green star, the baleful eye of the fire-snake.

'Might or might not be the place, John.'

'We'll never know till we look, will we?'

'I won't even answer that. Do you think you can sneak in behind that cruiser while it's busy with our Starwolf friends?'

'I can try.'

'Sure you can try. But don't get too biggity just because you bulled down a Starwolf. One cruiser found us, but if one cruiser was all they had on guard they'd never have sent it away to look. There must be another one waiting planetside, watching to see if we slip by. And they'll know by now that we have.'

'Thanks, Bollard,' said Dilullo. 'Now go back down and encourage your drive-units.'

He set the course for the green sun.

They dropped back into normal space dangerously near to a band of drift between the two little outer worlds of the system of the green star, and they hid there, pretending to be an asteroid circling lazily with all the others in the misty, curdled light, the thick nebula gases glowing icy green here instead of the warm gold around the yellow stars. It made Dilullo feel cold and oddly claustrophobic. He found himself gasping for breath and wondered what was the matter with him, and then he remembered how once when he was a child he had lain drowning at the bottom of a pool of still green water.

He shook the nightmare away, reminding himself that his father had come in time to save him, but that Daddy wasn't here now and it was up to him.

He went into the navigation room to check with Bixel. There was a lot of clutter on the long-range probe scanner screen. It took a while to sort things out, but there was no doubt about the result.

'Another heavy cruiser,' Bixel said. 'On station by the planet, flying an intercept patrol pattern. We haven't got a chance of getting past him.'

'Well,' said Dilullo, 'at least we know we're in the right place.'

He went back into the bridge room, shoving past Bollard in the doorway. Bollard said, 'What now?'

'Give me five minutes to think up a brilliant plan,' Dilullo said.

Chane beckoned to him. He was standing beside Rutledge at the radio control center. Rutledge had opened the ship-to-ship channel, and Dilullo could hear voices crackling back and forth in Vhollan.

'That's the two cruisers – the one fighting the Starwolves and the one at the planet ahead,' Chane said. 'They're doing an awful lot of talking.' He smiled, and again there was that touch of pride only half hidden. 'They sound pretty upset.'

'They have a right to be,' said Dilullo. 'Not only us invading their privacy, but a flock of Starwolves. Go get Thrandirin up here. He can translate.'

Chane went out. Dilullo listened to the voices. They did sound upset, and increasingly so. Because he had made the relatively short jump in overdrive, the actual lapse of time since they left the battle was not great, and it sounded as though it was still going on … the two cruiser captains were shouting back and forth at each other now, and Dilullo grinned.

'Sounds like one of 'em is yelling for help and the other one is telling him he can't come.'

He fell silent as Chane came in with Thrandirin. He watched the Vhollan's face, saw his expression change as he heard the heated voices on the radio.

'The Starwolves are giving your cruiser a hard time, aren't they?' he asked.

Thrandirin nodded.

'Will the one at the planet go to help him?'

'No. The orders are quite clear. One cruiser is to remain on station at all times, regardless of what happens.'

The voices on the radio stopped yelling and one of them said something in a cold, hard matter-of-fact tone. After that there was a silence. Dilullo watched Thrandirin's face, not unaware of Chane standing behind the Vhollan with a half-smile on his mouth and his ears pricked forward.

The second voice answered in what sounded like a brief affirmative. He could almost see the face of the man making it, a man heavily burdened with decision. And Thrandirin said angrily, 'No!'

'What did they say?' asked Dilullo.

Thrandirin shook his head. Dilullo said, 'Well, if you won't tell us we'll wait and see.'

They waited. There was no more talk from the radio. The bridge room was quite silent. Everybody stood or sat like statues, not sure what it was they waited for. Then Bixel's voice came sharply over the intercom.

'John! The one at the planet is breaking out of pattern.'

'Is he coming this way?'

'No. Heading off at an angle of fourteen degrees, with twice that much azimuth. Going fast.' And then Bixel cried, 'He's jumped into overdrive. I've lost him.'

'Now,' Dilullo said to Thrandirin. 'What did they say?'

Thrandirin looked at him with weary hatred. 'He has gone to help the other cruiser against the Starwolves. He had to make a choice ... and he decided that they were a far greater threat than you.'

'Not very complimentary to us,' said Dilullo. 'But I won't quarrel, since it leaves the planet clear.'

'Yes, it does,' said Thrandirin. 'Go ahead and land. There's no one to stop you now. And when our cruisers have finished with the Starwolves, they'll come back and catch you on the ground and stamp you flat.'

Bollard said, 'For once I agree with him, John.'

'Yes,' said Dilullo, 'so do I. You want to turn back now?'

'What?' said Bollard. 'And waste all the trouble that we've been through?'

He hurried off to his drive-units. Chane, full of private laughter, took Thrandirin away.

Dilullo took the Merc ship out of the drift and full speed in toward the planet.

XV

It would have been easier, Dilullo thought, if they knew what they were looking for. But they didn't, and they didn't even know how long they had to look for it, except that it might not be long enough. Dilullo had found a chance to speak to Chane alone.

'What's your guess? You know them; you've been in actions like that before. How will it go?'

Chane had said, 'The Starwolves are fearless, but not brainless. One heavy cruiser they would gamble with, and as you heard, they had it in so much trouble its captain was screaming for help. But two heavy cruisers ... no. Even without the losses they must have had, that's too much weight for them. They'll pull out.'

'Out of the fight? Or out entirely?'

Chane shrugged. 'If Ssander were still calling the turns, it would be entirely. The squadron's been away from Varna for a long time, much longer than it planned to be. It's run into trouble it wasn't expecting and can't handle ... two heavies. Ssander would have balanced the knife ... the killing end against the head ... and reckoned that it was wiser to live and let vengeance wait until tomorrow. I think they'll go.' He smiled. 'And when they do, those two cruisers will be back here in a hurry to clean up their less important problem.'

'Don't forget that you're part of that problem,' Dilullo reminded him.

Now the Merc ship scudded low across the curve of the planet ... lower than Dilullo liked. But the atmosphere was oddly thick, muffling the little world in an almost impenetrable curtain. After he got down through it far enough he understood what made it that way. The world seemed to consist of one vast dust storm, whipped and driven by tremendous winds. Where he could see it, the surface was all rolling dunes and rock. In some places the dunes had flowed over the ridges and the stiff reaching pinnacles; in others the rocks were high and strong enough to hold back the dunes, and in the lees of these grotesquely eroded walls were long smooth plains, showing a darker color than the piled dunes. Dilullo was not exactly sure what that color was. The sand, or dust, might have been anything from light tan to red, back on Earth, but under the green sun the colors were distorted and strange, as though a child had been perversely puddling them together to see what ugly muddiness he could invent.

'Not exactly a place you'd pick for looks,' said Dilullo.

Gomez uttered something uncomplimentary in Spanish, and Chane, who was haunting the bridge room again and peering over their shoulders, laughed and said, 'If someone wanted to hide something where nobody would be likely to look for it, this would be the place.'

Bollard's voice came over the intercom from engineering. 'See anything yet?' When Dilullo told him no, he said, 'We'd better get lucky pretty soon, John. Those cruisers will be back.'

'I'm praying,' Dilullo said. 'That's the best I can do right now.'

They swept over the night side, peering for lights; seeing none, they headed into a dawn that flushed chartreuse and copper sulphate instead of rose. Beyond the dawn, where the sun was high, a range of black peaks rose out of the dunes, their buttressed shoulders fighting back the waves of sand. On the other side of the range – the lee side protected from the prevailing wind, on a fan-shaped plain as smooth as a girl's cheek – was the thing they were looking for.

At the moment he saw it Dilullo knew it could not have been anything else; that, in fact, subconsciously, he had known what it would be, ever since Chane came back from the Vhollan warehouse with the pictures and the analyzer disc that registered nothing.

It was a ship. His brain told him it couldn't be a ship, it was too colossal, but his eyes saw it and it was.

A ship like nothing he had ever seen before or even dreamed of. A ship so huge it could never have been launched from any planet; it must have been built in space, taking shape in some nameless void under the hands and eyes of Lord knew what creators, a floating world alone and free, without binding sun or sister planets. A world, long and dark and self-enclosed, and not designed to stay forever in one fixed orbit, but intended to voyage freely in the vastness of all creation. This far it had voyaged. And here it lay, beached at last on this wretched world, its massive frame broken, lost, dead and lonely, half buried in the alien sand.

Chane said softly, 'So that's what they were hiding.'

'Where did it come from?' Gomez said. 'Not from any world I know.'

'A ship that size was never built just to run between the worlds we know,' said Dilullo. 'There isn't any technology in our galaxy that could have built it. It came from outside somewhere. Andromeda, perhaps … or even further.'

'I don't think that that thing was ever supposed to land on any planet … and if that is so, the pull of gravity would be enough stress to break it,' Chane said.

'Look!' interrupted Dilullo. 'They've sighted us.'

There was a small huddle of metal-and-plastic domes at the foot of the cliffs. Men started running out of them as the Merc ship came down lower. Other men appeared out of the broken side of the monster ship, ants crawling from the carcass of a giant that had overleaped the dark gulf between the island universes and had killed itself in the leaping.

Dilullo spoke sharply over the intercom to the whole company. 'We move as soon as we land. I think these men are specialists, civilians, but some of them may put up a fight, and there may be a guard force. Use stunners and don't kill unless you have to. Bollard ...'

'Yes, John!'

'Man the assault chamber and cover us. After we have secured the position, we'll establish a defense perimeter around both ships as fast as we can. I'm going to land as close as I can to the big one. The cruisers won't be able to clobber us with their heavy weapons without damaging the big one, and I don't think they want to do that. Pick what men you need, Bollard. Okay, we're going in.'

Then the Merc ship was down on the green-umber plain, with the massive ragged flank of the alien craft looming up beside them like a mountain range of metal. Dilullo cracked the lock and went out through it at the head of the Mercs, with Chane running easily at his shoulder like a good dog. The Vhollan specialists, much alarmed, were running about and doing a lot of shouting but not much else. They were not going to be a problem, Dilullo thought, and then he saw the other men.

There were about twenty of them, white-haired Vhollans in uniform tunics, looking ghastly in the green glow. They seemed to have come out of the great ship. Perhaps they lived in it, guarding it even from their own people so that no unsupervised act could occur, no unauthorized fragment of material be removed unseen. These men had lasers, and they moved with a nasty professional precision, heading straight for the Mercs.

Bollard let go with a round of gas shells from the ship. The Merc ships did not carry much heavy armament, since they were primarily transports designed to get the men to where the action was. But they did often have to land or take off in areas of intense hostility, and so they carried some weaponry, chiefly defensive. The non-lethal gas shells were very effective at breaking up offensive group action.

The Vhollan soldiers coughed and reeled around with their hands over their eyes. Most of them dropped their lasers on the first round because they could not see to shoot and were therefore likely only to kill each other. The second round took care of the laggards. Mercs with breathing masks completed the disarming and rounding up. Others had the civilians in hand and were looking into the domes for a place to put them.

'Well,' said Chane, 'that was easy enough.'

Dilullo grunted.

'You don't look very happy about it.'

'In this business things don't come easy,' Dilullo said. 'If they do you generally wind up paying for it later on.' He looked up at the sky. 'I'd give a lot to know how soon those cruisers will be back.'

Chane did not answer that, and neither did the sky. Dilullo got busy with Bollard, driving the Mercs to set up the defense perimeter, hauling out every weapon they had, including the samples, and setting men with power tools to make emplacements for them, blasting pits in the sand. Other men brought out the siege-fences of lightweight hard-alloy sections that had been useful to the Mercs on many hostile worlds, and set them up. They worked fast, sweating, and all the time Dilullo kept watching the sky.

It was an ugly sky, murky and dull. The sun looked like a drowned man's face … there was that drowning symbol again … glowing with sickly phosphorescence through the dust and the nebula gas. It stayed empty. The wind blew. They were screened from the full force of it here by the cliff wall, but it made screaming noises overhead, ripping past the pinnacles of dark rock with furious determination. A fine spray of sand drifted down, into the eyes and ears and mouth, down the collar, sticking and grating on the sweaty skin.

Dilullo was versed in strange worlds, in the taste and feel of the air, the sensation of the ground under his feet. This one was cold and gritty, sharp-edged, unwelcoming, and, though the air was breathable, it had a bitter smell. Dilullo did not like this world. It had turned away from the task of spawning life, preferring to spend its eons in selfish barrenness.

Nothing had ever lived here. But something, someone, for some reason, had come here to die.

Bollard reported to him at last that the perimeter was established and fully manned. Dilullo turned and looked up at the mountainous riven hulk looming above them. Even in the heat of preparation he had been conscious of it, not only as a physical thing but as a spiritual one, an alienness, a mystery, a coldness at the heart and a deep excitement hot and flaring in the nerves.

'Is Bixel manning the radar?'

'Yes. So far, nothing.'

'Keep in close touch and don't let him get sleepy. Chane …'

'Yes?'

'Find out which one of those specialists is in charge of the project and bring him to me.'

'Where'll you be?'

Dilullo took a deep breath and said, 'In there.'

The Vhollans had jury-rigged a hatchway in one of the broken places in the great ship's side. Other rents in the metal fabric had been covered with sheets of tough plastic to keep out the wind and the sifting dust.

Dilullo climbed the gritty steps to the hatchway and went through it, into another world.

XVI

Chane walked under the loom of the great ship, toward the dome where the Vhollans were being held. He was not thinking of either one at the moment. He was thinking of two heavy cruisers and a squadron of Starwolves, somewhere out beyond that curdled sky … wondering how the battle went, and who had died.

He did not like this feeling of being all torn up inside. He hated the Starwolves, he wanted them dead, he knew they would kill him without mercy, and yet …

Those hours on the Merc ship had been some of the hardest of his life. It was all wrong to have to fight your own kind and cheer on the man that was beating them because you told him how. Chane could never remember a time when things had not been simple and uncomplicated for him; he was a Starwolf, he was proud and strong, full member of a brotherhood, and the galaxy was a glorious place full of plunder and excitement, all theirs to do with as they wished.

Now, because his brothers had turned against him, he was forced to herd with the sheep, and that was bad enough, but the worst of it was he was beginning to like one of them. Dilullo was only human but he did have guts. No Starwolf could have done better. It hurt Chane to say it, even to himself, but it was true.

Damn. And what were they doing out there, those swift little ships biting and tearing at the cruiser? They had it in bad trouble, that was certain, or the second cruiser would never have gone. Chane smiled with unregenerate pride. The Vhollans had handed this world to the Mercs on a silver platter, rather than run the risk of the Starwolves breaking through.

One heavy cruiser the Starwolves could handle. But not two. *I should be out there*, he thought, *helping you, instead of being glad the cruiser held you and hoping the second one will blast you to atoms.*

As they would probably blast him and Dilullo and the rest of the Mercs when they came back.

Well, that would take care of his problems, anyway. He despised all this prying about inside himself, trying to sort out emotions he had never been forced to feel before. So the devil with it.

The dome was before him and he went in. The Vhollans were penned together in what seemed to be a lounge or common room, under the watchful eyes and ready stun-guns of four of the Mercs, headed by Sekkinen. It took a few minutes to cut through the half-hysterical gabble after Chane explained to Sekkinen what Dilullo wanted, and began questioning the civilians in galacto. Eventually they came out with a lean, studious-looking Vhollan in a rumpled blue tunic who stared at the Mercs with a superciliousness mixed with the fright of the scholar confronted suddenly by large and violent men. He admitted that his name was Labdibdin, and that he was chief of the research project.

'But,' he added, 'I wish to make clear that I will not cooperate with you in any way whatever.'

Chane shrugged. 'You can talk to Dilullo about that.'

'Don't lose him,' said Sekkinen.

'I won't lose him.' Chane took Labdibdin's arm, and he put his strength into the grip so that the Vhollan winced in pain and then looked at Chane, startled by such strength in a human grasp. Chane smiled at him and said, 'We won't have any trouble. Come along with me.'

The Vhollan came. He walked stiffly ahead of Chane, out of the dome and back over the cold sand, under the tremendous sagging belly of the ship. The thing must be a mile long, Chane thought, and a quarter that high … it was quite obvious now that it had never been intended to land.

He began to be excited, wondering about the ship, where it had come from, and why, and what was in it. The keen Starwolf nose scented loot.

Then he remembered that Dilullo was running this show, and his ardor cooled, for Dilullo had all those odd ideas about ethics and property.

He pushed the Vhollan with unnecessary force up the steps and through the hatchway.

A gangway bridged a twenty-foot gap of empty darkness that went down deep below the level of the sand, into the bowels of the ship. At the end of the gangway was a transverse corridor running fore and aft, as far as Chane could see in both directions. Work lights had been rigged by the Vhollan technicians. They shed a cold and meager glare, unfitting to the place, like matches in the belly of Jonah's whale. They showed the sheathing plates of the corridor to be the same pale-gold metal he had seen in the warehouse back on Vhol. It must have had great tensile strength, because it was relatively undamaged, buckled here and there but not broken. The whole corridor tilted slightly, the floor running unevenly uphill and down. Even so, the floor-plates were not shattered.

The inward wall was pierced by doorways set at intervals of fifty feet or so. Chane went through the nearest one.

And found himself perched like a bird in the high midst of what looked like a cosmic museum.

He had no way of estimating the space it occupied. It went high overhead and far below, deep down beyond the level of the sand outside, and on either hand it stretched away into dimness, lit here and there by the inadequate work lights.

He stood on a narrow gallery. Above and below there were further galleries, and from them sprang a webwork of walks that spanned the vast area spider-fashion, all interconnected vertically by a system of caged lifts. The lifts and the walks were designed to give access to all levels of the enormous stacks that filled the place, marching in orderly rows almost like the buildings of some fantastic city. The pale-gold metal from which they and the walkways had been constructed had again proved its toughness; the original perfect symmetry had gone with the inevitable buckling and twisting, walks were skewed and stacks leaned out of true, and probably there was damage he couldn't see, farther down, but on the whole it had survived.

And there was enough rich plunder here to keep four generations of Starwolves happy.

Chane said to Labdibdin, in a voice hushed with awe, 'These must have been the greatest looters in the universe.'

Labdibdin looked at him with utter scorn. 'Not looters. Scientists. Collectors of knowledge.'

'Oh,' said Chane. 'I see. It all depends on who does it.'

He moved forward along the canted walk, clinging to the rail and urging Labdibdin ahead of him. The transparent windows of the nearest stack showed only an imperfect view of what was inside. The tough plastic had cracked and starred in places. But there was a way in from the walk. He scrambled through it and stood in a large room crammed with cushioned cases.

Cases of stones: Diamonds, emeralds, rubies, precious and semi-precious stones from all over the galaxy. And mixed with them were other stones, chunks of granite and basalt and sandstone and marble and many more he couldn't name. All stones. All together.

Cases of artifacts: Curved blades of silversteel from the Hercules markets, with fine-wrought hilts, and crude axes from some backward world; needles and pins and pots and buckets and chased gold helmets with jeweled crests, belt-buckles and rings, hammers and saws … bewilderment.

'This is only a tiny sample,' said Labdibdin. 'Apparently they meant to classify later on, when they would have plenty of time … probably on the homeward voyage.'

'Homeward where?' asked Chane.

With a look of strange uneasiness, Labdibdin said, 'We're not sure.'

Chane reached out and touched one of the cases that held the jewels. The plastic cover was cold under his fingers but he could feel the heat of the red and green and many-colored stones like a physical burning.

Labdibdin permitted himself a bitter smile.

'The cases were power-operated. You passed a hand, so, over this small lens, and the lid opened. There is no power now. You'd have to blow it open.'

'Impractical, right now,' said Chane, and sighed. 'We might as well find Dilullo.'

They found him without trouble, a little farther along, looking at a collection of boxes of dirt. Just plain dirt, as far as Chane could see.

'Soil samples,' said Labdibdin. 'There are many such, and collections of plants, and samples of water, and minerals, and gases ... atmospheres, we suppose, from all the worlds they touched. Endless artifacts of all sorts ...'

'What about weapons?' Dilullo asked.

'There were some weapons among the artifacts they collected, but the sophisticated ones were permanently disarmed ...'

Dilullo said, 'Don't play vague with me. I don't care what they collected. I'm only interested in their own weapons, the weapons of this ship.'

Labdibdin set his jaw and answered, biting his words off one at a time as though he hated them: 'We have not found any weapons in this ship, except the useless articles in the specimen cases.'

'I can't blame you for lying,' said Dilullo. 'You wouldn't want to give us a weapon to use against your own people. But half the Cluster is talking about what you have here ... the super-weapon that's going to conquer Kharal ...'

A faint pinkness crept into Labdibdin's cheeks, the nearest thing to a flush that Chane had seen in these marble-skinned people. His fists clenched and he pounded them up and down on the railing in a kind of desperation.

'Weapons,' he said. 'Weapons.' His voice choked. 'My own people keep pushing and pushing and pushing, wanting me to find weapons for them, and there aren't any! There is not a sign of a weapon in this ship. There is no record of a weapon of any kind. *The Krii did not use weapons!* I keep telling them that and they will not believe ...'

'The Krii?'

'The ... people who built this ship.' He shook his hand in a wild gesture intended to take in all the collection stacks. 'In all these, in *all* of them, there is not one single specimen of a living thing, not a bird, not an animal, not a fish nor an insect. They didn't take life. I'll show you something.'

He went away from them, half running. Dilullo looked at Chane. They both shrugged, puzzled by the man's violence, not at all believing what he said.

'Keep a close eye on him,' Dilullo muttered, and they ran after the Vhollan, Dilullo a bit slowly on the canted metal walk – it was a long way down – Chane skipping lightly on Labdibdin's heels.

He led them to a service lift, rigged by the Vhollans and run by a portable generator. They got into it and it dropped them rattling down and down, past level after level of the stacks with the bits and pieces of a galaxy hoarded in them. Then it stopped and Labdibdin led them forward into a great oblong chamber that had obviously been a coordinating center for the ship and was now serving the same purpose for the Vhollan technicians.

Some of the original furniture was still there, though the Vhollans had moved in a few sketchy conveniences. It gave Chane a start when he looked at it. The height of a table made him feel like a child in grown-up land, but the contoured chairs that went with it were too narrow to accommodate even his lean bottom. No wonder the Vhollans had brought their own.

He saw the smooth-worn places on the chairs and table, the many subtle marks of use. Here someone or something had sat and worked, manipulating a built-in mechanism of some sort with banks of keys that were not intended for human fingers, had worn the keys smooth and bright, and worn a deep hollow in the unidentifiable padding of the chair.

'How long?' asked Chane. 'I mean, how long would they have been on the ship?'

'That's a silly question,' Labdibdin answered tartly. 'How long is long? By their reckoning or ours? Years or decades, or perhaps only months. And I wish I knew. I wish I knew! Look here.'

He stood in front of a pedestal, quite high, made from the pale-gold metal. It had a console in front with an intricate arrangement of keys. 'It has its own power-unit, independent of the ship,' he said, and stretched his hand out to it.

Chane laid his own hand on the back of Labdibdin's neck and said softly, 'I can snap it between my fingers. So be careful.'

'Oh, don't be a fool,' snarled Labdibdin. 'Weapons, weapons! You're the same as they are at Vhol; it's all you think of.'

A shimmering appeared in the air above the pedestal. Labdibdin turned to Dilullo and demanded, 'Will you allow me to proceed?'

Dilullo was watching everything, the Vhollan, the room, Chane, the array of unfamiliar and unguessable articles ranged here and there for study. He seemed to be watching outside the ship as well, picturing the ugly green sky in his mind and wondering when the cruisers would appear in it. He seemed to be listening for something, beyond the great engulfing silence of the ship.

He nodded to Chane, who stepped back. Labdibdin, muttering, picked up a pair of very odd gloves with long slender rods curving out from some of the fingers. He pulled them on and began pecking delicately at the console keys.

A three-dimensional image took shape in the shimmer on top of the pedestal. Chane stared at it and asked, 'What is the thing?'

'You're an Earthman and you don't know?' Labdibdin said. 'It's keyed from there.'

Dilullo said, 'It's a species of bird on Earth. But what's the purpose of this demonstration?'

Labdibdin snarled, 'To prove what I was saying. The Krii did not take life, not of anything. They collected images only.'

He pecked with the rods at the console. In quick succession images appeared and vanished … insects, fish, worms, spiders. Labdibdin shut the instrument off and turned, flinging his gloves away. He looked at Chane and Dilullo, a haggard, harried man beneath his scholarly arrogance.

'I wish to heaven somebody would believe me. There seems to have been some kind of a defensive system, a powerful screen that they could use to protect the ship. We couldn't get it to work.'

Dilullo shook his head. 'It wouldn't work here, even if you had the power for it. A screen works in space but not when a ship has landed … the force is instantly grounded and dissipated.'

Labdibdin said, 'That's what our technicians said. But anyway, one thing is sure … the Krii did not use offensive weapons!'

Chane shook his head. 'That just isn't possible.'

'I'm beginning to believe him,' said Dilullo. 'The Krii, you called them? You've deciphered their records, obviously.'

'Some of them,' Labdibdin admitted. 'I have the best philologists on Vhol here, working themselves into breakdowns. I tell you, they've pushed us and pushed us until we're all ready to drop, insisting that we come up with what they want, something to knock a world apart with. They don't seem to care half as much about the ship itself … or the real knowledge we might gain from it.' He ran his hand lovingly over the table edge. 'Stuff from another galaxy, another universe. A different atomic table … totally alien life-forms … what we could learn! But we have to waste time with all research oriented toward finding the weapons that don't exist. We're going to lose so much …'

'Another galaxy,' said Dilullo. 'Different atomic table … I made a pretty good guess. How much do you know about these … Krii?'

'They were devoted to learning. Apparently they had embarked on a project to study all of creation … one guesses at other ships in yet other galaxies, performing the same task of collecting samples. Their technological level must be unbelievably high.'

'Still, they crashed.'

'Not quite. A crash landing, rather … and of course this ship was never meant to land. Something happened. The relevant parts of the ship are pretty well demolished, and the records relating to the crash naturally very brief and sketchy, but it seems obvious there was an explosion in one of their power-cells, which damaged their life-support system so extensively they could not hope to make the voyage home. Of course nothing in this galaxy would do them any good in the way of substitute or repair. They seem to have chosen this world deliberately, because it is isolated and uninhabited, well hidden in the nebula ... and it was only by the merest accident that a Vhollan prospector looking for rare metals happened to find it.'

'Suitable place for a graveyard,' said Dilullo. 'Did you find any bodies of the Krii in the wreck?'

'Oh, yes,' said Labdibdin. 'Yes, indeed, we found a number of them.' He looked at Dilullo with haunted eyes and added, 'The only thing is ... they don't seem to be dead.'

XVII

They were deep in the very heart of the ship, walking down a long corridor with their footsteps ringing hollow from the metal vault, echoing away behind them to be lost in silence. The lights were sparse here, with long dim intervals between.

'We don't come here very often,' said Labdibdin. He spoke very softly, as though he were anxious not to be heard by anyone or anything but the two Earthmen. From his first bristling hostility, the Vhollan had softened to an astonishing degree.

He's a driven man, Dilullo thought. *It's a relief to him to talk to anyone, even us ... to break that stifling bond of secrecy. He's been imprisoned here for too long a time, practically entombed in this ship with ... with whatever I am about to see, which is enough to make his shoulders droop and his knees give way a little with every step. He's ready to crack, and small wonder.*

The footsteps sounded indecently loud in Dilullo's ears, and somehow dangerous. He was acutely conscious of the silence around him, the vast dark bulk of the ship that enclosed him. He saw his own smallness: an insect creeping in the bowels of an alien mountain. What was worse, he felt like an intruding insect, impertinently making free with someone, or something, else's property.

Dilullo wondered what Chane was thinking. He didn't give much away. Those bright black eyes seemed always to be the same, alert to every sensation, interested in everything, but never introspective. Perhaps that was a better way to go through life, just taking everything as it came, day to day, minute to minute, never worrying and never trying to get beneath the simple outward surface of things. It was when you got to thinking that things became complicated.

Or was Chane really as matter-of-fact as he always seemed? Dilullo suddenly doubted it.

Labdibdin held up his hand. 'We're almost there,' he whispered. 'Please go carefully.'

The smooth floor and sheathing of the corridor became a series of overlapping collars. 'To take up the shock,' Labdibdin said, making a telescoping motion with his hands. 'The chamber is mounted in a web of flexible supports, so that almost nothing short of complete annihilation of the ship could harm it.'

Dilullo went carefully, lifting his feet high so as not to stumble.

There was a doorway, open, and more of the dim Vhollan lights beyond. The doorway was exceedingly tall and narrow. Dilullo stepped through it, his shoulders rubbing on both sides.

He had some idea of what he was going to see. And yet he was not prepared at all for what he saw.

Beside him Chane uttered a Varnan oath, and his hand strayed automatically to his stunner.

If he were truly a wolf, Dilullo thought, *he would be snarling with his ears flat and his hackles up and his tail tucked under his belly. And I feel like that right now, myself … or perhaps, more accurately, I feel like a shivering ape-ling huddled in the night while Fear stalks past.*

Because these things were Fear. Not rational fear, which is a survival mechanism. No. This was the blind and mindless fear that cringes in the flesh, the xenophobic shrinking of the protoplasm from what is utterly alien and strange.

He could see why the Vhollans did not come here often to visit the Krii.

There were perhaps a hundred of them. They sat in orderly rows, each one upright in a high and narrow chair, in something of the attitude of the old Pharaohs: the nether limbs close together, the upper ones, with the long delicate appendages that served them for fingers, resting on the arms of the chairs. They wore only a simple drapery, and their bodies had the appearance of dark amber, not only in color but in substance, and in form they might have been either animal or vegetable, or a combination of the two, or a third something that defied analysis in the terms of this galaxy. They were very tall, very slender, and they seemed to have neither joints nor muscles but to flow all together like the ribboned weed that sways in tidewater pools.

Their faces consisted mostly of two big opalescent eyes set in a tall narrow head. There were breathing slits at the sides of the head, and a small puckered mouth that seemed pursed in eternal contemplation.

The eyes were wide open and they seemed to stare, all one hundred pairs of them, straight into Dilullo's heart.

He turned to Labdibdin, to get away from that staring, and he said, 'What makes you think they're not dead? They look petrified.'

But in his bones he knew that Labdibdin was right.

'Because,' answered Labdibdin, 'one of the records we deciphered was a message sent by them *after* they crash-landed here. It gave the coordinates of this system, and it said' – he ran his tongue nervously over his lips, looking sidelong at the rows of eyes – 'it said they would wait.'

'You mean they … sent for help?'

'It would seem so.'

'And they said they'd wait?' asked Chane. 'Looks to me as though help never came and they waited too long.' He had gotten over his first shock and decided the things were harmless. He went to examine one more closely. 'Didn't you ever dissect one, or do any tests, to make sure?'

'Try touching it,' Labdibdin said. 'Go ahead. Try.'

Chane put his hand out tentatively. It stopped in midair some eighteen inches from the body of the Krii, and Chane caught it away, shaking it. 'Cold!' he said. 'No, not really cold ... icy and tingling. What is it?'

'Stasis,' Labdibdin said. 'Each chair is a self-contained unit with its own power supply. Each occupant is enclosed in a force-field that freezes it in space and time ... a little warp-bubble wrapped around it like a cocoon, impenetrable ...'

'Isn't there any way to shut it off?'

'No. The mechanism is self-encapsulating. This was a survival system, very carefully constructed and thought out. In a stasis field they require no air, and no sustenance, because time is slowed to a stop and their metabolic processes along with it. They can wait forever if they have to, and be safe. Nothing can get at them, or harm them in any way. Not that we wanted to harm them.' Labdibdin looked at the Krii, hungering. 'To talk to them, to study them, to know how they think and function. I've been hoping ...'

He stopped, and Dilullo asked him, 'Hoping what?'

'Our best mathematicians and astronomers have been trying to work out some kind of a time-factor. That is, to translate *their* time of transmission of the call for help and *their* estimate of how long it would take the rescue ship to reach them. It isn't at all easy, and our people have come up with four possible dates for the arrival of the rescue ship. One of them is ... approximately now.'

Dilullo shook his head. 'This is all going a little too fast for me. I have an intergalactic ship, then I have its whole crew sitting here staring at me, and now I have another intergalactic ship on the way. And it might be coming, like now?'

'We don't *know*,' said Labdibdin despairingly. 'It's only one of four estimates, and a "now" might mean yesterday or tomorrow or next year. But that's the reason Vhol has been pushing us so hard here, just in case ... For myself, I've been hoping it would come while we're here, hoping I'd have a chance to talk to them.'

Chane smiled. 'Don't you think they'll be angry when they find you've been meddling with their belongings?'

'Probably,' Labdibdin said. 'But they're scientists. I think they'd understand ... not the weapons part, but the rest of it, the wanting to know. I think they'd understand that we *had* to meddle.'

Again he was silent, and very sad. 'This whole thing has been a terrible waste,' he said. 'Rushed and hurried and all for the wrong objectives. The only chance we'll ever have in my lifetime, certainly, to learn even a little about another galaxy, and the stupid bureaucrats back on Vhol can't think of anything except their piddling little war with Kharal.'

Chane shrugged. 'Everybody has his own idea of what's important. The Kharalis would be more interested in knowing that there isn't a super-weapon out here than they would be in learning about fifty galaxies.'

'The Kharalis,' said Labdibdin, 'are a narrow and ignorant lot.'

'They are that,' Chane said, and turned to Dilullo. 'The Krii aren't being much help either. Don't you think we'd better get back up?'

Dilullo nodded. He took one more look at the ranks of the not-dead but not-alive creatures, sitting so patiently in hope of their resurrection, and he thought that their alienness went deeper than the matter of form or even substance. He couldn't quite analyze what he meant by that, and then he thought, *It's their faces. Not the features. The expression. The look of utter calm. Those faces have never known passion of any kind.*

'Do you see it too?' Labdibdin said. 'I think the specie must have evolved in a gentle environment, where it had no enemies and no need to fight for survival. They haven't *conquered* anything ... I mean in themselves. They haven't suffered and learned and turned away from violence to seek a better path. It just was never in them. Love isn't in them either, by the way, judging from their records. They seem to be completely without visceral emotions of any kind, so they can be good with absolutely no trouble at all. It makes me wonder if their whole galaxy is different from ours, without all the natural violences that obtain on our planets ... climatic changes, drought, flood, famine, all the things that made us fighters in the beginning and gave us survival as the victor's crown ... or whether the world of the Krii was an isolated case.'

'As a human I have to stick with my visceral emotions. They may make us a lot of trouble but they're also all what makes life worth living. I don't think I envy the Krii too much,' Dilullo said.

Chane laughed and said, 'I don't want to be irreverent, but our dead look more alive than they do. Let's go. I'm tired of being stared at.'

They went, back along the hollow-ringing corridor, and this time Dilullo had a queer cold prickling at his back, as though the hundred pairs of eyes still watched, piercing through metal and dim light to follow him.

How they must have wondered, studying the strange wild natives of this star-jungle, the lovers, the killers, the saints, the sufferers, the triumphant damned.

'I don't think it means very much,' he said suddenly, 'to *not* do something, unless you've wanted very much to do it.'

'That's because you're human,' said Labdibdin. 'And to a human perfect peace is as good as death. The organism decays.'

'Yes,' said Chane, with such vehemence that Dilullo was startled into smiling.

'He doesn't mean just war, you know. There are other kinds of fighting.'

'Right. But to a flower, say, or a tree—'

The tiny transceiver in Dilullo's pocket-flap spoke with Bollard's voice. 'John,' it said. 'Bixel's got those two blips on his radar.'

'Coming,' said Dilullo, and sighed. 'What price perfect peace?'

XVIII

Labdibdin had been sent back to the domes with another Merc, and Chane sat in the bridge room waiting to know why Dilullo had wanted him here instead of on what was presently going to be the firing line. Through the door of the navigation room he could see Bixel hunched over his radar screen, following the approach of the cruisers. Rutledge was handling the ship-to-ship radio. Dilullo and the captain of one of the Vhollan cruisers were talking on it.

The Vhollan's voice came in loud and clear. *Senior captain*, Chane thought, *with spit, polish, and efficiency crackling in every word of his bad galacto*.

'I will offer you this one chance to surrender. Your only other alternative, as you must realize, is death. I surely don't have to point out to you the hopelessness of fighting two heavy cruisers.'

'Then why do it?' said Dilullo dryly. 'Supposing I did surrender? What would the terms be?'

'You would be returned to Vhol for trial.'

'Uh huh,' said Dilullo. 'It would be so much simpler for you just to turn out the firing-squad right here ... simpler and *quieter*. But assuming you really did take us back to Vhol, then we could plan on either A: execution for penetrating military secrets; or B: rotting in a Vhollan prison for the rest of our lives.'

He looked over at Chane with lifted eyebrows. Chane shook his head. So did Rutledge. Bixel, who was listening over the intercom, said, 'Tell him to go—'

'You would at least have a chance to live,' said the Vhollan. 'This way you have none.'

'My men seem to have a different opinion,' Dilullo answered. 'They say no.'

The cruiser captain sounded impatient. 'Then they're fools. Our heavy beams can blast your ship.'

'Sure,' said Dilullo. 'Only you won't use them because if you do you will also blast this big prize package you're supposed to be guarding. Why do you think I cuddled up so close to it ... because I loved it? Sorry, Captain. It was a good try.'

There was a pause. The cruiser captain muttered something in low exasperated Vhollan.

'I think he's calling you names,' said Rutledge.

'Very likely.' Dilullo leaned to the mike. 'By the way, Captain, how did you do with the Starwolves?'

'We drove them off,' said the Vhollan curtly. 'Of course.'

'Of course,' said Dilullo, 'but not without some damage. How is the other boy feeling, the one that was screaming so loud for help?'

'I don't think he's feeling too good, John,' said Bixel. 'He's yawing around a lot, as though some of his drive-tubes weren't functioning just right.'

Chane thought, *The Starwolves would have had him if the second cruiser hadn't come up. It must have been a great fight.*

He wondered if Ssander's brothers had survived it. If they had, he was still going to have to face them some day. They wouldn't give up, and sooner or later …

But he was proud of them.

The Vhollan captain was giving Dilullo one last chance to surrender, and Dilullo was saying no.

'You may get us, friend, but you'll have to fight for it.'

'Very well,' said the captain, and his voice was cold and flat and hard now as a steel blade. 'We'll fight. And no quarter, Dilullo. No quarter.'

He broke off transmission. Chane stood up, impatient, his belly tight with anticipation. Rutledge looked up at Dilullo.

'That's telling them, John. By the way, do you have any plan at all for getting us out of here?'

'Something will come to me,' said Dilullo. 'Are you tracking them, Bixel?'

'Tracking. They're coming in now …'

'What's the heading?'

Bixel told him, and Dilullo went to the viewport. Chane joined him. At first he could see nothing in the dirty green murk. Then two dark shapes appeared, very distant, and small. They grew with enormous swiftness. The constant screaming of the wind outside was drowned in rolling, booming thunder. The Merc ship trembled once, and twice. The cruisers swept past, high over the crest of the ridge, went into landing position, dropped their landing gear, and disappeared behind the ridge.

Dilullo sighed, much as though he had been holding his breath. 'I hoped they'd do that.'

Chane stared at him, surprised. 'They just about had to, if they were smart. They can't use their heavy beams against us … as you told him … but we're not hampered. We could have peppered them with our portable missile launchers. I was hoping they'd be foolish enough to land within our range.'

'Maybe they did just that,' Dilullo said. He pointed to the wall of cliffs, the jagged fingers holding back the sand. 'Do you think you could climb up there?'

He knows I can, thought Chane … and said, 'It would depend on how much I had to carry with me.'

'If you had two men to help you, could you muscle one of those portable launchers up to the top?'

'Ah,' said Chane. 'Now I see. The ridge screens us from their heavy beams, so if we took off on a low trajectory they couldn't stop us. But they could come right hot on our heels and catch us in space, unless ...'

'Exactly,' said Dilullo. 'Unless they couldn't.'

Chane said, 'I'll get in there.'

Dilullo nodded and lifted the transceiver button. 'Bollard?'

Bollard's voice came back thready and small. 'Yes, John.'

'Pick me the two strongest men you can think of, break out some coils of heavy duty line, detach one missile-launcher from your perimeter, and get them all assembled. Don't forget the ammo, about ten rounds.'

Chane said, 'Make it twenty.'

'You won't have time,' said Dilullo. 'They'll uncork their lasers and blow you off the ridge before you could fire that many.' Then he paused, looking at Chane. He said into the transceiver, 'Make it twenty.'

'You don't want men,' said Bollard's voice. 'You don't even want mules. You want ... yes, John. On the double.'

Dilullo went to the door of the navigation room. 'Stay with it, Bixel.'

Bixel looked at him, round-eyed. 'But why? The cruisers are down now, and he said the Starwolves had gone, so ...'

'Just stay with it.'

Bixel leaned back in his chair. 'If you say so, John. This is easier than getting shot at.'

'Would you like me to stay with the radio?' asked Rutledge.

'No.'

Rutledge shrugged. 'No harm in asking. But I might have known. You're a hard man, John.'

Dilullo grinned bleakly. 'Let's go see how hard.'

He beckoned to Chane. They went down from the bridge room to the open lock, and out into the cold gritty air and the shifting sand.

The Mercs were deployed along the defense perimeter, dug in behind the assault-fence or manning the emplacements. They were waiting quietly, Chane saw. Good hard tough pros. They would be fighting for their lives in a short while ... just as long as it took the men off the cruisers to get organized and make the long march around the end of the cliff wall. But nothing was happening now and so they were taking it easy, tightening their collars to keep the sand out, checking their weapons, talking back and forth unconcernedly. Another day, another dollar, Chane thought, and not a bad way at all to make a living. It wasn't like the Starwolf way, of course. It was a job and not a game; it lacked the dash and pride. These were hired men, as against the freebooting lords of the starways who had no masters. But since for a while at least he was denied the one, the other wasn't too bad a substitute.

'Still think you can do it?' Dilullo asked. They were walking down the line toward where Bollard was hauling one of the portable launchers out of its emplacement and shouting orders about regrouping and closing the gap. Chane looked up at the cliffs, his eyes narrowed against the dust.

'I can do it,' he said. 'But I'd hate to get caught halfway up.'

'What are you hanging around for, then?' asked Dilullo. 'Concentrate on their drive-tubes. Try to disable both cruisers, but take the undamaged one first. Watch out for return fire, and when it comes, run like hell. We'll wait for you … but not too long.'

'You just worry about holding them off here,' said Chane. 'If they crack the perimeter we won't have any place to run to.'

The coils of heavy-duty line had arrived, thin hard stuff with little weight to it. Chane draped one over his shoulder and took up one end of the launcher cradle. Bollard had provided him, as ordered, with the two strongest men in the outfit, Sekkinen and a giant named O'Shannaig. Sekkinen took the other end of the cradle. O'Shannaig loaded himself with the missile belts … nasty little things with warheads of a non-nuclear but sufficiently violent nature. They couldn't kill a heavy cruiser. Applied in exactly the right places, they could make it hurt.

Chane said, 'Go.' And they went, running in the soft sand, under the belly of the monster ship, and then out from under its ruined bow, past the huddled domes where the Vhollan technicians were locked up. Chane suddenly remembered Thrandirin and the two generals and wondered what Dilullo would do with them.

Sekkinen began to blow and flounder, and Chane slowed down impatiently. He was going to have to pace himself or wear out his team too early. O'Shannaig was doing better because he had his arms free. Even so, he was sweating and his steps had lost their spring. It was hard going in the sand. The weight of their burdens pressed them down so that they waded in it, and it slipped and rolled and clutched their ankles. They found themselves on solid rock at last, right under the loom of the cliffs.

'Okay,' Chane said. 'Sit a minute while I have a look.' He pretended to be panting hard, to match their panting, and moved away slowly, craning upward at the black cliffs.

They looked sheer enough, standing straight up in a monolithic wall until they broke at the top into those eroded pinnacles that tore the passing wind and made it shriek.

O'Shannaig said in his quiet burring voice, 'John must be daft. 'Tis not possible to climb yon, not with all this around our necks.'

'With or without it,' said Sekkinen. He looked at Chane without love. 'Unless you can pass some kind of a miracle.'

XIX

Chane didn't know about miracles, but he knew about strength and obstacles and what a man could do if he had to. No, not a man, a Starwolf. A Varnan.

He walked along the foot of the cliff, taking his time. He knew the men from the cruisers would be moving by now and that if he did not reach the top of the cliff before they came around and spotted him, he was going to be caught with either the launcher or the ammunition or one of the other men dangling helplessly midway and it was going to be bad. Even so, he did not hurry.

The wind was going to be a problem up there. In the dead calm under the cliff, he could look up and see the wind, made physical by the sand it carried in smoking clouds from the dune. Wind like that could carry away a man, or a missile launcher, with equal ease, even though it might drop them sooner.

He wished the drowned sun would burn a little brighter. That was one reason the cliff looked so smooth. The flat dim light did not show up the faults and roughness. Green on black ... that didn't help any either. Chane began to hate this world. It didn't like him. It didn't like life of any kind. All it liked was sand and rock and wind.

He spat the taste of dust and bitter air out of his mouth and went on a little farther, and found what he was looking for.

When he was sure he had found it, he lifted the transceiver button and said, 'I'm about to see what I can do about that miracle. Bring the stuff along.'

He rearranged the coil of rope and his other gear so that nothing stuck out to catch, and he began to climb up the chimney he had found in the rock.

The first part of it wasn't so hard. The trouble came when the chimney washed out and left him on a nearly sheer, nearly vertical face, halfway to the top. He had thought the face was roughened enough to give him a chance, and he had gambled on it. It turned out to be very poor odds.

He remembered that other climb he had made, down the outside of the city-mountain on Kharal. He wished with all his heart he had those gargoyles here.

Inch by inch he worked his way up, mostly by the sheer strength of his fingers. After a while he found himself in a kind of hypnotic daze, concerned only with the cracks and bulges of the rock. His hands hurt abominably; his muscles were stretched like ropes to the breaking point. He heard a voice saying over and over in his head, *Starwolf, Starwolf*, and he knew it was telling him that a man would quit now, and fall, and die, but that he was a Starwolf, a Varnan, too proud to die like an ordinary man.

The shrieking wind deafened him. The hair of his head was plucked and tweaked with such sudden violence that it almost blew him off the rock. A shock of panic went through him. Blown sand bit into his flesh like a shot. He cowered tight against the cliff-face, looked up, and saw that he had reached the top.

He was still not home free. He had to worm his way a little farther, laterally now, below the crest of the ridge until he was in the lee of a pinnacle. He clambered up into a kind of nest in the eroded rock and sat there, gasping and trembling, feeling the rock quiver under him with the violence of the wind, and he cursed Dilullo, laughing. *I'm going to have to stop this,* he thought. *I let him sucker me into one thing after another because I have to show off how good I am. He knows that, and he uses me. Can you do it, he asks, and I say yes …*

And I did it.

A tiny voice sounded under the noise of the wind. 'Chane! Chane!'

He realized now that it had been calling for several minutes. He lifted the transceiver.

'Sekkinen, I'm sending down the line. You can toss a coin, but one of you is going to have to come up here with another line. Third man to stay down and make fast. We'll have to haul the stuff up.'

He found a solid, sturdy tooth of rock to anchor the line on. Apparently O'Shannaig had won the toss, or lost it; it was his long body that came gangling up the cliff, his red-gold hair and craggy face that appeared over the lip of the hollow. Chane laughed, panting now in all honesty. 'Next time I'll ask them to send me a small weakling. You weigh, my friend.'

'Aye,' said O'Shannaig. 'I do that.' He flexed his arms. 'I was pulling, too.'

They sent the second line down. Sekkinen made both of them fast on the launcher and they hauled it up and wrestled it into the hollow, and then brought up the belts.

'Okay, Sekkinen,' said Chane into the transceiver. 'It's your turn now.'

They hauled him up in double-quick time, a big and tough and very unhappy man, who crawled into the hollow muttering that he was never built to be a monkey on a string. The hollow was getting overcrowded. Chane knotted a line around his waist, and a second one over his shoulders. The second one was hitched at the other end to the launcher.

'This is the tricky part,' he said. 'If I blow off, catch me.'

With Sekkinen paying out and O'Shannaig snubbing around the rock tooth, Chane slid out of the hollow and over the crest, into the full fury of the wind.

He didn't think he was going to make it. The wind was determined to fly him into space like a whirling kite. It hammered and kicked him, tore his breath away, blinded him and choked him with sand. He hugged the pinnacle, finding plenty of handholds now where the full force of erosion had been at work, working himself around to the windward side. He was at the crest of the great dune now, and it was like riding one of the giant waves on Varna's lava beaches, high and dizzy, breathless with the spume. Only this spume was hard and dry, flaying the skin from his face and hands. He cowered and crawled in it, and presently the wind was pinning him flat against the rock and he could see the cruisers resting down at the foot of the dune.

He could also see the tail end of a line of armed men marching out of sight around the end of the cliff.

There were hollows on this side of the pinnacle as well, where the softer parts of the rock had been gnawed away. The wind fairly blew him into one and he decided not to argue with it; this would do as well as another. He spoke into the transceiver.

'All right,' he said. 'Up and over, and watch yourselves.'

He braced himself in the hollow, right at the front, with his back against one wall and his feet against another. He laid hold of the second line and began to haul it in, hand over hand.

Praying as he did that the launcher wouldn't get away from his friends and fall down the cliff – because if it did, he would go with it.

It felt as though he were hauling on the rock itself. Nothing moved and he wondered if Sekkinen and O'Shannaig were not able between them to manhandle the launcher up and over those vital few feet of the crest to where he could get a purchase on it. Then all of a sudden, the tension eased and the launcher came leaping at him in a flurry of sand and he shouted to them to snub it. It skidded and slowed to a stop, the belts trailing after it on the snub line.

Chane heaved a sigh of relief. 'Thanks,' he said. 'Now get on back to the ship, quick. The Vhollans are coming.'

He wrestled the launcher into position in front of the hollow, a two-man job. While he was doing it, O'Shannaig's voice, maddeningly slow, replied that, 'It wouldna be richt to go without you.'

In desperation, Chane shouted into his transceiver.

'Bollard!'

'Yes?'

'I'm in position. Will you tell these two noble jackasses to clear out? I can run faster than they can; I'll have a better chance without them. When these lasers cut loose, I don't want to have to wait for anybody.'

Bollard said, 'He's right, boys. Come on down.' From the noises he heard then, Chane gathered that since it was an order, Sekkinen and O'Shannaig were going down the ropes a lot faster than they had come up. He finished laying out the belts and slapped the first one into place in the launcher.

'Chane,' said Bollard, 'the column has just come in sight.'

'Yeah. If I don't see you again, tell Dilullo ...'

Dilullo's voice cut in. 'I'm listening.'

'I guess not right now,' said Chane. 'I'm too busy. The cruisers are practically underneath me. The wind is murder, but these missiles don't much care about wind ... One of these cruisers has taken a beating, all right. I can see that.'

He laughed. *Good for the Starwolves!* He centered the guidance hairs until they met exactly on the clustered drive-tube assembly of the undamaged cruiser.

Dilullo's voice said, 'I'll bet you a half-unit that you don't get off more than ten.'

Dilullo lost. Chane got off ten in such quick succession that the first laser didn't crack until he had turned from the bent and smoking tubes of the first cruiser to the already slightly battered ones of the second. The heavy laser beam began chewing its way along the crest ... they didn't have him zeroed yet, but they would in a minute. Rock and sand erupted in smoke and thunder. Chane got off four more and the second laser unlimbered and blew the dune not thirty feet below him into an inferno. Then, all of a sudden, the lasers stopped and the launcher stopped and there wasn't any more sound of battle.

And a great shadow passed overhead and blotted out the sun.

XX

Eerie quiet; eerie twilight. Chane crouched in the hollow, his neck hairs prickling. He tried the launcher mechanism and it was dead under his fingers, as though the power-pack operating the trigger assembly had gone out.

The laser-pods on the cruisers remained dark and silent.

'Bollard!' he said into the transceiver. 'Dilullo! Anybody!'

There was no answer.

He tried his stunner and that was dead too.

He looked skyward and he could not see anything, except that somewhere up there in the murk and dust and nebula-mist something hung between the planet and the sun.

He fought his way out of the hollow and back over the crest to the other side, taking up his life-line as he went, swinging free for dreadful seconds as the wind took him around the corner and dropped him back into the place he had started from. He could see the Merc ship, the defense perimeter, and off to his left the men from the Vhollan cruisers fanned out into an attack formation with anti-personnel weapons. A couple of the Merc gas-shells had apparently burst among them a little before, because some of them were reeling around in the characteristic fashion and wisps of vapor were still shredding away on the wind. Other than that, everybody was just standing and staring at the sky or fiddling with weapons that had inexplicably stopped working.

Chane went down the line hand-over-hand to the bottom of the cliff, and started running.

Out on the plain, in the dusk of that great shadow, the Vhollans seemed to be smitten with a sudden panic desire for togetherness. Their outflung line receded, coiling in upon itself. It became a mob of frightened men, expecting attack from they knew not what and demoralized by the realization that they had been deprived of any means of defending themselves, beyond their bare hands and pocket knives. Chane could hear their voices clamoring, thin and far away under the wind.

He knew how they felt. Stripped and naked, and worse than that … at the mercy of something or someone too powerful to fight, like tiny children with paper swords against a charge of militia. He didn't like it either. It made him scared, an emotion he was not accustomed to.

He heard orders being shouted up and down the Merc line. They were beginning to fall back on the ship, hauling their useless weapons with them. But as he passed the domes, Chane met Dilullo and a couple of men.

'The Krii rescue ship?' asked Chane.

'It has to be,' Dilullo answered. 'Nothing else …' He looked skyward, his face a bad color in the unnatural twilight. 'The radar isn't working. Nothing's working. Not even the hand torches. I want to talk to Labdibdin.'

Chane went with them to the dunes. It was dark inside and sounds of near-panic could be heard. Rutledge had replaced Sekkinen as door-guard, and as soon as he saw Dilullo he ran toward him, demanding to know what was happening.

'My stunner doesn't work and the transceiver … I've been calling …'

'I know,' Dilullo said, and pointed to the door. 'Let them out.'

Rutledge stared at him. 'What about the Vhollans? What about the attack?'

'I don't think there's going to be an attack now,' said Dilullo, and added under his breath, 'At least, I hope not.'

Rutledge went back and unlocked the door. The Vhollans poured out in an untidy mass, and then paused. They too began looking up at the sky, and babbling. Their voices had become oddly hushed.

Dilullo shouted for Labdibdin, and presently he came jostling through the crowd, with several more of the scientists on his heels.

'It's the ship,' said Labdibdin. 'It must be. This force that has inhibited all power equipment … and all weapons, too, hasn't it …'

'It has.'

'… is a purely defensive device, and the Krii were masters of non-violent means of defense. We were using weapons here, you see. I could hear the lasers up on the ridge. So they stopped us.'

'Yes,' said Dilullo. 'You're the expert on the Krii. What do you suggest we ought to do?'

Labdibdin looked upward at the hovering shadow, and then at the great dark derelict that bulked so large on the sandy plain.

'They don't take life,' he said.

'Are you sure of that, or just hoping?'

'All the evidence …' said Labdibdin, and stopped. He was awestricken before the might and the imminent nearness of the Krii ship.

Chane said, 'What difference does it make? We don't have anything left but our claws and teeth. It's up to them whether they kill us or not.'

'That being the case,' said Dilullo, 'what do you think, Labdibdin?'

'I'm *sure* they don't take life,' said Labdibdin. 'I'm staking my own life on it. I think if we don't oppose or provoke them in any way, if we go back into our ships and …' He made a helpless gesture, and Dilullo nodded.

'And see what happens. All right. Will you take that message to your cruiser captains? Tell them that's what we're going to do, and urge upon them as strongly as you can the wisdom of doing likewise. It seems pretty obvious that this whole thing is out of our hands now, anyway.'

'Yes,' said Labdibdin. 'Only ...'

'Only what?'

'A few of us may come back ... to watch.' He looked again at the mighty derelict, in whose dark belly the hundred Krii sat waiting. 'Only to watch. And at a distance.'

The Vhollans streamed out over the plain toward the milling mob from the cruisers. Chane and Dilullo and the other Mercs hurried back to the Merc ship.

'How did it go on the ridge?' Dilullo asked as they went.

'Good,' said Chane. 'It'll take them a while to make repairs on those cruisers ... neither one's in shape to get off the ground.' He smiled wryly. 'Your plan worked just fine. We can take off any time now.'

'That's nice,' said Dilullo. 'Except we don't have any power.'

They both looked skyward.

'I feel like a mouse,' said Dilullo.

Rutledge shivered. 'Me, too. I hope your Vhollan friend is right and the cat isn't carnivorous.'

Dilullo turned to Chane. 'Are you worried now?'

Chane knew what he meant. *Starwolves don't worry*. He showed the edges of his teeth and said, 'I'm worried.'

Starwolves are strong, and that's why they don't worry. The weak worry, and today I am weak, and I know it. For the first time in my life. I would like to claw their big ship out of the sky and break it, and I feel sick because they made me helpless. And it was no trouble to them to do it. They just pushed a button somewhere, a flick of one of those long stringy digits, and the animals were suppressed.

He remembered the passionless faces of the Krii, and hated them.

Dilullo said mildly, 'I'm glad to know there's something that can get you down. Are you tired, Chane?'

'No.'

'You're fast on your feet. Run ahead and get Thrandirin and the generals out of the ship. Tell 'em to go to blazes with the rest of the Vhollans. If the Krii decide to let us have our power back sometime, I want to go, and I don't want to bother dropping our guests off at their home planet. I don't think it would be very healthy.'

'I doubt it,' said Chane, and took off running.

And as he ran, he thought, *Here I go again. Why didn't I just tell him I was tired? Pride, boy. And when you were a very little boy your father used to tell you how it went before a fall.*

I guess he was right. It was pride in what I had done in that raid that made me fight with Ssander when he tried to cut in on my share of the loot.

And here I am. Not a Starwolf any more, not really a Merc, either ... just living on their sufferance ... and at this moment I'm not even a man. Just an annoyance to the Krii. And if that isn't a fall ...

He reached the ship, fighting his way through the Mercs who were loading in the weapons and equipment, on the chance that it all might work some day again. It was pitch dark inside, the only light coming in through the open hatchways, which of course would not close now. He groped his way to the cabin where the three Vhollans were locked up, let them out and guided them down, and when they stood outside he watched their faces and smiled.

'I don't understand,' said Thrandirin. 'What is it? I see our men going away without fighting, and the light is strange ...'

'That's right,' said Chane, and pointed at the vast loom of the wrecked Krii ship. 'Someone else has come looking for that. Someone bigger than us. I think you can kiss it goodbye.' He gestured skyward. 'For there's another just like it up there now.'

The Vhollans stared at him like three night-goggling birds in the weird dusk. 'If I were you,' said Chane, 'I'd get going. You can talk the whole thing over with Labdibdin ... while we all wait.'

They went. Chane turned to help with the loading, which had all to be done by hand.

They were concentrating on the most valuable items and they were working awfully fast, so they had a good part of the job done when there began to be a new sound in the sky, and Chane looked up and saw a big pale-gold egg sinking toward them out of the shadowy clouds.

In a quiet voice Dilullo said, 'Into the ship. Just put everything down and go.'

Only about a third of the men were working outside, passing the things through the cargo hatch along a kind of human belt that extended to the storage hold. They did what Dilullo told them, and Chane thought he had never seen an area cleared so quickly. He followed Dilullo and Bollard up the steps to the lock, moving in a more dignified fashion, perhaps, but not much more. Chane's heart was pounding in a way it had not done since he was a child waking from a nightmare, and there was a cold, unpleasant knot in his middle.

The open and unshuttable lock chamber seemed dreadfully exposed.

'Whole damn ship's open,' Bollard muttered. There was sweat on his round moon face, and it looked cold. 'They could just walk in ...'

'Can you think of anything we can do about it?' asked Dilullo.

'Okay,' said Bollard. 'Okay.'

They stood and watched while the big gold egg came and settled gently onto the sand.

It sat there for a time and did nothing, and they continued to watch it, and now Chane had a feeling it was watching them. They were in plain sight if anybody wanted to look real hard, though they were taking pains not to be conspicuous. It was probably dangerous, and they should go farther in. But that was no protection either since they couldn't close the hatches, and they might as well see what was going on. The Krii would know perfectly well they were here anyway.

The Krii, when finally they did appear, seemed not to be interested one way or the other.

There were six of them. They emerged one after another through a hatchway that opened low down in the side of the egg, extruding a narrow stairway. The last two carried between them a long thin object of unguessable purpose, shrouded in dark cloth.

Very tall and slender, their seemingly jointless bodies swaying gracefully, they moved in single file toward the great ship. Their skins, Chane noted, were not quite so dark an amber as those of the Krii he had seen frozen in stasis. Their limbs were extremely supple, the long-digited hands looking almost like fronds stirring in the wind.

They walk so tall, he thought, *because they're not afraid of us. And if they're not afraid, it must be because they know we can't hurt them. Not* won't *hurt them.* Can't *hurt them.*

They did not even look at the Merc ship. They never turned those narrow high-domed heads to left or right to look at anything. They marched quietly to the entrance and went up the steps and disappeared inside the enormous wreck.

They were in there a long time. The men got tired of standing in the lock and clawed their way in the darkness up to the bridge room, where they could be more comfortable and still watch.

Bollard said, 'So far, they're peaceful.'

'Yes,' said Dilullo. 'So far.'

The golden egg sat on the sand and waited, its long rows of ports gleaming dully in the dim light. It did not have the conventional drive-tube assembly, Chane noted, and there were no external signs at all of what kind of power was used. Whatever it was, it functioned in the inhibiting force-field where nothing else did. Naturally. A defensive device wasn't much good if it immobilized you along with your enemy.

He saw movement in the entrance to the great wreck, and he said, 'They're coming back.'

The six came out, and after them the hundred.

In single file, forming a long swaying line, they marched out of the dark tomb where they had waited … how long? Their garments fluttering, their large eyes wide in the dimness, they marched across the blowing sand and into the golden shuttle-craft that would take them to the rescue ship, which would take them home. Chane looked at their faces.

'They're not human, all right,' he said. 'Not one of them is laughing, or crying, or dancing, or hugging someone. They all look as peaceful and harmonious as they did when they were ... I was going to say "dead," but you know what I mean.'

'No visceral emotions,' said Dilullo. 'And yet that other ship has made a tremendous long voyage to find them. That argues emotions of some sort.'

'Maybe they were more interested in saving the experience these Krii have had, than in saving the Krii themselves,' said Chane.

'I'm not interested either way,' said Bollard. 'I only want to know what they're going to do to us.'

They watched, and Chane knew that from the open lock and the cargo hatch the other Mercs were watching, waiting, and tasting the bitter taste of fear, just like he was.

It wasn't that you minded dying so much, though you didn't look forward to it. It was that you minded the way you were going to die, Chane thought. *If these long limber honey-skinned vegetables decided to finish you, they would do it coolly and efficiently, and so remotely that you wouldn't even know what hit you. Like gassing vermin in a burrow.*

The last of the hundred entered the shuttle-craft and its hatchway closed upon them. The golden egg hummed and rose up into the whirling dust and cloud and was gone.

'Now maybe they'll let us go?' said Bollard.

'I don't think so,' said Dilullo. 'Not just yet.'

Chane swore a short fierce oath in Varnan, the first slip of that kind he had made, but Bollard didn't notice it.

He was too busy looking at the fleet of golden eggs that had appeared, dropping one after the other until there were nine neatly lined up on the sand.

Dilullo said, 'We might as well make ourselves comfortable. I believe we're going to have a long wait.'

And long it was. Just about the longest wait that Chane could ever remember, penned up in the little iron prison of the ship. They ate cold rations, lived in the dark, and looked hungrily at the open hatchways that mocked them. Toward the end Dilullo had to use all his powers of persuasion, including his fists, to keep the men inside.

Presumably the officers of the Vhollan cruisers were having the same trouble, and presumably they succeeded, because the Vhollans kept clear. Once or twice Chane thought he saw figures moving the dust-whirls underneath the cliff. It might have been Labdibdin and some of the other technicians; probably was. If so, they did their watching from a discreet distance.

There was one comfort. The Vhollans couldn't use this interval to repair their tubes. Not unless they did it with little hammers and their bare hands.

Chane paced and prowled, and finally sat moping, sullen as a caged tiger.

Outside the Krii worked steadily, neither slow nor fast, keeping a methodical rhythm that rasped the nerves just to watch it. They never once came near the Merc ship. As far as they were concerned, it seemed, the Merc ship did not exist.

'Not very complimentary,' said Dilullo, 'but let's keep it that way. Maybe Labdibdin is perfectly right and they don't take life. That wouldn't stop them from having some highly effective method of suppressing people, the way they suppress machines, and their idea of the seriousness of resultant damage to the organism might not agree with ours. Lord knows what their metabolism is like, or their nervous systems. You can wreck a man pretty thoroughly and still leave him living. They simply might not understand what they were doing.'

Chane agreed with him. Still, it was hard to have to look at the irritatingly remote and lofty creatures day after day and not want to try rushing out and killing a few just to vary the monotony.

The shuttle-craft came and went, disgorging various equipment, taking the Krii technicians back and forth. A considerable amount of work was being done inside the wreck, but of course there was no way of knowing what that was. Outside, the Krii were setting up a complex of transparent rods that gradually took the form of a tunnel. They built that out from the entrance of the ship to a distance of about thirty feet, and then at the end they erected a kind of lock-chamber. At the ship end, the tunnel-like structure was sealed to the opening by a collar; they left only a narrow aperture for the technicians to go and come.

One day, light appeared suddenly through the rents in the ship's hull.

'They've got the power on again,' said Dilullo. 'Or jury-rigged a replacement for it.'

'How do they run their generators when we can't?' Chane demanded. 'They're in this inhibiting field too.'

'They developed the inhibiting field, and would know how to shield their own equipment against it. Or their power system may be so different from ours ... I mean, they don't even have the same atomic table.'

Chane said, 'However they do it, they're doing it. And if they've got the power on, all those cases will open up ...'

All those cases of jewels and precious metals. The loot of a galaxy, the way he saw it. It made his mouth water. Even the Starwolves had never aspired to such splendid heights.

A golden egg attached itself to the lock-chamber at the end of the tunnel.

Chane pressed close to the viewport, with Dilullo and Bollard beside him.

Nobody said anything. They waited, feeling that something decisive was about to happen.

The tunnel-like structure of crystal rods began to glow with a shimmering radiance that made its outline blur and shift. The radiance intensified, flared, then settled to a steady pulsing.

Things began to appear in it, gliding smoothly and swiftly from the great ship to the golden egg.

'Some kind of a carrier field,' said Dilullo. 'It makes the stuff weightless and kicks it along ...'

Chane groaned. 'Don't give me any scientific lectures. Just look at that. *Look* at it!'

The loot of a galaxy went by, just out of reach, streaming steadily from the hold of the Krii ship into the golden egg; into a series of golden eggs that operated in an endless belt-shuttle, loading and rising and returning in a circular pattern.

The loot of a galaxy.

'And they're not even going to spend it,' Chane said. 'They're going to all of this trouble just to *study* it.'

'Blasphemy, according to your ideas,' said Dilullo, and grinned at Chane. 'Don't cry.'

'What are you talking about?' asked Bollard.

'Nothing. Except our friend here seems to have a frustrated case of sticky fingers.'

Bollard shook his head. 'The devil with our friend. Look; they're loading all the specimens the expedition gathered. When they're finished, what then?'

It was not a question that was intended to be answered, and nobody tried.

But eventually the answer came.

The last items went down the carrier field and the glow died. Methodically the Krii dismantled their equipment and returned it into the clouds. The great hulk became dark again and now it was empty, drained of all use and meaning.

Finally, and at last, one of the Krii walked toward the Merc ship. It stood for a moment, very tall, swaying slightly with the wind, its great passionless eyes fixed on them.

Then it flung up one long thin arm in an unmistakable gesture, pointing to the sky.

It turned then and went back to the single golden egg that remained. The hatch closed, and in a moment the trampled sand was empty.

All of a sudden the lights were on in the Merc ship and the generators were jarring the bulkhead as they jolted into life again.

'He told us to go, and I think I know why,' said Dilullo. He began to bellow urgently into the intercom. 'Secure hatches! Flight stations on the double! We're taking off!'

And they took off, going like a scalded rocket in a flat trajectory that took them away from the cliff wall at an angle too low for the Vhollan laser beams to bear on them until they were out of range.

Dilullo ordered the ship into a stationary orbit and told Rutledge, 'Get that camera working. I've a pretty good idea what's going to happen and I want to record it.'

Rutledge opened the pod that held the camera and turned the monitor screen to ON.

Chane stared with the others into the screen that showed them what the camera was seeing.

'Too much dust,' said Rutledge, and manipulated the controls, and the picture cleared as the camera saw with different eyes, exchanging a light-reflectant image for one composed by sensor-beams.

It showed the great wrecked ship, lying monstrous on the plain. It showed the ridge and the two Vhollan cruisers beyond; the cruisers seemed like tiny, little miniatures for children to hang on strings and whirl around their heads.

After a while Rutledge looked at Dilullo, and Dilullo said, 'Keep filming. Unless you want to go home broke.'

'You think the Krii are going to destroy the ship?' asked Chane.

'Wouldn't you? When you know people have been meddling and prying with it, people with much less technological skill than yours but with much more warlike natures … would you leave it there for them to study? The Krii couldn't remove everything. The drive system, the generators, all that would be left, and the defensive mechanisms. Given time, the Vhollans might learn how to duplicate them in terms of our atomic table. Besides, why else would the Krii have told us to get clear? They wouldn't care about our fight with the Vhollans, and whether we got away or not. I think they didn't want us to get killed by any action of theirs.'

The image remained static on the screen, the vast dark broken outline of the ship quite clear against the sand.

Suddenly a little spark flashed down and touched the hulk. It spread with incredible swiftness into a blinding flame that covered all that huge fabric of metal from stem to stern and ate it up, devoured it, crumbled it to ashes and then to atoms, until there was nothing left but a mile-long scar on the sand. And presently even that would vanish.

The Vhollan cruisers, shielded by the ridge, were unharmed.

Dilullo said, 'Shut off the camera. I guess that shows we did our duty.'

'We?' said Rutledge.

'The Kharalis hired us to find out what was in the nebula that threatened them, and destroy it. We found it, and it has been destroyed. Period.' He looked down at the Vhollan cruisers. 'They'll be getting busy on repairs now. I don't see any more reason to hang around.'

There wasn't a man aboard who wanted to quarrel with him.

They climbed up out of the atmosphere, and out from under the shadow that had oppressed them for so many days, where the giant ship had hung between them and the sun.

Whether by accident or design, Dilullo chose a course that took them, not close but close enough to see …

Close enough to see a vast dark shape breaking out of orbit, beginning the long voyage home across the black and empty ocean that laps the shores of the island universes.

'No visceral emotions,' said Dilullo softly, 'but, by God, they've got something.'

Even Chane had to agree.

The Mercs had expansive ideas about doing some celebrating and Dilullo just let them go ahead and try. As he had foreseen, they were too tired, and those off duty were glad enough to crawl into their bunks for the first decent sleep they had had in so long they couldn't remember.

Chane, not all that exhausted, remained in the wardroom for another drink with Dilullo. They were all alone now, and Dilullo said, 'When we get to Kharal, you'll stay in the ship and make as though you never existed.'

Chane grinned. 'You don't have to talk me into that. Tell me, do you think they'll pay over the lightstones?'

Dilullo nodded. 'They'll pay. In the first place, nasty as they are in some ways, they keep their word. In the second place, the films of that monster ship will so impress them that the sight of it being destroyed will make them glad to pay.'

'You don't plan to tell them that it wasn't really us who destroyed it?' Chane asked.

'Look,' said Dilullo; 'I'm reasonably fair and honest but I'm not foolish. They hired us to do a job, and the job is done, and we're pretty well battered up from it. That's enough.' He added, 'What will you do with your share when we sell the lightstones?'

Chane shrugged. 'I hadn't thought about it. I'm used to taking things, not buying them.'

'That's a little habit you'll have to get over if you want to stay a Merc. Do you?'

Chane paused before answering. 'I do, for the time being, anyway. As you said before, I haven't got any place else to go … I don't think you're as good as the Varnans, but you're pretty good.'

Dilullo said dryly, 'I don't think you'll ever make the best Merc that ever was, but you've got capabilities.'

'Where do we go from Kharal?' Chane asked. 'Earth?'

Dilullo nodded.

'You know,' said Chane, 'I've got kind of interested in Earth.'

Dilullo shook his head and said dourly, 'I'm not too happy about taking you there. When I think of the people there walking up and down, and looking at you and not knowing you're a tiger impersonating an Earthman, I wonder what I'm getting into. But I guess we can clip your claws.'

Chane smiled. 'We'll see.'

If you've enjoyed these books and would like to read more, you'll find literally thousands of classic Science Fiction & Fantasy titles through the **SF Gateway**

*

For the new home of Science Fiction & Fantasy . . .

*

For the most comprehensive collection of classic SF on the internet . . .

Visit the SF Gateway

www.sfgateway.com

Edmond Hamilton (1904–1977)

Born in Youngstown, Ohio, Edmond Hamilton was raised there and in nearby New Castle, Pennsylvania. He was something of a child prodigy, graduating from high school and undertaking his college education at Westminster College at the young age of 14; he dropped out aged 17. A popular science fiction writer in the mid-twentieth century, Hamilton's career began with the publication of his short story 'The Monster God of Mamurth' in the August 1926 issue of *Weird Tales*. After the war, he wrote for DC Comics, producing stories for Batman, Superman and The Legion of Superheroes. Ultimately, though, he was associated with an extravagant, romantic, high-adventure style of SF, perhaps best represented by his 1947 novel *The Star Kings*. He was married to fellow SF writer Leigh Brackett from the end of 1946 until his death three decades later.